ARCHFORM: BEAUTY

Tor Books by L. E. Modesitt, Jr.

ARCHFORM: BEAUTY

L. E. Modesitt, Jr.

TOR®

A Tom Doherty Associates Book
New York

ARCHFORM: BEAUTY

Copyright © 2002 by L. E. Modesitt, Jr.

Edited by David G. Hartwell

This book is printed on acid-free paper.

A Tor Book
Published by Tom Doherty Associates, LLC
175 Fifth Avenue
New York, NY 10010

www.tor.com

Tor® is a registered trademark of Tom Doherty Associates, LLC.

Library of Congress Cataloging-in-Publication Data

Modesitt, L. E.
   Archform : beauty / L.E. Modesitt, Jr.
      p. cm.
   "A Tom Doherty Associates book."
   ISBN 0-765-30433-3
   I. Title.

   PS3563.O264 A89 2002
   813'.54—dc21   2001059655

First Edition: July 2002

Printed in the United States of America

0 9 8 7 6 5 4 3 2 1

For Tom Doherty,

the most underappreciated man in publishing.

"Great art is beauty."

"An elegant solution is beautiful as well."

"The beauty of words is lost behind the power of image."

"The beauty of politics lies in how effectively power is shared and transferred."

"A good family is a beautiful one."

ARCHFORM: BEAUTY

Chapter 1
Vienna, 1824

As the last notes of the orchestra fade into oblivion, the audience surges to its feet, the applause thundering across the hall.

The tottering, wild-haired conductor remains facing the orchestra, as if afraid to turn, until the concertmaster, tears streaming down his cheeks, steps forward and takes the conductor's arm, guiding him to face the audience. The conductor finally smiles as he takes in the ovation he can see, but not hear.

But the smile that crosses the creased and pallid face is part joy, part wonder—and part horror that none recognize or sense but the conductor, who is also the composer. Both horror and wonder are lost in the applause that storms across the city, an applause that is darker than the night outside, an applause for music that casts a shadow far wider than any know and for far more years than any could guess.

Chapter 2
Cornett

Synsil looked at me over the music stand that she always set too high, every Tuesday, as if to erect a barrier between us. Her singlesuit had a pattern of angled stripes of cream and blue that made her look thinner than she already was. Her eyes were dark brown, like a cow's, almost ready to fill with the tears that her pride and family background wouldn't let her shed. After only a semester of teaching her, I was more than a little tired of her need to always save face. She shook her head slightly, and her bobbed black hair shivered.

"Synsil," I began slowly, standing up from the piano bench and moving away from the antique Steinway, "you have a good instrument, but singing is not just talent. If you want to be good, you have to practice more. You have to practice the way I've shown you." It was almost hopeless telling Synsil that, but I had to try.

"Professor Cornett . . . I do try. It's just not fun." She rushed on before I could say a word. "I used to look forward to singing at the Academy. Now, it's just work."

"Anything you want to be good at takes work," I pointed out. "Singing's no different."

She looked at me, with that stubborn expression I'd come to know too well, and said, "If singing isn't fun, maybe I shouldn't keep taking lessons. It's not as though I could really make a living at it."

I made a living at it, and so did others. That kind of a living was a lot better than settling in as a corporate sariman, no matter how high the pay and benefits were for multilateral servitude. "I do, but if that's the way you feel, maybe you shouldn't."

"You do rezads. That's not the same."

"It *is* the same." I was trying hard to be patient when I really wanted to strangle her. "I couldn't get work if I couldn't do exactly what the studio wants vocally. I only get a few minutes to study the music before each session. You can't do that unless you understand music and your voice." When she didn't say anything, I added, "I also get gigs as a classical singer." Those were almost all art song recitals for one filch or another in southside. Those recitals were a matter of prestige for the filch, because you can't rez art song. But it paid, and paid well, if infrequently, and those were the nights I really enjoyed, because I could make beautiful music. I wasn't going to try to explain that. You can't explain beauty to people who don't feel it.

"My father says that old-style singing will be gone soon."

"People have been saying that for almost three centuries, ever since the electronic age began. Almost three thousand years ago, Aristotle wanted to get rid of the singers and poets." I smiled. "We're still here." Still trying to bring beauty into a world that seemed to want less and less of it.

"You should talk to my father."

That was the last thing I wanted to do. "You need to decide what's best for your future, Synsil. Your parents can't live your life for you. What do *you* want?"

"I always thought I wanted to be a rezpop singer. Or maybe rezrom."

"Do you like Elymai?" I asked. Most of the younger students soaked in and praised the romantic resonance slop that Elymai put out—I had a hard time calling it singing.

"She's good."

Synsil was wary. That I could tell.

"She has the same kind of background I do. It's hard to get where she is without a good education and training. If you want to be that good, you need to practice. You need to practice the way I've shown you." I paused, then added, "It's up to you." I kept my eyes fixed on her. She needed to know I was serious.

After a moment, she looked down. "I suppose I should practice more."

"If you don't, you won't have a chance to find out if that's what you want to do." She might not anyway, but now wasn't the time to get into that. She had to get serious about *something*.

My words brought the hint of a thoughtful expression, but all she said was, "I'll see you next week."

I looked at the back of the door after she left. Then I took a deep breath. I wondered why I bothered. I knew why. If I didn't, who would? Yet, did it matter whether classical singing remained alive in a culture where music had become ever more amplified, modified, synthesized, and simplified? Where it was on the brink of being able to mold emotions, whether or not the listener wanted to be molded? It mattered, I told myself—for about the fiftieth time since Monday.

Then, my internal links told me that I had five minutes to get to my class. I slipped on my blue jacket and picked up the data-case in one hand and my notes in the other. I closed the door to my office, such as it was, and walked down the corridor. I kept

a slight distance from the students as I slipped past the choral
room where Jorje's Modern Choir was still practicing. Thankfully, when I went by, they were doing a Vaughn Williams
piece—traditionally. I had to grit my teeth when they did Bach
with resonance, and that was minimal rez. But the audiences
loved it.

Tuesdays and Thursdays were my longest teaching days. Each
had two student lessons, and an hour and a half section of Music
101B—The Understanding and Appreciation of Music.

I slowed behind two tall figures, listening.

". . . Nayad said she sings rezads for her cake . . ."

". . . Chorima was going to take lessons from her, till she
found out she doesn't teach rez stuff . . ."

". . . still not understand why they make us take the course.
Most of it's boring . . ."

". . . no one listens to it . . . except the last weeks. Actually
talks about rez music . . ."

". . . bet she doesn't know all that much . . ."

". . . Chorima said she does . . ."

I kept a smile to myself as I followed them into the lecture
hall. I remembered Chorima—a tallish Asian girl. She'd actually
done well in the 101 class the semester before.

As he took a seat in the lower tier, the dark-skinned and more
angular student—Ibrahim D'Houd—glanced back as he realized
I might have heard his words. He smiled nervously.

I returned the smile, then stepped behind the podium console.
I laid my notes on the top, open to the first page, and slipped
the databloc into the slot. If I'd wanted to, I could have programmed it to play from my office console, but that was wasted
time, so far as I was concerned. The university didn't pay me
enough for that extra time.

I just stood there until quiet settled over the lecture hall. It
didn't take long.

"The results of your tests are in your personal files, in case
you haven't checked. Most of you did well. A few of you still

don't seem to understand that you need to study." I scanned the faces in the tiered seats of the hall. With more than a hundred students there, I still didn't know all the faces. I shuddered to think what it would be like if I had the two hundred the hall could hold. "Do any of you have questions about the test?"

There weren't any, but there usually weren't. Those who had questions either saw me after class or asked them over the link.

"We're going to be hearing and seeing a symphony from one of the great composers who bridged the Classic and Romantic Periods with his music. Just as Bach might be considered the father of the fugue, this composer might be considered the father of the modern symphony. The symphony we're going to hear is generally considered a Classic symphony, although the third movement is scherzo form, rather than minuet, and foreshadows the changes in the symphonies to come . . ." I could tell I'd lost them and glanced around, picking a sleepy-looking face in the fourth row—one I knew. "Daffyd? Do you know who the composer is?"

"Beethoven," he replied.

"That's right. We'll hear parts of his Ninth Symphony next week, and you'll be able to hear the difference. Now . . . listen."

The databloc held videos of the Nyork Phil performing Beethoven's Fifth. Even though the holoviews alternated between players and pan shots of the entire orchestra, which just showed instrumentalists playing, I'd found that the students didn't listen as well or hear as much if I only played a straight audio. They had to watch something to get their ears working. Music by itself meant nothing to most of them.

After the selection ended, I waited a moment before I began to speak. "The first four notes of what you heard—da-da-da-dah—in a way they were used as an early form of resonance music. Not when they were composed, but later." That got a few puzzled expressions. I waited before I asked, "Does anyone know when?"

"Weren't they some form of code in the First World War? At the beginning of the InfoRev?"

"Not exactly. They did have something to do with war and symbolism. Can anyone else tell me when and how?"

The vacant faces showed that they weren't about to provide an answer.

"During the Second World War, the British Broadcasting Corporation prefaced all its foreign language old-time radio broadcasts with those four notes, as a symbol of victory. Those four notes also represent the letter 'V' in Morse code. So that the physical impact, as well as the meaning, make the 'V for Victory' notes one of the first documented uses of resonance. A limited form, certainly, but . . ."

So far, so good. No one had fallen asleep. Not yet, anyway. I hated to think about their reactions when I got to the later composers—like Bartók and the five-part archform structure he'd invented and used for his *Concerto for Orchestra*.

". . . next week, we'll get to another composer whose music was also used as the basis for early resonance motivation . . . For now, we'll look into the structure of the late Classic symphony, the way it evolved from Mozart onward . . ."

I flipped my hair back from my face, and from there I went into examples of development, with short excerpts from various works, mostly Mozart, since he was the most regular.

All the time, I kept thinking about Synsil, and her comments about making a living as a singer, because I hadn't been totally honest. She had been partly right about it. Except for the handful of high opera singers kept by the old Met, the Kirov, and the Royal Opera, most of us had to use our abilities in a scattering of fields—from rezads to the occasional art song gigs to teaching. And the teaching positions got fewer and fewer every year. I was lucky to have gotten even a solid adjunct position at UDenv. But it did allow me to keep singing . . . and making beautiful music.

I smiled and said, "The next excerpt is from Mozart's Haffner Symphony. He wrote this symphony in less than two weeks in 1782, yet some scholars think that it is technically one of his best . . ."

As I activated the databloc, I couldn't help thinking that Mozart hadn't had it all that bad. He didn't have to have his compositions tweaked electronically for cheap emotional effects. Also, he'd only had to please one patron.

Chapter 3
Chiang

I stepped into the Department foyer off the underground garage. Like everything in DPS, the foyer was done in muted gray and forest-green. Smelled like pine, roses, with an overtone of oil. I released the hold on the gatekeeper, could feel the rush of data pouring into me, then the priority override.

Lieutenant Chiang! Captain Cannizaro wants you soon as you're on duty.

Even on link, I recognized Sarao's voice and back-linked. *On my way.*

I took the ramps briskly, didn't run. Stopped running through the Department years ago. Didn't seem to matter. Street's the only place to run, and only there if you've frigged up bad.

Never open your links to your work until you're there. You do, and you work all the time. Learned that one the hard way a long time back. One day, linked into main ops, and caught an allpers alert. That was the beginning of the Tularo Trouble. Before I could unlink, Cannizaro caught me on-net, called me in. When I got back home a week later, Catalya was gone with the twins. Might have been better if I'd been like Ahmed. He spent a month in rehab. Family clustered all around, worrying. Me, I came home tired to empty rooms.

Catalya had gone back to Porlan, left a note. Said when I wanted to give up the Department she'd be there.

VRed her, and we had talked. She wouldn't budge. I don't like ultimatums. Never did. Figured that if I gave in on that, I'd be giving in on anything. VRed the twins every night till they grew up and went off on their own. Estafen's still in Porlan, but Erek moved back to the east coast. Still VR them, more like once a week, now. Think they're beginning to understand, but you never know.

After that, Cannizaro insisted I go trendside. She'd just made lieutenant, then, insisted she needed someone like me. Guess she was right. I made sergeant along the way, then lieutenant four years ago, when she took over the Department, and I got her old job.

Someone had to put the trends together, study all the facets, try to figure out what was going to happen before it became too big. That lesson, we learned from Tularo. In Denv, that was me. Lieutenant Eugene Tang Chiang. Official title was Trends Analysis Coordinator. Had just six people under me, but the job was a lieutenant's because the trends head has to have had street time and credibility. Need that to brief the District Coordinator and his staff, work with the SocServ types, and hold the right kind of chill in dealing with the media netsies.

Didn't take me long to get to the captain's office. It was on the third level, overlooking the square, with the old state capitol to the east and the dozen remaining dinosaur towers to the west, all set in the middle of the Park. Lots of trees and green grass. Grass was green, even in winter.

I stepped into the office. Captain had done it in light blue, with darker blue trim. Very restful. She'd paid for it from her own pocket. Most of the other offices, mine included, were off-white.

"Close the door." Those were Cannizaro's first words.

I dropped into the ergochair at the corner of her desk console. Captains and lieutenants were the only ones who rated desks. Couldn't have been more than a half dozen in the building. Then, outside of the dispatchers, there weren't much more than a dozen bodies there at most times. Patrollers and dets don't do much good if they're not out on the street. The netops people were all in the annex, on the other side of the garage. I couldn't take that, patrolling the net for scams, larceny, and general misreps. Did it in training, long years back. Understood the need, but hated the job. Even hated analyzing their weekly reports. Didn't miss a word, though. Couldn't afford to.

I looked at the captain.

She didn't look like a Cannizaro. Except in her eyes, a penetrating black. Thin long face, squarish body, short blond hair, worry lines running from the eyes that had seen too much. "Chiang . . ."

When she used my name like that, it wasn't good. Meant trouble in Denv. I waited.

"Your weekly report . . ." That was all she needed to say.

"Something's going to happen." I shrugged. "Can't say what. Start getting upticks in the little stuff . . . ODs, car delinks, TIDs . . . always happens before something breaks. Lot of upticks, too many for coincidence."

"District Coordinator Dewey is up for reelection. He's got an opponent with creds. Unlimited creds." Cannizaro's voice was flat.

Dewey had always supported the Department, even when no one else had, even as far back as Tularo.

"He's being opposed by Jared Alredd. Son of Aylwin Alredd. The younger Alredd claims the Department lets matters get out of hand before acting. Old broken windows school."

"Can't tell you what's coming down, Captain. Only that it is."

"As soon as you know . . . ?"

"You'll know." I'd always let her know. First.

I got a nod and a faint smile, as much as I ever got, before I stood.

"Even when I'm off," she added. "Use TP code."

"Stet, Captain." Then I headed down to my second-floor corner office.

Stopped outside in front of the consoles. Duty coordinator was Sarao—brunette, intense. Her name sounded like "sorrow." It fit. Sometimes gave me grief. Practiced antique combat with sword and board. Married old-style to a body-sculptor, but refused to let him sculpt her. Good choice, I thought.

"Resheed's report is in your linkfile." She looked at me, but she was still monitoring the inlinks.

"Thanks." It always was. Resheed was dependable. Then, all of trendside was. "Thoughts?"

"Like you said yesterday, something's coming down."

"Captain's worried."

Sarao nodded, her attention really on the feeds she was getting. Then she blinked and looked at me. "Happy faces all over the place—at the Pavilion, on the shuttles. Face scans show a good ten percent increase in soop use—or something like it."

More soop use meant that people weren't happy, turned to the designer exhilarant. But they couldn't stay sooped forever. Lot of jobs required a nanite cleanjob before taking over a console or a system. Then, most folks on soop were either students or servies, sometimes permies. Wondered at times if soop could make life better for a permie. Then, should it be? People didn't get permanent nanite behavior mods unless they'd been convicted of two violent offenses or three significant offenses.

"Any localization?"

"Everywhere but southside and the towers." Sarao's voice was dry.

We both laughed. Hard laughs. Southside and the towers were gate-private. Nothing happened there in public. Rumors about the filch orgies came up, but private was private so long as no one got hurt. Wondered about that, too, after the Halburt clone scandal. How many others had been offed silently and replaced with more tractable clones? Had any? Who could tell?

Trendside you learn early that you don't guess. Not about the filch. Hard evidence, that's fine. But you don't fish there. Not without the captain's backing and full milspec nanite armor.

"I'll read it."

I walked through the door. It opened to my aura, then closed. My office was small, a third the size of the captain's. Just enough room for the desk and the console and two ergochairs in front of the desk. Leaning forward, I could see sunlight glittering the gold leaf dome of the antique state capitol—back when a state meant something. Now it was a museum. Couldn't see the Continental Complex, down south beyond southside. Could almost feel it, though, at times.

Called up Resheed's daily update, direct-link to my implant. Didn't tell me that much. ODs up, nothing to flag any group. Except age—all were under twenty-five. Then, more than eighty percent always were. A handful of vehicle delinks, including one electrolorry. The netops reported a new scam targeted at the netless, offering them "free" access. Wasn't, of course. Area comm section had taken over on that.

Data and more data. There's more to public safety than data. Data doesn't feel. Crime happens because people feel. You feel what they do, the data makes sense.

I tried NetPrime News—the local reports. Best of the worst. Again, direct-feed. Just closed my eyes and let the words and images appear. Didn't care much for holo projections off the net. Crap blown larger remained crap.

Most newsworthy item was a bit about the west-coast wygs were modifying scanner glasses. Mods let the perps see who had nanite body shields, make it easier to pick victims. Just what we needed. Another gadget to make public safety tougher. Wish someone had told the Department. If the street hadn't been quiet, probably wouldn't have been on news at all. I flashed a memo to the captain, suggested it be disseminated Department-wide.

After that, checked all the incomings. Mostly routine. Only things new were a rash of phony soop sprays that were only glucose with a boost and the theft of lorries for house smash-ins. Mass overwhelmed most house shields. Also, a notice of higher DPS deductions for health care. That was because of improved internal nanite diagnostics. Took more equipment to read and repair.

Higher health care, water surcharges—not one thing it was another.

Almost two hours later before I stretched and walked back out to the consoles.

"Going to run the towers? Or westside?" asked Sarao.

"Westside. Can't get into anything in the towers. Not without appointments or a cause warrant. See me going to the regional advocate asking for one just to prowl because I feel something's coming down?"

"Too bad they don't let us do more of that."

"Never have. Never will."

"How long?" Sarao looked at me.

"Long as it takes. I'll be on link if you need me." Didn't need to say that, but it made people happier to hear it. Even Sarao, and she knew better.

Ask why I go out? Why I don't link? People don't talk. They don't talk in person sometimes, either. But the way they don't talk tells stories, too.

Went back down to the garage. To transport. Entered my codes through GIL link. Linking ID to gene codes—genetic identity link—made a lot of the old-style crimes almost impossible. Almost. Next came the code for recon. System paused, like always. Recon was a special code. Only trendside could use it. I got a white electral. Nothing special except a beefed-up comm unit and military-level defscreens.

Electral was recoded just for me by the time I crossed the garage. Door still squeaked. Always would. Smelled like plastics inside. That wouldn't change. Touched my hands to the stickwheel.

Cleared for recon. Estimate return.

"*Fourteen hundred.*" I always spoke, but linked when I said it.

The gates irised wide. Took the west tube and came out beyond the Park and towers. Westside's on the other side of the river, if you can call the Platte a river. The metroplex quarters fan out from the Park. Northside's production; eastside's transport and sariman housing; southside is filch, wish-filch, and upper sariman. Then, there's westside—trades, servies on the way up, servies on the way down, and a scattering of netless blocks—the downs. DPS links worked there, but not much else.

Could have taken the express tube, but you don't learn much underground. Instead, I went over the Elletch Bridge. Saw all the servies in their old scooters or on the shuttle glideway headed to southside or northside. Off the bridge, I turned north on the Bryant Guideway, then west past the Westside Fields.

First stop was Morss's Galleria. Fancy name for an old-style pool joint with a couple of formulators that served food at four times the cost of home units. Mornings were slow. Only a side table was used. Two old ex-servies. They leaned on their cues as much as used them. Both watched when I walked in. Was wearing a dark blue singlesuit—sariman business style. They still watched.

Morss moved to me quickly, then stopped. "It was looking to be a beautiful day. Been a while, Lieutenant."

Morss always said that. Could have been talking to him the day before. Still tell me it had been a while.

"Little stuff. Lots of it." Didn't look at him, exactly. Not with the scar running from the corner of his mouth to his ear. Just waited, my eyes mostly on the street.

"You always had a sense 'bout that. Remember the time you walked to Gian's, then walked away? You couldn't a been ten. Chou and his boys goin' over Gian."

"Gian didn't forget."

"Sure didn't." Morss shook his head. "Today . . . this week . . . nothin' I know about." He frowned. "Was Luke's kid Al. Disconnected the overrides and safeties on his dad's lorry. Ran it off the guideways and into Clear Creek."

Didn't sound like what I needed. "Know why?"

"No one does. He didn't tell no one. Not even his girl. She been crying nonstop, they say. Young Al, he was a quiet kid, mostly. Been to FlameTop concert last night. Found him early this morning. Luke was real broke up. His boy was a good kid."

"Sorry for them both. And the girl."

"You might know her, Lieutenant. Tasha Lei."

"Zhou Lei's daughter?"

"His youngest. Zhou wasn't too happy about the two of them. Never said much, but I could tell."

"You think it was a screen?"

Morss shook his head. "Naw. Zhou figured it wouldn't last. Al never stayed with a girl more than a few months."

Made a mental note to my linkfile to check out the accident. "Anything else?"

"Remember old Arturo Kemal?"

"Went with his daughter once."

"Say he's about to die. Hanging on for now. Only ninety. Drank too much. Nanites can't beat that. And last week, maybe the week before, his grandniece Antonia died. Rock climbing up north somewhere. Old Arturo was all broke up."

"He does love his family." That was about all I could say for him. "Hasn't Chris been running the outfit, anyway?"

"Has for years. You're not his favorite, Lieutenant."

I laughed. "Never was. Not after his sister. He still got Grayser on the heavy equipment?"

"Far as I know." Morss stopped. "Boys tell me Chris is working to make it all legit. Put stuff in place once he takes over official-like. He claims he owes it to his kids. Got a lot of creds from someplace—all legal Bulsor says. Chris has some idea about spinning the heavy stuff off to someone no one heard of. Guy's an ex-wyg that came out of the Ellay desert."

I laughed. Kemal going legit? Even with their big company, and all their credits, the family couldn't walk straight with a laser guide. Been true of Kryn, too.

We talked for another half hour. Didn't offer me any more insights.

When I left, the ex-servies stopped their game and watched. So did Morss. He was still watching when I eased the electral back toward Bryant.

Second stop was Westside Physical Systems, only about a klick southwest of Morss's place. Small office building with a formulation shop behind it. No other electrals around. So I parked right in front of the door. Like all DPS electrals, the white one self-locked the moment I stepped away.

Inside, there was a foyer, a counter, and a permie at a console behind the counter. Walls, floor tiles, countertop—all were maroon, all spotless.

The permie looked up from the console. "Yes, ser?"

"Lieutenant Chiang, Department of Public Safety. Here to see Kama." His full name was Kamehameha O'Doull. I'd never used it. Hadn't asked how the Hawaiian in his past met the Irish in NorAm, either. Kama was more than two meters tall and well over 120 kilos.

"I'll tell him, ser." The servie went link, his eyes blank. Then he said, "He'll be right here, ser."

Kama slipped out of the back room. Hard to believe he was so big. No fat, and he moved like a dancer. He wore a spotless white coverall. The shiny boots were black.

"Trouble, I see." Kama grinned.

I grinned back, then shrugged helplessly. "How's business?"

"Fine. People still need plumbing and pipes along with their nanite-based house systems. You're lucky you caught me in." The grin vanished. "You still owe me a game of chess."

Owed him that game of chess for more than twenty years. "I know. You'd beat me. You always did."

"That's not the point. It's a game of beauty."

"If you say so." I wasn't sure that was the point. If we both linked, usually got a draw, based on old grandmaster games. If not, Kama won in twenty moves, maybe thirty. That was beauty? "Just asking. Got a feeling something might be happening."

The contractor's eyes narrowed. "I've never liked your feelings, Eugene. Is it anything I should worry about?"

I shrugged. "Couldn't say. That's why it's a feeling. Minor offenses up. Pols worried. No one says much."

"You could be wrong."

"Been wrong before. Be happy if I am. Anyone building a fortress?"

"I wish someone would. Business is a little slow, except repairs here in westside." He laughed. "Something always goes wrong here. You have to make dozens of little service calls to make ends meet."

"Too bad you can't do service southside."

"Most of the filch mansions have self-repair systems. Here, who can afford them? Only business I get there is either new systems, total disasters, or upgrading whole systems."

"Getting any of that?"

"Maybe one every other week, about the same as always."

"Each one more elaborate?"

"Why else would they upgrade?" Kama smiled more broadly.

"So it would take a cargo lorry loaded with lead at full velocity to break into one of those filch palaces?"

"For most. Some would take more. One place has a fuel cell power room that would run half of westside."

"That has to be Alembart."

"You can guess all you want, Eugene."

"What about the McCall thing? That your system? Pretty horrible."

Kama shook his head. "Brazelton's. He's a hundred times our size. He's got system techs. They do it by the link manual. I do all that myself. I couldn't afford a tech."

"Bet your system designs are better."

Kama smiled. "Probably, but from what I can tell, it wouldn't matter. McCall reengineered it. That's what your DPS techies claim."

"What do you think?"

Kama frowned.

I waited.

"McCall is a solicitor. What solicitor knows nanite systems that well?"

I nodded. "He used to work for O'Bannon and Reyes. O'Bannon was pretty close to Chris Kemal."

"Do you know something?" Kama raised his eyebrows.

"With privacy laws, who *could* know?" I offered a grin. "Chris Kemal . . . heard anything?"

"We're not exactly friends. His circle is higher than mine, Eugene. It's much higher. You've been closer to him than I have."

I waited.

"I haven't heard anything. They say Kemal's hurting. Dewey doesn't like him, and neither does Senator Cannon. Kemal's been seen with Heber Smith lately."

"Heber Smith?" I hadn't heard that name.

"He's the campaign manager for Alredd. They don't call him that. He says he's a business consultant, but it's no secret that Alredd's going to take on Dewey in the summer election. Alredd's also backing Hansen against Cannon in the fall."

"Because Cannon mandated the guideway study and the changes in the maintenance requirements?"

"Something like that," Kama said.

"Kemal wants the guideway repair business back?"

"He never had it. Brazelton did."

I snorted. "Brazelton had the business, before it went to GSY. Creds behind it were Kemal's. He wants a return on those creds."

"I'd guess so. Wouldn't you?"

I'd have guessed a lot more. So would Kama. "Heard Arturo's hanging on. Might die."

"He already died where it counts a long time ago."

I sighed. Loudly. "I may be back."

"You're worried."

"Goes with the job."

"Remember . . . you owe me that chess game."

"How could I forget?" How could I? Owed him since before I'd gone to the DPS Academy. Kama never forgot anything. Never would. Might not tell, but wouldn't forget.

I walked out to the electral, standing by itself out front. Kama watched me from the door. Sometimes felt that everyone watched me.

Had barely pulled away when Sarao linked me. *Lieutenant . . . Captain wants to know if you've found anything.*

Nothing. Might help if I knew what I was looking for.

She asked to be linked if you came up with anything.

I'll do it.

That was the way it went all day. Knew I was on the edge of something. Just didn't know what. Couldn't even figure out where to ask. Or what.

Got back to the garage at fourteen-forty. Took a few minutes to satisfy the transport system. Needed a statement if I was back more than fifteen minutes past the estimate.

Stopped by the captain's office before going to mine. She looked worried. Worried and tired.

"You didn't find anything, did you?"

"Nope," I admitted. "Something's coming. Street's too quiet. Too . . . normal."

"Not all the problems are on the street." Cannizaro leaned back in her ergochair and smiled faintly. "They never have been."

"No. But the slick problems cause street problems, and big slick problems cause big street problems."

"You think it's a slick problem or a filch one?"

"I don't know. Let me work on it."

"You're the last of the street cops, Chiang. After you, things will change."

Shook my head. "Always be street cops, Captain. Just fewer. Two kinds of perps—the sariman and filch slicks, and the twisted servies. Need people who know both." I knew servies and permies and the netless. Didn't know the slicks. They were for the netops types. Even as I thought that, knew I'd have to look deeper into the netops reports.

"Let me know." That was all the captain said.

"Soon as I do." I walked out of her office and down the ramp to mine.

Sarao raised both eyebrows as I neared the consoles.

"Just more feelings. Need to look into some things."

"Anything I can check on? Screens are slow now."

"Not yet. Don't know where to point you."

"Whenever."

I smiled.

Back in my corner office, I called up lorry accidents. Three flashed into my mental screen. Second one was in Clear Creek. Medical had added info since the morning. Young Al had been drinking. Alkie levels just below impairment. No other drugs. Baseline nanite body protectors way down. No infection, and no sign of past injury before the crash. Probably Luke had been short of creds, put off his son's annual medcheck. Bad idea, but hadn't killed Al. Crash had.

Still bothered me. Couldn't say why. But had more incomings to check on, and my own report to the captain. No hurry to get home. Nothing to get home for.

Linked to the system again. Could always check on Heber Smith, and some of Kemal's other associates. Maybe . . . some tie with McCall . . . maybe there was something . . . somewhere . . . that would tell me my feelings were right.

Chapter 4
Munich, 1941

Torches blaze around the rear of the hall, lighting the red, black, and white banners topped with bronze standards.

> *"Wie zuerst ich dich fand*
> *Als feurige Gluth,*
> *Wie dann einst du mir schwandest*
> *Als schweifende Lohe:*
> *Wie ich dich band,*
> *Bann' ich dich heut'!"*

The massed voices blend into an echo that reverberates up into the darkness of the Kongressaal. The outspread arms of the copper eagle stretch above the hooked cross and the brass bowl where red flames lick at the gathering darkness.

The lower notes echo from the pipe organ, the tones resonating

through the vast hall under the Deutsches Museum, rippling the
crimson banners that seem to drip blood upon the black-clad
honor guard below.

". . . Wie ich dich band,
Bann' ich dich heut'!"

As the music fades, indrawn breaths punctuate the silence of
the dark. Presently, the words begin, almost as if a continuation
of the Wagnerian resonances.

". . . a heritage beyond price, an honor beyond honor . . .
those who gave their souls for the freedom and future of our
people and for the eternal greatness of the Greater German Reich.
Germany, *sieg heil!*"

"Sieg heil! Sieg heil! Sieg heil!!!"

The refrain echoes like thunder into the upper reaches of the
Kongressaal, shaking the Deutsches Museum from beneath, shak-
ing the ground around, and rippling into the darkness far beyond
Munich.

Chapter 5
Parsfal

I was buried in the southwest corner of the lowest level of the
university library. My eyes burned as I flicked past image after
image in the reader, hurrying through decades of information
quickly, trying to locate old photos and stories not in the link
archives—or even fragments of stories that could be twisted as
needed. I already had some possibles that I'd scanned into my
office archives, two about Walter Cheesman, one about Moffatt,
and a couple about territorial Governor John Evans, and some
from later governors of the former state of Colorado. I got tied
up with some articles about a political organizer named Robert

E. Lee, who was sometimes called "the general," but who wasn't one. That was the trouble with liking your work. Besides being single, that is. I had to fight to stay on the subject at hand. NetPrime wasn't paying me for psychspinning, or straight historical research, but for usable slants for PrimeNews.

Parsfal! Where are you?

I winced at the volume on the link. Bimstein always over-boosted. In an earlier age, he would have yelled, like Yeats's rough beast slouching toward Bethlehem, except that Yeats never envisioned his beast yelling as the center fell apart. And Bimstein wouldn't have understood a gong-tormented sea, or even a wine dark one. He would have made some caustic remark and told me to get back to work.

Where I said I'd be—in the old university library. You wanted background on the southern water diversion.

Why did you have to go there?

Because the old newspaper stories were microfilmed or fiched or whatever, and it would have cost too much to convert them to electronic storage. So no one did.

What will that give us?

The same as always—the impression that we look into things much deeper. That we, above all other newsies, understand the depth of the stories we cover, and provide a beauty of coverage that no others can emulate. I paused. *While providing color and other titillations from those safely dead and beyond the shelter of the libel laws.*

I could sense Bimstein's snort over the link. *Don't be too long. Kerras says he's going to need your touch on something else. It must be big. He won't say what.*

Kerras never said what he was working on, not unless Kountze landed all over him. And whatever he was working on was big, whether it was a three-cred miscredit in the local housing assistance office or a rash of detentions of invisibles or a massive kickback from the Martian Republic to MMSystems for leaking the design of the latest asteroid tug's debris screens. It hadn't been called a kickback, of course. The Republic had just paid what it called an early delivery fee for some standard power modules. With Kerras, the current story was always big, and he was always upset if he didn't get the big ones, like the PDF asteroid stories that Kountze had given Brianne deVeau two years ago, after the Belters had "miscalculated" and sent all sorts of rock heading earthward. Water asteroids were easy to destroy or divert, compared to mining debris, and Kerras had wanted that one, but Kerras hated all Belters, and didn't care that much more for the Martian Republic.

Parsfal?

Just finishing up. Be back in less than an hour.

Bimstein didn't answer, and I just got his simmie. So I broke off even before the simmie could offer to take a message.

The regional water diversion was coming up before the NorAm Senate, and the debate would be heated because of the continuing drought, and the low flows in both the Rio Grande and the Colorado. Phenix had put population caps in place, and wanted Denv to do the same—or send more water south. That was already getting big play in the Denv District Coordinator's election, and I wanted some deep background quotes, historical quotes, or statements that sounded real and that no one could dispute. Then, who was going to dispute pre-Collapse quotes, anyway? Kerras needed stuff that would show the issue was more than words, that it went back a long time.

What I was doing would take more work once I got back to the office, because I'd have to refine the personae that resembled the historical figures, and then spend an extra hour—or more—getting the details right. But it worked. The segments for which I'd done the research and creative re-creations had the highest ratings of any local news provider. They always did.

I shut down the reader, and closed my portable scanner, then walked over to the records custodian—a permie who'd been watching me for almost two hours, since there was no one else down in the archives. I extended the case that held the old records. "Thank you."

"Glad to be of service, ser." His face wasn't quite blank, but he wasn't smiling, either.

With a nod at the poor man, even if he had deserved permanent nanite reprogramming, and was bound to tell the truth at all times, I took the ancient circular steel stairs that must have been two hundred years old and hurried up to the main level and then out into an overcast late March day that was as cold as early February, without the snow, a day that all the instruments would agree was a dark cold day, even if it weren't in January.

I'd debated calling an electrocab, but Bimstein wouldn't have allowed it as an expense, and I didn't want to eat the fare. Instead, I walked across the gardens east of the library and then south along the ancient boulevard, hurrying most of the way, until I reached the local shuttle station. There were a good fifteen people waiting already, and that meant a shuttle was likely to be arriving soon. I could have linked and called up a schedule, but what good would that have done? The shuttle wouldn't arrive any sooner.

Most of those on the platform were students. They were the ones in multicolored singlesuits, without jackets, or with sleeveless vests, or, occasionally, with a jacket, but one left open. They clustered mostly in groups, looking as though they didn't want to be there, as if taking a shuttle were somehow beneath them. Then there were the junior faculty types, looking not all that much older than the older students, but then with nanomeds, no one looked much older than grad students, except in the eyes, until the last decade of life, when even nanomeds didn't help. The faculty types wore either solid-colored singlesuits with jackets over them, or tunics and trousers and jackets.

I usually wore a singlesuit with a jacket over it, but that was more for convenience, with the moving around that could come at any time in digging up stuff for NetPrime. The tunic, trousers, and jacket were what I preferred, but I never got to wear them enough.

Once on the shuttle, I listened. It was useful and sometimes even interesting.

"... sometimes ... rather be an invisible ..."

"... nah ... they get caught ..."

"... Dagmar ... got accepted by A-Square for pilot training ..."

"... wouldn't catch me driving a steel closet through the Belt ..."

"... lots of creds ..."

"... see those meteors last night ..."

"... ice chunks ... sloppy mining ..."

"... claim that Elymai and Aristo are clones ... link-programmed to sing ..."

"... eyes don't look that way ..."

"... cleanup programming take care of that ..."

"... think about that filch McCall?"

"... did it, if you ask me ..."

I got off at the OldTech station on the low ridge that split the true filch part of southside from the part where the less affluent filch and high sariman types lived. I couldn't see that much difference, especially not compared to my tiny quarters. At least I had a stand-alone house in the small historic district, even if the walls did date back more than three centuries and the covenants required that I not change the exterior. It was the only thing I'd gotten from my grandmother. Worth about half a small filch mansion, but you couldn't buy half of one, and I couldn't afford the other half. Damned if I would live in eastside or east southside with the sariman types, either. I supposed that made me a snob of sorts.

The OldTech station wasn't much more than an antique brick platform, with a slate tile roof and nanoscreens to break the wind. Only two of us got off. The other was a woman in the singlesuit of a CommInspector. I just hoped she wasn't headed for NetPrime, but she walked eastward. Could be headed for either NorNet or one of the indies.

The wind had turned warm by the time I left the station, a spring chinook that appeared from nowhere and had me opening my jacket before I'd walked a hundred meters. Another two hundred brought me to NetPrime—a low pale green marble structure with clean lines that rose out of grass that was green even under the snow in full winter.

The building was nestled into the ridge, with four levels below ground, and three above, meeting the environmental requirements for non-obtrusiveness. The tech areas were mainly on the third and fourth levels down, but I was lucky. Issues research was semi-tech, and that put me on the first level down, and off the main garden courtyard. So I had natural light through the courtyard skylight. What I didn't have was much space. My cube was all of two and a half meters square, and most of it was taken up with shelves—filled either with datablocs or several dozen hard-copy, old-style books that had never been converted to electronic storage, not that I'd been able to find. One was a gem— *Statistics from Colonial Times to the Present.* Of course, the "present" had been almost two hundred years before, but the numbers were fascinating. More than three hundred million people just in the old USA section of NorAm? Unbelievable.

I had barely passed through the archway that held the concealed security scanners when my link buzzed.

Parsfal? You back yet? Kerras came across the links as thin and whiny, for all that his voice was mellifluous in person and over the net. Mellifluous—beautiful word, even if I did have to keep it for myself.

Just heading down to my place. Got a couple of sweet hist-slots for the diversion piece. You'll love them.

I might. How long?

How much time do I have?

NorNews doesn't run national for almost another hour. Need to jump them. Bimstein says you've got thirty, pushing it.

You'll have something.

Thanks.

How good it would be was another question. I'd hoped for an hour, although I'd already linked the scans of the old photos I'd taken in the university library to the simmie-building program with commands to construct, but the tweaking required to make the images look real on a holo projection could take the hours I didn't have.

Hurrying down the ramps, I barely avoided ramming into Eldiego—the RomNews anchor. His late-afternoon slot had a nine percent share of the total sectoral news market—close to phenomenal in a fragmented fullnet system where a two percent share for a single slot was considered respectable. Eldiego smiled, and I grinned back sheepishly. The man never seemed upset.

Parsfal? Kerras, again.

I'm working on it. That was almost accurate, even if I weren't quite to my cube.

We've got some advance stuff on the McCall murder.

Murder? Thought she was trapped in her electral when it caught fire and the nanite system expanded to contain the blaze. Programmed wrong.

SlashBurnNews already out with a story that the regional advocate's office is going to indict. Claim that her husband reprogrammed the system against her electral. So we're behind. Need an angle. When you get the hist-slots done, need background on him, and on elaborate murders of the filch. You know . . .

I know. Later . . . or you won't get these.

He was gone, and I was brushing past Istancya as she left her cube and I slipped into mine, linking into the system to check how the constructor had rebuilt the simmie of the long-departed Colorado State Governor Evans. The problem was that there weren't many photos from when he'd been governor, and most were from his later years. So I needed some regression there, trimming and darkening the beard, adjusting the skin tone and tension . . . a lot to do in not that much time.

Before I knew it, the link was buzzing again.

Only got ten minutes for the hour-top slot.

Done. Feeding to Metesta now. Bimstein got on my nerves, but there wasn't any help for it. He might lizard me endlessly, but he let me work my own way.

Thanks. Try not to push it so close. Sometime this afternoon, in between, while you're looking into the McCall stuff . . . also need a few facts on the Legislature's funding for local education and something on the nanomed support level for immigrants.

We try . . . but digging up the old stuff and verifying the new takes time.

Again, he was gone, and I had to cut off his simmie. He was like that.

Before I went to work on the McCall murder stuff, I wanted to see how much Metesta used in the final cut for Kerras's water piece. I called up the running cut for the news, watching on the screen, rather than having the holo field fill my cube. The first image and voiceover I got was an image of a starburst, followed by an intense point of light, and trails of light flying in all directions before fading.

"That was the PDF successfully destroying an errant water asteroid headed toward Earth. We'll be back in a moment with the details . . ." I skipped ahead to Kerras's piece, which ran later in the national news roundup.

"Here with Senator Cannon just outside the Senate chambers is Les Kerras." The field cut to the tall senator with the deep blue eyes and striking white-blond hair. Cannon offered the viewers an engaging and warm smile, projecting a palpable warmth and concern.

"Senator Cannon, you've opposed the Southern Diversion ever since you were first elected to the Continental Senate. Why?"

"The Southern Diversion is nothing more than filch-food. Filch-food for the southwest. Eastslope needs its water. Formulators don't make water. Every liter that goes south raises the cost for the people of Deseret that I represent. It's that simple. Diversion means higher prices. Diversion's theft with fancy words." A wider smile followed. "It's also theft from the people of Denv. Theft that could lead to population caps here."

I had to smile. Every sentence was short, and there were plenty of five-second cuts for the instanews types. No one was going to outsimplify Cannon. And he'd also placed himself in favor of protecting both the people of the NorAm capital and his own district. He didn't miss many angles.

Kerras voiced over. "That was Senator Cannon, about water diversion. Diversion fights go back a long way. Back to the first territorial governors. Here's what they had to say."

The simmie of Governor John Evans was almost perfect, with the well-trimmed dark beard, the vest, and the wide lapels of the frock coat, and the deep resonant voice. "Besides the Denver Pacific Railroad, the Denver Union Water Company was what made Denver into the state capital and the only tolerable place in the western wilderness. . . . Take away the water, and you would have nothing but the savages of Sand Creek."

Then came the simmie of Governor John Vanderhoof. "I stand on the principle that you shouldn't build dams that take water and provide nothing in return. Diversion is theft, nothing more."

I was pleased with the hard-eyed look that I'd managed to inject into that simmie. Of course, they hadn't quite said what I'd had them say, but it was close enough, and certainly accurate in an overall historic sense.

Kerras's voice-over followed. "There you have it. For over three hundred years, the people of Denv have had to fight for their water. Senators Elden Cannon and Kristine Patroclas are carrying on that fight against the filch interests of the Southwest."

Kerras had provided the senator with coverage almost as good as a rezad, one of the new ones, for free, and I'd helped, as usual, even if I didn't care much for Cannon. Then, I didn't care much for politicians of any kind. Patroclas was a pleasant cipher, and that was why Kerras had used Cannon.

I couldn't rest on self-satisfaction, though. I had to get back to digging up numbers and examples for Kerras that would fit the McCall case. After all, PrimeNews was "news with a difference," the difference being the slight gloss we added with hist-slots and numbers, or with any other slant we could find, and it was my job to find the slant.

After wandering out to the break room and getting a beaker of orange juice from the formulator—charged to my account, of course—I went back to my cube to start on the background to the McCall murder case.

My first cut at statistics didn't do much good. As I'd suspected, while there were NorAm enumeration blocs that were categorized by income levels, the blocs were regular squares and didn't fit the actual Denv quadrants. Nor did the overall stats help much. Less than two percent of NorAm population was filch, but the filch weren't distributed equally. Most were in centers—probably ten percent of the Denv area population was filch—or in secluded locales where they had private retreats. Springs was about average, while places like Pueblo and Collins had nearly no filch. Durngo and Aspen were each nearly seventy percent filch, and had been for centuries, but two areas of less than a thousand people didn't affect the area percentages much.

I tried an overlay of filch housing patterns on the census blocs, and geographically, it came out that sixty percent of the land in southside was filch estates, but southside as a whole, even with the near filch and the high sariman, only held about ten percent of the Denv area population. That was rough, very rough. And if I came too close, then the District Advocate might come down on PrimeNews for privacy violations.

There *might* be a way, but that would take time, which was short. I ran a full archive search—both of the news-to-print files and the holocast files—just using the terms "filch" and "murder." Less than fifty matches in the past ten years.

That seemed odd, far too low. So I expanded the time frame

to fifty years. That showed up with 270, also seeming low, but enough to work with for refined scans. I definitely had some work ahead of me. I also had to dig up some of the education and immigrant support figures—if I could find them.

Then, I had to offer the PrimeNews slant.

Chapter 6
Cannon

"Good morning, Chairman Cannon." Halberstem greeted me as I walked up to the GIL verifier at the members' door to the Economics and Commerce Committee hearing chamber.

"Good morning." I offered a smile. "How's Andrea?" Andrea was his daughter. She'd just gotten her law degree and certification as a solicitor in the Deseret District bar. Lovely girl, and bright. Too bad she hadn't found the right man yet. But she had time. The verifier light flashed green. It always did. We hadn't had someone try to impersonate a senator in more than twenty years, not at the capitol in Denv, anyway.

"She's fine. She'll be starting with Higgins, Scolino, and Knaak next week. She's excited." Halberstem smiled. "She really appreciated the leather case, Senator."

"It was my pleasure." And a reminder to Halberstem that I rewarded families as well for their father's—or mother's—loyalty. "Give her my best."

I was among the first in the members' chamber behind the dais. It was a severe long room with several consoles against one wall and two small oblong conference tables with straight-backed chairs around them.

"How long will this be?" asked Owen Ridings, the newly elected senator from the Piedmont. His long red hair was tied back in the rediscovered colonial fashion, except Owen was anything but colonial in outlook.

"Too long, Owen." I grinned. "It's a simple technical bill, and most of the members understand it." The hearing was a markup session on legislation to streamline the functions of NASR—the NorAm Securities Registry.

He groaned.

With a nod, I slipped through the door to the main hearing room and took my place in the chairman's seat in the middle of the curved and raised wooden desk-dais—real oak, and dating back more than a century. The hearing room was less than half full, and most of those that were there were either securities solicitors or their paralegal staffers.

Owen followed me in and took his seat at the left end.

I sat there for four minutes, until ten o'clock sharp. "This committee will come to order. The business at hand is consideration of S. 127, legislation to provide technical improvements in the organization of the NorAm Securities Registry." I glanced around.

"Mr. Chairman," announced Senator Peres, sitting at the far left side of the dais, "I have an amendment at the desk."

"The clerk will read the amendment," I began.

"I ask consent that the reading be dispensed with, Mr. Chairman. Each senator has a hard copy and a linkfile."

"So ordered."

"This amendment," Peres continued in her growling low voice, "is designed to clarify reporting requirements for significant shareholders. Under the current requirements, for example, trusts held by non-immediate family members are not considered under the control of a single entity. Nor are irrevocable trusts to minors, even when the trustee has orders from a guardian who may also hold a significant bloc of such securities. This amendment requires reporting of such circumstances and makes failure to report such holdings a class one administrative felony, the same as failure to report significant holdings under current law. A fuller description is on each committee member's link."

"A moment for objection, Mr. Chairman?" That was Teddy Ohlsenn, a predictably conservative senator, which was good because he hadn't been the most predictable or the brightest of securities solicitors before he had been elected senator from the High Plains District.

"Two minutes."

"The senator's amendment will do nothing but reduce the protections of the privacy laws, without providing any real protection for either investors or for the institutions whose share trading is being regulated by NASR. More importantly, it will increase the work hours of both the NASR registry section and of every institution traded on any level one exchange. In effect, the amendment will add nearly two percent to operating costs. I've sent a cost analysis to each of your committee-links. If you would just look at the figures, you'll see what I mean."

I smiled. It was a nice speech, and the facts were in the links, just as Teddy had said, neatly prepared by CASD. It didn't matter. The speech and facts were for the record. CASD already had the votes to defeat the amendment.

"Are there any other points?" I asked.

"A point of information, Mr. Chairman," Peres requested. "A question for the distinguished senator from the High Plains."

"A question for information purposes only." I knew what was coming. So did Ohlsenn.

"Were the figures you provided developed by the Continental Association of Securities Dealers?"

"As the senator from Baja has surmised, CASD did provide the figures. They are the only organization outside NASR with the expertise and data to do so."

"Let that be noted," replied Peres.

"So noted." I nodded. "The vote is on the amendment. Please signify yes or no."

The lights before each member lit. Eight red, three green, and the amendment was defeated.

"The next amendment before the committee . . ."

The markup lasted all morning, until after one o'clock, when the committee voted to send the bill to the full Senate, by the

vote margin that had characterized most of the amendments—
nine to two.

After graveling the markup to a close, I ducked back to the
members' room. There were sandwiches on one of the conference
tables. Whenever a committee meeting went past noon, Halberstem had them on a tray there, under my standing instructions,
along with various beverages. I'd found that even that simple
gesture made the other committee members less fractious in long
meetings.

I took a turkey and bacon sandwich—formulated, but from
one of the regal units, so that it was almost as good as the real
thing. Hungry as I was, I finished it in minutes.

As I took a cup of water, Jo Jaffrey looked up from the end
of the table where she was nibbling on one of the vegetable sandwiches—cucumbers, I thought. She swallowed and said, "We
need to talk, Elden. I have the figures you asked for on the coastal
reclamation legislation."

"Next week? It won't come up for at least a month."

She smiled. "I won't forget." She had silvery hair, probably
natural, one of those genetic throwbacks that nanites didn't correct. She could have colored it, but she wasn't that type.

"I know." I laughed. "I do know."

"Until then. I'll call you."

I nodded and finished the second sandwich before slipping out
and walking the back corridors to my office.

There, Ciella was waiting. "All of your appointments are on
your linklist, Senator." She tried to conceal a frown. She had nice
long legs and a good smile, even if she wasn't smiling at the
moment. The rest of the package was just as good.

"Thank you." I'd known they were, because she was good and
always had them listed, but I enjoyed looking at her. I'd have
enjoyed more, but that wasn't in her job classification, and it
wouldn't have gone over well with voters, especially women. Or
with Elise. I wasn't the kind that could get away with that. A
man has to know his limits, especially in politics. "I may have

to change some of them, once I meet with Canthrop. I'll let you know. I'll also let you know when I want to leave for St. George on Friday."

"Yes, Senator. Is that all?"

"For now, Ciella. Thank you." I gave her a warm smile, the paternal and friendly one, before I walked into my office. There, I went to the window and looked out on the hills to the south and west. After the cold and overcast of the past week, the sunlight was welcome, and it would make what I had to do less difficult. People are always easier to persuade when they feel cheerful.

Denv was a far better place for a continental capital than any of the old national capitals. Anyway, all of the major ones, except MexCity, were underwater or uninhabitable, and Denv was close enough to Deseret District to make the travel easy.

Thirteen forty-two . . . you have eighteen minutes before the Canthrop appointment.

I clicked off the link reminder and seated myself behind the desk. Then I studied the holo projection that I called up in front of the desk. The first briefing item Ted had provided was the NorAm contribution to the World Patrol. Below that were the amendments that had been announced as being offered. D'Amico's wasn't there. He always waited until just before the debate deadline.

Ted, add in an amendment from Senator D'Amico that proposes a twelve point five percent increase in the WP contribution . . .

Is that on the WP funding resolution?

None other.

How . . . I mean, it wasn't listed . . .

I know. But D'Amico will offer it. Do the same kind of analysis on that one and add it in. I cut off the link so he could work on it.

The second legislative item was the contribution to the Planetary Defense Force.

How much of the PDF contribution goes to the asteroid watch and protection program?

There was a pause. *Twenty-nine point seven percent, ser, I mean, sir.*

Thank you. I smiled. Ted Haraldsen was a good young man, already married, but he needed to get away from the unisex salutations. Men and women might be legally equal, but they were different, and the Senate wasn't the NorAm Guard or the WP or PDF. He'd learn.

I needed to get through the legislative items before Canthrop arrived. There'd be all too many things to handle afterward.

The fourth item bothered me. Always had. It was funding for baseline nanite and link enhancement for immigrants. The only immigrants NorAm got in large numbers were from Afrique, and those were required under the 2310 Protocol. We never should have agreed to that, but no one had anticipated that so many immigrants would be pouring out of Afrique more than half a century later. What was done was done, and we had to look to the future and set—or reset—the right precedents.

Ted?

Yes, sir?

The enhancement funding . . .

Do you want to offer your amendment from last session?

No. I'd thought about it. Not exactly. Let's trim it to ten percent of the total cost and have that repaid at one percent per year for ten years, and give a three-year grace period before it starts. That's only asking them to repay ten percent. Have each immigrant pay it through an income tax surcharge. You can work out the details.

Yes, sir. Even through the link, Ted sounded puzzled.

Don't worry about it. And draft me a short statement that explains that my interest is twofold. I believe we must always retain the principles that government works for everyone and that prosperity must go to all people, and must be paid for by all people. And I believe that this principle applies to high and low alike. Intimate that I'll be looking into filch abuses of this principle as the session continues.

Yes, sir.

Sometimes, politics was beautiful. The amendment would serve more than a few purposes, especially in dealing with Hansen in the campaign, but he wouldn't even see it coming until it was too late, if I handled it right. Who looked at amendments to minor line items? Until they made the news, no one did.

I leaned back in the big black leather chair and smiled, letting myself think about the beauty of it all for a minute, but only for a minute. There were twelve other items to read through and consider.

Before I knew it, the link chimed. *Dr. Canthrop's here, Senator.* I recognized Ciella's words even on link. Lovely girl.

Send him in. I cut the holo display and waited.

Canthrop had been a graduate economist who'd gone back and gotten his legal degree and then been a clerk assistant to the NorAm Advocate General before serving as the Advocate Counsel to the Public Affairs Committee. After ten years there, he'd opened his own firm. I'd been one of the first to retain him. I knew talent—and rewarded it.

Canthrop sank into the black leather armchair opposite the desk, brushing back his wispy blond hair. He had circles under his eyes, and I hadn't seen that before.

"Looks like you've had some long nights, Bill."

The consultant nodded. "You would, too."

"What's Hansen up to?"

"That'd be the last of your worries, Senator."

Canthrop was good, but sometimes you had to humor him, and it was one of those times. "What should be my worries?"

"Roberta Menstyr."

"Never heard of her. Should I? Freelance advocate? Representative government agitator?"

"You and I both wish that. You're going to be seeing a lot of new rezads in the next few months. By the way, your family's basically Mormon, right? English stock?"

I wasn't sure what he was getting at. So I let a touch of a frown show. "You know that. Why?"

"What netsys does your family usually track?"

"Is this—" I decided to play it straight. "I forgot. You don't joke. All right. I'll link. NorNet—you know, NorNews, the . . ."

"I know. Its coverage has gone from over fifteen percent to ninety percent of all English-stock NorAms for market share. That was another of her tests." Canthrop rubbed his forehead. It didn't do much for his thin hair. I always wondered why he hadn't done something about it. "Most of that's in the last three months. Not all that obvious, of course, because genotypical English stock—enough for rhythmitonal resonance to work—only comprises around seventeen percent of the current NorAm population. But others are catching on."

"Bill . . ." I said knowingly. "Isn't this at the edge of privacy material?"

"It probably is." His voice was tired. "That's the least of my problems. Or yours."

"It works, then?" I couldn't believe that. People had been trying to use resonance as a persuasion tool and worrying about it for half a century. Most holonet ads already used rez as a basis, even without whatever Canthrop was talking about. "I thought it was only good for getting the younger folks into music." I grinned humorously.

"Her version works. It really works. It has for a long time in the right conditions. There are records. Beethoven started it. Wagner gave it a push, and Goebbels and Speer orchestrated it for Hitler. Menstyr actually figured out the genetic basis and the mathematical resonances. At least five other firms besides Talemen Associates are working on ad campaigns based on the new developments, but Menstyr got herself a patent on some of it, I think. She'll probably get pretty wealthy . . . if she can live with herself nights."

"People have been playing around with resonance effects for almost fifty years. All the popular music uses it in some way or another. But so far no one's been able to put the overtones into the net—bandwidth problem, as I understand it. Why will this technology or whatever it is work when earlier versions didn't?"

"Senator . . . it works. Does it matter exactly how?"

I supposed it didn't. Not that I was all that clear on rhythmitonal resonance, except for how it generally worked, and that it did with music, especially on the emtwos, but I wasn't about to admit that. "It matters enough that I'll feel more comfortable if you'll tell me more." More important, I might not know the technology, but I knew people, and the way he explained it would tell me more than the technology behind it.

Canthrop concealed a sigh, or tried to. Then he squared his shoulders and pulled out a thin bound folder. He extended it toward me.

"Hard copy?" I raised my eyebrows. "We are skirting privacy."

The consultant rubbed his forehead. "Could be, Senator. I'm not about to put this through any link. You want to read it . . . read it now."

That was going to shoot the afternoon's schedule, but Canthrop usually had a point. And he looked worried. More worried than I'd seen him. I took the thin report. The cover was blank. So was the second page. The third page started talking about the history of the studies of resonance. I knew that. By the fourth page, I was reading intently.

. . . PET-monitored brain scans indicate a significant differentiation between the metabolites of neurotransmitters of those subjects identified as carriers of RTR-1, the segment studied for susceptibility to rhythmitonal resonance reaction . . .

The consistent and well-replicated finding that RTR-1 carriers demonstrate neuromotor and associated cortical resonance reactions to class one rhythmitonality patterns also indirectly supports a neurobiological hypothesis that rhythmitonal susceptibility is genotypically imprinted. . . .

Results in line with the supportive CBF findings were recently reported in a study using BEAM technology for computer averaging of EEG tasks during cognitive tasks involving decision making (Elyysiet, 2358). More specifically, increased patterns of reactivity were found in the frontal areas of the subjects, relative to controls. Despite their apparent support for rhythmitonal susceptibility, these sorts of investigations will require careful replication before much confidence can be placed in their conclusions. . . .

Results are also needed on subjects who have clear psychopathologic disorders in order to determine the specificity of the preliminary findings concerning RTR-1 susceptibility to culturally attuned rhythmitonal resonances. . . .

Culturally attuned rhythmitonal resonances? I nodded slowly. "Does Hansen know anything about this?"

Canthrop shrugged. "I couldn't say."

"Hadn't we better design the campaign around this? Or have it as a strong component?"

Canthrop managed to close his mouth. "Are you suggesting . . ."

"Bill . . . rezads have been legal for close to thirty years, or longer. This is an applied and scientific form of rezad. Neither the Senate nor the Supreme Justiciary is going to declare this version illegal, and certainly not before the next election. So we use it first and better or we place second in the election. Second, as you recall, is losing."

I waited a moment, then smiled warmly, and began to explain, gently. "You're worried, and I can see why. If an unscrupulous candidate started to use this . . . well, it wouldn't be good. That's why we have to use it first, and in a positive way, reinforcing all the good things we've done, why we've done them, and why they've been good for the people, especially the everyday people." I paused, mostly for effect. "I'd bet we could even develop a message that would create a certain skepticism about negative rezads, couldn't we?"

Canthrop nodded slowly. "I suppose so, but I wouldn't know.

We'd have to go through Talemen. Or pay them some sort of royalty."

"Whatever it takes. We do want this to be a positive campaign, Bill. I'm sure you can see why it's important to get out front with a very positive effort."

"Ah . . . it's just that I'm a bit surprised, Senator."

"You wouldn't want me to wait and then have to fight a negative campaign?" I offered another smile. "I read about one of the old machine politicians, years ago, and I still remember what he said. You have to give people a reason to vote for you. If you do that first, you make it twice as hard for your opponent, because he has to give them reasons why not to vote for you, and then why they should vote for him."

"I suppose so." Canthrop was still puzzled by why I'd decided to act so suddenly, but I could see where this could go, and that was why it was important we got the jump on Hansen. He didn't have the kind of resources we did, and by the time he raised enough he'd have to campaign on our ground—if I understood the implications, and I was pretty sure that I did. That was one of my talents, seeing things early.

Bill would understand once we got working on it. He was a good man at heart.

Chapter 7
Lanta, 2367

The sleepy-eyed sariman staggers down the hard but warm ceramic tile of the wide hallway. Even the replicated mosaic seems to pulse with the rhythmic beats that vibrate the closed door of the end bedroom. He stops before the door and knocks on it. There is no answer. He knocks a second time, harder.

Frowning, he overrides the lock through his link, then stands back as the door opens.

The blond-haired child watches the holo projection, listening . . . transfixcd.

"For the fun and sun, to play all day . . .
stay with NorPlay . . . stay with NorPlay . . ."

The words resonate into the bedroom. The child watches the pair of blond children his own apparent age frolicking across the crisp green grass.

"What are you watching?" The man rubs his stubbly jaw, letting his eyes and ears track toward the projected image. He pauses, then watches as the commercial finishes to the distorted strains of a Strauss waltz.

"NorPlay . . . that's where I'll stay . . ." The boy's voice unconsciously mimics what he has just heard.

"Jared?"

"Yes, Dad?" The towhead looks up at his father. "NorPlay's more fun than the others. That's all right, isn't it?"

The sariman shakes his head, finally looking at his son as the three-dimensioned cartoon figures replace the pair of children and resume their high-pitched antics. "I don't know." He purses his lips. "I guess so." His eyes blink momentarily in an echo of the resonances of the modified waltz. "I guess so."

Chapter 8
Kemal

The morning light poured through the skylight, and I glanced at the ancient wristwatch. It had been my great-great-great-grandfather's when he had come from the old Turkey to NorAm. The time was nine thirty-five. That left almost an hour and a half before the memorial service started.

"Are you all right?" Marissa looked at me. She was standing

in front of the mirror on her side of the bathroom. She blotted away the tears. She'd always liked my father. She said he was cute. He'd always played to the women, even when he could hardly speak at the end. His eyes would twinkle, and he'd grumble something. They loved it.

"I'll be fine. It wasn't exactly a shock." I straightened the suit coat and checked the tie in the mirror. It was hand-knotted, in the half Windsor I'd picked up from Damien years ago. The suit was a Bellini, hand-tailored, double-breasted, navy-blue, with the faintest pinstripe. I never wore black.

"He was your father," she said.

"I loved him." I had loved him. I had respected him more before he turned to drinking. I preferred to remember him as he had been—strong and decisive, a leader among men. "The last years have been hard."

She stepped away from the mirror and touched my cheek. "I know." Her eyes were still bright, and she looked away for a moment.

I couldn't help a faint smile. Even upset, she was beautiful. She'd always supported me. I'd never understood men who had beauty and grace in the women they married and then went out and played around with lesser women.

"Thank you." I put my arms around her and bent down. I kissed her neck gently, careful not to disarrange her hair and jacket.

We left the bedroom together.

Alyssa and Roderik were waiting in the open foyer at the top of the staircase. They'd come in the night before. Roderik had come from Southern University in Cedacity. He was getting a masters in finance. Alyssa had flown from her job at TriCon in Portlan, but she planned to spend a few days after the service at the family compound at Aspen. Mother was with them. She was all in black. Roderik wore a deep gray pinstripe. His sister was in a black suit with a white blouse.

"We're ready, Father," Roderik announced.

I looked at him. There was never much sense in saying the obvious. It made you look weak. Or stupid.

Marissa touched my arm. "Chris," she said softly.

"We should go." I let the others go first. Marissa and I followed them down and through the front entry. I could feel the tingle of the defense screens as we stepped out into the cool air.

Armand stood in the access booth above the portico. He was in charge of maintenance at the house. In fact, he oversaw the systems of more than half the family. Everyone agreed that we needed someone we could trust. I nodded to him.

He returned the nod stiffly.

The dark green electral was waiting under the portico. Nathan had the doors open.

"We should be back in about two hours."

"Yes, ser."

I checked the electral's defense screens before we pulled out of the lane and through the property gates. The screens were fully powered and in the green. It was less than a klick to the main guideway east. Two minutes later, I turned onto the guideway and locked in the system. I programmed the electral to make the turn when we reached the Southside Parkway.

"Don't go too fast, Christopher." Mother leaned forward.

"The system sets the speed," I pointed out with a laugh.

Marissa looked at me again. She was right.

"I can request a slower speed, if you'd like," I added.

"No. That's fine. I didn't want you driving too fast at a time like this. You shouldn't drive fast when you're upset. You have enemies who would use that."

She was right about that, and I lowered the programmed speed.

Even using the bridges and guideways, it was more than a half hour before we pulled into the reserved space in the garage below the KC headquarters in southside. Father had questioned the building when I'd first suggested it. It had become a mark of where we as a family were headed. Even he'd admitted that years ago.

Fred and Morrie were waiting for us. Fred got the door for Marissa, and Morrie opened the one for Mother.

"Everything's set, Mr. Kemal," Fred said. "Just the way you ordered."

"Thank you."

Fred led the way to the private inside ramps. That way, we could reach the auditorium quietly.

I'd picked the auditorium in the KC headquarters for the memorial service. Most companies didn't have auditoriums or real meetings. They did it all VR. It's not the same. People who work for you need to see you. They have to know what you're made of. The other thing is that having people come to meet with you reinforces the feeling that they work for you. You let them use VR presence, and they feel too independent. Those were things I'd learned from my father early.

That's why the company had an auditorium and a large conference room between the chairman's office and the president's office. I'd already moved from the president's office to the chairman's office the night before. Tomorrow, matters would be clear to those who didn't already understand. In a family-held organization like KC, there couldn't ever be any doubt.

Morrie escorted Marissa, Mother, Roderik, and Alyssa to their seats in the front row. Fred stayed with me, in the wings offstage.

The service was scheduled to begin at eleven. While we waited, I used the monitors Fred had arranged to study the audience. More than half of those in the hall were family. The others were KC executives and senior people in the various subsidiaries. Some had brought family, like Josef Domingo, who headed CerraCraft. Most hadn't.

My nephew Stefan was sitting in the second row. He was wearing a beige singlesuit. It was open at the neck. He wore a gold collar chain, and he'd thrown on a black jacket over everything—for my father's memorial service. Stupid little fop. He was grinning as he talked to the girl beside him. I hadn't seen her before. That wasn't surprising. Stefan spent credits as though they fell on him like sunshine. That was something else I'd have to face more directly now, with the KCF trusts.

Alyssa turned in her seat and looked at Stefan. His grin disappeared. I smiled. She'd done it without a word.

Stefan's younger brother Ivan just looked straight ahead.

I scanned the rest of the audience. There were about four hundred in the hall.

How many? I sent the question on link to Paulina. She was watching on monitors from my office on the top floor.

Three hundred sixty-seven. James O'Bannon just arrived below with his wife. José Reyes is behind him. Evan McCall came early. He's in the fourth row.

Thank you, Paulina.

The solicitors should have been there, after everything, and all the business KC had provided for them. Especially McCall. He was smart about law, but he'd let his wife sway him too much. That was another thing about Marissa. She left business to me.

Senator and Mrs. Lottler have also just arrived, and so has District Coordinator Dewey.

Lottler wasn't a surprise, not after all the support the family had given him. Dewey, that I couldn't figure, unless he was honestly paying his respects. He had nerve, though.

The service began with a march, from one of the ancient operas—*Aida*. That had been one of Father's requests. He'd always liked to hear it. At the end, I'd had to turn up the volume so high that it shook the walls of his bedroom. But he'd smiled.

When the last notes died away, Padre Borges stepped from the other wing. It had always seemed strange that my father had been one of the few remaining Catholics. It had been his choice. The Kemals had been Muslims, generations back, and then modernists, but Mother had been a Catholic, and Father had loved her. He'd also become a friend of the Padre.

So there I was, watching a Catholic priest offer a benediction to an agnostic descendant of Islam. I couldn't deny that Borges had been a comfort to Father. So had the bottle.

Then, Ricardo Spiropoulos came to the podium. He'd retired as senior vice president of KC a year earlier. He'd been with my father for thirty years, and I'd promised to let him stay as long as he wanted. In the end, he'd decided on a handsome retirement, and he'd left happy, which was what both Father and I wanted. That was the way it had to be.

I wondered what he'd say.

Ricardo coughed. He cleared his throat. Finally, he started. "I knew Arturo for more than forty years . . . Arturo had a dream. I wasn't a dreamer. But he said that he'd dream, and I'd help him make it real. But it wasn't just us. There were lots of good people, and there still are . . . Arturo had a way of making everyone laugh, even at the most serious times. He wanted people to be happy. . . ."

We both knew there were people who would never be happy. We'd talked about it.

". . . he wanted everyone to feel they contributed and that they were a part of a family . . ."

That was true. In what we did, people had to feel that they were a part. They had to share the responsibility, the liabilities, as well as the rewards. That went for solicitors, too.

". . . most people did . . . He built an organization and a legacy, and not many men can claim that in this day and age. And, most of all, to his last breath, he was my friend. He remembered after I retired. He called. He sent notes. How many business leaders are remembered for that? . . ." Ricardo choked up on the last words. I couldn't make them out. Some of those in the audience were weeping, too.

Then it was my turn. I stepped from the wings and walked to the podium in the center of the stage.

The podium had its own defense screens. There was no sense in being foolish. I tried to keep a low profile, but no multilateral president is without enemies. KC wasn't a large multi, but it wasn't small, and we were definitely growing quickly. Far more quickly than NASR would have liked, if they had known.

I looked out across the audience. Then I waited. You have to let people become just a little nervous.

"My father was a family man. He loved his family. He would have given everything to us. But he was a good father, and he knew that giving everything would have left us even poorer in spirit." I offered a sad smile. "So he was a wise father, as well. Like all children, I didn't understand him until I was a father. . . .

"He also loved the people of KC because they were family, too. He knew that without that kind of feeling an organization is only an empty bureaucracy. . . ."

Even though I'd planned it all, and had the words feeding to me through the link, there were times when I had to stop and collect myself. But a man can be upset at his father's memorial service.

". . . We're all sitting in a great building. Some have said that it will be a monument to my father, a testament to his vision. I hope not. I hope that his testament will be in the words he said that others remember. In the small kindnesses he did for others. In the memory of his laughter, and his joy in life . . ."

I managed to get out the last words, and then stood there as the closing dirge played.

I didn't know what it was. Mother and Padre Borges had picked it.

Fred was waiting for me in the wing. Morrie escorted Marissa, Mother, Alyssa, and Roderik back to the wing. Mother's eyes were even redder than before the service, and Marissa had been blotting away tears.

Alyssa looked at me and mouthed, "Stefan." She gave the faintest headshake.

I nodded, just slightly.

We walked to the inner ramp and back down to the garage.

Fred and Morrie made certain we were safely in the electral. They watched as I eased the electral out of the KC garage, past security and through the screens.

Once we were clear of the screens, Marissa leaned toward me.

Her voice was low. "That was touching, dear. He would have been proud of you. He always was."

No one said anything until we were on the Parkway headed back north. We needed to get to the house before the rest of the family arrived for the wake. My sister Barbra was particularly punctual. Kryn would take her time.

Then Mother leaned forward. "Christopher, you must be careful. There are many who choose to believe that you were only acting for your father." Mother had always worried.

Then, my father had always been a careful man, except when he drank. After Leon's death, he'd drunk all the time, even after we'd taken care of Gietta in a way that made sure no one would take us lightly. Even so, Father had kept drinking. That had been for ten years. Except for his public appearances, when he pulled it together, he'd been a silent and quiet drunk, except around Mother, Marissa, and the other women in the family. They'd made him a happy drunk.

"I'll be careful." That was an easy promise to keep.

"The rest of you," Mother went on, "you must also be careful. You must take care of your health and your families." She half smiled as she looked at Roderik and Alyssa. "When you have them, that is."

Marissa reached out and squeezed my hand. I still marveled at my fortune in her.

Chapter 9
Cornett

The antique Steinway dominated my office, if you could call the space that. Really, it was just a practice room with a tiny corner console and two chairs—nanite synthwood, supposedly mahogany. Oh, yes, there was the single music stand, also synth-mahogany. I'd had to put up the corner shelves over the console, three sets, and they were all overflowing with sheet music and a few of my reference books.

I guess I was old-fashioned in more ways than one, but you can't learn art song, or any music, from a console. Some of the rezrap and rezpop singers have it linked right into their heads. Most of them sound like they were reading it, rather than singing it. Singing isn't just hitting the notes with the right words. The old composers had styles, and you have to know the style to make the song sound right. And you have to practice. I tried to work in at least an hour a day, but that was sometimes a problem, because practicing is something you have to do before you get too tired or frazzled, or it does more harm than good. That means practicing early in the day. That has always been hard for me because I'm not a morning person, and because my teaching at the university was in the morning and early afternoon.

Today, the rezrappers and poppers don't practice. They just spew it out. The systems reformulate the sound as they attempt to sing, add in the rhythmitonal resonances based on the audience profile, and everyone thinks it's wonderful.

Whatever it is, it isn't music, and it isn't artistry. The problem isn't new. There's always been a conflict between excellence and popularity. It's just that the more technology gets into the act, the more likely it is that special effects overshadow excellence, and artistry's lost.

Reflecting upon that once more, I took the *26 Italian Songs and Arias* from the music stand to put it back on the shelf after Michelle had left. She was my only student on Wednesdays. I had six private students through the university. Besides Michelle, I had one on Mondays, and two each on Tuesdays and Thursdays. Those six were in addition to the section of music appreciation I taught on Tuesdays and Thursdays.

After shelving the music, I took my jacket off the hook behind the door, getting ready to leave for home and a quick lunch. I certainly couldn't afford to eat at a uniquery, not on my income, and I ate at the student center far too much anyway.

After lunch, I'd have to head out to OldTech for a rezad session with Mahmed.

There was a single rap on the door. "Luara?"

I recognized Jorje's voice and sent a link pulse to the door, which opened to admit him.

His dark eyes radiated concern as he hurried in. "You were leaving? This will only take a moment, but you should know."

"Know what?"

"I just got the preliminary Arts College budget . . ."

"Music got cut again," I suggested.

"Another twenty percent. The trustees have approved a cut in the in-person credit hour requirements, and raised the allowable link and self-taught hours. The dean wants to cut the service program. We're carrying three sections of appreciation. He says the numbers only support two. We have to consolidate into two larger classes. That's more cost-effective. We also need to offer courses that are more relevant."

Jorje and I *were* both the vocal and music service program, but I was the adjunct, and he was on a multiyear firm contract.

"Larger classes will show that we're keeping in-person classes cost-effective?" I hated the whole idea of cost-effectiveness in education, but teachers had been attacked for not being cost-effective from since the time of Socrates, if not before.

"I know how you feel," he temporized.

"Do you?" I could feel my voice rising. He didn't have a clue to how I felt. That was for the best. Jorje was a nice man, but like the word "nice" itself, he was somewhere between totally self-serving and sweetly ineffectual. That was probably why the dean kept him around. "Is there any chance . . . ?"

He shook his head. "I can offer you the new class on rez-prep. It's three credits. You've got the degrees and experience. I know you don't like it, but it's all there is."

"I'll take it." What other choice did I have? "But I'm also going to see the dean."

"I can understand that." He nodded. "I did want to tell you before you heard it elsewhere."

"I've heard it."

"Well . . . that was all." He bobbed his head, then turned.

Still holding my jacket, I watched him leave. Automatically, I put it on and then gathered the music I wanted to look over that night.

Another cut in the arts, all in the name of economy. As I stepped through the door, letting it close behind me, I wondered why I was even at the university. My brother Raymon thought I was crazy. So had my ex-husband Michael.

Before he'd totally given up on me and on artistry, Michael had been very vocal about it. "The tests show it, Luara. You could be a top NorAm administrator, or a manager in any one of a dozen fields. You could be filch. You're wasting your time at the university. There's no money in old-style music. No money and no future."

I certainly wasn't looking at much of a future. But how could I give up the beauty of making music—or teaching? Without the university contacts, I wouldn't be getting the gigs that I was. Or even the rezad work.

Raymon understood my love for music, in a way. He shared our father's views. Both had suggested, if I wanted to make music a career, that I go into rezpop. Rezpop wasn't music. Entertainment, high-paying entertainment, but not music.

I walked slowly past the choral room—and Jorje's rehearsal—and then out of the Fine Arts building. Along the lower garden corridor, shielded by nanoscreens, and in the spring sunlight, the year-around yellow roses offered a fragrance that was almost overpowering. Ahead was the university screen gate, and beyond it, the maglev station that served the south end of the university.

Before I left the protections of the university, I ran a self-check. My internal nanites said I was fine. Then I touched the heavy silvery bracelet on my right wrist. The nanoshield was on standby. I'd never needed it, but my father had given it to me three years earlier after a student had been frozen and stripped at UBoulder.

It had been triggered only once. That had been a year ago, when a student high on soop had mistaken me for his girl and tried to hug me from behind. The screen had thrown him almost into the maglev car I'd been about to board. He'd just picked himself up, like all the soopers, and grinned.

The screens brushed over me as I stepped between the stone pillars and onto the hard granite stones comprising the walk that led to the station. There were only two others on the platform, under the arched canopy. Both were students, a couple, and they were engrossed in each other, their voices intense, but so low I couldn't make out a word.

Less than five minutes later, the eastbound shuttle arrived. The couple hurried through the forward door. I took the rear and slipped inside the shuttle car just before the doors swished shut. I turned back to look out through the armaglass.

As the maglev pulled away from the platform, a dark-skinned, bearded student panted up onto the platform. He looked blankly at the departing shuttle, then started to shiver all over. His face was flushed. I took another look and swallowed. His face was covered with a bloody sweat. He raised a hand and then pitched forward onto the hard stone pavement.

Without real thought, I pulsed a link to the DPS.

Student collapsed on the university transit platform, south station. Bloody sweat, and possible seizure. Needs medical attention.

Your report has been received. A medvan is on the way. Thank you.

I hated the metallic feel of an autosponder, but I'd made the report. That was all I could do. I couldn't even see the station by the time I'd finished. What had happened to him? Some sort of disease? I'd never seen that sort of a bloody sweat. What could it have been? I would have said it was a seizure, but after thinking it over, it wasn't like any seizure I'd read about. Then, I'd never seen a seizure.

Finally, I tried to think about the afternoon, wondering exactly what the rezad would be pitching. High-end electrals? Formulator inserts for special menus?

My stop was the fourth one, on the inner edge of eastside, bordering one of the historical districts that had escaped the devastation of 2131. I liked looking at the mix of architecture as the maglev shuttle neared my station. There were gray-tile-roofed bungalows of a type I'd never seen anywhere but Denv, a geodesic dome comprised of an early composite that shimmered with a light of its own, a small-scale replica of an antebellum plantation house, a centuries' old art deco brick house with half its windows made of glass bricks.

I got off alone, as I usually did in midday. There was a faint hum as I passed through the platform scanners. I wondered if they needed some maintenance.

The walk home was pleasant, because I always took the path that bordered Park East. The green of the grass jarred slightly with the bare-limbed elms and the bare flower beds. Only universities and the filch had year-round flowers outside. I'd given up on trying to grow them in the conapt. Somehow, I either watered things too little or too much.

I reached the lane. Then I had to look at the boringly clean lines of the conapts that formed Eastside Courts. The conapt wasn't what I'd have chosen, if I'd had a choice. I hadn't had one. It had taken every demicred I'd had just for the option, and almost all of my pay as an adjunct instructor of voice went to the monthly fee. I might actually own it in sixteen years and ten months.

The door waited until I pulsed it to open, and the interior link system reported, *Interior is empty. Balcony scanner is inoperative.* The scanner on the upstairs balcony off my bedroom had been inoperative for almost a year. Someday, I might actually have enough spare credits to have it repaired or replaced. *You have three messages.*

From whom? I pulsed the door closed and surveyed the small front foyer. There was dust on the replica antique marble-topped plant stand. Another sign that the nanetic cleaning system needed refurbishing, as if I had creds for that also.

Mahmed Solyman, Raymon Cornett, and Aleysha Bunarev.

Mahmed. I ordered. *Project.*

The image of the dark-haired and dark-skinned production manager appeared, bowing slightly. "Luara. You're scheduled at fourteen hundred. I'd like you to do two, instead of one this afternoon. Full pay for both, but I'll need you at thirteen-thirty. Let me know."

Full pay for two rezads. That was the first good news in weeks, since the invitation to sing at the Clayton soirée, but the soirée wasn't for another week. I wouldn't see the credits until after that. Mahmed flashed the creds to my account within hours after we wrapped.

Because I could actually sing, I'd managed a side business moonlighting as a backsinger for rez-based net commercials. They didn't have to spend the time correcting my voice, and the manipulations were simpler. I was cost-effective. That left me with very mixed feelings—pride over my competence and dislike of the whole idea of cost-effectiveness. The credits were more than necessary. A few more sessions, and I might actually be able to pay for the deferred maintenance on the cleaning and house defense nanite system. I didn't want to think about the scanner.

I linked to Mahmed—and got his simmie. *This is Mahmed Solyman of Crescent Productions. If you would leave . . .*

Mahmed, this is Luara. I'll be there just before thirteen-thirty to do two rezads. See you then.

Raymon had just been calling, in his twice-weekly brotherly fashion. Nothing special. I'd get back to him when I came home after the session at Crescent. Aleysha was my neighbor and wanted to know if I'd seen Solomon, her cat, an animal who did nothing to deserve the name. I hadn't, and left a message that said so.

Within the kitchen formulator, the magic nanites hummed and hissed, and after several minutes the ancient appliance groaned and finally produced an edible pasta primavera. I was so hungry

I ate all of it. I wasn't about to ask the formulator for wine. The last time I'd been tempted and tried that, I'd gotten something that verged on vinegar. Even the best formulators didn't do wine and subtle flavors well.

Before I knew it, I was walking back to the shuttle station. I glanced up at a sky that was showing more and more clouds to the west over the Rockies. With my luck, it would be pouring by the time I finished the rezad recording sessions.

The shuttle was mostly empty, again, but it would be crowded by the time I finished at Crescent. Mahmed's small production outfit was in the lower level of one of the older buildings in OldTech. That meant transferring to a South Ridge shuttle. Even so, it was a solid fifteen-minute walk from the OldTech station on the path beside the winding lane barely big enough for a single electral.

When I got to the building, I had to dig in my linkfile for the passcode. The gate took forever, or so it seemed, before it pulsed, *You may enter. You are cleared to the lower level by the left ramp.*

After I passed the gate, I walked slowly, trying to catch my breath, because I'd hurried from the station.

Mahmed was waiting in the foyer outside the square box they called the studio. "I got your message. I'm glad you could do it." He handed me a folder. "This one's for Beauville. You've heard of them—upscale mostly hand-finished interior furniture, the stuff you can't just pop out of an industrial formulator."

The words—I couldn't call them lyrics—were somewhere between mediocre and not-quite awful, and the melody was reminiscent of early twentieth-century English art song, as if they'd taken something and shifted it, and I couldn't quite pin down what it might have been. That could have been because they didn't really understand the modal basis of some of those songs.

In the end, after I'd spent some time going through the music, I just walked into the studio and stood on the big "X." I used a headset for the music feed, because music has to be auditory and not link-channel, and sang the lyrics.

We followed the usual pattern, which meant that the first run-through was exactly as written. The second was the way I thought it should be, and the third was the way Mahmed interpreted it.

Mahmed was smiling when I finished the third take. "You can make anything sound good."

I wasn't sure about that, but he was thoughtful to say it. "Thank you." After a moment, I added, "The second set?"

"The music and words are outside. Do you want a break?"

"I'd like some water, and some time to look them over." I took off the headset and brushed back my hair. No matter how I fixed it, it was so fine that some of it kept drifting across my forehead.

He nodded, and we walked out into the office area. "Are you doing any real singing? Anywhere where I could hear you?"

"I'll be doing an art song recital at the university in the fall. I'm singing a soirée performance in a week or so."

"Filch show? To prove their superiority in taste?"

"They pay," I pointed out wryly. "Not too many people want to hear unaugmented vocal music these days."

"I'll be there for your recital." He handed me the second folder.

He would be. He'd been there for my last. He'd been there for my first, and that was how I'd gotten into doing rezads. He wanted to help me so that I'd be around to sing art song, and I helped him by giving him clean lines to work with, which kept his costs down.

It still bothered me at times, but working singers in our world—those who don't want their voices twisted and turned by technology, those who want to preserve the inherent beauty of voice and song—we don't have much choice. We probably never have had.

Music—and its beauty—was continually getting shortchanged. That was one reason why I was going to see the dean, even if it did no good. That was more than likely to be the case.

Chapter 10
Kemal

By Tuesday, I was officially the chairman of KC Constructors, rather than the unofficial chairman. It didn't change anything. I'd been the executive officer for almost ten years.

There was always something. I needed to talk to Heber Smith about the elections. Dewey was getting to be more and more trouble, and I'd never liked Cannon. Cannon was too sanctimonious. He kept asking questions about CerraCraft. There weren't any problems with CerraCraft, but he thought there were. Dewey was worse. He'd wanted to help his cousins, and he'd gone out of his way to get Cannon to sponsor and pass the guideway divestiture laws. That was right after we'd invested in Brazelton and expanded operations into most of the NorAm Districts. I could do without both Dewey and Cannon.

Heber was out. He'd call back.

I started to review the plans for expanding the club business in Lanta and Porlan, and then into smaller cities. That would help the alkie formulation leases, too. The more diverse sources of direct credits, the better—especially with the Republic deal working out as it had. People were less likely to question where KC and KCF were getting credits if they thought we were pulling in millions from the clubs and alkie business. The new rezrap helped, too, a lot, because it boosted alkie consumption. Too bad a few kids were oversensitive, but there wasn't anything that didn't have side effects for someone. I had to avoid shellfish—unless I wanted a whole raft of nanomods. Marissa had a problem with red wine—the real stuff, not the formulated kind. That was life.

Mr. McCall is here for his one o'clock. Mr. Kemal.

Thank you. Paulina. Have him come in.

Evan McCall looked more like an accountant than a solicitor. He had a thin face and deep-set eyes. His right eye twitched. That was something new.

The door closed, and I could sense the privacy screens. Most people didn't notice, but the screens were automatic in my office. That made matters simpler. I didn't record anything inside the screens, either. That was asking for trouble. Most people in charge of things never understood that. Put what had to be done legally in recorded form, and nothing else.

I got up from the desk and walked over to the bar in the corner. I poured out an orange juice. It was real, not formulated. Then I offered him the glass. "You look like you need this."

He took the glass. His smile was both wry and nervous. "I could. The DPS is hounding me again. About Nanette's accident."

"Sit down." I took one of the seats at the conference table.

McCall took the other. He took a long, slow swallow of the juice. "You know that I can't even reset my own desk console and gatekeeper without a prompting program. The DPS keeps badgering me about Nanette's death. I don't understand how it happened." His voice quivered, just a touch. That was very unlike the controlled solicitor. "They've been asking me about marital problems. About quarrels. They don't believe me."

"I believe you." I knew he hadn't had anything to do with it. It was too bad things had turned out as they had, but it was inevitable with a wife like his. Family is important, but women have to know who makes the decisions.

"You're the only one." He shook his head. "I just don't understand why. It had to be an accident. Nanette didn't have any enemies. Not a one."

As far as her psychology practice went, he was probably right about that. She should have stayed with psychology, but she'd been about to push him too far. The linkbugs had shown that, and KC didn't need NASR or other regulators looking into KC and the rezrap-alkie link. Later, it wouldn't have made any difference, but she wouldn't have waited. I knew the type. "It's tough when the government doesn't believe you."

He took another sip of the juice. He set down the glass and

handed me a thin folder. "That's why I'm here. I wanted to let you know that everything is in process on the estate. It's only a formality, but it's all under control. The file explains it all, the timetable, and the process. If I'm not available, Marc Oler knows the basics, but not the details. He doesn't need to know those."

"Good." It had taken years to work it out so that it would be only a formality. What would go through probate was only a few hundred million, all to Mother. There were also a few special bequests and donations. The visible estate was large enough so that no one would look deeper. Even if they did, there was nothing that any prudent filch family would not have done. Setting up the transfers and trusts had been far from simple, and had taken years. Now, I only had to worry about insubordinate nephews. "You do good work, Evan. You always have." I stood. "Good luck with the DPS."

"I'll need it." He stood slowly.

I half clasped him on the back. "Just hang in there. Everything will turn out for the best."

"Thanks, Chris."

After McCall left, I linked to Paulina. *See if you can get Emile Brazelton here after my meeting with O'Bannon. Put it on the schedule as guideway progress.* I always gave Paulina a subject for each meeting.

Yes, ser.

The next problem was far simpler. I put through a holo call to Mother. She was where she always was after lunch. She was in her study writing letters the old-fashioned way. She wore another black dress. Outside of the fine lines around her eyes, she could have passed for one of my sisters.

"How are you feeling?"

"As well as ever, Christopher. You don't have to check on me every day."

"I can't call my own mother?" I laughed. It was a running joke.

"You're good to call. I almost never hear from Kryn, but you and Barbra are always so good. Did you know that she sent over some hand-baked cookies she made? Italian sugar cookies, no less . . ."

We talked about cookies, and the children, and about how so many families had no sense of loyalty. After twenty minutes, I said good-bye.

That gave me time to check the third quarter financial reports on the KC subsidiaries. That was supposedly Poul Therault's job, but I couldn't ask the Vice President of Finance intelligent questions if I hadn't studied his reports.

Mr. O'Bannon is here, Mr. Kemal.

Have him come in.

I stood.

O'Bannon walked into the office and settled into the chair across from the desk. He gave me a lazy smile. He was a big man with perfect white teeth, set off by his dark skin and short black hair. "Nice office here."

"It's not that much bigger than the old one." I sat down. "How is the Burling project going?"

"We've managed to acquire the rights to the last three sections. Another week, and everything will be registered."

"Under the K2 subsidiary." I didn't want any confusion about that. K2 handled only real estate. Everything there could have been handed to District Coordinator Dewey, and he couldn't have found a single misplaced comma or a quarter credit unaccounted for. He still would have tried to find something and then complained publicly that we were hiding it.

"I'm assuming," O'Bannon said easily, "that there will be a sale at some future date."

"Assume all you want, James." I laughed. "At some point, you'll be right. K2 is a property dealer, and we can't make credits there without selling."

I knew what he was thinking. He had to wonder why I wanted farmed-out and reclaimed land in the eastern part of the Denv District. It couldn't be used for agriculture. Development was limited to less than one percent of the total land area. With enough land, one percent was more than enough for a privately owned and operated orbiter base and terminal, and neither the PD or the PDF would be able to do a thing about it.

"The rumor is that McCall is going to be indicted for murder." O'Bannon looked squarely at me.

"If the DPS or the District Advocate thinks he killed his wife, then he will be. I don't speculate on the law, Counselor. That's your expertise."

O'Bannon nodded slowly.

"How is he taking it?"

"He's very upset. He won't talk to me or to José. You know he took Marc Oler and Caron Hildeo with him."

"Will that pose a problem?"

O'Bannon tilted his head. "Until this business with his wife, I wouldn't have said so. Evan has always been extremely professional. I don't even know the details of what he set up for you. As his senior partner, I could have asked, but I felt you preferred matters to be kept . . . compartmentalized."

"It works better that way. Most times." I shook my head. "Poor bastard. He's lost. He doesn't know what hit him." He didn't, yet, and it was better that way.

"It's too bad. He's the best privacy solicitor in NorAm."

I nodded. Even the best had their limits. Part of my job was to recognize those limits and deal with them. "What about the co-op agreement with Talemen?"

"They're willing to sub-license and to ignore any previous infringements." O'Bannon laughed. "Neither of us is calling it that. They get the royalties on all VR and home entertainment sets. They have exclusive rights in VR production. We have the rights to use the technology in clubs and live performance spaces. They can license it to clubs, but we get the royalties, less a ten percent placement fee."

"We'll sign it, if that's what it says." Most times, I would have pushed for more. At the moment, we'd take what came easy, and look to expand later.

O'Bannon nodded. "That's what I'd recommend."

"Is there anything else I should know about?"

He frowned. "I can't think of anything." After a moment, he looked at me. "Is there anything else? I don't want to waste your time."

"For now, that's it."

We both stood, and I walked around the wide cherry desk. We shook hands, and O'Bannon left.

Most business leaders wouldn't have seen people in person. Too many relied on link or holo meetings. There's no substitute for sitting across from someone. I caught feelings and hints I couldn't have, even with full VR.

Before long, Paulina linked in again. *Stefan Saul is here.*

I'll come out and get him in a minute.

I let him wait ten minutes while I checked the legislative status flags. There was nothing we hadn't anticipated. Then I went out to the outer office.

Stefan was standing, looking out the window toward the Rockies. He wore a dark green singlesuit, and a conservative light green wool jacket. Both were new. He was also without the gold neck chains. My sister Barbra wasn't stupid. She'd clearly seen the look Alyssa had given Stefan at the memorial service.

"Come in, Stefan." I smiled and stepped back into the office.

"Yes, ser." Stefan was a centimeter or two taller than I was. The way he slouched, he looked shorter.

After I pulsed the door closed, he started to sit down, almost carelessly. Then he stopped and looked at me.

"Go ahead."

He sat on the dark green leather armchair that was set opposite the far corner of the desk. He didn't look at me, not directly. "You asked to see me, ser."

I settled behind the uncluttered desk and waited for a minute, still smiling, before I began. "Your grandfather was very fond of your mother. I'm sure you know that."

"I've heard that, Uncle Chris." Stefan's face said he didn't believe a word.

"He wanted her, and you and your sisters, not to have to

worry financially. That's why he set up the trusts. He also didn't want you to rely on that income for anything more than a generous basic income. That means one thing. If you want a more luxurious way of life, you can't rely on your trust."

"Uncle Chris, I just asked about what was in it. Is that a crime?"

"I understand you also asked if you could sell any of the securities."

"I just wanted to know how it worked, ser."

I didn't believe that for a minute. "I understand." I smiled again. "It's really very simple. There are two kinds of securities in all the KCF trusts. Some provide annual income. Some produce longer-term capital growth. It's a balance. The trustee could invest more credits in income-producing securities, but in years to come, you'd have less and less income. Or he could invest in those providing capital appreciation. That way, the value of your trust would be much greater over time, but you'd have very little to live on now."

"Ser . . . with all due respect . . . the amount that my mother and my sisters and I are receiving amounts to much less than one percent of the value of the trust."

"That's not surprising, Stefan. Only about ten percent of the holdings are invested in income-producing securities. The majority is invested for longer-term growth. That's so that the capital will be there for your children and your children's children."

"So we scrape by so that you—" He stopped abruptly. "I'm sorry, ser."

I looked hard at him. "I scarcely think that an annual income of over two million credits is scraping by, Stefan. There are filch in southside who don't have incomes that substantial."

"Things are more expensive than when you were young, Uncle Chris. I've tried to be careful, but there's not enough there."

Careful? Not enough there? I'd called up his expenditures. He'd purchased two electrals, just in the past year, and a second house in the Redford Preserve. The house had been twenty million by itself. KCF's general trust had taken the mortgage privately, collateralized against his own trust assets, because I hadn't wanted the transaction made public. Stefan didn't know that. He'd just happily signed the papers. He wasn't so happy about the one hundred twenty thousand credits a month coming from his account to repay the mortgage.

"What do you want from me?" I asked politely. "I'm not the trustee. The trusts are irrevocable. I can't change the terms."

"You mean you won't." He got a pouty look.

"I can't. Talk to your solicitor."

"You picked the family solicitors. You won't give the details to any other solicitors, and the ones you picked won't let me do anything you don't want."

I certainly hoped not. That was the whole idea. "They'll tell you exactly what the terms of the trust are. It wouldn't matter what solicitor you talked to. It wouldn't change the terms." That much was certainly true.

Stefan didn't say anything. He was trying not to show anger. He was doing a poor job.

"I don't think we'll ever agree on this, Stefan. It doesn't matter. I can't change the payouts on the trust. You'll just have to figure out how to deal with it." I stood up.

He sat in the leather chair for a moment, then abruptly jumped up. "Yes, ser. I will."

He was also going to complain to Barbra about how stingy I was. He wasn't about to understand. Nothing I could do would change that.

Emile Brazelton is waiting, Mr. Kemal.

Tell him I'll be right with him. I'm almost done here. "If you'll excuse me, Stefan. I have another meeting."

"Yes, ser."

I followed Stefan out. "Give my best to your mother."

He didn't answer. I didn't think he would. He wasn't smart enough.

I motioned for Brazelton to come in. He looked like an average sariman. Brown hair, brown eyes. Not big, and not small.

"That was your nephew, wasn't it?" he asked as the door closed behind him.

"One of them. That was Stefan." I didn't bother to sit down.

"You asked for me?"

"I need another job taken care of. The one we talked about before. He knows enough to figure it out. He isn't sharp enough to know he knows. If he gets into DPS custody, Kirchner could figure it out."

"Kirchner won't make trouble."

"You know that. So do I. But Cannizaro could. She's got Chiang, too."

"You don't like Chiang."

"He dated Kryn once, when we were in school and still living in Old Westside. He looked at Father, and he looked at me. He took Kryn out. He was a perfect gentleman. He showed her a wonderful evening. He sent her an old-fashioned note thanking her, and then said that he'd never be in her class. Kryn wouldn't speak to me for a month."

"Smart man."

"Too smart. Especially now. Cannizaro's put him where he has access to everything."

Brazelton frowned and fingered his chin.

"McCall's distraught," I said. "He's very upset. If the DPS or the District Solicitor charge him with the murder of his wife, he could do anything. We need quiet right now. He's tough about the law, but he's not tough in any other way."

"You think he might commit suicide?"

I shrugged. "Who knows? He loved her a lot. I understand that. Most people would, I think." I paused. "We're also working on some angles to straighten out the guideway problem. You may have to give us a hand there."

Brazelton nodded. He wasn't happy, but what choice did he have? Without the buyout of his company, he would have been a permie pushing a broom in northside. The Justiciary doesn't like massive embezzlement and fraud. Now, he made more credits, and his company was prospering, and we kept him on the personal straight and narrow. It was a good deal for everyone.

"You understand."

He nodded again.

"Let me know."

I watched as the door opened and he walked toward it.

I tried to make deals that benefited everyone. That was the beauty of what I did. I'd learned a long time ago that you can't keep a family or a business going if you're not giving as well as getting.

It was a pity Stefan hadn't figured that out. I had hoped he would.

Chapter 11
Chiang

Wednesday came. Open file search showed nothing on McCall. Case bothered me. Indictment had been announced, but no details. Homicide wasn't saying anything, except what they had to. McCall even came up clean in the internal DPS file. Nothing. Not an overdue electral registration, an illegal turn, not even an emissions tax penalty for his house. Only public data were scholarly articles on things like the extended right to privacy. Was listed as a speaker at a number of solicitors' professional meetings. Same smiling face every time.

Checked accidental deaths reported in Denv over the past five years. DPS didn't get all of them. Not one filch. Didn't surprise me. True accident, and the filch had doctors and solicitors to take care of the formal stuff. Accident like McCall's wife, same thing happened. So . . . no report in the DPS files. Servies and permies— they reported accidents, and most of them were. The filch . . . I wondered.

More I saw and read, the more McCall bothered me. But I

didn't think it was wise to lean on anyone in DPS. Not on a feeling.

Looked out my window at the Park. Another sunny day. Been a cloudy winter, and the sun was welcome.

Direct-linked Resheed's report. ODs remained the same, roughly, up from the year before, but no longer rising. The netless scam numbers were down. Probably would be until the scammers came up with a new angle—in another week or two. The netops section reported the latest ID theft techniques. Read through it, then decided to go over to the other side and talk. I always learned more face-to-face.

I started to get up from behind the desk. A flash link blazed in from CDC in Lanta. Read through it. Phrases leaped out at me, the kind I didn't want to see.

Ebol4 strain has appeared in Nyork and Nengland districts . . . as with ebol3, a pairing of SAD nanites with a modified ebola virus . . . longer incubation and contagion period . . . greater risk of spread, particularly among netless or those with only baseline nanomeds . . . cold weather version thought to have been engineered by Agkhanate Talibanate for use against Russe Hegemony . . . extraordinarily infectious and will provoke a high fever and occasional convulsions even among populations with full-spectrum nanomeds . . . greater risk to public safety personnel . . . recommend additional nanomed boosters for those in close contact with vulnerable populations . . .

Another bioweapon coming out of the undeclared West Asian conflicts. All we needed. World Patrol kept the lid on heavy weapons. Recsat systems were good for that. Didn't do null for bioweps.

Linked with Sarao. *CDC flash. Make sure it's an allpers. Patrollers need to take care with low-level invisibles.*

Oh?

Stet. Didn't explain why, but didn't have to. Yet. Two kinds of invisibles—those removed from the NorAm database illegally, like by Kemal's operation, and those imported from West Asian areas. No point in admitting they existed. Not when DPS couldn't do anything except with the ones we caught.

Looked back out to the Park, waiting. Still sunny and green. Not so bad when the snow covered the grass, but felt wrong in late winter and early spring when the trees hadn't leaved out.

Done, Lieutenant, Sarao linked back.

Thanks. I stood and walked out of the office.

Sarao looked up from the consoles. Still needed screens to handle more than one visual input.

"Going to the other side. Had some questions about the netops report."

She nodded.

The ramps were empty. They should have been. So was the lower lobby off the garage. Could smell a hint of ozone—restraint loops. Always smelled that way when someone was carted in under restraint.

Passed Sorgio on the way up. Nodded at each other.

Netops was quiet. Sergeant Darcy was by the consoles.

"Lieutenant."

"Sergeant. I was going through your latest report. Someone else counterfeiting GILs?"

She offered a professional smile. "It's more elaborate than we'd have suspected. They take a T-samp from the victim, then implant the phony GIL in place of a real one, surrounded by an Isup barrier. The GIL reads positive, and so long as no one takes a samp . . . it works."

"What about the victim?"

"Disabled, usually, in some sort of accident. Badly mugged, in some cases. Usually high sariman, or independent professional."

"Where no one else watches the personal or business accounts closely."

"Stet."

"Why not dead?" I asked.

"Then the worldnet closes down that GIL, and the feits can't get at the victim's assets. Usually, it's someone well off and single, but not filch. Filch have barriers, and advocates. And families who get upset at disappearing assets."

"How long will this last?"

"Month . . . two. Netpros already flooding the nets with the scam stories, and offering services to protect assets. Be too much trouble, and too low a return before long."

I nodded slowly, before asking, "You deal with the McCall thing?"

Her eyes and voice were cold. "That's not a trend, Lieutenant."

Gave her a smile. "Not yet. Like to see that it doesn't become one. May be more of one than anyone realizes."

Her eyes softened. Not much. "How do you think so?"

"Privacy barriers. Not that many filch. Can't get death breakdowns. So you can't spot any trends there. We're looking into it." I smiled.

"You think the filch have more accidents?"

I shrugged. "Shouldn't have. They have more safeguards."

"More gadgets means more to go wrong."

"Could be."

"No one bets against you, Lieutenant . . ." She left the implications there.

Understood what she meant. I'd better have more than a feeling if I wanted to push into filch territory. "Just looking at what everyone can see."

Darcy nodded.

I walked back down the ramps to the garage-level foyer. Then walked back up the ramps to my corner office. Walked slowly, thinking.

Chapter 12

Words evolve, perhaps more rapidly and tellingly than do their users, and the change in meanings reflects a society often more accurately than do the works of many historians. In the years preceding the first collapse of NorAm, the change in the meaning of one word predicted the failure of that society more immediately and accurately than did all the analysts, social scientists, and historians. That critical word? "Discrimination." We know it now as a term meaning "unfounded bias against a person, group, or culture on the basis of racial, gender, or ethnic background." Prejudice, if you will.

The previous meaning of the word was: "to draw a clear distinction between good and evil, to differentiate, to recognize as different." Moreover, the connotations once associated with discrimination were favorable. A person of discrimination was one of taste and good judgment. With the change of the meaning into a negative term of bias, the English language was left without a single-word term for the act of choosing between alternatives wisely, and more importantly, left with a subterranean negative connotation for those who attempted to make such choices.

In hindsight, the change in meaning clearly reflected and foreshadowed the disaster to come. Individuals and institutions abhorred making real choices. At one point more than three-quarters of the youthful population entered institutions of higher level learning. Credentials, often paper ones, replaced meaningful judgment and choices . . . Popularity replaced excellence . . . The list of disastrous cultural and political decisions foreshadowed by the change in meaning of one word is truly endless . . .

Was that merely an aberration of history? Hardly, for the same changes in language today reflect our own future. Take the word "filch," now applied to the wealthiest of the wealthy. The original meaning was "to steal slyly in small amounts, to pilfer." When the longer term ("filthy rich") previously used was resurrected after the second collapse, the contraction and the theft "overtones" of the original meaning of "filch" fit admirably the social needs of the time. The growing application of this term to those who are more than moderately successful clearly reflects a widespread social unrest and dissatisfaction with those who control the wealth and power of our present-day society . . .

> T. Eliot Stearns
> *Historical Etymology*
> Lanta, A.D. 2241

Chapter 13
Parsfal

I came in early on Wednesday to make some time to chase filch murder and death stats, before Bimstein started linking every ten minutes. It didn't matter. I'd barely gotten into the background when the link buzzed.

Parsfal? Take a few minutes this morning or early this afternoon and get me some updated stuff on hurricanes and recent and historic shifts in the Gulf Stream. Paula Lopes is doing a piece tomorrow on the impacts on the Caribbean and on why the last five years have seen arctic winters in the British Isles.

Who gets the feed?

Kirenga. Also, see if you can run a twenty-second comparison/ contrast between Cannon and that old historic governor—Van-

derhoff, was it?—on the Southern Diversion, something with a twist. Work in Patroclas if you can. Have to run.

I knew what he wanted on the comparison—either paint Cannon as a principled man in line with the past or a schemer betraying the past—and Patroclas as well-meaning, but ineffectual. That meant more work on Cannon and Patroclas, to see where their votes lay on diversion and environmental issues. I added the water and weather assignments to my "to-do" list, and went back to where I'd been.

All I'd come up with the night before on the McCall background was pretty typical. A former associate with O'Bannon and Reyes, an honors graduate of UDenv Law, with two grown children, he had just started his own office as a solicitor. Handsome and apparently personable, at least from the comparatively few bytes available on him. He'd been a featured speaker at a number of solicitors' conferences, and he made a habit of publishing articles on his specialty, which was privacy law.

I read one of them. He could write, assuming he was the one who wrote it. And he was careful. Solicitors had to be, reportedly, but every word was used and chosen with care. Not a poet with words—more like an accountant. Not so much beauty there as economy and precision. Certainly nothing like Yeats or Keats or even Exton . . . it reminded me of an old poem . . .

Was he free? Was he happy? The question is absurd.
Had anything been wrong, we should certainly have heard.

Except Evan McCall hadn't been happy about his wife, apparently, and perhaps more. Yet, in the end . . . I had nothing. There wasn't even anything specific about his children or their names in anything. I'd wanted to have something on the follow-up with the indictment. It was a juicy sort of case. Everyone loved to watch a filch get it—or escape it, if he did so with style. McCall and his wife had been the vid-perfect couple, and there hadn't been a sign of trouble. All that meant was that Evan

McCall was not only personable, but very bright, even beyond the letter of the law.

I tried his office, but only got a simmie, and a very simple message. "The offices are closed until further notice. If you have an urgent legal problem, you may reach Marc Oler . . ."

I tried that link code, but just got Oler's simmie, promising to return any calls. I asked him to contact me.

After that, I did call up the death stats, and even cross-indexed them by income and cause. For most of the population, the numbers were just as I'd have expected. Except that in the higher income categories, there were no breakdowns by income and cause—just a notation—"privacy protected." There were so few filch deaths that any data would reveal the families? Unless I could find an angle, it looked like I'd have to drop that for a time.

Unless . . . maybe that could be a sidebar story, something about the fact that, in just another way, the filch were different. Our lives are open screens. All we see of the filch are beautifully decorated covers, like the covers of old-style books. They're shielded by the privacy laws, even statistically, by their nanite-protected houses, by their credits, and by other filch—like McCall himself.

I hated the direct route, but there was no help for it. So I had to try McCall's old firm. I put through the link, full VR, if edited to show me in a tidy office with bookcases behind me.

"O'Bannon and Reyes, may we help you?" The dark-haired and dark-eyed woman answering the VR link was a real person, not a simmie. That in itself was impressive, and doubtless meant to be.

"This is Jude Parsfal, from NetPrime. Is Mr. O'Bannon available?"

"Just a moment, Mr. Parsfal." The holo image blanked and then reappeared, images of a modernistic building, a large dwelling, filch style, a small dwelling, and what looked to be an antique machine shop.

"Whatever your legal needs, O'Bannon and Reyes is here to help you . . ."

The staid old-style commercial blanked off, to be replaced by a dark-skinned and distinguished-looking man of considerable size. "James O'Bannon, Mr. Parsfal." After the briefest of pauses, he added, "I've already talked with Les Kerras. I don't know that there's much more that I can add, Mr. Parsfal. Or should. Mr. McCall's case rests with the Justiciary."

"Les is the one who gets the on-net images. I'm the one who gets backgrounds and facts, that sort of thing. I've read through some of Evan McCall's articles and presentations. He seems to be regarded as an expert in the field of privacy law."

O'Bannon laughed. "If there are any aspects to privacy law Evan does know, I'd be very surprised. He is very good."

"He set up an independent practice. Isn't that a little odd, given how all aspects of law tend to intermesh?"

"Hardly. Privacy law is one of the handful of areas where it makes sense. Clients who feel they have a need for privacy will feel more comfortable in dealing with a single solicitor. Also, privacy issues can usually be handled discretely from other legal issues. Evan does have two junior associates, for areas that might be related."

"Related?"

"Intellectual property, and disposal or direction of property— wills, bequests, gifts, powers of attorney, that sort of matter."

"Mr. McCall seems extraordinarily personable. Is that an asset for privacy solicitors?"

"That's an asset for anyone, don't you think?"

"Does he have any hobbies or interests besides law?"

"As almost anyone could tell you, Evan is very focused. I wish you well with your inquiries." He smiled, and I was looking at the wall of my cube.

About the only thing I'd gotten was what I already knew— that Evan McCall's practice dealt with people who didn't want anything known about them. And that he specialized in the kinds of law that dealt with things people wanted kept quiet.

The rule of thumb is that no one is more than six people removed from anyone else. So who did I know that might get me closer?

The first name that came to mind—that would do any good—was John Ashbaugh. We'd gone to school together, and he'd gone on to become a securities solicitor.

I was lucky because he was in.

"I can't help you much, Jude."

"Professional ethics?"

"I don't know enough about Evan McCall to worry about professional ethics. I just know what everyone knows. He is the best privacy solicitor in Denv, and he's spent nearly all his career with O'Bannon and Reyes. He was the one who handled their top clients like Kemal, Ching, and Sandoval. He also has a sidelight in intellectual property. He mixes well with everyone, even some smaller fabricators like Brazelton, although Brazelton has expanded enormously since it was acquired by KC." John smiled and shrugged.

"Is there anyone you could suggest who might be able to tell me more?"

He frowned. "I can't think of anyone, except Maeda Forsala, but she still would be bound by solicitor-client privilege—"

"She an associate of his?"

"The word is that she was retained by Nanette McCall. That was common knowledge."

I should have seen that coming. Three would get me five that Forsala is a domestic relations solicitor.

"You might be able to find out something from Dean Smythers. He was at UDenv when McCall was on the *Review* there. The dean might be able to fill in something about his school years. And his regular tennis partner is Walt Kerrigan." John shrugged once more. "That's about all I know."

And all he was about to say. "Thanks. I appreciate it."

The holo image vanished, and I mulled over what John had told me while insisting he hadn't told me anything—and how it fit the pattern with Kemal.

Kemal was the head of KC Constructors, and KC had been the target of the guideway legislation that Cannon had rammed through. Kemal reportedly underbid the design, engineering, and construction, and got the maintenance contracts in return. It hadn't been that simple, of course, because certain of the guide assemblies had been proprietary, and Kemal wouldn't sell them to other contractors except at a price high enough to ensure they couldn't underbid him on maintenance. John had explained that to me, once, as well, and my understanding was simpler than the reality, but, essentially, that was what it had amounted to. Cannon's bill had required open architecture and applied the proprietary design laws to both NorAm and district public works and infrastructure projects.

According to everyone, Kemal and his family had a shady background, but nothing had ever been proved. The more recent rumors were that Kemal had been expanding into everything, that he actually was the majority owner or silent partner in firms like Sandoval's and Brazelton's, and a good twenty others across NorAm. But so long as he had registered ownership of less than ten percent—or five in the case of military or PDF suppliers, privacy law shielded disclosure in the media, although the appropriate legislative committees had access, and so did the NorAm Advocate General. I shook my head. Kemal wasn't my problem at the moment.

John had as much as told me that McCall's wife was about to start a divorce or separation, and that *wasn't* common knowledge, which meant I couldn't use it, because there was no way to prove it. He also was pointing out that McCall had some clients who were less than savory.

Walt Kerrigan was an advocate who had once been an aide to former Senator Owen of Deseret. All I knew about Brazelton was that he was the head of a firm that specialized in nanite control systems and designs.

Back to the files.

Parsfal? Bimstein blasted through the link.

Yes?

Got anything on McCall?

Some . . . tracking down some other leads right now.

Put it aside. It'll hold. Start your routines looking up stuff on Super-C.

Super-C? I didn't know what he was talking about.

Old term. Supercavitation. Someone just blew a Russe maglev orbiter down . . . somewhere over the Pacific. Used an old-style Super-C torp-missile. Could have been anyone. Fingers are point-ing at the Agkhanate.

Who was on the orbiter?

Just the Foreign Secretary of the Martian Republic, the ExSec of the Duma, and a dozen others equally exalted. Rehm is han-dling the people facts. Want some background on how and why someone could have gotten one of those old torp-missiles, how come it was still working, how they work . . . all the tech stuff you do so well. Half hour.

I gulped.

Do it! I winced at the volume. *Then you've got another half hour on McCall, and not a minute more, before you get back on the orbiter story.*

I'm on it. But Bimstein was gone, understandably.

Finding the background on supercavitation was easy. It had been first developed more than three centuries earlier by the old USSR before its collapse. Prototype rocket-propelled ocean tor-pedoes had been sold to whoever would buy them. The problem hadn't been speed; they'd been ten times faster than the old-style torpedoes. The guidance systems had been poor, and the range limited by the wire control system. The next breakthrough had been nanitic deformulation of water, adapted by Russian scien-tists. That allowed an easier bubble formation, but that devel-opment had apparently been abandoned with the development of maglev propulsion and the satellite surveillance and patrol sys-tem adopted under the PDF compact. Except it hadn't, not if someone had used the technology. But who?

I shook my head. That wasn't my problem. Bimstein wanted more tech facts.

I got to work. I was almost finished when he was blasting through my skull with his overboosted linking.

Parsfal?

Where do you want it fed?

Kirenga's handling it. How much?

Four minutes in thirty-second chunks.

Any good?

Fair. I had to be honest. There hadn't been time to do better.

Try to do better for the follow cast.

You want me to drop McCall for now?

No. Still hot locally. No more than a half hour, and feed it to Metesta. Then dig up more tech stuff on terrorists and what the Agkhanate has done. Keep it on the tech side. Rehm's handling the people and politics.

Stet.

After that . . . there's something about another biowep that CDC says is hitting NorAm . . . ebol4 . . . See what you can find on that.

Another backgrounder was all I needed.

After trying to sort out what I could find on Walt Kerrigan and Emile Brazelton, which wasn't much, I did take a few minutes off and watched the holo image of the orbiter story as it went off live. I deserved that for all the sweat, before I got back to the McCall backgrounding.

"Tragedy over the Pacific—and a high official of the Martian Republic is dead."

The image showed a night sky that could have been anywhere, followed by a blinding flare.

"This is Les Kerras. A little more than an hour ago, an official Russean maglev orbiter was destroyed by an antique nuclear missile. The attack occurred as the orbiter returned from the geostat station above the Pacific. What you just saw was the re-creation of that destruction. Recsat surveillance confirms that the missile was launched from somewhere under the Pacific Ocean . . .

"Early indications are that part of the design of the missile used dates from before the Collapse. The weapon used a technology known as supercavitation to travel a considerable distance underwater at high speeds before breaking the surface and accelerating to take out the orbiter. The acceleration was great enough to have required a custom-formulated monomolecular and multioxygenated metallic solid fuel . . ."

I was proud to have dug up that one.

Parsfal! Bimstein's link was tight, not loud.

I froze, rather than sighed. The timing wasn't exactly wonderful.

I'm here.

I'm putting through a Commander Resoro of the PDF.

Maybe I'd been too resourceful.

Mr. Parsfal? There was no image, just a chill voice.

Jude Parsfal. I acknowledged. *What can I do for you?*

We'd be interested in knowing how you determined the fuel of the device that attacked the Russean orbiter.

That was simple enough. The range of orbiter speeds is in a number of netfiles and research sources. I went to the OTA files. Then I used a nav program to determine the velocity required to intercept from a mid-Pacific location, and then I fudged around with the weights of old nukes, figured some modernization, and with that mass came up with the necessary ejv. Good old basic math indicated it had to be an exotic fuel, and one that probably had to have been formulated with an industrial formulator. That pretty much limited—

You didn't talk to anyone before you looked into this?

Bimstein gave me a half hour to put some background facts together, Commander. I'd have been lucky to have even found one person who could have told me anything in that time.

You may be hearing from someone.

Once again, I was left alone at my console. And I was still supposed to come up with more for the McCall piece, and then get back to digging up more on the orbiter incident—and then the bioweapon thing. Whoever Marc Oler was, he hadn't gotten back to me. I had the feeling he wouldn't, and it would be a while before I could devote the time to chasing him down.

Chapter 14
Cornett

Wednesday morning was usually an easy morning, but since I had my appointment with the dean at ten-fifteen, I had to get up earlier to fit in everything. For some reason, the formulator wouldn't accept any of the breakfast menu codes. I'm anything but a morning person. I don't even watch the news. I couldn't ever eat a heavy meal first thing in the morning. I ended up with tasteless cheese, and some crackers, washed down with water. I couldn't even have made an omelet or something from scratch, or boiled water for coffee or tea, because my larder was bare. Organic ingredients weren't exactly cheap.

The only good thing was that I still managed a good hour of practice on the first part of what I'd be singing at the Clayton soirée. My cords were clear. I felt that I'd really managed to work the songs into my voice. The practice was good, so good that I ended up running late.

The maglev shuttle was off schedule, which never happened, except when I was behind schedule. I was going to have to hurry when I got to the university, in order not to be late for my appointment with Dean Donald.

As I stepped off the shuttle, the piercing ululations of an emergency medvan echoed across the university grounds. All of us on the platform looked around. I couldn't see the medvan, and I was running too close to being late to spend time searching.

I heard a second siren as I entered the Administration building, a four-hundred-year-old brownstone that had been a copy of an even older structure. The sound died away as I took the stairs up to the second floor. The Arts and Humanities section was in the back—the smallest and most crowded of the various university offices.

Malenda looked up from her console as I entered. "Good morning, Professor Cornett."

"Good morning." I glanced from her to the open door to Dean Donald's office. It was an old-style six-panel oak door, with brass knobs. It wasn't automatic or hooked into the link system. The dean was standing there, waiting.

Wharton Donald was a head taller than I was, but probably not more than ten kilos heavier, and I was scarcely that heavy anymore. How could I be when I couldn't even get a decent breakfast out of my formulator? He smiled all the time. He was smiling as he waited in the oak-framed doorway of his office, bobbing his head.

"Luara . . . do come in. Do come in. Professor Ibanez had told me you might wish to speak to me." He stepped back into his office, and I followed.

"I did. That's why I made the appointment." Of course, Jorje would have warned the dean. Jorje was looking out for Jorje. "I told him that I wanted to talk to you. He didn't seem to have any objections."

"I am always here to talk to faculty. How can we maintain a smoothly functioning university without open communication? Please sit down and tell me what is on your mind." He closed the door and motioned to one of the synthleather chairs—red, trimmed with black—in front of his desk.

Smiling benignly, he walked past me and seated himself. Then, he leaned back in the reclining leather desk chair that almost swallowed him. "You have added such a dimension to our music program. And Professor Ibanez has told me about how uniquely qualified you are to teach the new rez-prep course. You know, these are difficult times for higher education. Student numbers are no longer increasing, and we need to provide those courses which the students feel will best prepare them for the jobs that are open . . ."

"There's a problem with that," I blurted. "There are several."

He frowned.

"Students don't know enough to know what they need. Also, they don't know what courses will provide lifetime preparation, and which are just short-term vocational prep courses. You aren't doing them any favors by catering to their present whims."

"Whims? Luara, dear . . . we have some of the brightest students in NorAm. Surely, you wouldn't consider their career plans as mere whims? Don't you think that you're selling them short?"

I forced myself to smile. It was hard. "I think we have a lot of bright students, Dean Donald. But intelligence is not the same as experience. We live in a technological age, where heavy industry has been replaced by formulation. Don't you think that career patterns and industry can change quickly? As you said at the last convocation, the most important role a university can play is to teach its students to think."

"Ah, yes. That is indeed what we must do." He smiled again. "I don't believe you told me why you wanted to see me."

There I'd gone again, tossing aside my carefully thought-out opening. I returned his smile. Mine was false. I wasn't sure his was. "Professor Ibanez had mentioned that you were considering reducing the number of music appreciation sections from three to two."

"Efficiencies of scale, Professor. In this time of tightened educational funding, we are forced to seek such efficiencies."

I managed to twist what I'd thought about earlier in response. "Efficiency isn't the same as education. The music appreciation section I'm teaching now already has more than eighty students in it. Even with a carefully prepared nanetic background on each student's face and name, it's difficult to make sure that they're all getting the material. No teacher can scan a class any larger. Once you lose the ability to assess their comprehension, it might as well become a link class. It's no longer education. It's just an assimilation of a lot of facts and names and a few partial melodies. I believe, and I hope you do, that education is the process of learning to think across a broad spectrum of academic disciplines. Music has been a critical discipline. Current studies and some even validated centuries ago prove that the study of music improves mathematical and critical thinking. Link classes don't. There's no way they can convey the intricacy or the beauty of music."

The dean spread his hands. "I wish I had been able to bring you to the hearing before the trustees. But there's little that I can do now. There's only so much money for traditional studies. We received the rez-prep funding as an outside grant, and that's on a year-by-year basis. I had so hoped that you would be able to use it to generate greater in-person numbers . . ."

"I certainly plan to, but it's not the same as basic musical understanding. It will help a few in getting a job. It won't generate more critical thought." Especially when students didn't care much for thinking. I suspected they never had, but once, I hoped, faculty had had more power in ensuring that students had to think in order to get through the courses. Then, maybe that was unfounded nostalgia on my part.

"The trustees look so carefully at our numbers . . ." The dean shrugged again.

"My numbers are up," I pointed out.

"I'm certain you'll show the same success in the rez-prep class." He smiled broadly.

Did I really want to point out that the falling numbers in the appreciation classes were due to the fact that Jorje taught two sections—lackadaisically—and I taught only one? He had a long-term contract. Mine was year-to-year.

"I know you've done the best you can, Dean Donald," I lied. "I really felt that you should know that I'm deeply concerned about this. I'll continue to do my best, but when I have only been teaching a third of the sections, obviously I cannot generate numbers all by myself. I feel deeply that the students are the ones being shortchanged by this decision."

"Your concern for the students does you great credit." He leaned forward in the chair. "I do so appreciate your coming to see me. I can certainly see why you're so effective as a teacher. You have great passion for your subject."

In short, I'd been too passionate. Again.

He smiled yet again and stood.

I wasn't really through, but what else was there to say? I'd been hit with another decision made by politicians and bureaucrats who understood nothing except numbers and votes cast by a spoiled population. So I eased myself out of the chair and murmured, "Artists are passionate. That's what makes us artists."

"Indeed, indeed."

That was my appointment with Dean Wharton Donald, tool and spineless bureaucrat.

Instead of cooling off as I walked down the stairs, I just found myself getting angrier and angrier. Not only had it been decided before anyone had talked to either Jorje or me, but the people who had decided it knew nothing about education or what went on in a classroom or a lesson. They weren't interested in having students learn to think, no matter what they said publicly. They just wanted the impressions. Just as Wharton Donald wanted to create the impression of being a caring dean.

There was another series of sirens that accompanied my angry walk across the campus to the Fine Arts Center. Had there been some sort of accident? I just wished one had happened to Wharton Donald, the spineless mouse. He didn't even have enough backbone to make a good rat.

A group of students was milling outside the lecture hall, which doubled as the choral room, waiting for Jorje's appreciation class to get out.

". . . let them launch it underwater a long ways from anywhere. Who could tell?"

". . . say the Martians pressuring the PDF . . ."

I wondered what they were talking about. Had the sirens had something to do with it?

"Professor Cornett, what do you think about it?" The questioner was the roommate of Rachelle, who I'd have to face in a lesson on Thursday. I didn't recall the girl's name, just her face.

"Are you talking about all the sirens? I don't know. It's been a long morning already."

"You haven't heard? Someone used an old-style nuke on an orbiter that was carrying the Foreign Secretary of Mars. It was a Russe shuttle."

I stopped. I must have looked stunned. I felt stunned. A nuclear missile? "When?"

"Just about an hour ago."

Why would anyone risk something like that? Was any political belief worth that kind of destruction? "It's . . . insanity." I was having trouble grasping the fact.

"The new ebol4 bug . . . that's likely to kill more people." Someone back in the group offered that.

What ebol4 bug? "They're both insane." I felt like I was repeating myself. I've never been very good at making brilliant coherent statements when I'm caught off guard. I shook my head, and was saved when the door to the lecture hall opened and disgorged scores of students fleeing Jorje's class.

Ebol4 bug? Was that what had happened to the student on the shuttle platform? I shuddered at the thought of how few seconds had separated us.

After a moment of hesitation, I made my way down the corridor to my own office. Surprisingly, Mershelle wasn't standing outside, waiting, although I was there only a minute before the hour. She was almost always early. I pulsed the door. It opened, and the lights went on.

You have one message, the office link announced. I could have set it up to link to my home system, but if I had, I'd have been at everyone's mercy all the time. The people I wanted to hear from knew my home codes. So did those who had to reach me, like Mahmed. In the mood I was in, I never wanted to hear from the dean or Jorje.

I went to the gatekeeper. *Message.*

Raymon's image appeared. He was in his office, wearing what

I called his doctor's uniform—the white tuniclike shirt and the dark trousers. *Hope you're somewhere where you can backlink. It's urgent.*

I'd been expecting a message from Mershelle, not my brother. Raymon almost never bothered me at the university. I hated linking when I didn't have to, and I called up a holo projection. It wasn't that big, less than half size because that was the limit on the office console.

"Office of Dr. Cornett. May we help you?" asked the simmie receptionist.

"This is Luara, his sister. I'm returning his call."

Within a minute, his image appeared. He looked just as he had in the message. "Haven't you heard?"

"About the nuclear attack on the Russe shuttle? I just found out."

"You haven't heard about Michael?"

"I never hear from him." My stomach still clenched at Raymon's tone of voice. While it hadn't worked out with Michael, and things had been bitter at the end, I certainly didn't wish him ill.

"He's dead. This new ebol4 biowep."

"Michael's dead?" I just looked at the holo image of Raymon. Michael . . . dead? The social reformer and activist? The man who never said no to anyone? The man who wanted to rebuild society whether it wanted rebuilding or not?

"I found out this morning."

"When . . . how . . . How did he get it?" I finally asked.

Raymon offered a sad and sympathetic smile. "With all the people that come to him? Who could tell? Does how really matter? When are you free?"

"After my next lesson. Why?" I could tell that I was just reacting. Sometimes, I hated myself for that. After each time it happened, I'd ask why I didn't think things through more.

"I want you to come to the office. Take a cab, not the shuttle. I'll pay you back."

"Would you mind telling me why? What's so urgent?"

"Ebol4's nasty. You need upgraded meds."

"Raymon . . . I'm a singer . . . I can't afford . . . And what does it matter, with orbiters being destroyed with nuclear weapons?"

"We'll muddle through that. The Republic still needs too much from Earth to launch an attack. Besides, I can't do anything about that. I've only got one sister, and I can do something about that. I'm paying. I'll see you at my office as soon as you can get here. Clarice will be looking for you. And stay away from people you don't know. Or those you do." His face was tight—strained.

"I have one lesson. I'll come right after that."

"Promise?" His voice was intense.

"I promise." Absently, I flipped back my hair.

"Good."

After I broke the link, I just looked blankly at the Steinway. How long, I wasn't sure. Then I got up and checked the music that Mershelle was supposed to be working on and put it on the music rack of the piano. I still had to teach, even if the world was going crazy around me.

But it was hard to concentrate on music—and its beauty—under such circumstances. Michael . . . dead? We seldom talked, but he had been a big part of my life for a time, and I had been drawn to his idealism. The problem was that his idealism was even more all-consuming than my passion for music—and that very little else had worked past the initial attraction.

I shook my head. I'd been so angry with the dean. In some ways, it all seemed so small, at least compared to bioweapons and a nuclear weapon. But . . . maybe they were all part of the same problem. Maybe, people weren't thinking. Or thinking about matters too small, instead of seeking thought and beauty. Then, maybe I was just looking for a justification for my anger.

After another ten minutes, it was clear that I had no lesson to teach. Mershelle never showed up, and she hadn't left a message. So, fifteen minutes later, I left and headed out to Raymon's office. On the one hand, my instincts were that I doubted that I'd be exposed to the new virus. On the other, my more rational side pointed out that students got exposed to *everything*. They always showed up to tell me they were sick, as if to prove it, rather than leaving a message. Then, there had been the young man on the platform. Raymon was right, but I didn't have to like it. Still, I closed the office and walked toward the station.

I didn't hear any more sirens while I waited for the maglev, but none of us on the platform got very close to each other.

Chapter 15
Chiang

I had to take Wednesday morning for my annual DPS physical. Physical and tests took less than an hour. Waiting between tests took the morning and lunch. Did give me nanomeds against the ebol. Saw about thirty other DPS types getting them as well. Got to my office at thirteen-thirty.

Sarao looked up from the consoles. Her short brown hair was shorter than usual. "Captain called. I told her you were getting your annual. She said not to bother you."

"She say what she wanted?"

Sarao shook her head. "Very polite. Calm."

"What's new?"

"Backstreet bodyshop ops are up. Couple more disappearances from northside." She offered a cynical smile.

We both knew the two were related.

"What else?" I looked at her. "We got ebol4 jumping from continent to continent. Filch don't get hit unless they're careless. Those that do, they get full nanetic therapy and self-clone re-placements. Poor sariman, if he gets hit with ebol4, choice to watch himself die or get a hacksmith washjob organs, and has to live from saldrop to saldrop paying for isup. Servies and per-mies just die." I glanced toward the consoles. "Death rates?"

"Not a trend yet. Up five percent from the beginning of the

week. Disappearances will rise, mostly in permies from northside, some from westside." Sarao's voice was flat.

Stats like that have a terrible and inevitable beauty. "You put out an allpers on bodyshops?"

"It's ready to go. Wanted your approval. It's in your pending links."

"Good. What else?"

"More ODs last night."

"On what?"

Sarao shrugged. "Soop in their systems, but how can anyone OD on soop?"

Winced at that. Soop was an exhilarant, but the docs claimed no long-term effects. Except too much could set a heart racing. Not fatally. "Overdosing on soop? Can't be done."

"Some alkie there, at least in one, but doesn't make for an OD," Sarao confirmed. "You might see something I didn't."

Alcohol mixed with soop? Kids used soop, mostly. Most adults used alkie. Some crossover. "That it?"

"Besides the usual? I didn't see anything else."

"Thanks. I'll check the allpers first." I walked into the office, glanced out at another sunny and cold early spring afternoon, and then pushed a link to the captain. Got her simmie.

Captain, Lieutenant Chiang, returning your link. She wasn't in.

Then I went to the daily trend report. Sarao was right. Showed ODs up again. Went through them case by case. All young, all under thirty chronological, most under twenty-five, and three underage. All had the kind of heart stoppage associated with pharmacological effects. Only two drugs identified were soop and alkie, and no trace of anything else foreign. Soop had no known toxic effects, and the alkie levels weren't that high. The death certs all gave heart failure, cause unknown.

Put in a search request on the effects of combining alkie and soop. Got an answer almost immediately. Negative. Twenty years of studies said no cross-toxic or negative health effects existed.

Went back and studied the blood tests on the three that had in-depth studies. Not one had any other foreign substance in the blood. Still bothered me. Went back through all the reports for the day, but couldn't find anything.

Sat there for a time, then sent a search through the files, checking all suicides. Found five like Elcado, starting four months earlier. The earliest one caught my attention. Erneld Cewrigh. Drove parents' electral into the CeCe Reservoir. Even redirected the air-cushion feature to boost it over the restraining field at the boat ramp. Very ingenious. No drugs except alkie, and not much of that. None before that.

The link pulsed, and I acknowledged.

Chiang . . . Kirchner here. Kirchner was the lieutenant heading homicide.

Yes.

Thought you ought to know . . . McCall committed suicide.

Why should Kirchner care if I knew? *How did that happen? When?*

Half hour ago. He was under nanite home restraint, surveillance, everything. He turned off all the safeties in the house and jumped onto a flagstone courtyard. I thought you'd be interested.

A fall killed him, with a filch's internal nanites?

From a six-story tower? A tall six-story tower. Even on link, Kirchner's irony came through.

The McCall thing was really beginning to stink. *Anyone else around? Recsat surveillance?*

Funny thing. Area went blank just before he jumped, maybe five minutes. Got the jump. No one near. We're waiting on an autopsy. Let you know if anything turns up.

Thanks.

Just sat there, wondering. How had Kirchner known? Only ones I'd talked to were Darcy and Sarao. I pushed the link. *Sarao?*

Yes, Lieutenant?

You talk to Lieutenant Kirchner about the McCall case?

No, ser. Not to anyone.

Thanks. Meant Kirchner hadn't known, but had wanted me to know. As much as saying that the case stunk, and that someone had restraint loops all over him . . . and over homicide.

Stood, walked to the window. I looked out. McCall had known something. Something deadly to someone. But he was a privacy specialist, the last guy about to spill anything. Meant that his trial for his wife's death would reveal whatever it was. Revelation needed McCall alive, and it had to be less likely to be revealed with him dead. Have to think about that. And talk to someone.

Finally walked out front.

"I thought you'd be leaving soon," Sarao said.

"You know me too well."

She shrugged. "I know you don't like loose ends. Neither does Captain Cannizaro. That's why you're in charge of trendside."

"Maybe. Be going out to westside first. Don't know where after that. Be on link if the captain wants me."

"We'll find you."

Didn't want to be found. Not yet.

Got the green electral from transport and headed west. First stop was Westside Physical Systems. Kama might know something.

Same permie as last time was at the console behind the spotless maroon counter.

He looked up at me. "He's not here, Lieutenant."

"Know where he is?"

"He's on a job, ser."

"Suppose it's an important one?"

"He says all jobs are important."

"Do you know where I could find him?"

"He didn't say, ser."

That had to be true. Nanite permie treatment forbade lies. Kama knew that. Meant he didn't want it known where he was. Could have been lots of reasons.

"Is he on link?"

"No, ser. Not now."

"Tell him I was looking for him."

"Yes, ser."

Walked back out to the green electrocar. Never cared much for green in vehicles. Fine for grass and trees. I linked to Sarao. *Need a trace on an electrovan. Aldus four-six. Probably in southside. Registered to either Kamehameha O'Doull or Westside Physical Systems.*

Reasons?

Need to find the driver. Possible witness, but not material. Make it look good.

You don't ask for much, Lieutenant.

I never do. See what you can do.

Detrus owes me. We'll see.

Thanks.

Decided against dropping in on Morss. Instead, I decided to find Luke Elcado. Again, couldn't have proved a thing, but had the feeling Al's death and the other suicides were somehow tied into . . . something. Hoped I could find out what before Cannizaro asked me.

Luke ran what some called a portable uniquery. Provided and delivered stuff that couldn't be nanite-formulated—mostly exotic foods. Most customers were sariman, with enough creds for small luxuries, not enough creds to have staff to provide them all the time the way the filch did. Except some filch still used Elcado's Specialties and had stuff home-delivered. That's how good Luke was.

His business was at the east end of westside, not three hundred meters from the Platte Greenway. Close to the tubes and bridges so his electrolorries could get to eastside or southside quickly.

Luke never believed in unnecessaries. Customer area was gray-walled, five meters by five, half of it behind a counter. Counter held defense screens. Behind that was where Danyse usually sat. She was his daughter, doubled as bookkeeper, order-taker, and receptionist. She wasn't there.

Black-haired, hard-faced older woman looked at me. "Yes, ser?"

"Lieutenant Chiang to see Luke."

Looked like she thought about asking for ID, then her face blanked as she linked. A moment later, her eyes refocused. "He'll be right here, Lieutenant."

"Thank you."

Her face blanked again as she took an inlink from somewhere, possibly an order.

I walked to the end of the counter, then back. Always been hard for me to stand still.

The door at the end of the counter opened, and Luke looked out. He motioned.

I followed him through the door, down a short hall, and into his office. It was gray. No decorations. Besides the chairs, console, and flat table desk, the only other item was a fullphase holo projector.

"Gene—I mean, Lieutenant. Ah . . . what . . ."

"Sorry to hear about Al. He was a good kid."

Luke looked down. "Thanks for the flowers. And the note. Katya thought they were nice." He didn't meet my eyes. "What do you want?"

"To talk. No trouble. Information. Had a couple of cases like Al's, just in the last few weeks. Wanted to talk to you about Al because he was a good kid."

Luke frowned.

"It's simple. Some of these kids . . . they've been in so much trouble it would take weeks to unscramble everything involved."

"Lieutenant . . . he . . . he killed himself. Why he did, that's a DPS matter?"

"It might be. Can't say more. Not yet. But there's no trouble for you or Al. Won't be."

"With ebol4 and nuclear terrorists, you worry about why my son—"

"Luke." Made my voice hard and very cold. "DPS can't stop the Talibanate or Russe terrorists. And we're not CDC. When a good kid delinks a lorry and drives it into a river for no reason, and when he's not the first . . . maybe we can do something."

"Tasha . . . did she put you up to this?"

"No one at DPS has talked to her. You don't care for her, do you?"

"I don't care one way or another . . . now."

I sighed. Don't usually. Sometimes it helps. "We all need help one day. Today, I need help. You might need it tomorrow."

He was the one to sigh. "All right. What do you want to know?"

"What Al did the night before. Anything you can remember."

"He asked to get off work early. An hour early so he could take *her* to dinner. At a uniquery."

"Must have cost him a lot."

Luke smiled, a faint sad smile. Shook his head. "We supply about four places. We get dinner passes. Gilda and I never use them all. Al wanted one for The Right Bank—Wilm Bruff's place. He wanted to impress *her*."

Bruff's place was where the young filch and the high sariman went. Cost a bundle of creds. "I'm sure he did."

"He always wanted to impress her."

"Then what?"

"He said they were going to a FlameTop concert. The rezpopper. He's local, sings at the Moulin Noir."

"Anything special about the concert?"

"Al said FlameTop had a new reztwist. *She* told him that. Something that would make him a big rez star before long." Luke shook his head again. "Never did understand that rez stuff. Then, I couldn't keep time if I had a pro dancer on each elbow."

"Do you know what this twist was?"

"I don't know what it was. Al didn't say."

Asked him a few more questions, but it was clear he'd told me what he knew.

"Know where I could find Tasha? She still live at home?"

"No. Al said she had her own place, with another girl. It's not listed. She works for one of those comm outfits—the ones that you call up when there's an ad on the net. AnswerQuik, I think."

"Thanks, Luke." I stood up.

"You think this will help someone?"

"Hope so. Really do."

He nodded, and I left. Poor bastard.

Once I got in the electral, I considered, then linked to the office.

Sarao? Any luck with the trace?

Detrus is out on some assignment. She'll be back in a half hour. So they say. You want me to try Sansky?

No. Sansky went by the screen, and then some. *Going to track down another mystery of sorts.*

Oh?

The suicides. Till later. I broke the link. AnswerQuik was in eastside. A link pulse got me a simmie. I asked for Tasha Lei.

She's on duty. Might I take a message?

No. *I'll try her later.*

If she was on a standard shift, she'd still be there. Wished I knew what I chased.

Took me nearly an hour. Two medvans blocked the ramp to the Elletch Bridge. Checked the DPS net, discovered a driver with ebol4 had passed out. Electral stopped safely, but when DPS patroller saw the blood everywhere, called in meds and decontamination. Snarled things for a time. Shuttle would have been faster, but I couldn't abandon the DPS electral. Might need it later, too.

Detrus hadn't come back, either. Nothing was going well.

AnswerQuik was in a long building in the complex just barely in eastside, four klicks north of OldTech. Had a real guard, behind a double screen. Good two meters of muscle. Some of it between the ears.

"Looking for Tasha Lei."

"No visitors, ser."

"Lieutenant Chiang, DPS. I just need to talk to her for a few minutes." Pulsed the official ID and backed it with the DPS/GIL counter.

"Ah . . . just a moment, ser. I'll have to check with the supervisor."

I stood there, waiting.

In less than two minutes, a thin-faced woman—dark-haired, Korean gene-back—appeared behind the screen. Didn't look at me, studied the ID and codes. Finally, she looked up.

I smiled. Couldn't hurt.

"Lieutenant . . . might I ask what interest you have in Tasha?"

She could ask. I didn't have to answer, but there was no reason not to.

"She's in no trouble." Not yet, anyway. "She might have been a witness to something. DPS wants to know if what she saw . . . if she saw anything."

"That's what you all say."

I smiled again. "I'd still like to talk to her."

"We can't stop you, Lieutenant. I hope you'll be kind. It's been hard on her."

"Understand."

"I hope so. You can use the job interview room. It's the door on the left there. She'll be out in a moment."

Walked over and opened the door. The room wasn't more than three meters square with three chairs and a side table next to the wall. Didn't sit down.

A woman walked in—black hair, piercing green eyes with the slightest tilt to them, a touch of dark bronze to her skin. Small, but very alive. Could see why young Al had been hooked. Couldn't see why Luke didn't like her.

"Lieutenant? I'm Tasha Lei."

"I know your father." Gestured to the chairs.

"I am certain you do." She sat down. "Genyse said you needed to talk to me."

"About Al Elcado." I paused. "Why he died . . . there's a mystery there."

"He drove an electrolorry into Clear Creek. He didn't have the high-level nanomeds that would have saved him." She swallowed.

"It happened to several others in the past few months. Records don't show a pattern of deaths like that before. Hoped you could answer a few questions."

"Could you just ask them . . . please?" Tears hovered in her eyes.

"You went out with him the night before."

"Yes."

"Understand he took you to The Right Bank."

"Oh, Lieutenant. He wanted to impress me. I wouldn't have even agreed to that if it had come out of his pocket, but his family gets passes. It was important to Al that he could take me someplace like that."

"You went to dinner alone, the two of you?"

"Yes."

"Did he eat anything strange? Different?"

She frowned, trying to remember. "No. He had tournedos with bearnaise salsa."

"Drink?"

"No, not at dinner."

"Did anyone approach you two?"

"No one except Wilm. He just offered his regards to Al and asked him to give his greetings to Al's father."

"You went from dinner to the concert? Where was it?"

"Yes. At the Moulin Noir."

"Tell me about the concert."

"Just a concert at the Moulin Noir. We had seats halfway back, near the middle."

"How many people were there?"

"Five hundred, maybe. It was full, but it's not that big."

"Who was singing?"

"FlameTop. He's on the way."

"You been to hear him before?"

"I'd heard him once before in February, with Elyna."

"Elyna?"

"My roommate. We rent a conapt not far from here."

"Was it the same concert?"

She shook her head. "He's better now. He'll be doing the big houses and tours before long. The first time I heard him, he was still . . . he wasn't as good."

"What was the difference?"

"The rez—he's really got it integrated into the song and the music now."

"You told Al that FlameTop had a new twist. What was that?"

She tilted her head, impatiently. "I just told you—the way he integrated the rez."

"Does anyone else do it that way?"

"I don't know—what does this have to do with Al?"

"I'm trying to find out." I offered a smile. Hoped it was sympathetic. "Just a question or two more. Did you have drinks—alkie—at the concert?"

"Al had a few drinks, alkie, I mean, but only two or three. He didn't have any at dinner. He said three was his limit."

"After the concert?"

"He took me home. He didn't stay long. I never saw him again." Her eyes were bright. Tears would come.

"Did you have anything to drink?"

"I'm old-fashioned, Lieutenant." A crooked smile crossed her face. A tear oozed from the corner of her left eye. " 'Sides, I can't drink."

"Can't?" Wondered at that response.

"I'm allergic to alkie. Could be fixed with heavy nanomeds, but . . . where would I get the creds for those? And why?"

I nodded.

"If you think of anything else that might be strange, please let me know."

She nodded. Wasn't agreeing.

"Thank you. I can't think of any other questions. I might have to get back to you, but it would only be for one or two questions." I stood, then bowed slightly.

She nodded and slipped out the back door.

The big servie guard didn't even look at me as I left.

Still couldn't see why Luke disliked her.

Needed to talk to FlameTop—if I could run him down. And his band, whatever the instrumentalists were called. Also needed to talk to Kama, to find out more about the ODs, and what else had happened while I'd been out. Hoped that the DPS medics had a handle on the ebol4. Feared that they didn't.

Chapter 16
Cannon

In some ways, it had been a trying day from the very beginning. More than a dozen newsies had contacted me about the orbiter attack, but Ted had anticipated everything. He'd had a draft statement ready within minutes. He'd gotten almost everything right, beginning with the condemnation about such a terrible act to my regrets to the families and friends of those so cruelly ripped from life and my belief that the PDF would find those responsible. We had to take out the part about them being punished, because that was unlikely to happen. If I did say something like that, Hansen would be trumpeting my failure to keep a promise and my ineffectiveness in every ad and solicitation—beginning in two weeks and lasting through the election.

Then, as a result of the events with the Russe shuttle, all debate on the pending appropriations measures had been suspended. That would mean longer days in the weeks ahead. Because of the orbiter disaster, no one contacted me about the ebol4 situation, but I had Ted working on that, too. The disease was going to be a far bigger issue over the weeks ahead. Most people didn't have that much sympathy for either Russe or the Martian Republic. The Republic was gouging us on space-delivered raw materials, and people still remembered that the second Collapse had been triggered by the Russe default on the environmental cleanup debts they'd incurred. The voters of NorAm would screen out the Martians and Russeans, but they weren't going to forget deaths closer to home. Those deaths would keep occurring. Even the newest drug treatments were largely useless, and only stepped-up nanomeds worked. Most servies couldn't afford them, and neither could the government, not for millions of people. The virus was virulent enough that it could be contained, but the early estimates were as many as a million servies and permies could die. That was if nanocontainment worked at all the medical facilities and if the disease didn't mutate into something worse. Even under the best of circumstances, too many people would die. I didn't have that much sympathy for the permies—they'd chosen their lot—but most of the servies were hardworking people.

There wasn't any point in announcing how bad it would be. If we did, there would be panic, and more people would die. So we all talked about the problem of the disease, and made sounds as if the current efforts would limit it—which they would. Just not enough.

On top of that, Alberico was still trying to add the Southern Diversion to every bill that he could, and I had to spend over an hour on a VRlink with the Continental Water Administrator explaining why it was a bad idea. We didn't need population caps in both Denv and Phenix, and especially not in St. George. Ted's briefing points had been right on target, but I'd have to repeat the effort with more than a few decision makers in the Executory.

Even Ciella hadn't felt well, for some reason, and I'd insisted that George send her home early. She'd be grateful for my insistence, and there were times when you couldn't buy gratitude. So it was a good idea to stockpile it when you could. Especially among the people who worked for you.

All in all, I was happy to leave the office.

Elise was in the foyer when I walked in. She was leaving the formal living area.

"Elden . . . I didn't expect you so early, with all that's happened today."

"Did you get your nanomed boost?"

"You just walk in the door, and that's what you ask? With

the possibility that the Republic is going to start throwing asteroids and everything else at us? My, aren't you the concerned
representative of the people?" Her dark eyebrows arched perfectly.

I stepped forward and hugged her. "I've made statements and
reassured people, and that is about all I can do about terrorists
or the Agkhanate or whatever African warlord it might be. I love
you, and I care. I can do something to make sure you're safe
from this new strain of ebol. It's vicious. And, no, I can't say
that in public, either."

Elise actually hugged me back for a moment before stepping
away. "Terrorists blowing orbiters out of the sky. Another bioweapon gone mad." She shook her head. "Why? Where will it all
end?"

"The orbiter business . . . I think there will be a statement from
the Agkhanate in a day or so. The Talibanate leadership will
announce that they have discovered the group that did it, and
have confiscated the materials and the bases. They'll say that the
guilty will be punished, and that it was truly regrettable. Then,
they'll add words to the effect that given the continuing Russe
irresponsibility both in terms of ecologic cleanups and intransi-
gence in dealing fairly with Islamic populations in southern Russe
that the world could expect no less, and that until those issues
are addressed, there is always the possibility that extremists will
take matters into their own hands . . ."

I shrugged.

"Elden . . . I see that the day hasn't improved your mood."

"No. That's the best possibility. I always hope for the best."

"I don't think I wish to hear the worst." She raised the antique
porcelain watering jug she had been carrying and glanced toward
my study. "I realized that your cacti needed water. You never
do."

"If I do, I overwater them." I followed her into the cherry-
paneled study. "The ebol4 could be an accident, or it could be
an indirect attack on the EC or us. You wipe out a chunk of the
servie and permie population, and people suffer, and they get

upset. It strains the medical systems, and that increases costs and hurts the availability of other treatments. That hurts more people. After that, it really hits the service industries. Fewer servies means they can bargain for higher wages. Costs go up, and we all pay a second or third time."

"Who would do that?" She dribbled water over the miniature barrel cactus and then over the bonsai Joshua tree. "Would they be that cold-blooded?"

"About half the world, and they would be. There's not too much the Legislature can do." I paused, then added, "Bill's worked out a new approach for the campaign."

Elise raised her dark eyebrows, in that way that meant she didn't exactly approve of my dealing with a campaign now. But then, she didn't approve of a lot. Why was she still with me? Because the alternatives were worse.

She finally spoke. "Which campaign?"

"The one against Hansen. Mine. It's likely to be most effective on the emtwo level."

"I hate that term."

"I didn't coin it. Some writer did centuries ago. Kornbluth, I think."

"It's still a euphemism, and one that dehumanizes people."

"I sometimes wonder if they are human," I mused, knowing that would get her going, and that she wouldn't think so carefully before she thought.

"Marching morons—that's what it means. Is that how you think of your dear, dear constituents?"

"Some of them are. Some of them are far brighter than I am. It takes all kinds, as your brother Eric is always saying."

"It's expressed in scientific terms—em squared. And don't we owe everything to science?" Elise's voice could get bitter enough to cut down redwoods, not that anyone would allow that these days. Such a contrast between her voice and her beauty. She was more regal-looking than an ancient princess. It served her well in her position as a talent assessor for NorNet.

I laughed. "You put it so well."

"So just what are you and Bill going to do?" she prompted, which I knew she would, given the choice between discussing the day's disasters, the emtwos, and a campaign strategy. Of course, she could have walked into the living room, with its view of the Rockies, but I would have followed her.

"It's based on resonance advertising and . . ."

"They tried that thirty years ago, and it was a flop, Elden. You're letting Bill use that?" She laughed.

"There's a new twist to it."

"With you there's always a new twist, except the ones offering it are usually redheads—"

"Elise . . . you know . . ."

She sighed tiredly. "I know you never *do* anything. You're so afraid you might get caught that the only thing you screw is the public." She offered that brittle smile. "You were going to tell me about the new campaign."

"For one thing, we're going to kick it off early, and we're going to make it *very* positive."

"That's a new twist."

I ignored that jab. "We can reinforce the positive aspect with the new rezads. The same message with different background and music for each demographic group and net outlet."

"Won't that be too expensive?"

I shook my head. "No. We can use the same holo images in all markets, if we're careful. The rez and music parts are different, but they're the least expensive. Bill's lined up a production outfit that specializes in that. Very reasonable."

"You always want everything to be reasonable, Elden. It's too bad that the world isn't more obliging."

"I've never expected that."

"By the way, speaking of Eric, he linked earlier. He wants to see you." Elise stretched, catlike, smiling. "He'll be here in about fifteen minutes. Would you like something to eat?"

"I would, and I appreciate the offer." I grinned.

"It's ready, I think. The menu code for the formulator was as complex as I've seen. It took half a databloc, but it's supposed to be good. I thought we could eat on the balcony."

"*What* is it?"

"A peanut chicken dish that was very popular three centuries ago. The Soaring Sophisticate re-created it from old files discovered in the ruins of Ellay."

While I wasn't thrilled about formulator-created chicken or peanuts, Elise seemed interested and intrigued, and she was intelligent and most beautiful. "Let's try it."

She smiled. "Despite everything, Elden, you do try. It's one of your most endearing traits."

So we sat on the balcony, where the screens blocked the wind, but not the late day sunlight, and ate. Elise was right. The chicken was actually good, especially for a change. I told her so.

"Thank you." She smiled, warmly, and not cuttingly. "By the way, I did see the doctor this afternoon, right after you linked. Did you?"

"I have an appointment at eight tomorrow. Earliest they could fit me in."

"Good. You may be one of the more powerful men in the Nor-Am Senate, dear, but you see too many people to take chances."

She was right about that. Then, for a woman, especially, she was right about many things. I'd learned that over the years. I did listen and learn.

"How do you feel about the Russean orbiter?" I asked.

"Testing the pulse of the people?" Her question was gentle, not biting.

"Wondering."

"I hate to see people die for posturing and gestures." She shrugged. "I know it happens. It always has. The Russean people keep making messes of their country. They have for centuries, and this is another example. I guess what will happen will happen. I worry more about things like the ebol virus and the PDF asteroid patrol not catching that mining debris."

I didn't get a chance to comment because the system announced, *Eric Christensen is here.*

Tell him we'll be right there.

We stood and carted the dishes into the kitchen, and then walked to the front foyer, where I pulsed the door to let Eric in.

Eric had Elise's dark brown hair and the same large brown eyes. Somehow, they were luminous on her, and almost protruding on him. He nodded as the door closed behind him. "You're looking good, Elden. You, too, Elise."

"So are you," I replied.

"I'll leave you two." Elise smiled brightly and stepped down the hallway to her private study.

Eric and I followed her, but only to the first open door, the one to my study. I went in first. I pulse-linked, and the study door shut after Eric followed me inside. The nanite-based privacy screens went on as well. I sat down behind the desk and motioned for him to sit wherever he wanted. He took the replica cherry captain's chair.

"What do you want?" I figured it was easier, and quicker, to ask. Otherwise, after a half hour of wasted small talk, Eric would slide into whatever he had in mind.

"What do you think about the ebol4 thing?"

"You know what I think. It's a mess. It's probably a bioattack from either West Asia or Afrique, and no one can afford to make that accusation because there's no way to prove it—or even come close."

Before I could say more, Eric added, "You know that Alberto Martini died last December. Someone has been buying blocks of MMSystems from the family. Your investigation of the fusion tug and power module business made the stock a real steal. Too bad you couldn't cash in on it."

"Did you?"

Eric laughed. "Conflict of interest on two fronts. CWC is a competitor of MMSystems in some markets, and I'm your brother-in-law. Mikhail would have dismissed me on the spot."

"What about MMSystems?" Eric wouldn't have mentioned it without reason. He never did.

"Whoever controls it has a handle on the future. They control the fusion tug business, and deep-space power cells, and those mean leverage over all deep-space industries."

"That's been obvious for years." I still didn't see exactly where Eric was going, but even the general direction was disturbing. "And the family wants to sell?"

"Let's just say we think there are . . . shall we say, extenuating circumstances."

"What sort of mess has young Martini gotten himself into?"

Eric shrugged. "We don't know, but we think he's the one selling. Mikhail thought you might know or be able to find out."

It might be worth it, but I'd have to be very careful. "I assume that's not the only reason why you're here."

"Not totally. But I did want to hear what you were saying. Or not saying." He cleared his throat. "There are a lot of contracts at stake in the Southern Diversion. Word is that Kemal will be coming after you."

"I couldn't expect anything else." I paused. "There aren't that many contracts. It's not as big a thing as the fusion tug investigation. Why are you concerned?"

"You mean you don't want Kemal to turn all of Phenix into westside?" Eric grinned and gestured toward the wide window, toward the mountains and the warrens of Denv's westside.

That threw me, but only for a moment. I decided to play along, to see what else Eric would say. "What am I supposed to do? Both the Capital District and Deseret District get hurt by it. The drop line is the same. Less water means a lower effective population cap and greater density for Denv, and half the towns in Deseret. Formulators don't make water, not cost-effectively, and people hate population caps." I glanced at the amused smile on Eric's face. "You didn't come here to get me to spout forth on the diversion issue. You know where I stand, and it's where the retained solicitor for CWC would want me to stand."

"Actually, it is. Mikhail worries about anything that might hurt his legacy. He always talks about the Cewitto foresight."

"Mikhail Cewitto, the prognosticator?" I laughed warmly. "Or Mikhail Cewitto, head of CWC?"

"He's been right about most things," Eric pointed out. "Mikhail's especially worried about where this might lead. Kemal's backing Alredd, and Heber Smith is working for Hansen."

"I though the changes to the guideway law were what Kemal wanted."

"He does. He especially wants a change in guideway maintenance requirements. The Capital District Coordinator's election is in less than three months. Alredd's going after Dewey. With Kemal's money . . . and less than visible resources . . ."

"Alredd can't beat Dewey. Even with Kemal behind him."

"No. But what if he makes the diversion an issue in the co-ordinator's election? That allows him two campaigns, both in Denv and in your district."

"We've already got something in the works."

Eric smiled—a polite unconvincing expression. "McCall used to work for O'Bannon and Reyes."

"They're Kemal's retained solicitors."

"McCall was just indicted for murder, you may recall."

"I heard that."

"He committed suicide this afternoon."

"How?" I didn't like the way Eric said it.

"He turned off his screens and jumped off a sixth-floor balcony."

"Interesting." It was more than interesting. More like chilling. "You're telling me it was murder. Again."

"The verdict will be suicide." Eric stood. "Like I said, Mikhail's worried. He'd like to offer any help he can."

"I appreciate that, Eric. I really do."

"We'll do what we can, and anything else that we can work out." He stood up. "Think about it."

How could I not think about it? Then, I wasn't Evan McCall—

thankfully. There was certainly no doubt that Hansen would be getting more than a few million creds—or the equivalent in some untraceable way—in support from Kemal. That wouldn't be obvious until after Alredd lost to Dewey in the coordinator's election. Even with Kemal's billions, Alredd couldn't beat Dewey, but that election could make mine tougher. A great deal tougher.

Maybe Bill and I would have to supplement the positive rezads with some targeted ones, not exactly negative, but raising questions about Hansen's motivations. That might work, but we'd have to really lay on the positive stuff first, so that we had a foundation. We'd have to be careful, very careful.

I also needed to find a way to find out what was happening with MMSystems. That wasn't exactly in my personal interest, but it could backfire all over me if I didn't know what was going on there.

I nodded. Politics was intricate . . . and beautiful in its own strange and deadly way.

Chapter 17
Parsfal

By Wednesday afternoon, I hadn't gotten much farther on McCall. I had found and modified the statistics on hurricane frequency and the shifts in the Gulf Stream for Bimstein, and provided some graphics. I'd also run a vote survey on Cannon, but hadn't figured out how to slant the comparison piece between Cannon and Vanderhoof, or how to include Patroclas. Then, after I'd finished with the PDF commander, I'd finally managed to dig up some facts on the previous ebol strains, and then repackage the warning symptoms put out by CDC into something simpler. I couldn't have done it if Istancya hadn't given me a hand with some of the digging.

Kountze told Bimstein to assign Paula Lopes to handle the

ebol4 story, and he did. She had a soothing manner, and what else could we do? Every other year, it seemed, there was another bioweapon that got loose. The post-Collapse lines of Drew came to mind.

> The white death came, and then it left,
> its scalpel neither swift nor deft . . .

For a moment, I just sat there.

When I finally got back to the McCall stuff, I'd tried a search on Nanette McCall and came up with a few references, but not many. She had been a physiological child psychologist, well respected, who had published several articles on aspects of post-puberty psychology as affected by physiology. Again, there was nothing to indicate friction between the McCalls, except perhaps that she was always referred to as Nanette Iveson.

Walter Kerrigan had been a senatorial aide for years, before starting his own consulting firm, which specialized in imaging, not surprisingly, since Kerrigan had been a speechwriter and general newsie-flak for Senator Fontana. He was about five years older than McCall. I made a few links on Kerrigan and discovered he had an impressive list of clients, and few of them were politicians. Kemal was reputedly one of them, but none of my contacts could confirm that. They'd all heard it, but that didn't make it true.

I wondered about link-calling Maeda Forsala and was about to swallow the screen and do it.

Parsfal? Bimstein was louder than ever, link limits or not.

I'm here.

What else do you have on McCall?

Not much. I just got back to that one. First, you had me on Super-C. Then, you wanted storm stuff in the Caribbean, remember? Because that hurricane was the earliest on record. And then the ebol4 material. And the water comparison for the Southern Diversion, because of the historic low flows in the Colorado. Why do you need more on McCall?

You haven't heard? He jumped off a tower. Onto a stone courtyard. Squashed flatter than flat. So what do you have?

You've got what I have.

The damned filch committed suicide, and you tell me you can't find anything more on him?

I winced at the violence of Bimstein's link, and I had to wait a moment before replying. *You had me working on all the other stuff, and there's not much there. I can't even speculate without something, but I do have an idea.*

An idea? Better be good.

The filch are different. We're all open screens . . . see their images, and that's all you see. McCall is a perfect example . . . vid-perfect solicitor. Yet he's been indicted for murder. How much of the filch don't we see? What really goes on behind those nanite screens? I checked on his wife, and his closer acquaintances. It's the same thing there.

Hmmm . . . have to think about that. I'll get back to you.

I almost laughed. What he meant was that he was going to see if anyone else could find anything on McCall, and if no one came up with anything, then . . . then he might buy my approach.

I swallowed hard and tried the link to Maeda Forsala's office. I was scarcely surprised when I got a simmie, dressed in a dark suit with a pale mauve blouse.

"This is Maeda Forsala. Please leave a link code and a message."

Since her greeting was spoken, old style, I activated the speaker and projection and spoke my reply. "Ah . . . this is Jude Parsfal of NetPrime. I'm trying to track down some information . . ."

The simmie projection wavered and was replaced with a second image. This one also wore a dark suit, but the blouse was cream, and the dark hair was longer and swept back. "Mr. Parsfal . . . how might I help you, if I can?"

"I'm a researcher with NetPrime, ser. I'm trying to find out more information about Evan and Nanette McCall . . ."

"Someone told you that she had retained me, I'm certain."

Her response surprised me, but I just answered, "That's what

I'd been told, but it didn't seem to track . . ." I was gambling with that, hoping I'd read it right.

"Bravo, Mr. Parsfal. You're the first of several who seems to have done the background work. For that, you can have the information." She smiled, and her teeth gleamed like a shark's. "It's not a violation of privacy. Nanette was not a client of mine. She never contacted me, and you may quote me on that. So far as I know, she was happily married to Evan."

"Is it possible she might have contacted another domestic relations solicitor or advocate?"

"Possible, but highly unlikely. We'd known each other personally for years."

Left unspoken was the fact that Forsala had the reputation for being the best at that sort of thing. "Why do you think this rumor is being circulated, then?"

"I cannot speculate on that. That's your job, Mr. Parsfal."

"Mrs. McCall—"

"She went by Nanette Iveson, except on social occasions, or when the children were involved when she was younger."

"Nanette Iveson was well known as a physiological child psychologist."

"She was indeed. She was not as social as Evan, and she was far more perceptive."

"I see." I thought I did, but how could I ask the right questions? "Had you heard that Evan jumped from the tower at his home and died early this afternoon?"

The startled expression on her face was a clear answer that she had not. "No. I hadn't." After a moment, she added, "I had never thought of Evan as that decisive. But one never knows." She paused, but not long enough to let me ask another question. "I don't think I can add anything else, Mr. Parsfal. Good day."

I was looking at nothing and collapsed the blank holo projection. I'd been as much as told that the rumor was false, and that McCall didn't have the guts to commit suicide. That was just wonderful. I had less than nothing of substance there—except that Nanette Iveson had not been seeking a divorce.

I managed to find Kerrigan's firm's link codes and tapped them in, only to discover he also required a holo projection link.

"This is Jude Parsfal of NetPrime—"

The simmie vanished. A dark-haired and rugged-looking man of that indeterminate age that was so common appeared. "What do you want?" He sounded annoyed.

"Ah . . . any information you can provide on Evan McCall. You were his closest friend."

Kerrigan laughed, bitterly. "So you can twist things yet another way?" He paused, and his face smoothed. "I apologize, Mr. Parsfal. Since we've never talked before, I may be assuming what might not be true."

"I'm sorry. I've been given the job of finding background. Frankly, there's very little there, and half of what is supposedly common knowledge isn't even true." That was stretching it slightly, but it wouldn't hurt. "I hate to bother you now, after the latest . . ."

Kerrigan straightened up. "The latest? He was indicted for murder. That was crazy enough, but . . . there's more?"

"He committed suicide by jumping from a tower a little while ago."

Kerrigan looked totally stunned. "I can't believe that."

"The recsat system has it on databloc."

Kerrigan shook his head. "I wouldn't . . . I don't see how . . ."

"I'd heard that you were often his tennis partner. You knew him fairly well?"

"As well as anyone . . . Are you sure about the suicide?"

"That's the DPS report."

"I can't believe it. He was friendly to everyone. This has been so unfair."

"Some have said you only knew him through tennis . . ."

"We saw each other socially sometimes, but usually . . . on the tennis court. We played most Saturdays. Evan was a good player, not great, but good. He didn't talk much. He never did."

"I understand that he and his wife were very close."

"You wouldn't know it from the way DPS has handled it." He offered another bitter laugh. "Yes, they were. Evan couldn't have laid a hand on Nanette. First, he loved her too much. It was evident in everything he said or did. Second, he was a technical idiot. He was always having to have his staff readjust his holo projection or his link settings."

"Why do you think the DPS charged him, then?"

Kerrigan shrugged. "That would be the kind of speculation that I'd rather not engage in. I'd guess that they were misled, but that would be a guess, and it's not for attribution."

"Would you object to a report that said sources close to the family believe DPS was misled?"

"If you think that might be the case . . . I don't know. It's only a guess."

"Can you think of anyone who might want to see McCall dead?"

"Are you thinking he was murdered?"

"I don't know what to think." That was definitely true.

"Evan?" Kerrigan frowned. "No one personally, that's certain. Everyone I know who knew him liked him. I don't know anything about his practice. He was a privacy solicitor, and he never said a word about a client in the whole time I knew him. I wouldn't know one of his clients if they walked up to me or if someone handed me a list."

"Do you know anyone who might?"

"Only his junior associates. Knowing the way Evan was, I'm certain they wouldn't say anything to the media. They might have said something to DPS."

I offered a few more questions, but Kerrigan had said what he was going to say, and it hadn't been much. Then I put in another call to Marc Oler, but only got the simmie.

I went through the thin file on Emile Brazelton. It was suggestive. Brazelton was the head of the nanite-based fabricating firm that KC Constructors had hired for the control systems of the shuttle guideway system. KC was Kemal's firm. According to

John Ashbaugh, Brazelton had been a client of McCall's. But so had KC Constructors. I was debating how to approach that when Bimstein's overboosted link seared through my skull.

Parsfal? What have you got on McCall? Now!

Everyone liked him. He was deeply in love with his wife. He never ever talked business even with his closest friends. Someone put out a rumor that the McCalls had been having trouble and that she had retained a solicitor for a separation or divorce. It isn't true.

You sure of that?

I got a confirmation and an allowed quote from the solicitor. Also got another source that won't be quoted directly but will allow a quote as a source close to the family. The source claims that DPS was misled, that Evan McCall wouldn't and couldn't have laid a hand on his wife.

Hmmm . . . guess we'll play it the other way.

The other way?

McCall was truly in love with his wife. He was so distraught by her accidental death and the charges that he'd murdered her that he couldn't take it and jumped.

Do we know that? I asked.

We know that they were in love. Got some other confirmations on that from Rehm. We know they didn't have problems. The DPS has just apologized for its hasty action and said that Nanette McCall's death could easily have been caused by an inadvertent misadjustment in the nanite field parameters. They've confirmed that McCall couldn't have readjusted the system.

That was even stranger.

You can wrap that up. Send what you've got to Metesta. Then, get back on the ebol background. Five deaths in Denv yesterday, and ten so far today. And I still don't have the last water diversion piece I asked for.

After Bimstein broke the link, I put together the "source" quotes on McCall and fired them off to Metesta. Then, I just sat in front of my console. That was the news business. McCall had been hot, and now Kerras or someone was doing a wrap-up on the story, probably with a tragic overtone, lamenting the situation, with at least a sideways slam at DPS. And I was supposed to forget it and concentrate on ebol4 and the horror it was likely to bring to Denv and NorAm.

I shook my head, and the old lines crept into my mind.

The world is weary of the past
Oh, might it die or rest at last . . .

Sometimes, I felt that way. Sometimes, there was too much to be weary of, and too little of beauty and grace.

And I had the feeling that the McCall case was a tiny sliver of something far, far larger, something I couldn't even imagine—or have the time to pursue. I decided to finish up the latest diversion segment so Bimstein couldn't hold that over my head. He'd hold something else.

Chapter 18
Kemal

After I stopped by the KC MedCenter for the nanomeds to deal with the ebol4 outbreak, my first appointment on Thursday was with Heber Smith. The meeting would be short. After I met with Heber, I had to talk to O'Bannon about the impact of the orbiter attack. The attack hadn't helped anything. Because of the new fusion tug technology, it might attract attention to the upcoming corporate meeting of MMSystems. It would increase tensions between the Martian Republic and Earth. Increased tensions sometimes led to bad government decisions and greater scrutiny. KC didn't need any of those.

The ebol4 outbreak was going to make matters bad enough.

I'd already made sure Marissa, the children, and the rest of the family got their upgrades right after I did. If I didn't take care of family, who would?

I put those thoughts aside and went out to greet Heber Smith. He'd taken the company flitter from St. George the night before.

He looked rested when he walked in. "Somehow, the office fits you, Chris." He grinned. "It's good to see you."

"It's good to see you. It looks like you slept well."

"I did. I had dinner with my daughter and her family last night. We've got another grandson."

"Family's important." I gestured to the conference table.

We both sat down, our backs to the view. There wasn't much, since it was cloudy, and even Mount Evans was obscured.

"You've got a problem with District Coordinator Dewey," Heber began.

"We've always had problems with Dewey. Everyone thinks he's so clean, and that we're so crooked. We're honest. We've told the world that we oppose him. He runs on the idea that we're corrupt thugs." I snorted. "His cousins run GSY. He gets Cannon to put through that divestiture legislation. They benefit, and he's honest? We built the new shuttle system, but because we built it, we can't maintain it. We can do it better and cheaper, but we're not allowed to. They get most of the profits, but it's clean? The Justiciary bought that crap, too. So we can build systems, but we can't get the maintenance contracts. Or we can let someone else build crap, and take a loss for two years upgrading it through maintenance. That's good government?"

"It's good politics," Heber pointed out.

I had to laugh. "You're right. We'll have to do something."

"You still have another problem with Dewey."

"What?"

"He's working with the NorAm Economics and Commerce Committee to draft another piece of legislation." After a moment, Heber went on, "He wants to limit the royalty markup on proprietary technology to one hundred percent of production costs. That's for public works projects. It wouldn't apply to contracts between private parties. Our counts show that it might pass."

"What else?"

"He's talking about hiring a forensic accounting team. It won't be called that, but that's what it amounts to. He wants to show that—"

"GSY can do a cheaper job on major projects once they can steal our technology. Politicians like Dewey need to be shot. Or drawn and quartered. They have no idea of the years we've spent in upgrading Brazelton's operations, the engineers we've supported, the design and development costs. All they look at is the markup over the direct production costs. So we need to make sure Alredd wins the election."

"We can't. It's not possible, Chris. Dewey's got such a base among the servies, close to seventy percent. He's got sixty percent of the sariman, and forty percent of the filch."

I understood the numbers. What I didn't understand was the forty percent of the filch. Dewey was a populist demagogue. He'd drain every filch he could. And forty percent would vote for him. "You're sure of that?"

"Absolutely."

"How much more can we give to Alredd?"

"Even through all the avenues you've got, less than three million."

"Find out how much. Talk to O'Bannon, and make sure every single credit is absolutely legal. Then tell me what checks to write."

"You're throwing the credits away."

"No. I want every single credit we send from now on targeted against Dewey's support of whatever Alredd can call filch projects. The guideway legislation, the Southern Diversion, and anything else. Talk to O'Bannon. See if there's a way those ads can be run into Deseret District. If not, have Hansen use the same stuff, pointing out that the Dewey-Cannon conspiracy—call it that—is designed to take Deseret credits and pour them into the Capitol District."

"Cannon will still win. Hansen's facing more than an uphill battle."

"This time. We have to think more for the long term, my friend. Senators come and go. We'll help Cannon go."

"Cannon's one you don't want to tangle with, Chris. He'll let a lot slide, but if you attack him, or threaten him, he gets his back up."

"Then we don't apply force to him. We apply it to the things and people he cares about."

"You don't want to make an enemy of the man, Chris."

"Heber . . . he's already an enemy. The question is what we do about it. And about Dewey."

"I don't know that you can do much about Dewey."

"I'll have my mother pray for a miracle," I suggested. "We could use it."

"I hope she prays well." Heber smiled.

"Some of her prayers have been answered." Then, we both knew that we couldn't count on divine intervention. Not without help. "You're staying for the weekend?"

"No. I'll leave tomorrow. Ruth's sister is hosting a family get-together tomorrow night."

"Have a good time."

After Heber left, I had some thinking to do. Dewey would ruin KC, just on principle, because he didn't understand economics or business. Some of what he had in mind would undermine the arrangement with the Republic. I had some ideas, but, again, I didn't get far.

Mr. O'Bannon is waiting, Mr. Kemal.

Send him in.

O'Bannon slid into the office and eased into the chair he always took at the conference table. He was like a black tiger.

I sat down across from him. "What's the word?"

"Your friends are upset. As you instructed me, I told them that the attack was carried out with obsolete technology. I also pointed out that NorAm orbiter wouldn't have been as vulnerable—"

"The vulnerability was mostly because the Russeans don't like to cross anyone else's airspace. The Agkhanate had to know that. The Russeans also couldn't track the attackers. They can't retaliate."

"Can you?"

"Why would I want to, James? The attack just shows the problems of dealing with the Russeans."

"The Republic might want to."

"They'd get better terms on paper. Not in practice. They know that. Their hands are tied. They have to deal with EurCom or NorAm, and they have to let this attack pass. Oh, they could line up a metallic asteroid and accelerate it at Earth. They could build up enough velocity to make its deflection impossible, but they couldn't aim it well enough to hit Kabul. They could destroy civilization and possibly humanity on Earth. That destroys the source of their technology and all their markets. So it's an empty threat. That's why they're helping us. A direct takeover would be viewed as far too unfriendly, but they want MMSystems in more friendly hands."

"Hands they can control by threatening exposure," O'Bannon said.

"It's not in their interests to expose me, and it's not in mine. Besides, what we're doing is perfectly legal."

"Until the NorAm Senate finds out."

"Even in cases of continental emergency, ex post facto legislation is banned. That's what my distinguished solicitors told me. Now . . . what else did they say?"

"They understand that you are not in a position to do anything about the disaster, but they would like to make the point that once can be accepted, as a necessary evil. Twice will require action."

I snorted. "What action? Any direct action hurts the Republic more. They're not stupid."

"I agree. That is, however, what they said." O'Bannon smiled. "What do you want me to tell them?"

"Everything is under control. They'll have more favorable directors in a month, and a completely favorable board and executive officer in fourteen months. Suggest to them that they take a more aggrieved position and a less combative one. Something along the lines of how they're risking their talented people to supply Earth's raw materials needs and that they shouldn't also have their diplomats being killed as well."

"You have a rationale for that? They'll want to know."

"They can't keep their plans secret forever. Everyone knows that they could devastate Earth. The only reason they don't is that it would also destroy them. That will change. The more they build a reputation for forbearance, the less the continental legislatures will be forced to posture and threaten."

"Makes sense to me. You think they'll buy into it?"

"They should."

"You want me to tell them that?"

I shook my head. "Suggestions are one thing. Demands are another. Always suggest."

"And if they don't buy it?"

I laughed. "What have we lost? They're the ones who lose. I can always sell back what we've bought—over time. Or I can offer it to the highest bidder."

"You plan to make a profit, I assume?"

"Don't I always?" I paused. "What about the MagSys takeover?"

"You have to go slow there, Chris. It's going to take another year to get a plurality, and that's a small minority plurality. It might be worth two seats on the board, if that."

"Keep at it." I hadn't expected any more.

O'Bannon cleared his throat. "What about McCall?"

"What about him? He's been charged with murder. We've talked about it. What can I add? I don't believe he did it, but you never know about people. That's why I try never to push people into a corner. Cornered cats, rats, dogs, and people all bite." I didn't corner people when I could avoid it. I dealt with them before they felt cornered. At least, when I could. I'd waited too long with McCall. That was because I had needed him to finish matters.

"You think he'll reveal anything?"

"You never know, but I don't think so."

After O'Bannon left, I had a few minutes before lunch to go over the Dewey problem. That was one I'd have to resolve quickly. There's nothing more dangerous than a public crook who thinks he's honest. I had some of the details worked out. In my head. Plans were safer there.

Then Paulina linked in.

Ashtay Massin is here. He says he doesn't have an appointment, but he won't take long.

Send him in. I pulsed the door open. Ashtay never wasted my time.

Ashtay Massin walked into the office. He was the trustee of the KCF trusts. He was built like an ancient weight lifter. He had wavy brown hair and green eyes. He didn't look like an accountant or a solicitor. He was both.

"What's the problem?" I closed the door, then motioned to the conference table.

He sat down first, knowing that was my preference. "You know me too well, Mr. Kemal." Ashtay would never call me Chris. I liked that.

"Your nephew Stefan. He came to see me early this morning. He's already pledged his interest in his trust as collateral for a loan from Mountain Asset Management. He gave me the papers, so that I'd know."

I forced a smile, then shook my head. "You know the young ones. I'll have to talk to him. How much is the loan?"

"Ten million credits."

"He can't pay that. They have to know that. He'll be in default in three months."

Ashtay nodded. "If he defaults, we'll have to pay it. If they contend the application was fraudulent, then we may have to divulge the assets."

"Unless we pay it off before that happens." What Stefan had done was blackmail, pure and simple. He knew I didn't like publicity, and a Kemal defaulting on a secured loan was the last thing that needed to be news.

"I don't have that authority," he pointed out. "All I can do is obligate the interest and income, and put out a credit block on Stefan. That's why I thought you should know."

"I'll have to talk to him. We'll make sure it doesn't go to default." I sighed. "The young ones. Some of them take a while to understand."

Ashtay nodded sympathetically.

"Since you're here," I went on, "are we set for the MMSystems annual meeting?"

"I'll have the slate of officers for you to look at by the end of next week. We'll leave young Martini as president for a year. We'll also leave Bunanev, St. Pierre, and Emin on the board. That's what you wanted, wasn't it?"

"We'll have to handle it that way. The board's terms are staggered. You're sure Martini will propose the slate?"

"Does he have any choice?" Ashtay's smile was grim. He didn't approve of how I'd set Rafael Martini up.

"No. That was his choice." Business was business, and the young fool should have known better than to try to play around. His wife's family was old-line, very wealthy and very powerful, with their controlling interest in InterCred. The Fontaines had their own ways of expressing disapproval, and Rafael needed the credit they could provide. Badly.

Ashtay waited before asking, "Is there anything else, Mr. Kemal?"

"Not right now." I smiled. "Thank you for letting me know about Stefan. I'll be talking to him this afternoon. We'll work something out."

After Ashtay left, I headed down to Poul Therault's office to have a luncheon meeting.

We discussed the financial picture for the coming year, and all the contingencies that we needed to consider. I didn't eat that much.

By one, I was back in my office, working out the details of the Dewey plan.

Mr. O'Bannon for you, on holo, Mr. Kemal.

I'll take it.

O'Bannon's image was as big as he was. He had a somber look. "Have you heard, Chris?"

"Have I heard what?"

"About Evan McCall."

"I haven't heard anything new. Not since the indictment."

"He just committed suicide."

"What?" I shook my head. "That's hard to believe." That certainly was true enough, and a measure of Emile's ability. "How? Why? Does anyone know?"

"The DPS isn't saying anything. The orbiter mess and the ebol4 outbreak have kept it quieter than it could have been."

"Poor bastard." I felt sorry for McCall. He'd never quite understood—except the law. His wife had been the practical one, until the Cewrigh woman had gotten to her, and that hadn't left me much choice. "Let me know if anything else turns up."

"I will." O'Bannon paused. "What are you going to do about privacy matters?"

"I don't know." I gave a rueful smile. "You're my oldest solicitor. If you have a suggestion, let me know."

"We might be able to work out something with Caron Hildeo. She understands."

O'Bannon was telling me that Marc Oler didn't. "See what you can do."

He nodded. "Until later, Chris."

I looked out the window. Nothing was simple. It never was.

Paulina . . . would you please see if you can find my nephew Stefan?

Yes. Mr. Kemal.

I leaned back in the ergorecliner, thinking. There might be a way to solve several of my problems at once.

I have Stefan for you. Mr. Kemal.

Thank you, Paulina. I called up the holo display. Stefan was back into a beige singlesuit, with the gold chains.

"Stefan, you're concerned about money?"

"I told you I was."

"You did." I nodded understandingly. "Do you have the morning free on Monday? I'm playing golf with Emile Brazelton, but let me stop by before that. We can take a drive. Maybe you can join us. We can work out something. I've thought about it. It could be you're right. Houses and electrals are more expensive than when I was your age. Thirty percent more expensive, Poul tells me."

He looked dubious.

"Look, Stefan. When you collateralized that loan, Ashtay notified me. There are better ways to handle that. If you feel that desperate, we need to talk, and to work out something. You can't handle that kind of repayment for very long. The trust is a lifetime trust. There's nothing either of us can do about that. I hope you know what that means."

He tried to hide a look of defiance.

"Think about it. This is going to cause your mother a great deal of concern. I'd rather work with you to find a way to work this out." I smiled. "Have I ever not done what was best for the family?"

"No."

"I'll pick you up at quarter to nine on Monday morning."

He looked like he might refuse, but thought the better of it. "All right."

"Quarter to nine on Monday," I said it again. "We'll figure out something." I broke the connection.

Now, all I had to do was work out the details with Brazelton. I also had to make sure that the Smythers business was under control.

Chapter 19
Cannon

Canthrop's office was in the complex to the east of the government center, a corner suite on the northwest. It was just before eight forty-five on Friday when I arrived outside his door. I was early, but he'd see me, and that meant less wasted time for both of us.

When I stepped inside, Canthrop's receptionist looked up with a smile. "Senator Cannon. I'll tell him you're here."

"Thank you."

Her face blanked as she linked, and I studied the office, although I'd certainly been there often enough. All the furniture was neo-Queen Anne, slightly more ornate than I would have chosen, but not overpowering.

The receptionist was statuesque, redheaded, with a small straight nose, pale blue eyes, and flawless complexion—at first glance, a woman you'd want to get very close to. But she was almost an emtwo. I could see that from the eyes, the very vacant eyes. They were the kind of eyes that followed everything and reported everything, and understood only the most basic of implications of those actions. That she was his receptionist said something about Canthrop as well, but I'd known that about Bill for a long time.

She looked at me again with those not-quite-vacant eyes. "He said for you to go on in."

I nodded and stepped toward the old-fashioned door that I had to open with the bronze lever handle. Canthrop was standing beside his desk, looking westward at the mountains, still snow-covered at the top.

"You're early," he said as he turned.

"I don't have much choice. It's going to be a long day. They all will be for the next few weeks. Between the orbiter mess and the ebol4 disaster, not to mention the budget appropriations, the increased strain on the PDF because of the carelessness of the

Mars Belters two years ago, and, of course, the Southern Diversion . . ." I laughed. "What do you have?"

Canthrop gestured toward the folder on the corner of the desk. "There it is. This is the voice-over. We'll use your voice, with rez overtones, but everyone will hear it as your voice. I wanted you to look at it. If you like it, we can go right over and record it. If not, we'll make the changes, and we'll record whenever you can."

I picked up the folder and opened it, then began to study the script.

> . . . I'm Senator Cannon. I'm *your* senator. Every day I'm working to create a better life for you. You have dreams for your future, for your family, for your children. Those dreams are my goals . . .

In its own way, it was classic. Simple and spare, and a direct but positive appeal, with the implications that failure to vote for me would be a victory for the filch and for the greedy who would rob the hardworking people of Deseret of their last credit and laugh while doing it.

"What do you think?" Canthrop pushed back a wisp of his thin blond hair.

"I'd like to add a phrase at the end. Something like, 'When we share dreams, there's nothing we can't accomplish together.' " I smiled. "We can just add that and record it this morning."

Canthrop frowned, then murmured the words. ". . . When we share dreams . . ." Abruptly, he nodded. "Good sentiment, good words, and they'll fit."

"Fit? Of course they'll fit."

"I meant with the rez tags. It's better that they're your words."

"You mean my words have to fit with this resonance?"

"Well . . . if we want the full effect," Canthrop admitted. "We're pretty constrained in some ways."

"Just so you're not twisting my words into something that's not what I said."

"You'll approve every word, like always."

"Good."

He frowned, then smiled. "Took a minute to find the cue. Here's one of the musical motifs we'll be using as a tag."

As the music filled the office, we listened. There was something about the short melody, even though it seemed to ramble, in a way. It was less direct than I would have liked, but Canthrop was right. There was an appealing feel to it. After hearing it, I would have voted for me. Then, that bothered me, because only about half the people in Deseret District were from the same background as I was.

"What do you think?"

"It appeals to me. But what about those who aren't like me?"

Canthrop's smile got wider. "That's the beauty of this approach. Here's the motif for those of the Latin-Hispanic background."

The second selection struck me as more emotional, more . . . overt . . . but was too direct for me. That was probably a good thing, according to what I'd read up on about rezads.

"Now . . . you understand, Senator, that while the words will be the same, the graphics, the music, and the background and resonance will change to match each netband and soshgroup . . ."

"That's what the campaign is paying you for, Bill." I grinned back at him. "Speaking of paying . . . is this going to break us?"

He shook his head. "Nope. The production costs are low because we're just using you, the singer, some pretty fundamental graphics, and the tech people—"

"Tech people? That was pretty costly the last time."

"Different technology, different company. We're using Crescent Productions. Almost a one-person operation, but good technology and a better price. They've been doing some high-end stuff commercially, and it's plush at a servie price. The biggest cost will still be the net time."

"That doesn't change." I understood that. Getting access was always the most expensive part of anything in a modern society. That was one of the advantages of incumbency.

"Do you have another hour?" Canthrop asked. "If you do, we can wrap this all up this morning."

An hour. That would be tight. Especially with my having to go to St. George at six in the afternoon. But time would get even tighter in the days ahead. Ebol4 would get worse before it got better, and the same was true of the maneuvering and debates on the pending appropriations—and anything could happen with the outfall of the Russe orbiter mess. And I still wondered what might come from the McCall mess. I'd met McCall just once, at a fund-raiser, but he hadn't struck me as the kind of man who would either murder his wife or commit suicide. Some people are professionals at numbers, like Canthrop, and others excel in other things. Politicians are professionals at knowing people, and all my years in dealing with people told me that McCall hadn't committed suicide. Which meant that Kemal was somehow behind it, and that I'd best be very careful.

It could well affect my campaign before it was all over.

"Senator?" Canthrop prodded.

"I was thinking. I can work it in." I smiled. "Let's go."

"It's only up in OldTech," Canthrop said apologetically.

"We can take my electral, then, and I'll drop you back here on my way to the Legis building." Maybe we wouldn't be too late, and I'd been careful to be at most committee meetings on time. Face-time and gratitude—you could never stockpile enough of either. Not in politics.

Chapter 20

The ancient Romans understood the danger beauty posed. The word "beauty" comes from Old French (*beaute*), which in turn derived from the Latin word "*bellus*," meaning handsome, fine, or pretty. Yet the Latin word for "war" is "*bellum*"—a difference of one letter, and at the end of the word, indistinguishable from the neuter form of the adjective (also "*bellum*"). The Roman goddess of war was Bellona.

The Romans believed that war had beauty, perhaps a terrible beauty, but a beauty all the same. Why else did Caesar write so movingly about war? And why did the Romans make dying in the service of the Mars a far more honorable and glorious death than did the earlier Greeks, from whom they stole so much?

Interestingly enough, while Venus was the Roman goddess of love and beauty, studies show that she evolved from a comparatively weak and generally benign goddess in the Greek *Iliad* to a goddess of both compelling beauty and treachery in later Greek and Roman poems.

Even the term "belladonna" is Italian for "beautiful lady," but it refers to the herb from which the poison atropine was extracted. Throughout human history, beauty has been and continues to be regarded with great suspicion. Those who would define it are often called to task, and their efforts dismissed with the old cliché that beauty is in the eye of the beholder.

Yet . . . individuals have attempted to describe and define deities. Cultures have striven to create art of great beauty, whether in hard and tangible stone, or in the intangible and fleeting creations of music and song. Beauty is accepted as an attribute of creations or of individuals, but never as an absolute. Religions and cultures have attempted to define other so-called abstracts in hard terms, abstracts such as justice, mercy, compassion. Yet any serious scholar who attempts to define beauty in the same terms runs the risk of ridicule or ostracism . . .

Why do people so fear the ideal of beauty that stands by itself, unlinked from creations or individuals? Is it because so few can appreciate it? Understand it? Or because beauty is transcendent, and those who can define it within themselves have climbed an intangible step above the masses who, like the ancient Romans, find their beauty in destruction?

> Exton Land
> "Paradoxes of Beauty"
> *Etymology Quarterly*
> March, A.D. 2365

Chapter 21
Cornett

I'd almost not checked the news over the weekend. Curiosity had gotten the better of me by Sunday evening. Besides, I'd have to emerge from the cocoon of my conapt on Monday morning. I had to face both the university and the rest of the world—unless there happened to be a good reason. I was looking for such a reason, but didn't find it.

Ebol4 cases were increasing, but they remained scattered. The DPS was urging people to take extreme care. They also asked everyone to report anyone with the warning symptoms, but not to touch them. I certainly hadn't gotten that close to the unknown man on the shuttle platform, even if I'd had no choice. I still wondered if he'd survived. Most with the bloody sweating faces hadn't from what I heard on the netnews.

Nothing else had happened so far with the Russe orbiter. Drug overdoses from some unknown cause were up slightly in Denv, but no one had any ideas why. The PDF announced that they would be able to contain the debris from the mishandled asteroid mining by the Mars Belters. So there was nothing to do but go on with life. Such as it happened to be.

Except for music, life wasn't much at that moment. It wasn't the first time music had been the only good thing in life. After Michael, there had been Gordon. Gordon had drifted away. Maybe I'd given him a push, once he'd discovered I wasn't a singing doll, but actually had opinions about things. I hadn't met anyone else who seemed to care about music, or any kind of artistic beauty. But then, I had met very few men—or women— who did.

So Monday found me at the university. There I swallowed my pride once more, and signed my agreement to teach rez-prep both for the summer interterm and for the fall term. After that, I taught my single Monday lesson to Abdullah, the only man I was currently teaching. He was a quick study, and always learned his music. He also made no secret that he was taking lessons from me because he wanted to become a rezpopper. Even so, teaching him was a joy, and I looked forward to that part of Mondays.

More than once he'd told me, "Professor Cornett . . . I watch you. You can sing anything. I even hear your voice on the rezads sometimes. If I can sing anything, then, even if I do not become rich and famous, I will make a living from singing."

He worked hard, and he had a good voice. Most of the time, those two weren't enough, but I wasn't about to put it that bluntly. I just suggested that success in the arts depended partly on luck, as well as on talent, skill, and determination.

When I said that, he always gave me a broad smile. And the next lesson he was even more prepared. I wished more were like him and like Amina, who I taught on Thursdays.

After teaching Abdullah, and after working in another half hour of practice for the Clayton soirée—mainly "Frauen liebe and Leben"—I caught a shuttle north from the University station. I wasn't sure I should, but I knew I'd regret it if I didn't go to Michael's memorial service. After that, I'd have to hurry back south, to Crescent, for another recording session with Mahmed.

There were only about half as many people on the shuttle as usual. Once again, everyone stayed separated. No one said much. My destination was outer northside, the fourth stop. From there I had to walk to the Community Center. The grass was as green in the park that flanked the walkway as it was in eastside, but the trees seemed lower, almost stunted. The buildings to the north of the park were set in plain greenery, with little landscaping. The grass looked like a carpet that had been painted green and rolled out around the buildings. Most were fabricating formulation centers, from their windowless appearance.

At the north end of the park was the Community Center where they were holding the memorial. In the synthstone-floored lobby was a simple sign on a pedestal: MICHAEL MORRIS MEMORIAL SERVICE, MAIN CONFERENCE ROOM. I followed the arrow. Footsteps followed me as others drifted into the Center.

The conference room was just a long hall with antique block walls. There were no decorations, paintings, or hangings. The walls were coated with the white synthplaster used in every permie dwelling in NorAm. I looked over the hundred or so chairs. About half were filled. I sat down in the back. I wasn't sure I should have come, but Michael had been a part of my life for ten years. As much as I hoped for a sense of closure, I knew I wouldn't get it. But I'd still had to come.

It was to be a memorial service—with no ashes or remains in any form. The Department of Public Safety had insisted on immediate and total cremation of all ebol4 victims, but a holo projection of Michael filled the space to the right of the old-fashioned oak podium. The figure was almost of a stranger. He didn't look familiar. When we'd been married, he'd worn a beard, short and square-trimmed, but the man beside the podium was younger-looking, clean-shaven, wearing a maroon tunic over white trousers and shimmering white boots. He was the image of youthful idealism. That wasn't surprising, since poor Michael had never grown up.

I sat there numbly, watching as more people filed into the room. His brother and his mother came in, and a man in a black singlesuit seated them in the front row. A thin brunette sat next to them. I didn't know her. That wasn't surprising. Our parting had been bitter.

Another man in a black singlesuit appeared and stood at the podium. He just began to speak. There was no introduction, no preamble.

"Michael Morris was the director of the Community Center for fifteen years. He never turned away from a problem or someone in need . . ."

That had been the difficulty. For Michael, all problems were equally important. I'd never been an admirer of the filch and still wasn't, but they weren't the cause of society's miseries. They were the symptom. When credits are all that count, everything except the pursuit of those credits is debased. Poor Michael, the professional server of the permies and the servies, could never quite grasp that. He might have given it lip service, but he was always convinced that if he could just get more credits from the government, the filch, and the foundations, he could rebuild society.

". . . when he came to northside, the Community Center was two rooms in the back of General Formulating. Today, we have an employment and counseling program that served five thousand people last year alone. We have a full youth program, and a complete youth athletic center . . ."

I smiled, if sadly. In his own way, Michael had done a lot, and people would remember.

". . . all this because of the energy and dedication of one man. Michael Morris was not a saint. We all know how angry he could get, but he channeled that anger . . ."

Michael's anger wasn't something I wanted to remember. It hadn't been channeled in any constructive way with me. He'd wanted me to go into business where my abilities and presumably my credits would help him with fund-raising and political activity that would change society, or at least Denv. He'd helped the poorest servies and the permies of northside. I hadn't seen any change beyond that. He'd never listened to my thoughts on it.

Or why I thought music and beauty were every bit as important as jobs and credits. I thought that they were more important, but I'd never dared to say that. In the end, there had been too much I'd never dared to say.

". . . northside will never see another Michael Morris . . ."

By then, I was having trouble reconciling the image of the man they all knew and loved with that of the man I had once loved. I sat through the rest of the memorial, and then slipped out right after it was over.

As I walked back to the shuttle station, I thought. I felt sorry for Michael, and for his family, and for the woman who had loved him—she'd sobbed silently through the entire memorial. I was sorry, too, that Michael hadn't lived to finish what he started. Yet I had to wonder. Nothing had ever been enough for Michael. Would another twenty years have meant more? Another fifty or a hundred? Or would he have become ever more bitter? Or had he mellowed? I didn't know. I never would, not really.

All that was certain was that we'd had very different views on what mattered in improving people's lives. Michael had felt that the answer was in the material, and I'd had to question that. As a whole, our society was richer than any before it, and yet there were still bioweapons and terrorism across the entire globe, and tensions between Earth and Mars despite more and more material affluence. There were still students glassy-eyed on soop, murders despite ever more restrictive surveillance and improved nanite shields, and a quiet dissatisfaction that verged on desperation.

Or was that dissatisfaction merely my own projection?

I didn't know that, either.

I made the OldTech station with time to spare, and could take a leisurely walk to the building housing Mahmed's small production company. The old and slow entry system checked my codes, in the same plodding routine, and finally cleared me. I went down the ramps.

Mahmed was waiting, as usual, just inside the door that bore the golden crescent moon, and the words "Crescent Productions."

"You may not want to do this one, Luara." Mahmed looked embarrassed. "It's political."

"If I can sell furniture, why not politicians?"

"Even for Senator Cannon?"

I knew Cannon was a senator, and I'd heard his name on the news. When the political news came on, I usually turned somewhere else or just tuned it out. What had the politicians ever done for beauty and the arts? Not much since the Emperor Joseph, I suspected. "Let's see it."

"Here's the music and text." Mahmed extended the music, crisp, and obviously freshly printed.

In the space outside the recording area, I looked over the words, and then the music. The words were more obscure than usual, at least for a rezad, where the punch was usually direct and short.

And he cast his vote, strong, for you, for me,
over the filch, standing there where he should be . . .

After humming the melody, I realized I knew it, or a version of it. But from where? I couldn't place it, but I knew it from somewhere. That would probably make singing it harder, but not impossible.

"What do you think?" asked Mahmed, anxiously.

"I can do it. It's no worse than upscale furnishings." No better, but no worse.

"I'll need more takes for this," Mahmed pointed out.

"That's fine." I couldn't complain. He paid well and on time. Besides, I wasn't all that eager to head back to my conapt and think about the day.

We went into the studio and did run-throughs, eight in all.

Only when I came out of the studio did I realize what I'd sung. It was an adapted version of a song by Ralph Vaughn Williams— "The New Ghost."

And he cast it down, down, on the green grass,
Over the young crocuses, where the dew was . . .

I had to wonder why Senator Cannon was setting political ads
to English art song, but I knew nothing about campaign ads,
except that I detested them.

"You up for another?" asked Mahmed. "Standard rate."

Of course I was. Thanks to the rezads, I actually looked to
have more creds than pending expenses. I also wanted to stay in
Mahmed's good graces, because what I saw coming at the university wasn't promising.

The second ad was another one for Cannon, with a more florid
text. The music, when I hummed it, was only vaguely familiar.
After a moment, I realized that it reminded me of a song I'd done
by Granados. That probably meant that the original song or music had been done by Granados, or at least by someone of the
same school.

That only involved four takes. After we finished, I turned to
Mahmed. "What are you doing with this?" I had to ask.

Mahmed looked embarrassed. "It's for his campaign. They pay
well . . . you understand that."

I did, indeed.

"I've been trying to get into the new rezad business, but you
have to pay Talemen Associates. All of the additional equipment
is mine, but I have to pay them a royalty. It's the new twist on
rezads, and it's technically better. They sent over a set of parameters. Had to add another board. Looks a lot like the custom
work my brother did for some rezpopper."

"What rezpopper?" I didn't care, but it was almost as if he
wanted me to ask.

"Cold Ice." Mahmed laughed. "Said he got the idea from a
competitor. Stole it, that's more like it. But the setup's legal, so
long as you pay Talemen."

Rezads that were technically better? Better at what? Persuad-
ing people? I shivered.

"Are you all right?" Mahmed was immediately solicitous.

"I'm fine."

"Are you sure?"

"Yes."

"Good." Mahmed smiled.

"Another?" I asked.

"If you're up for it."

"If you're paying," I countered.

"Senator Cannon is paying, but with you, we're giving him a real bargain."

Mahmed wasn't being hurt by it, either, I knew. All in all, I did four separate rezads for the good—or not-so-good—senator. I might even have banked enough credits to pay for the overdue repairs to the conapt.

Chapter 22
Kemal

I left the house a little after eight-fifteen on Monday morning. That was because the club was in southside. Stefan lived there as well. He had been the first of the family to move there from the northwest. His place was about two miles from where Marissa and I were building the new house. For me, the move made sense. The new house would be less than ten minutes from the KC headquarters. For Stefan, the move was strictly for the address. He had no job, just his trust income. His place was a good half mile east of the Southside Parkway, almost in the southern part of eastside. It was an imitation Renaissance villa, and small. Around five hundred square meters, with three garage bays. He had no children. His girlfriends came and went. He didn't think much about family.

As I entered the oval drive, I could see Stefan waiting under the small portico. He was wearing a beige singlesuit. I slowed and linked to Emile. *Beige—the second shade on the chart.*

Beige, second shade. I have it.

Good. See you later. If Emile hadn't had the proper shade, then I would have had Stefan put on the one in the backseat, but the less I asked of Stefan the better.

"You're early, Uncle Chris." Stefan slipped into the front seat.

I pulled out of the drive and turned south, toward the club.

I didn't say anything.

"If I could ask," Stefan finally said, "what do you have in mind?"

"You need more credits. I need a favor. It's that simple."

"Uncle Chris . . . I don't know about that kind of favor."

I laughed. "It's not that kind of favor. You know who Emile Brazelton is, don't you? He was in the office when you were there a couple of weeks ago."

"Yes . . ."

Stefan was definitely wary.

"You know he had problems, and we bailed him out. He's excellent at managing and developing technology. He just didn't have the capital. Or the contacts. He's also a good man at heart, but he had personal problems. They got in the way. Well . . . his first wife is vindictive. He's not allowed to see his son, but his son wants to see him. There's a Justiciary order out. That means they can use the footage from the recsats."

Stefan looked puzzled. That was good.

"You can help him see the boy for a couple of hours. There are two singlesuits in the back. You put on the maintenance suit over your own. I'll drop you off under the trees at the club, just inside the gates. You walk to the shelter at number three carrying the tool kit that's on the floor. You wait there. When we get there, you peel off the maintenance suit and put on Emile's sweater. It's loud and striped. You play fourteen holes with me, and then on seventeen we meet Emile, and you switch at the rain shelter there."

"That's it? How do I get back?"

"That's it. As for getting back, you walk back to the trees where I let you off and you take off the suit under the trees when no one's looking, fold it up so the logo doesn't show, and put it under your arm. Then you walk to the club and ask me for a ride. Don't explain. Just say that you saw me and thought you could save yourself some time."

He nodded.

"This will allow Emile to see his son. That means he'll be feeling better. He'll be thinking about the job, and not about the unfairness of not seeing his boy. You've done him a favor, and you've done me a favor. You know that I always pay off favors."

Stefan looked doubtful, but not that doubtful.

"If it were your mother . . . and some judge had ruled she couldn't see you, wouldn't you want to see her every so often?" I laughed. "It's in the middle of the morning."

"That's it?"

"That . . . and you don't tell anyone, because it could get Emile in trouble."

I could see Stefan figuring that he could leverage that into more credits. But he'd wait to try that. By then, it wouldn't matter.

"You do this right, and we'll take care of your loan—the way it should have been handled."

"How is that?" Stefan was more curious than snotty.

"I buy the note. It becomes a note to me, and I immediately forgive half of it, and give you the first year interest-free. Then, we'll see how you're doing."

He wanted more than that, but he also wouldn't have believed it if I'd given more. This way, he had the credits, and a year to spend them before trying to get more out of me. He'd take that.

"I appreciate that, Uncle Chris."

I laughed. "You need to get into that suit." I pulled the electral over to the side of the road, under some overhanging elms, already leafing out, so that he could climb in back. Once he was in the back, I pulled out again.

"You could have had Armand do this," Stefan ventured as he struggled into the maintenance suit. "Why me?"

"He's a permie. What would happen if he ran into someone? Or if someone asked him what he was doing?"

"That's true."

"Family's always the best," I pointed out. "I want to help you, but I don't want you to think I don't want at least a gesture in return."

Stefan said nothing for the few minutes it took to reach the club. The scanners checked the pass, and the gates opened.

I drove another fifty yards before pulling over and letting Stefan out under the ancient elms.

Stefan walked away through the trees, and then out along the side of the empty tennis courts. I could see the club logo on his back.

The club was empty—or close to it—on Mondays in early April. That was the way I'd planned it. I changed into my golf shoes in the locker room.

Emile was waiting for me in the golf shop, wearing a beige golf singlesuit, and a white cardigan with wide and bright green stripes. "You're late."

"I had to stop and have some words with Stefan. I dropped him off and let him walk back to his house."

We bought some balls. There was no one there, except the simmie of the pro. The transactions and images would be on databloc. Then we checked out the cart—also through a simmie. I guided the cart down the path to the first tee. There was no one on the course at ten past nine, except for a twosome two holes ahead. They were leaving the third green. I could see Stefan working his way toward the shelter, but taking his time.

The wind was coming out of the west. It was warm, not quite a chinook.

"Ten credits for the first hole?" I grinned at Emile.

"Why not? I like taking your credits." He gestured to the tee. "I'll give you the honors."

My drive on number one was a slice, but it was only off the fairway on the right side by about twenty meters. Emile was straight down the fairway, but about twenty meters behind me. My second shot landed in the bunker to the left of the green. His was on the apron. I blasted out of the trap, but came up twenty feet short of the cup, and two-putted. Emile chipped to within three meters of the cup and sank his putt for a par.

He grinned as he pulled out his ball. "Ten credits."

"Another ten on two?"

"You don't want to double?"

"With my slice?" I laughed.

Emile bogeyed number two, and I parred, and we both parred number three. That left us even after three.

Then I drove the cart over to the rain shelter between the number three green and the number four tee.

Stefan was already peeling off the maintenance singlesuit. "That got hot after a while." He looked at me. "That was a lucky putt on three."

"It was a good putt. You'll see on the next few holes."

Emile took off the green striped sweater and handed it to Stefan. Then he began to pull on the maintenance singlesuit.

"The sweater's awfully hot . . ." Stefan murmured.

"Just wear it for the next hole," I suggested. "After that you can drape it across the cart seat."

"Thanks very much, Stefan," Emile said. He nodded and picked up the tool kit. He walked back toward the maintenance yard off number seven, where a van with the GSY logo was waiting.

Stefan took out Emile's driver. "Good clubs." Then he looked at me. "We haven't played in a while. Twenty credits a hole?"

"If you're up for losing it."

He laughed, and so did I.

We talked. Not about money. Mostly about golf, and a little about his new Tija electral and how much power it had.

"You need to be careful with it," I pointed out. "It's high-powered and light, and that means it can roll over more easily than other electrals."

"You and Mother!" Stefan laughed. "I know how to drive, Uncle Chris."

"I suppose you do." I'd certainly been young once, but not that young at twenty-five. "Is the girl who was with you at the memorial service . . . ?"

"Cheryn? She's more of a friend . . ."

Stefan was a good golfer. He was better than I was, but not that much better than Emile. By the time we got to the seventeenth tee, he was up two holes, and because I'd pressed and lost a few times, he was up a hundred credits as well. It was good he was winning, but not an accident.

Emile was waiting, although his face was damp, as if he'd hurried. He took off the maintenance singlesuit and held it up. He'd left the tool kit behind where it would be added to the club's equipment. He hadn't used it. He'd used the GSY equipment.

Stefan took the singlesuit from Emile and slipped it on.

"I appreciate this, Stefan," Emile said. He meant it.

"So do I," I added.

Stefan gave me a faint smile.

"Thank you, Stefan," I added. "I'll start the loan transfer process as soon as I get to the office this afternoon. It will probably take about a week with all the legalities. I'll have to have the solicitors look at it."

"I appreciate your being so understanding, Uncle Chris."

"Family is what's important, Stefan." I grinned. "And the hundred credits will be in your account this afternoon. See you in a bit."

Emile and I watched as Stefan walked eastward along the creek.

"You think he'll say anything," murmured Emile.

"Not for a few days. Not until he's sure that the paperwork is all done, and he can count the credits as his. What will be, will be." I shrugged. "How about the other?"

"It's taken care of. A few days, no more."

Once Smythers and Dewey were dealt with, there wouldn't be any loose ends. I smiled. "Fifty credits for this hole?"

"Fifty?"

"I lost a hundred to Stefan. If I'm good and lucky for two holes, I'll break even. If I'm not, you get some pocket money."

"You'll lose two hundred."

"We'll see." I'd have lost ten times that to make things work. Emile laughed. "We certainly will."

My first drive went in the creek, and the second one landed in deep rough. Emile was in the fairway. Some days went like that.

Chapter 23
Chiang

Tuesday came, and I went straight to westside. Had intended to do that earlier. Couldn't. Was DPS duty supervisor Sunday. Monday had been a mess. Newsies had latched on to the ODs of unknown cause. I couldn't explain it. Medical couldn't. Everyone pointed fingers everywhere else.

Late Monday, found out that FlameTop would be rehearsing Tuesday morning. Not early, except ten hundred was early for a performer. He usually didn't rehearse that early. Could have gotten him after a night performance. Not a good idea. Performers are tired and on an adrenaline high. Bad combination.

I still wanted to track behind the McCall thing. Couldn't believe homicide had been wrong. Apologizing afterward? The apology didn't make sense. But McCall was dead, and I'd have to move carefully.

Going to see FlameTop was because I owed it to Luke, in a way, to find out about Al. Also knew if I didn't, I'd be swamped by other stuff Cannizaro thought was important. Like the ODs and the bodyshop ops that were going up with the ebol4. Knew I'd have to get on those as soon as I got back.

FlameTop was still at the Moulin Noir. Parking stack was almost empty. Maybe five other electrals. Two guards outside the theater club, both a head taller than me. Didn't feel like arguing. Just showed the credentials. Still took them five minutes. Finally, one's face blanked, and then unblanked. He looked at me. "You can go in, Lieutenant. He'll meet you on the stage."

"Thank you." Wondered if FlameTop had been using something to get started in the morning. That wasn't what I was there for. Inside was a combination second-rate uniquery and theater. Tables set in tiers that arced around and looked down on the stage area.

Walked down the dark center aisle between the tiers. Only light was on the stage. Little enough of that. Single figure wandered into the puddle of light just before I climbed onto the stage.

The name FlameTop fitted. Tall cone of flame-blond hair shaped into flame shape, probably a nanite field of some sort. "You the DPS type?"

"Lieutenant Chiang, DPS." I showed the credentials again.

He didn't look at them. "What can we do for you?" Every word was close to contemptuous.

"Everyone says you have a new twist on rezpop."

"That's what they say, Lieutenant." A cocky grin turned the slit in his face into a mouth. White teeth sparkled. "I can't believe you came here to ask me that. Unless you're a fan of new rezpop."

"Mind telling me what kind of twist?"

"So you can give it to someone else?"

"I wouldn't know a rezpopper from an ebol4 victim." Hate the cockiness some people have. Usually people who've got more than they deserve and think it's their due. "Don't want the tech details." Not then, I didn't. "Just an idea."

"I do it different. That's the idea."

"Louder? Or with different resonances?"

"Any punk can make it louder. Let's say . . . I just match mood and music to the rez. You'd have to be here."

"I understand that. But you're doing something new and different with the rez effects, right?"

He frowned, almost a sulking expression.

I waited.

"Something like that, Lieutenant. Something like that."

"I take it that whatever it is that you do gets some of your fans excited." Tried to keep the dryness and irony out of my voice.

"More excited than other rezpoppers. They wouldn't be coming back night after night, would they? Like I say, you have to be there."

Wasn't sure I could have stood that. I walked over to the shimmering black column that was at the edge of the lighted part of the stage. Studied the column, glanced to the far side, where there was another. Looked up. Triangular pyramid in the ceiling with the blunt end toward the audience. Looked like the same shimmering stuff. Looked new, too.

"These what project your twist?"

"For here. You need an adaptor for a home unit. Otherwise, you don't get the same effect."

"But I'd get some of it?"

"Some."

"You got a bloc of your new twist music? And one of those adaptors?"

"This a shakedown, Lieutenant?"

"I'll buy it for whatever you charge your fans."

"Thirty creds." He gave me that contemptuous smile. "Lori'll have one waiting outside. She has adaptors, too. They're two hundred."

Tried more questions. Didn't get far. FlameTop didn't know much more. Could have waited for his tech type, but that could have been all day. Could always come back.

Hated shuffling out nearly three hundred creds with tax, but if the bloc and adaptor were harmless, I could always give them to one of my nephews or nieces. Helen's kids were into that garbage.

Since I was out there, I tried Westside Physical Systems next. Sarao hadn't gotten a trace on Kama's lorry. Detrus was out— permanently. Ebol4 got her before she'd been scheduled for nanomeds. About half DPS had the new meds so far, mainly those

on the street. Said all DPS would have them in another week. I'd
bet two. Could only do so much so fast. Medical system was
swamped.

As I walked into Kama's place, the permie behind the console
looked up and told me, "He's in, Lieutenant." Didn't even wait
for me to ask.

This time, we went back to his office—also spotless and stark
white and purple.

Kama closed the door. "I heard you were looking for me, Eugene. That's not good for business, if it gets out."

"Heard anything about Kemal?"

"No. Have you?"

"Rumor is that he got a lot more creds from somewhere legal.
Also heard he's going to get deep into politics."

"Both could be. He expanded the main formulation plant.
Twice in three years. He's brought in top designers for Brazelton's outfit, and he's building a big place in southside. Brazelton's
doing the screens. They'd stop an asteroid."

"Friend told me Kemal was going legit."

Kama laughed. "Ninety-nine percent of what he does is technically legal. He could give all the dirty stuff to Grayser and his
new Ellay wyg, and never break a law, and he'd still be as
crooked as a Belter's orbit."

"McCall. Heard anything?"

The contractor shrugged. "I haven't figured out how you could
turn off a system's safeties from on top of a tower. Mine . . . you
have to have the windows and doors shut, and they won't accept
commands from the balconies. That's standard, especially if
you've got children, grandchildren, or elderly parents."

Another reason the McCall thing stank. "Anything else?"

Kama frowned.

"What about overrides? Could you override the system, one
of yours, since you built it?"

He shook his head.

"Could you design one with overrides? Overrides the owner
wouldn't know about?"

"I wouldn't. If that ever got out, I'd never get another job. That's a bad idea, and it defeats the whole idea of safeties."

"So . . . he'd have to have cut the power down at the main cutoffs, and then climb back up six flights? If you'd built the system?"

"If I had."

I nodded. That was all I was probably going to get there. Now. "Heard anything else?"

"No."

"What do you think about this new rezrap?"

"Didn't know you were into that, Eugene."

"I'm not."

"Neither am I. I've had to redo the stage protection screens at the Moulin Noir three times in the last week. He also had me beef the door screens to detect ebol4." Kama frowned. "I'm supposed to do the Red Moon tomorrow. Hassan told me that he'll pay for the screens. Something in the new rez makes them want more alkie. Not drop-dead flattened, but his alkie receipts are up about twenty percent. He's looking for someone to follow FlameTop. Maybe Cool Ice or whatever his name is, or someone else with the new reztwist." He shook his head. "Kids . . ."

"How good are the ebol4 screens at the door?"

"Four nines for someone who's really infectious. Less than fifty percent in the first day."

"Hassan freezes them on the spot and calls for a medvan?"

"He has one rented and waiting. No sirens that way. Says he's only had two cases."

Wondered about that.

I decided to stop by the Galleria, but Morss must have seen me coming. He wasn't there.

Finally got back to DPS at ten past noon.

First thing I did was hand the databloc and rez adaptor to Sarao. "Want these analyzed. New rezrap or rezpop. Want to know how it's different, if it has different physical impact, emotional impact . . . whatever. See if they can find a physiological effect. Oh . . . seems to boost desire for alkie—tell the techs that."

"Like I said, you want a lot."

"May not be enough."

Gut told me there was a link between the music and the suicides, maybe the ODs. Probably couldn't prove anything, but worth a try. Might even be more there.

Didn't even get my office door shut.

Chiang? You in DPS?

I recognized Cannizaro's tone after the first word. *Yes, Captain.*

If you've got a moment, I'd like you to come up.

I'll be right there. Had to be. Cannizaro never asked for me to come to see her unless there was trouble.

She flicked on the privacy screen as soon as the door was shut. Looked at me. Had circles under her eyes, circles that nanites weren't stopping. "Two things, Chiang. First . . . Dewey's dead."

"How?"

"His official electral went off the Elletch Bridge. The techs are still looking into it."

"Some sort of malfunction," I suggested. "Convenient for Alredd."

"That may be, but we'll have to be very careful."

Understood that. Alredd would likely be the next District Coordinator. The techs wouldn't find anything.

"You don't seem surprised, Lieutenant. Did you have some idea something like this would happen?"

"No, ser. It's clear afterward, but not before." I said nothing more, just nodded.

Cannizaro said nothing either.

"Don't like any kind of murder," I finally said.

"Neither do I, Chiang. What *were* you looking for in westside?"

"Reason for the spike in the suicides. Demographics didn't match. Also had some soop ODs. Not supposed to happen."

This time, the captain nodded. "That I can buy. We don't need to get hit with another round of things we haven't seen. What did you find?"

"I'm not sure. I'm having some analysis done."

"Very careful wording."

"Could be very strange, Captain. Don't want to say much. I could be wrong. Doesn't feel right, and the forensics don't fit." I tried not to sigh. "Anything more about Dewey?"

"No." Cannizaro didn't meet my eyes, not quite. That meant trouble. More trouble. "DPS has a problem."

We had many. I waited, finally asked, "Which one?"

"The McCall case. We look bad, very bad. I've just been contacted by a Hans Kugeler. He's a solicitor representing the McCall children. They want a further investigation of their parents' deaths. They also don't want it done by Kirchner and his people. They'd pushed for an outside group. I offered you. They considered, and Mr. Kugeler accepted."

Didn't like that, but I nodded. "What's the twist?"

"You have three weeks to provide a report acceptable to both DPS and the solicitor."

"Should I put in for early retirement now, Captain?"

Cannizaro raised her eyebrows. "You think it's that bad?"

"Worse, from what I've seen."

"Tell me."

"Talked to a nanite safety systems engineer. Filch systems are designed so they can't be shut off from open balconies. McCall would have had to have gone down to the power cutoffs and cut them manually. Then climbed back up six flights of stairs. Also, a spysat analysis told me that the area went blank for five minutes before McCall jumped. Came back on to catch his untimely death."

"I didn't know you were on the case, Lieutenant."

"Captain, ser . . . you once told me my job was to look at all cases and keep bad things from happening to DPS. So long as I kept it quiet and let you know. McCall case stinks, but I kept quiet, and I'm telling you. A lot more there I don't know."

Cannizaro smiled. Cold smile. "Good thing you're not in homicide."

"What do you want, Captain?"

"I want the truth. But . . ." She gave a very long pause. "Only the truth you can prove with absolute evidence. I don't want to fight Alredd and his backers."

That meant Kemal. Had his fingers into everything in Denv and across about half of NorAm. And he wanted more.

"If I can't . . ."

"We apologize . . . again . . . We even confess poor handling of the case."

"Three weeks?"

She nodded.

What she wasn't saying, and we both knew, was that if I couldn't unravel it all and prove it, with Alredd in his pocket, Kemal would practically own Denv in less than a year. Didn't want to think about how much of the rest of NorAm. "When do I meet Kugeler?"

"He'll be down at your office in less than an hour. I've told Kirchner to send you everything homicide has. Everything. He will."

Knowing Kirchner, he would. He'd be glad to dump it on me. He'd even smile. "That all, Captain?"

"Isn't that enough, Lieutenant?"

It was.

Cannizaro had to have told Kirchner before I met with her, because Sarao was waiting. She had an amused smile. "Lieutenant Kirchner brought by some files and some datablocs. Your desk is under them."

She was right. A pile of files, and a large stack of datablocs. Probably wasn't much on each bloc, but that meant they came from different sources. I started to sift through them. I had an hour. Forty minutes later, I was more worried. Homicide had been thorough. They'd gotten permission to search all of McCall's files. Ostensibly for suicide indicators. Nothing. Except the tech suspected that certain of his office files had been recently blanked. But selectively. There were files on all clients. There was a list of clients—marked "privacy protected." KC Constructors was listed, as was Brazelton, and a number of other individuals and firms. Some I'd heard of. Most I hadn't. Nothing was missing, according to the statements by Hildeo and Oler, his associates. No way to tell to what client the missing files had been attached.

All the statements . . . all the recsat shots . . . everything indicated to me that McCall and his wife had been murdered. Not one bit, not one statement, could point toward anyone. Had a decent case for murder. But unless I could find a suspect, the whole thing would go as either suicide or unsolved. Could probably push for unsolved murder, but that would hurt DPS and upset Cannizaro, and probably give Alredd a club of some sort.

The key was nanites. Dewey, McCall, and McCall's wife all had nanite system malfunctions or manipulations involved. Would have bet that Brazelton's hand was in it, pushed there by Kemal. Finding proof was another matter.

Lieutenant . . . there's a Mr. Kugeler here to see you. Sarao's link broke through my speculations.

Thanks. I went out.

Kugeler was a small and very dapper solicitor. Had a narrow face, dreamy eyes, kind that would have hidden behind spectacles centuries earlier.

"I am Hans Kugeler, Lieutenant Chiang. Captain Cannizaro has indicated that you have been assigned to provide a full report on the unfortunate deaths of Evan McCall and Nanette Iveson. Is that your understanding?"

I nodded, gestured for him to enter the office. Pulsed the door shut and triggered the privacy locks, and the scramblers. Nothing would record around us. Not within the misty gray wall.

His eyebrows lifted. The dreamy eyes hardened, but he didn't speak. Just settled onto the front edge of the ergochair.

I sat in my chair. "You've been retained by their children. Hope you can provide insight and some hard evidence as well."

"Evidence appears rather difficult to discover."

"Hard evidence, yes. We don't have much time."

"You don't have much time, Lieutenant."

Looked straight at him. "We want the same thing. You don't have any more time than I do. If I can't prove it was murder, with hard evidence, no one else will, either."

Kugeler laughed softly. "You think it was murder?"

"*Know* it was murder, both of them. *Proving* it is something else."

"Would you mind telling me why you think that is so?"

Leaned forward. "McCall loved his wife. Too much evidence of that. Someone planted a divorce story, in advance. McCall was a technical idiot . . ." Went on to explain all I knew and why and how McCall couldn't have committed either the murder of his wife and then killed himself. ". . . but almost none of that is hard evidence."

"If you can't discover this 'hard' evidence, what will you do, Lieutenant?"

"We have three weeks." I smiled. "If I don't . . . we'll see, then."

Kugeler nodded. "You have a reputation for honesty and tenacity. We will hope it is sufficient."

Hoped I had survivability on my side also. "So do I."

"What do you want from me?"

"First, you tell no one what I've just said. Not even the McCall children. I'll deny it. Second, need to go over the McCall house again, for starters." I gestured to the pile of datablocs. "Also need to go over these. Could we do the house in the morning? By then, I'll know what else I might need from you."

"I would assume that the children would agree."

"And you?"

"I will say nothing until three weeks is up—and nothing after that if I am satisfied that your report is accurate and as complete as possible."

"Eleven hundred tomorrow morning?"

He nodded once more.

I stood. So did he.

After Kugeler left, just stared at everything for a few minutes. Still had to run trendside, and still had questions about the suicides and ODS. Just hoped nothing else came up in the next few days. Especially not something else with a filch slick angle.

Chapter 24
Cannon

By Tuesday noon, right after lunch, I still hadn't gotten anything back from the feelers I'd put out about MMSystems. I had the committee staff asking all the space contractors for information on PDF-related contracts funded by the Legislature, and I'd had a few friends making inquiries. The fact that I hadn't heard anything was unsettling. People always wanted to hand over dirt about competitors or big government contracts—unless someone had a laser focused at their head.

Other matters were going far more smoothly. The appropriations bills were moving, and there'd only been token opposition to my immigrant repayment amendment. A few of the more isolationistic types were shocked, but I'd just smiled. Once the precedent was set, later, a year or two, we could see about ratcheting up the repayment rates for future immigrants. We'd get there, just a bit more slowly. That was another beautiful aspect of politics—there was always another way to get there.

Ciella linked in. *Senator, Mr. Christensen is here. He says he doesn't have an appointment, but he'll only be a minute.*

Tell him that's about what he'll get. I've got to go to committee. But send him in.

Yes, sir.

I was glad Ciella was back. I'd been worried that she might have been one of those affected by the ebol4 virus, but she'd said it had been a reaction to the nanomeds she'd gotten. It would have been a shame to have lost her. She was a truly beautiful girl.

Eric walked into the office, and I pulsed the door shut behind him. His face was tight. He'd never have made it in politics. I could read him like a blown-up holo screen, and so could any good politician.

"I see you've got more good news." I offered a smile, the ironic one.

Eric looked around. I understood what he wanted, and punched the hidden stud for the privacy cone projector. We were surrounded by a cone of silence, and a gray misty field. Nothing short of military equipment mounted just outside it could have made out what we said. There were some aspects of technology where I kept very current.

He sat down in the black leather chair across the desk from me. "Have you heard? Dewey died in an accident. It wasn't an accident."

I hadn't heard, but I'd been in committee meetings all morning. "How? Where?"

Eric snorted. "On the Elletch Bridge. His electral swerved through the guideway and rail. That's impossible, and we both know it. The electral hit one of the retaining walls below, and the fuel cells ignited. Not much left. Especially of the control systems."

"Those district cars have restraint systems and redundant safety systems. That does lend some credence to your observation."

Eric nodded. "By tomorrow, KC Constructors will be complaining that you killed him. The charge will be that you used politics to take the maintenance away from the company that built the system, and poor Coordinator Dewey died."

"An investigation will be inconclusive, I'm sure." I could hear the dryness in my voice. I doubted that it would be as direct as Eric predicted. Directness contains the danger of backfiring. Subtlety doesn't.

"No. It will show that the maintenance on the electral was poor. That won't be laid to you, but used in Alredd's campaign to point out the need for change in the coordinator's office. Also, someone high in the DPS might be in on this. Or at least the commissioner."

"Why do you think that?"

"The DPS apologized for the handling of the McCall case, and some of the nets are suggesting now that McCall committed suicide because of his wife's accident and because he was distraught over the unfounded charges."

I thought about that. "Someone doesn't want McCall's death investigated too closely."

"Has to be Kemal," Eric suggested.

"Kemal's too smart for that. There won't be a track to him."

"No," Eric agreed, "but there might be to someone who knew, someone like Brazelton or Sandoval."

"Two or three steps removed. It's suggestive, and you're probably right, but if anyone made the charge without proof, and there won't be any, Kemal would gut their assets under the protections of the privacy laws, and any DPS officer who pushed it would be suspended or involuntarily retired." I found myself pulling at my chin. "Have you found out any more about the MMSystems takeover?"

"You think it's related?"

"It could be. Or it could be coincidence." I frowned. "I've got some inquiries out, but no answers. I don't like it when I don't get answers."

"Most senators don't," Eric pointed out.

"That's not what I meant. When I don't get answers, it's trouble. If they don't want to tell me, I get well-formulated nonsense and placating platitudes. If it's a pain in the ass, but not a real problem, I get more detail than anyone could ever want. If it's something I have the right to know, but is classified for security reasons, I get an invitation to a briefing and more cautions about the sensitive nature of the information than you could imagine. Here . . . there's nothing."

Eric looked skeptical.

"I know. You have your doubts. But I'm getting answers on all my other inquiries. If I'd lost my office or my authority, I'd be stonewalled on everything. Everyone would decide I'm not a player. What all this means is something is about to happen, and no one wants to jump off the fence in either direction until they know which side to jump to."

"You think it's the MMSystems business?"

"It has to be, but you have to know something to ask the right questions or look for the right signs. Or bluff." It was still too early to bluff. That I could sense, and I've always been good at knowing that.

"Why don't you just call Rafael Martini and feel him out?" suggested Eric.

I laughed. There was no point in telling Eric I'd already decided to do that. Let him think it was his idea. "There is a certain beauty to the direct approach. He won't tell me anything, not directly." When I did call Martini, I'd have to handle it right, so that he'd reveal *something* by any reaction, or at least that he was hiding something.

"You'll find out," Eric said.

"If he'll talk to me."

"He will, if only to find out why you're calling."

"Could be. I'll think about it. In the meantime, I've got a committee meeting." I stood and flicked off the privacy screen.

With the smile of a man who knew something others didn't, Eric inclined his head, then turned and left.

Once the door shut, I linked. *Ciella . . . put through a call to a Mr. Rafael Martini, the chairman and president of MMSystems. Tell Mr. Martini—or his simmie or secretary—that Senator Cannon will be calling shortly on a secure connection. Then tell me what the response is.*

Yes, sir.

Then I pushed a link through to Steven Pagel, my committee counsel. *Senator Cannon here. I'm going to be a little late. Would you give my office a link if a vote or an amendment I'm interested in is coming up?*

I'd be happy to do that, Senator.

In the past people had speculated that legislative voting would be done remotely, with VR conferencing or multi-holo projections. It didn't work out that way because the projections were too good and any remote access system could be counterfeited or overridden. The only way to be certain someone was really that person was to have that person show up and pass a GIL scan on the way into the committee room or the Senate floor. Anything else could be and had been feited.

Senator. Ciella linked through, *Mr. Martini will be available for your call in fifteen minutes. He's in transit.*

Thank you.

Transit? I had my doubts. He probably wanted to record every word and gesture. That was fine. I was more than used to that.

Since there was little sense in leaving the office—it would take nearly five minutes to get to the committee room—I spent the time going through some of the briefing backgrounders Ted had prepared.

Exactly sixteen minutes later, I pushed through the holo call to MMSystems.

The holo image of Martini showed a dark-haired man with deep blue eyes and fair skin, who still looked in first youth, as opposed to nanite-prolonged youth. He smiled, but didn't speak.

"Mr. Martini," I offered.

"Senator Cannon. What can I do for you?"

"Perhaps I can do something for you, Mr. Martini." I smiled warmly, paternally. "You may know, or perhaps you don't, that I was a great admirer of your father, and what he had managed to accomplish with MMSystems."

"He did a great deal, but I have my doubts that admiration prompted your call."

"Oh, but it does, Mr. Martini. It does. I was distressed at the reports about the dealings with the Martian Republic." Another smile, this one understanding. "But even in the best of organizations, especially in transition, such things can occur. We all understand that." I could tell he knew I was about to drop something on him, and that meant there was something to drop.

"As I recall, the Executory's investigation cleared the company of any illegality." Martini tried his own smile. It wasn't bad. "But I do appreciate your concerns."

"Part of that might well be attributed to, shall we say, good will? And to your father's reputation. If anything else were to occur, not that I'm suggesting it will in any way, it might well be handled with . . ." I paused just briefly, "less delicacy."

"Senator, I do appreciate your courtesy, but someone must have misinformed you, and I would hate to have you spend your valuable time in an election year with concerns over such misinformation."

"Well . . . if that's the case, I certainly won't give it another thought." I smiled again, this time falsely, falsely enough that he could see it. "And I wish you the very best in continuing the family traditions. I'm most sorry to have bothered you."

"Senator, we all appreciate your concern for both NorAm and your constituents, and no one would ever consider a call from you a bother."

"Thank you very much, Mr. Martini." Still smiling, I broke the connection.

I couldn't prove it in the conventional way, but Martini was up to something, and I had the feeling that Eric had been right and that Martini was selling. The odds were that, somehow, either Kemal, or someone like him, was doing the buying, because MMSystems' capitalization was so large that it had to be someone who could marshal the credits without selling stock or other assets, and there were only a handful of people in NorAm who could do that. It wouldn't hurt to check, if I could figure out a way that wouldn't break the privacy restrictions.

Ted?

Yes, sir?

Have Alicia do some research. We need to know if anyone has been selling large positions in any equities over the past three months. Just have her run a search program on bloc equity volumes, say one percent or more of any major cap issues.

Yes, sir.

Either way, the results would tell me something.

I got up and straightened my coat. I was already late for the committee meeting, but Pagel would have linked if there had been a vote coming up. Later, I'd have to talk with Gilligan and Canthrop about the campaign. While they didn't need to know the in-depth background, we'd need to think about anticipating the attack ads that would be coming from both Hansen and Alredd.

Chapter 25
Parsfal

By Tuesday morning, I was tired of finding angles on another tragic ebol4 death, or spinning out the stats to show that the epidemic was nowhere near as bad as the CDC had predicted, because only two hundred thousand had died in NorAm, and merely twice that in EurCom, while deaths were trailing off as containment and nanomeds took effect. Donne may have told death not to be proud, but so far as I was concerned death had done himself proud enough, and that didn't include the continuing and rising death toll in Afrique and SudAm. Nor did it include the continuing deaths in Denv from the mysterious ODs.

Then, while I had finished another weather piece and more on the Southern Diversion, I was still dithering around with stuff on McCall, and getting nowhere. I should let go of old stories, but old stories didn't always let go of me. I'd put in another link to Marc Oler and gotten the same simmie message. I'd also left a message with Kerras, asking for contact suggestions, but he was link-blocked.

So I called John Ashbaugh. He wasn't in either.

With that, I prepared another stat update on ebol4 and fed it to Metesta, and then started on some temperature and weather stats as a favor to Istancya to repay her for helping dig me out when I'd been buried in the flurry around the ebol4 outbreak and the Russean orbiter destruction, now largely forgotten little more than a week later. The silence was truly amazing. Nothing had emerged. Nothing at all, unless you bought the Talibanate's story that despite the components being traced to the Agkhanate, no one there had anything to do with it.

Parsfal? Bimstein again.

I'm here. What do you need?

Some quick numbers to go with the Dewey death piece . . .

Dewey? The District Coordinator? When did that happen?

Where have you been? Less than a half hour ago . . .

Doing weather and temp stats . . .

Drop those . . . Dewey's electral went off the Elletch Bridge . . . get something quick on electral fatalities, and also anything you can on the costs of guideway maintenance in the Denv District . . . and anything else linked to that. Rehm's doing the personal background. Need that in a half hour.

I'll do what I can.

Once you feed that to Metesta, need some more backup on those education and nanomed stats. On the African immigrants.

How much do you need?

Go over it with Brianne. She's got the story. Something Cannon's done in the Senate.

He's always doing something. The last thing I wanted to dig up was statistics on the medical costs of treating immigrants. If they were for Kerras, he'd want something to imply the taxpayers would never get their credits' worth, and Brianne would want something to show that both the nanomeds and the education were great. I had problems with both, when I'd seen too many kids from westside and northside who couldn't afford any real health care.

Get on the Dewey stuff!

Bimstein was gone, and I had to start scrambling. The electral stats were easy enough. NorAm Transport Department had those. Only 973 fatalities in all NorAm in the previous year. I threw in a comparison to historical times, when more people died annually in internal combustion engine vehicle accidents than in some wars.

The guideway maintenance was harder. I couldn't really do that, so I fudged around it, by using the overall maintenance budget and the past year's admin and overhead costs, and standard contracting-out percentages, and then qualified the whole mess by noting that the figures were preliminary estimates based on existing public data. What else could I do?

Once I finished off the Dewey stuff and whipped it to Metesta, I took a deep breath, before starting in on the medical and educational stuff for whatever Cannon was up to. But my mind was still on the McCall story. It nagged at me, but I pushed it aside and linked to Brianne. There was no sense in giving her the wrong slant.

Brianne? Ah . . . this is Jude. What do you want on the immigrant stuff?

Jude . . . There was an impression of a sigh. *You know what I want. Everyone's treating these poor people like it was their fault that they had to leave Afrique. They're people, not numbers. Senator Cannon has this bill—it's an amendment he got attached to the health appropriations that will make them repay part of their nanomed and medical upgrades. Unless there's an outcry, it's going to become law, and that will establish a precedent . . .*

That people ought to pay for improved health?

Jude! Those people don't have our advantages.

I decided against arguing. *You want numbers and vignettes about what a contribution they make and how they've struggled to get here, and how the children of immigrants make a disproportionate contribution so that we get it all back and then some over the years?*

Don't be so sarcastic.

I wasn't. Is that the line you want?

Without the sarcasm, thank you.

How soon?

Five tonight. Feed it to Kirenga.

You'll have what I can get. I'm sorry. I didn't mean . . . I've been swamped.

That's all right. I understand. Bimstein's getting on everyone.
There was a laugh.

Thanks.

After that, I worked for nearly two hours on the immigrant numbers without Bimstein blasting through the link, and I guessed that he'd been satisfied with the Dewey stuff.

Parsfal? Les Kerras here. What did you want?

The McCall thing.

It's dead.

I know. It shouldn't be. Someone circulated a rumor that Nanette McCall was filing for divorce. It was wrong. Also, they didn't know her. She always went by Nanette Iveson. I've talked to a lot of people about Evan McCall. First, he was deeply in love with her. Second everyone agrees the man was a legal genius and a complete technical idiot. He couldn't turn off a nanite screen without written step-by-step instructions. Third, he used to be with O'Bannon and Reyes, and he had dealings with Chris Kemal . . .

Lots of people have to deal with Kemal . . .

It stinks, Les . . .

There was a long silence, and I wondered if he'd broken the link.

I might . . . might . . . be able to work it into a cast if you can get me something more, something solid.

How would I get that? I don't have any contacts with DPS, not in homicide.

You don't want to go to homicide. Go to DPS trends. Lieutenant Chiang. Eugene Tang Chiang. Solid westside boy. Don't use dazzle. Be direct and honest. Only thing he respects.

Lieutenant Chiang.

You got it. And if he'll give you something, then we'll see.

I nodded. Kerras didn't feel any better about it than I did, and he'd been told not to pursue it. He hadn't been told not to have me pursue it. I'd been right about it, but that didn't make me feel good at all.

I tried Chiang at DPS, but only got his simmie. I left a link-message.

This is Jude Parsfal at NetPrime. I was hoping you could help me with some trend information. I had decided to use the mysterious OD stuff as the entry. That was a legit question no matter what.

Then I went back to the immigration numbers. I did manage to unearth a study that showed that the children of immigrants made more credits than the average NorAm citizen, and using the baseline numbers, and calculating the numbers of immigrants, I could make a case that the children's taxes more than paid for their parents' medical costs, even with time-discounting. I knew Brianne would love that, and I was pleased that I didn't have to do too many statistical contortions to come up with that.

A holo image popped up in front of me.

"Chiang here. You called?" The man in the holo image wore a dark blue singlesuit that was close to the street uniform of the DPS—but wasn't. He was lightly bronzed with short black hair and a square face, and well muscled. He had the wary and polite look that all senior DPS types seemed to wear with their uniforms.

"Ah . . . yes, I did. Les Kerras said you might be able to help me on a couple of things. First, we've been hearing that ODs are up and that the DPS hasn't been able to find the drug causing the problem. We've reported it, but I was looking for more background, if you had it."

Chiang laughed, not mockingly, but ruefully. "Background only. Have been some deaths with OD symptoms. Moderate levels of soop, sometimes alkie, but always soop in their blood. No foreign substances in their blood. None. Contacted CDC. Twenty years of studies. No negative effects from those levels of alkie and no negative effects from soop. None."

"None? But people are dying, mostly young ones."

"Background only," Chiang reiterated. "*All* are young people. We've asked CDC to look into it. Has to be a city thing. So far, only showed up in Denv, Lanta, and Porlan and one or two other places. All population centers. Absolute numbers still low."

"Something that targets the young . . . hmmm. Can you suggest anyone else who might know something?"

"Could try CDC." Chiang's expression told me that they didn't know or weren't likely to tell me.

"I had another question. I did the background research for the McCall case—"

"Mr. Parsfal. That's a closed investigation. He committed suicide. The Department made a serious error. We admitted it."

I paused. There was something there. I knew there was. "I see. Well . . . Les Kerras said you'd set me straight." I paused. "Maybe I could stop by and chat with you about the ground rules of what I should ask and what I shouldn't. It could save us both time in the future."

"Could."

"What about tomorrow?"

"Nine hundred. Have to be short."

"Nine hundred it is."

There *was* something there. Chiang wouldn't have agreed so easily if there weren't. He also didn't want it on an open transmission.

I finished up the numbers for Brianne and fed the package to Kirenga, complete with fancy holo graphs and even an animated segment.

After that, I decided to look into the OD business more. First, I combed the nets. The numbers were there, but not the names, for the most part. By checking obits, news on all the nets, I managed to come up with six names. Six out of more than four times that number over the past week and a half.

With the privacy restraints, I could only find three names of others who might be family. I took a deep breath and made the first link, to a Donal Samelo.

All I got was a voice-over, not even a simmie. So I left a message.

"This is Jude Parsfal. I'm a researcher, and I was wondering if you could help me with some background information . . ."

No one cut in, and I went to the second name. This time I got a simmie, and a tired-looking woman appeared halfway through my spiel.

"What do you really want? You selling something?"

"No. I'm a researcher, and I'm looking into the causes of ODs . . ."

"You people never stop!"

I just waited.

"You want to blame everyone! Frederico was a good boy. He never even tried any drugs. The DPS said so."

"That's why I'm looking into this," I interjected. "We're looking into the possibility that it wasn't an OD . . ." I don't know why, exactly, I said that, but at times your instincts are better than your rationality.

She stopped and looked at me, as if I might actually be human.

Before she could say anything more, I spoke. "All I'd like to know is what Frederico did that night, anything different he might have eaten or done. Nothing more."

"He just went to the Red Moon, like I told the DPS. He and Carmencita had dinner here. We had carnitos and beans—"

"Flour or corn tortillas?"

"Corn flour."

"Any new or different salsa?"

"No. Same as I always make. Everything was the same."

"Do you know what he did at the Red Moon?"

"Carmencita said they just listened to this new rezrapper. Hot Ice or Cold something. They had drinks, non-alkie. Frederico couldn't afford any more."

"Did he have any soop before he left?"

"He had just a little jolt. Just enough to feel good for the music, he said."

"Did Carmencita?"

"They both did . . . but it was so little. The DPS said that couldn't do it. People been taking soop for years."

"How did they get there?"

"Took the shuttle and walked."

"Can you think of anything different? Anything at all?"

She shook her head.

I wished I could have thought of something more. Instead, I just thanked her.

The last name got me a high-class simmie, and no response to my message. After that, I sat back in my cubicle. There was something there, and I couldn't put my mind on it.

Finally, I put through a search on resonance advertising. I got thousands of references. I tried again, limiting it to recent scholarly articles. There was one, in the latest edition of *Physiological Psychology,* entitled "Culturally Attuned Rhythmitonal Resonance—Myth or Fact?" It wasn't what I recalled, but it would do, and I had the system print out two hard copies for me. It wouldn't hurt to see Chiang bearing gifts, so to speak.

You have an incoming from John Ashbaugh, the gatekeeper announced.

Accept. I flicked up the holo display.

"Jude, you left a message."

"I've been trying to reach Marc Oler for days. You know any way to get to him?"

John looked mildly surprised. "It's hard to reach someone who's dead."

"Dead?"

"He was one of the first victims of this ebol4 strain. I thought . . ." He shook his head. "There's no way you would have known."

"Who was McCall's other junior associate?"

"That's Caron Hildeo. She just accepted a position back at O'Bannon and Reyes, but as a senior associate. James was most solicitous, under the circumstances, even promoting her."

"It sounds that way." I shook my head. "It's still hard to believe that McCall jumped off a tower . . . such a bright man, and . . ."

"You're trolling, Jude."

I grinned. "How about biting then, John?"

"How could I do anything there? That's a murder that turned into a suicide, and I'm but a poor securities solicitor."

"So tell me something about securities." I grinned and tried to think of the most outlandish thing that I could, involving Kemal, because I wondered if he were somehow involved in the McCall thing. I figured that John might give me something else. It was worth a try. "Tell me that Kemal's outfit is involved in complex securities manipulations verging on the illegal and unethical."

John couldn't quite hide the jolt, and I pounced. "So what is he up to?"

"That's against—"

"He's not your client. You told me that years ago. Rumors aren't covered by solicitor-client privacy."

John sighed.

I stared.

"Rumor . . . and for background only, and if one word comes back about me, I'll never talk to you again. About anything. Ever."

"Agreed."

"Rumor is that he's using laundered funds to buy his way into legitimate space industry formulation."

"Speculation only . . . but would McCall have known that?"

John frowned. "He might have. He was Kemal's privacy solicitor. But Kemal used O'Bannon and Reyes, and even Flemmerfeld, Hayes, and D'Aboul."

"What sort of space industry formulation?"

"Something big. Maybe the biggest. I can't say more." His lips tightened. "I really can't."

"All right. I won't press. But . . . if something comes up, and more than a few people know about it . . . would you let me know?"

He nodded.

"Thanks, John. I'll let you know if I find anything else."

I was suddenly looking at a blank holo display, and I collapsed it.

I hoped I'd handled it right. There's a fine line between squeezing as much as you can and stopping short so that you can go back later.

The weather stuff I owed Istancya was still waiting, and I settled back at my console. I had a bit more research to do on the rezrap angle—where the "new" rezrappers were playing. I needed that because it was my angle with Chiang. All because the McCall story wouldn't go away. I wished I understood why.

Or maybe, it was as the Irishman had put it,

But something is recalled,
My conscience or my vanity appalled.

There were times, so many times, when the beauty of the words contrasted with the utility of what I did. Yet . . . didn't seeking and revealing truth have a beauty?

Didn't it?

There are advantages to having assets. One of them was the large indoor pool at the house. I swam a klick every morning before breakfast, more if I had time.

After I swam on Wednesday morning, I pulled myself out, then sat at my table. The smell of the orange trees and the humidity was welcome. So was the aroma of the coffee with the waiting breakfast. Breakfast was simple. Fruit, scrambled egg, dry toast, and juice. The fruit was a Valencia orange from one of the trees in the pool room.

I linked to the house net. *Armand? I'd like you to come to the pool.*

Yes, ser.

Armand had been a systems tech before he'd lost his temper and maimed a coworker, and then assaulted a DPS det. He'd been very good in the martial arts. Now, he was a permie, and in charge of maintenance for the house, and most of the family.

Armand was a very special permie. He'd cost me a great deal. He was like every other permie, except in two respects. His nanites were programmed so that he could not tell anyone what he talked over with me. Second, and most important, any instructions I gave him overrode the permie conditioning. They had to be from me in person and by voice. Other than that, he was a permie. He told the truth about everything—except he couldn't say anything about anything concerning me, and he couldn't say anything about anything I told him not to speak about. All he could say was, "I don't know."

Armand was perfectly happy with the arrangement. The nanites saw to that as well.

I'd finished the orange and half the egg and toast when Armand appeared. He was three centimeters shorter than I was, but with wider shoulders and black hair.

"Mr. Kemal."

"Please sit down, Armand." I turned on the privacy shield that screened the table—only my table.

Armand sat across from me.

"My nephew Stefan has become very careless, Armand."

"Yes, ser."

"He has a brand-new Tija electral. The kind with two fuel cells. Are you familiar with the system?"

"Yes, ser." Armand's voice was flat. Not so flat as that of many permies, but flat.

"Stefan has become very dangerous to the safety of the family. I'd like you to take care of it. The Tijas can become very unstable at high speeds. Could you make the Tija even more unstable?"

"I could, ser."

"And could you make sure that the fuel cells exploded when the Tija rolled? And that no one could escape? Without leaving any evidence?"

Armand frowned. He thought for a moment. "Yes, ser."

"I'm telling you to do that when you check the systems at his house today. If you leave immediately, he'll still be sleeping."

"Yes, ser."

"Let me know if you have any trouble."

"Yes, ser."

"Thank you, Armand. You may go."

"Yes, ser."

I released the privacy screen as he left.

Marissa crossed the pool deck from the exercise room. She was wearing pale green shorts and a matching sleeveless top. She carried her own breakfast—fruit, yogurt, dry toast, and a large mug of coffee. She sat down to my right.

"What were you talking to Armand about, dear?" asked Marissa.

"Some maintenance tasks. I want him to be extra careful in inspecting things."

"You're worried, aren't you?"

"I am. KC is becoming big enough to have enemies outside of Denv, even outside of NorAm."

"You've been big enough to have enemies across NorAm for almost ten years," she pointed out. "Senator Cannon has been after you for five years."

"He doesn't understand business. Somehow, he thought it was moral if Dewey rewarded his cousins at GSY, but immoral if we made money and cost the taxpayers less. It's all right to reward relatives if two companies are involved, but wrong if only one is." I laughed. "Politicians!"

"Coordinator Dewey seemed sincere," Marissa pointed out. "It was a shame that he died in that accident yesterday."

"Poetic justice, but I can't point that out. He wanted divestiture. That meant worse maintenance. He died because the maintenance was bad. Can you imagine what would happen if I said anything right now?"

Marissa sipped her coffee. "They'd say you were self-serving. They will anyway."

She was right about that.

"Barbra and I talked yesterday. She mentioned that you'd had a talk with Stefan about finances."

"I did. He went to Mountain Asset Management and got a loan collateralized against his KCF trust. He can't possibly pay the interest for long. We'll have to restructure it into something he can handle." I snorted. "It's almost blackmail, but I'll have to do it."

"Alyssa's good at reading people. She doesn't trust Stefan."

"I don't either, but he is family. That's why the trust is irrevocable and lifetime. It's also why I have to put a stop to his borrowing. Ashtay talked to me about a credit block on Stefan. I'd hate to go that far, but if this restructuring doesn't work, we may have to. We'll have to do something." That was just the way it was.

"Barbra wouldn't like that, dear. She's very protective of Stefan."

I sighed. "That's part of the problem. She's spoiled him." I refilled my cup. "Would you like some more?"

"Please, thank you."

We both sipped coffee for several minutes.

"Chris . . . you're worried, aren't you?"

"When am I not worried? I've got politicians who don't understand business, and suppliers who don't understand politics. I've got nephews who think that credits are free. I've got a son who's at the age where he thinks that I don't understand anything. You know what's worst of all?" I laughed ruefully.

Marissa waited. She'd heard it before.

"I've got it better than most people." I took a last sip of the coffee. "And I need to get dressed and on my way." I got up, then walked behind her chair. I bent down and kissed her neck. She always smelled wonderful. "See you tonight."

"We're having the D'Abouls for dinner, remember?"

"I won't be late." I hoped I wouldn't be. Family was important, and Marissa always had wonderful dinners.

Chapter 27
Chiang

I got into DPS on Wednesday before zero seven hundred. Early for me. Worried about the newsie I had to meet. And about the McCall mess. Sarao was waiting. She had that look.

"Now what?" I asked.

"Techs looked at your rez toys. They use more and different rez frequencies/overtones, whatever, and probably destroy hearing twice as fast as standard rezsong. There's a possibility of some metabolic effects, but . . ."

"They can't say anything more?"

"Right."

"Send them to CDC with a request for everything. Ask if exposure will enhance effects of soop or alcohol or modify it."

"CDC? They've got to be buried with the ebol1 mess."

Shook my head. "The viral types are. Sound and electronic exposure types won't be."

"It's your budget, Lieutenant."

"If I'm right, save us grief. If I'm wrong, Cannizaro will tell me I wasted my lab and consulting budget."

"You're here early. The McCall case?"

She was there early as well, anticipating why I was. I'd never told her. "That. Other stuff, too."

Wanted to study Resheed's summary report. Also wanted to look into the Dewey report. If I could get it out from under seal. Cannizaro hadn't said much about that. And the ODs and suicides. Even before that, needed to lean on Kama.

"Wouldn't want to be at your console, Lieutenant."

Times like these, I didn't either. I smiled and went into my office. Still gray outside.

First off, put in a call to Kama. Got his simmie. Strongly suggested he get back to me.

Then I read through the daily summary. More of the ODs without drug traces, but they were down. They'd been declining since the weekend. All involved soop at moderate or low levels. No new suicides.

Went back through the McCall stuff. Like an unpreserved corpse, smelled even worse.

Kama got back to me. Could sense anger and then some.

Eugene . . . you may be a friend from school . . .

But you don't like your old friend leaning on you. Wouldn't do it, except there's too much here not to. I need some special technical advice.

You didn't need to threaten me if I didn't get back to you.

The last time I was polite . . . went to your office . . . nicely . . . took three days to run you down. Don't have three days.

What do you want?

Want to send two techs to you—in the next hour. Remember
we talked about hiding overrides in nanite control systems? You
tell my techs what to look for and how to find it. Then you're
out of it. Otherwise, I get the advocate's office to have you ap-
pear as an expert witness at an indictment . . .

Eugene . . . I offer you help, and this is how you repay me?

You help me, and you won't be hurting.

That's what you say.

Have I been wrong? Since our last chess game?

I'm doing a new place in southside. Could they meet me there?
In an unmarked lorry, or DPS building inspector's car?

Can do.

Understood what he wanted. That I could do, and did. Got
the address, out on Old Carriage Lane. Good thing Cannizaro
had given me authority to draft any DPS experts I needed. The
techs weren't happy, either, but they took one of the unmarked
lorries.

After they left, I went back through the McCall docket that
Kirchner had dumped on me. Then went through it again.
Caught a few more items I could use—maybe.

Brazelton had offered a deposition on Nanette Iveson's death.
Notarized and authenticated document, saying that he had installed a standard system and that it had passed all tests. Nodded
to myself. Might have something there.

There's a newsie here to see you, Lieutenant. Says he's Jude
Parsfal. Claims he has an appointment.

I checked the time—zero eight five-five. I'd lost track of the
time. *He does. Forgot to tell you.* I got up, stepped out to meet
him.

Parsfal was short, muscular. Would have been heavyset centuries earlier. Didn't look like a net researcher. Carried a thin
manila envelope. Hadn't seen one of those in years.

"Ah . . . I'm Jude Parsfal, Lieutenant. I appreciate your taking
the time."

Motioned him in. When I pulsed the door shut, I also triggered

the privacy screen. New style. Silent. He stood until I motioned
to the other ergochair.

"We're screened."

"I can feel that." He smiled, cleared his throat. "Lieutenant.
Yesterday, we talked about two things. One was the rising number of ODs that seemed to have no cause. You had said that all
of the cases had soop in their systems. I did a few interviews and
a little searching. I can't prove anything, but I'll offer you a possibility."

Nodded for him to go ahead. News types get around. Might
actually have something.

"All those whose families I could talk to indicated that they
had been to see one of the new rezrappers right before they died.
They'd also had some dosage of soop. I have to wonder if somehow this new type of rezrap interacts with soop—at least for
some people." He shrugged. "Just a thought."

I found myself frowning.

"The new rezads have a greater effectiveness," he added, "and
some people are claiming that it's because they create a physiological effect, not just a mental one. There's even a study out on
it. But its effect is determined on a chromosomal basis."

"You're stretching, Parsfal. Like to solve this as much as anyone, but . . ."

"I don't think so." He pulled out several sheets from the thin
flat envelope he carried and extended them to me. "This is the
hard copy from the March issue of *Physiological Psychology*. It's
called 'Culturally Attuned Rhythmitonal Resonance—Myth or
Fact?' And it's all about how the new rez affects both physiology
and psychology. If it can do that . . ." He smiled politely.

"Still think you're stretching."

"It could be. You told me yesterday that this OD phenomena
was largely restricted to denser population areas, like Denv, Porlan. I'll bet there have been some in Lanta and Pitt, too, and very
few anywhere else. I did a search last night of the performances
of the 'new' rezrappers. So far, there are only a handful, and at

least the publicized performances have been in those four cities. You could check, I'm sure."

Had to admit Parsfal had the makings of a good trendie. Problem was that he might be right. Also, he was offering because he wanted something else. "Thank you. I will. You might be onto something." Smiled politely at him.

"There's another matter . . . the McCall case."

"It's officially closed," I pointed out.

He took a long breath. Deliberate breath.

I waited.

"It has an odor, Lieutenant. A very strong odor. To a disinterested observer, it might even appear as though everyone wanted it to go away quietly. Les Kerras said to be straight with you. I will be. First, Evan McCall was deeply in love with his wife. Second, after her death someone circulated a rumor that they were having marital problems. I checked it out. It was totally false, even to all the details. Third, Nanette Iveson was killed by a malfunctioning nanite protective screen that trapped her in her classic vintage electral when it caught fire in her own garage. Those screens are supposedly impossible to adjust that way, unless you're an expert. Evan McCall was a legal genius and a technical idiot who couldn't program his own holoscreen to receive a standard image. Fourth, McCall had been and presumably still was the privacy solicitor for Chris Kemal, but he had just left O'Bannon and Reyes to start a new firm. Interestingly enough, one of his two associates reportedly just died of ebol4, and the other immediately rejoined O'Bannon and Reyes. Fifth, Kemal is up to something very big, enough to make some very important filch most uneasy. Sixth, Kemal has been unhappy about the way District Coordinator Dewey interpreted the new guideway maintenance laws passed last year by the Legislature, and now Coordinator Dewey has just died in an accident—also involving malfunctioning nanites." Parsfal smiled politely. "Doesn't that suggest a bit more than coincidence, Lieutenant?"

It did. Meant I had even less time than Cannizaro had given me. "Seen some amazing coincidences over the years, Mr. Parsfal.

Certain you have as well." I paused. Parsfal didn't jump. Just waited. Not good. He knew what he had. "I trust Les Kerras. I don't know you. Trust is hard to come by."

He nodded. "I understand. If you want to give anything to Les, I certainly understand. That's no problem."

That was worse. Meant they both knew. Or—even worse—that Kerras had been leaned on and was using Parsfal. Had to play it as well as I could. "Mr. Parsfal. I will give you one bit of information. Only on background, and only on the condition it not appear in the news anywhere."

"I can only promise I'll tell no one, not even Les. I can't stop someone else from finding out whatever this is."

"Doesn't matter. If nothing appears, then I may have more for you. DPS is reviewing the McCall case for many of the reasons you have cited. We're early in the review. Can't say more now. I've told no one else."

Parsfal nodded. "Neither will I. Not until you tell me, *or* until another net announces the review."

That was fair. Didn't like it, but fair. "You keep your word, and you get the story from me before anyone else. You don't, and I'll never talk to you or Les again."

He nodded. "Fair is fair. Is that all?"

I liked that. He heard and didn't push. Could be I'd need him as much as he'd need me if the McCall case went where we both had it pegged. "That's all for now. Can't say now when I'll know what." True enough, but I'd better know more before long. I stood.

So did Parsfal. "Thank you. I hope the research article will help on the other."

"So do I." I released the screens.

After he left, I sat back for a minute. Parsfal was research, not T-head like Kerras. He didn't smell like a setup. Good setups never do.

Some things I could check myself. The suggestion that something was up with the rezrappers and the ODs. Called up the death reports, those we had. Parsfal's hunch had been right. The info wasn't there on all the OD reports. On the sixty percent that it was, all had been at a rezrap show within an hour of their deaths. Proof? It wasn't proof, but the correlation couldn't be less than sixty percent. Too high for coincidence. Checked the request that Sarao had sent out to CDC, then sent a follow-up noting the high correlation, and sending a copy of the study Parsfal had left.

Looked into another angle on the McCall case, Marc Oler. No real death report. Cremated at eastside Pinery Hospital. Small filch hospital. Cause of death: ebol4. Had to wonder if Parsfal knew, who else did? McCall left O'Bannon and Reyes. He was dead. So was his wife. So was his number one associate. Reported as ebol4, but cremated with no way to prove it. Number two associate, alive and well, and back in the fold.

Again. No proof, but a good pointer that McCall had known something. But what? The big deal that Parsfal hinted at? Could any deal be that important?

Laughed. I'd seen kids killed over a jacket or a ten-cred chit.

Trouble, Lieutenant? Sarao came in on the link.

Not yet . . . I laughed. *Not any more than already, and that's too much.*

At ten hundred, I checked out the white electral and started out for McCall's. The two techs met me on the Southside Parkway. We talked. They had met with Kama. They told me they could find what I was looking for—if it happened to be there. Then they followed me the rest of the way.

McCall place had a ten-meter-high green synthstone wall. Lane off Southside Parkway led to a gatehouse. Two guards there. One looked at me.

"Lieutenant Chiang, DPS." I gestured to the lorry behind me. "DPS techs."

Still got the cold stare. Rather than argue, I passed over the remote GIL that would authenticate me.

Three minutes later, the massive iron gate opened. Guard hadn't said a word.

McCall's place was strange—half pseudo-early twentieth-century art deco and half ancient Tibetan. More like an ancient Tibetan monastery. Set below and east of an artificial mountain close to a hundred meters high and nearly half a klick across. Mountain was dark gray rock sculpted in the shape of miniature Himalayan peaks. Couldn't even see the real Rockies for the pseudo Himalayas. All the outside walls were pale green synth-stone, smooth as glass.

Kugeler and a woman were standing under the flat-roofed portico in the entry circle. They didn't move when I got out of the electral. The woman was blonde. Looked like the vids of McCall.

I bowed to her. "Eugene Chiang, DPS."

"Irene Iveson," she replied.

She'd taken her mother's name. Another reason why I hadn't been able to track her.

"Can you tell me what you're looking for?" asked Kugeler.

"Evidence." I gestured to the lorry. "I'd like the techs to go over the house systems and those in the garage area, while you and Ms. Iveson take me through the tower part of the house."

"The DPS has been over the systems at least twice," Kugeler said mildly.

"These techs have special training." Hoped they did, and what Kama had given them was enough.

"I take it that you're looking for something definite?"

"Several things." No point in not admitting that much.

"What, if we might ask?" Kugeler persisted.

I offered a polite smile. "Rather not say, yet. Could be wrong. If you would show us to the control center?"

Control center was on the lowest level in the center of the house. Foyer led to an indoor pool and solarium on one side, corridor leading to the garage on the other, and control room right off the foyer.

Left Moorty and Alfonso there, and followed Iveson up a circular ramp. Walked past half a dozen sculptures set on pedestals in wall alcoves. Had no idea whether they were original or formulated duplicates. Made no difference. For stone, neither was cheap. Air smelled like expensive and real flowers. Probably grown in the solarium.

Iveson turned into another corridor with woven hangings—all in geometric patterns and bright colors. Double doors opened at the end, closed after we stepped into another foyer. Stark. No hangings, no paintings, no windows, just polished green stone floors, and a ramp that curved upward, through the open center of the tower.

Iveson stopped, looked at me. "This is the lowest level of the palatium—that's what Father called it. It's old Latin for palace."

That fit McCall. Didn't say so, though.

"There's a lift on one side," Kugeler suggested.

"I'd rather walk, if you don't mind. After we look at the rooms on this level."

"You're the detective."

First level had a large exercise room, attached steam room and sauna. Nothing extraordinary, except for the quality of the fixtures.

"There's another steam room and sauna off the pool," Iveson offered.

I nodded.

Second level had two guest suites. Luxurious guest suites with double baths and freshers attached to each. Furniture was hand-turned neo-Anne. Polished, but with a few scrapes. Rooms had been used. Not just for show.

Third level had a series of rooms. One seemed to be an art studio—on the north side. Another had endless floor-to-ceiling cases filled with small drawers.

"For Dad's stamps," explained Iveson.

Then there was a casual sitting room. Nothing special. Just a comfortable room with old-style acoustical sound reproduction equipment. New and expensive old-style acoustical reproduction equipment.

Fourth level had two offices on the west side, a wood-paneled library on the east.

"The one done in white and peach—that was Mother's," Iveson said.

"You've gone through all the files and datablocs, I assume?" Looked more at Kugeler.

"That was the first thing we did—after the DPS left," replied Irene Iveson. "There was nothing there."

"You were looking for something?"

"I still think my parents were murdered, Lieutenant. I was looking for any possible reason."

"Did you find one?"

She shook her head. "That doesn't mean they weren't."

She was right. I just nodded, and we walked up another level.

Top two levels were for entertaining. Fifth level had both culinary formulators, the kind used in uniqueries, and a complete kitchen with gas stoves and walk-in refrigerator. There was a large back staircase from the kitchen to the upper level. On the west side was a dining area off the balcony, with an elegant neo-Anne cherry table that stretched ten meters. Didn't even come close to filling the room. Nor did the matched sideboards. Any one of the wooden straight-backed chairs at the dining table cost more than all the furnishings in my small great room.

Top level was glass-walled all the way around, selective polarization for the glass. On the balcony, could see inside, more than ten meters away, glass looked greenish silver. Decor was also neo-Anne, with matched couches, end and side tables, armchairs, upholstered cherry side chairs. The whole interior space was unwalled—except for the central lift. Just a mid-chest-high wall around the access ramp. Could sense the safety field around that inner wall, though.

The upper four levels all had balconies.

One thing I noticed. There was no rez equipment. I kept looking. Neither Kugeler nor Iveson said anything.

Finally, looked at the daughter. "Did your parents have any rez equipment?"

She frowned. "Dad used to, in the listening room on the third level."

We went back to the comfortable room on the third level. As I'd noted the first time through, only old-style straight sound projection. Beautiful and expensive—precise—but not rez. That bothered me.

Iveson looked at me. "There used to be . . ."

"When was the last time you know it was here?"

"A year ago, when they had a party for Marcya. I've been here dozens of times since then, but I never really looked. It's not . . ." She paused. "Is that important?"

"Not directly." Like everything else. "We can go back down." Nodded at Kugeler.

We walked down the ramp. I thought.

The other thing was that it would have been easier for McCall to have jumped off the side of the inner ramp. Still almost a six-story fall onto hard stone. Except no recsat would have picked it up inside the tower.

The techs were waiting in the control area. I closed the door— manually—behind me, leaving Kugeler and Ms. Iveson in the foyer.

Lead tech was Moorty.

I looked at him. "What did you find?"

"We used a scope screener on the manual power cutoffs. Very, very interesting, Lieutenant. Not a single fingerprint anywhere. Not on the covers, not on the sides."

That didn't surprise me. My guts got tighter. "What about the system programming?"

"It's like you suspected, Lieutenant. Remote overrides. Could be triggered from outside the property. Or anywhere inside."

Looked at the second tech—Alfonso. "You agree?"

"Yes, ser."

"Ser?" offered Moorty.

I waited.

"We can't put this in the report, but someone inserted what I'd call taps in the system, then removed them. There was also a small unit mounted back here. Adhesive traces on the metal."

That figured, too. "I'll need a report. What you can report. Schematics or whatever. Two copies. One to Captain Cannizaro, one to me. And we'll need to seal the room and put it under constant remote."

They both nodded.

Cannizaro knew something was wrong. Had to have known from the start. Needed someone to prove it—or someone to get killed to blow it open. I didn't like either option. Didn't want it to go that far. If I couldn't find more proof, question might be how much I let Parsfal know—and when. Problem was that, like the comm types said, you can't send half a quark.

I smiled and opened the door.

"What did you find?" demanded Kugeler.

"Some more suggestions that your suspicions might have merit, Ms. Iveson." Admitted that because I didn't want them immediately bashing Cannizaro. "We need to see where they take us." Paused, then added, "We're going to seal and monitor the control room."

"You're admitting that there was a possibility of murder?" Kugeler persisted.

I looked at him. Hard. "Mr. Kugeler. I can't speculate publicly. There are some suggestive and unresolved matters here. There are several possibilities. First, unlikely as it seems, Nanette Iveson died in an accident, and Evan McCall committed suicide in grief. Second, a series of coincidental events, not murder, but not suicide, killed both. It has happened. Third, someone set up both deaths to appear as accident and suicide. Right now, there are problems with each of those possibilities. None fits neatly. What I feel, what you feel—they don't matter in resolving this. What matters is what DPS can prove."

Kugeler nodded.

Irene Iveson glared. "You aren't saying—"

"Irene," Kugeler interposed quickly, "the lieutenant is being more than fair. We asked for an investigation. He has listed the possibilities, and he is investigating. He has only been looking

into this for a little more than a day. He has already found more
than his peers have. I think that, for the moment, he is being very
open and fair."

I had to correct one thing. "Didn't find more overall. They
found a great deal. I happened to find several additional pieces
of evidence that may make more sense of what they found."

Kugeler smiled. He understood. "You will keep us informed,
Lieutenant."

"Yes. I will." Didn't have much choice on that.

Chapter 28
Cornett

Early on Thursday evening, I was standing just inside the foyer
of the conapt, checking the time. I was waiting for Marco. He
had an electral that was licensed for use in Denv, and he was the
only full-acoustic accompanist I knew who did. I certainly
couldn't afford the license. That was why Dad's '54 Altimus was
garaged at Raymon's.

Had it been a good idea to accept the gig? Did an adjunct
professor of voice at UDenv have a choice? The gig paid, and
not much non-rez singing did anymore. Even if the Claytons had
insisted they wanted someone who could sing both Golden Age
and art song, I had to wonder. I pushed aside the doubts. I didn't
need those before performing, and I was getting paid.

I found myself looking out at the drive. Marco was late. Not
late, I corrected myself. Not so early as you'd like, Luara. I
glanced out, catching a glimpse of my own reflection in the armaglass doors of the foyer. The blue gown had been a compro-
mise, not a performing gown, exactly, nor an evening formal, but
what did one wear to an old-fashioned soirée held by one of the
wealthiest filch in Denv? The cut flattered my figure. It was comfortable, and it did set off my hair.

I'd already warmed up in the conapt, slowly, because I had a fairly demanding performance ahead, in more ways than one.

When I saw Marco's battered Viera pull up in the cul-de-sac that served all the conapts on the south side, I stepped outside. I made sure the door shut, and the systems were armed. Then I turned. The sky was changing from a pale bright blue into that deep shade that came with first twilight. A beautiful shade, but I shivered as I looked up, wondering if we would see streaks of fire before long.

The Martians hadn't said anything, not really, about the destruction of the Russean orbiter or about the death of their foreign secretary. The PDF kept saying they had the asteroid debris under control, but if they did, why did they keep talking about it?

I was still a little numbed by Michael's sudden death, and by Mershelle's. I'd gotten a link message from Student Affairs. Like Michael, she'd been a victim of ebol4. She'd been a hardworking student, and like that, she was gone. Even in a modern world, life was fragile, and death could still be sudden. Too often it was still the good who died young.

Marco was holding the door to the Viera for me. He wore a simple black dinner jacket with the bow tie and black trousers that had marked male concert attire for centuries.

"Thank you."

"I even cleaned the seats," he said before closing the door.

I couldn't help but smile.

Marco threw himself into the driver's seat and continued, as if there had been no hesitation while he walked around the electral, "And I went through the Schumann a couple more times. It really gets to you after a while."

Almost all of Schumann's songs did. More than once I'd wished I could sing *Dichterliebe*—but he'd written it for the male voice, and it didn't transpose, not well.

"The Moore pieces . . . they're not all that special, except when you sing them, Luara. Klaus kept wondering why I was practicing them . . ."

I let Marco talk as he drove out the Connector, and then took Southside Parkway. We passed a huge place with golden walls. That was the Kuhrs mansion. I'd sung there two years earlier, at their youngest daughter's wedding. Farther south was an even larger mansion with greenish walls and a miniature mountain to the west.

The Clayton estate had no walls, just hectares of parklike green grass and trees and hills. The lane wound through the grounds until we reached the house itself, set on a rise overlooking a lake. The house was of rose marble and sprawled across the rise. In the center was a shimmering crystal dome at least a good fifty meters across.

"That's really quite something." For the first time, Marco stopped chattering.

He eased the Viera under the towering covered and columned entry portico at exactly five forty-five, forty-five minutes before the soirée was to begin. That was so we could have a few minutes of practice in the actual space, and so that he could accustom himself to the piano. He'd have more time than I would. He had to play background music for a half hour before I sang, and for the time between my two sets.

The Claytons had a doorman, tall and dark and impressive in a gold and black uniform. The uniform could have been military two centuries earlier, with its high stiff collar.

"Might I announce you?" The doorman smiled politely as he opened the door.

"Luara Cornett. I'm singing tonight. This is my accompanist, Marco DiMicelli."

His eyes blanked for a moment, the way that happens when a permie links to a system. I wondered what he'd done to merit readjustment. They claimed that it took three crimes or two violent ones, but I wondered.

"Yes, Ms. Cornett. They're expecting you . . . and Mr. DiMicelli."

Another permie appeared to open Marco's door. "I'll park it for you." He pressed a locator tag upon Marco.

The entry portico was floored in more of the rose marble. When we walked through the arches and open double doors, a tall and slender blond woman, wearing a swirled green Grecian chiffon that uncovered her left shoulder, met us.

"You must be the singer. I'm Alcesta Clayton—Roberta's mother. Roberta wanted an old-fashioned soirée, and her father insisted that there was nothing to do but have an acoustic chamber concert—the kind that they had before resonance."

When music was still music, I reflected. I was surprised that the daughter was agreeing to unmodified vocal music. I've always disliked singing for the post-ed group. They're too young to really understand, and old enough to think they're experts at everything. To them, music is good if they like it, and bad if they don't, and they use their considerable verbal skills to justify their unsupported opinions.

"You are that kind of singer, aren't you? I mean, you don't use all that equipment?"

"Just the piano, and my voice." I half turned. "This is my accompanist, Marco DiMicelli."

Marco bowed, smiling politely.

"Dorn will be so happy you're here. And so will Roberta." With another smile, she glanced back over her shoulder. "Here she comes. Well . . . I'll leave you two in her capable hands. It is her soirée."

"Very nice to meet you." I inclined my head.

So did Marco. He barely had recovered when the other tall woman reached us. She was wearing a black and red dress that was sheathlike, but not quite that clinging.

"Professor Cornett, I'm Roberta Clayton." She was tall, like her mother, but with jet-black hair and broader shoulders. Her eyes and smile were warm, but with the kind of warmth I associated with politicians, like Dr. Hinckle, the university president. "I'm so glad that you're here."

She offered another smile, this one confidential. "Father said that you'd be doing some Golden Age vocals, as well as the more classical pieces. Is there any chance that you will be singing 'My Funny Valentine'? It's Father's favorite."

"Actually, there is." I was singing it. It had been on the request sheet. I hadn't been about to ignore that.

"Good." She smiled a third smile. "Let me show you to the piano and the Crystal Room." She turned and led us along a marble-walled corridor to a green-carpeted ramp that circled downward.

The Crystal Room was the huge expanse under the rose crystal dome. It was part solarium, part garden, and partly an indoor formal courtyard. There were small tables set in an arc around a fountain. In front of the fountain, a three-meter-high white-bronze sculpture of a unicorn bowing his head to a maiden, there was a dais raised about five decimeters above the polished rose marble of the courtyard. On the dais was a three-meter concert Steinway, shimmering black, and seemingly untouched.

"It was tuned this afternoon," Roberta said.

Marco nodded acknowledgment.

"If you don't mind, I'll leave you two to do what you need to do. After you're ready, please feel free to eat or have something to drink. Everyone will eat as they please." Roberta gestured toward a long buffet table, covered with pale rose linen.

"Generally, I don't eat until after I sing," I explained.

"That's fine, too." With a last flashing smile, she was gone.

Marco just stared for a moment.

I smiled. Roberta Clayton had put on quite a performance, and the soirée hadn't even begun.

"It looks almost new," murmured Marco as he stepped up to the Steinway. "I hope it's not too stiff." He sat at the piano and ran his fingers across the keys. "Good sound. Not too stiff." He looked up. "Could we do just a bit of the Schubert? And then the second Poulenc piece?"

I stepped up on the dais.

We practiced for only about ten minutes. I had a hefty amount to sing later.

Marco and I got something to drink from one of the bars set

up around the Crystal Room. Actually, I had plain soda. He had a red wine of some sort. I wouldn't have anything until after I sang. The Claytons had four real bars with real bartenders and real fermented liquors and wines, not imitation formulated alkie. The bottles at each bar cost more than I made in a year, perhaps two, or even three. Even though I sang at soirées five to ten times a year, I still felt slightly out of place. It was sobering to sip a glass of wine, good as it was, that cost more than I made in a full day of teaching. So I didn't, until after I sang.

I laughed at myself. I enjoyed good wine as much as anyone. I only had the sobering thoughts after I left the ball, without either glass slipper, and returned to my more than modest conapt.

So Marco and I sat and talked. We didn't talk about music, but about everything from the way the ebol4 epidemic had come and started to go in less than two weeks to why Dr. Hinckle was close to useless as a university president, at least from the viewpoint of the faculty. Or the adjunct faculty, since both of us were mere adjuncts. As we talked, more and more elegantly clad couples slipped down the ramp and into the room. Marco slipped away to the Steinway and began to play.

Even though there were more than a hundred people there by six forty-five, not one had joined us. I wondered, not for the first time at a soirée, if I wore an invisible sign that proclaimed: "Hired Singer."

I was to do what amounted to two sets. I would begin with a series of art songs. Then I was to take a half-hour break before doing the Golden Age vocals. At seven o'clock, Marco nodded in my direction, and I walked to the dais and the piano.

After beginning with the easier Moore songs, I did a series of short Wolf pieces, followed by the Poulenc, and then by Schubert's "Gretchen an spinnrade." Along the way, I got some applause, and surprisingly, relative quiet. Then I did the Schumann "Frauen liebe und Leben," before finishing up the first half with the Evans piece, "Lives of Quiet Desperation."

I don't do many modern art songs for one reason. There aren't many. I had to search to find even the Evans piece.

We got more applause. I hoped it wasn't from relief. Marco announced that he would be playing for half an hour, and that I would be back singing Golden Age popular vocals right after that.

I slipped back to the table in the corner, stopping by the nearest bar to get more plain soda, before reseating myself.

A tall man approached and inclined his head. "Professor Cornett, I'm Dorn Clayton, Roberta's father. I won't intrude much, because I know you have more to sing, but I wanted to tell you how much I enjoyed the art song."

"Thank you." I meant it. Usually, I got polite thanks, and words about how important culture was.

"That was beautiful, especially the Schumann. I've always felt that Schumann was as great a composer as Mozart or Beethoven, but because symphonies are more popular, the art song composers are denigrated."

I wasn't certain I'd go that far. So I answered, "I love his songs."

He laughed. "Perhaps I overstated my case." He smiled. "I did prevail upon Roberta, and I'm very glad that I did."

"She is lovely."

"Very lovely, very bright, and hasn't the faintest idea of what is truly beautiful music. Like most of her generation."

What do you say to that? "She agreed to your choice. She must respect it."

He laughed, self-deprecatingly. "That was her concession to me. She's very astute, and very good at reading people."

"She does seem very capable."

"Oh, she is. But, I must go and not tire you." He paused. "Also, given recent events, I also liked the Evans piece." He smiled and quoted:

"Most lead lives of quiet desperation,
so vainly seeking divine inspiration,
ignoring the smile of a child just kissed,

the scent of roses after gentle mist,
the robin's song across a morning lawn,
following the soft-blazing orange of dawn . . ."

"There isn't much modern art song," I said.

"There isn't much modern art, Professor." He inclined his head. "I do look forward to hearing your second set."

As I sipped the soda, I composed myself, half listening to Marco play. I wondered at the difference between father and daughter. Before I knew it, Marco had nodded at me, and I was walking back to the dais.

I led off with a humorous number, one lampooning, in a way, classical song, something called "Art Is Calling to Me." That got both laughs and applause. Then came a series that led off with "What Good Would the Moon Be?" from a Weill drama, then "The Twelfth of Never" and "We Kiss in Shadow."

Midway through, I did Dorn Clayton's supposed favorite—"My Funny Valentine." At the end, I launched into one of the old musical numbers—"Climb Ev'ry Mountain"—which took a little effort, and then "Send in the Clowns."

I finished with a rousing old spiritual, "Ride on, King Jesus."

As I'd expected, there was much more applause for the Golden Age vocals than for the art songs.

"I'm starved," Marco announced.

"Then let's eat." As I headed toward the buffet table, we eased past a younger group. My ears are too keen, sometimes.

"No kick to the music."

"It's one track. All the old stuff is."

"Rezrap has more juice. Even rezpop does."

I kept walking, although I would have liked to say something. Hired help knows its place, but I was seething. I piled more food than I should have on my plate.

As I turned away from the table, a man spoke.

"You're Professor Cornett? I expected . . . someone different."

He was older, that I could tell from his eyes, but tall, with a warm smile and white-blond hair. He had the build of someone who worked out because he had to, not because he enjoyed it. I felt I should recognize him from somewhere.

"I teach at the university, but I'm only adjunct. The title of professor is a courtesy."

"I think I've heard you sing before," he added, "but I couldn't say where."

"I've sung a few recitals there."

"I fear I've missed those."

"What do you do?" I didn't want to ask his name. Since he seemed to think I should know, I wasn't about to prove my ignorance.

"I'm in politics." He smiled, as if amused. It was a rueful smile, and clearly not a condescending one.

"You look more like a distinguished historian." I didn't know exactly what to say. I didn't want to ask another question that would reveal I knew next to nothing about politicians. He was probably very important, or he wouldn't have been at the Claytons' soirée.

"I find that amusing. Historians are even less objective and more self-serving than politicians, and we're not known for being either objective or altruistic."

He was a politician. He'd say that. Just like Dean Donald or Dr. Hinckle would offer amusing self-deprecation, just before they capitulated and repudiated another aspect of thought and beauty.

"We do have a few virtues. For example, if we don't listen to our constituents we don't stay in office. How many people do you know who really listen?"

"Not many," I had to admit. "But just because that's what people want doesn't make it right."

"The Burke argument." He nodded.

I hadn't the faintest idea what he meant. I wasn't sure I cared.

"Edmund Burke—eighteenth-century Irish politician and political theorist. He argued that a politician owed his constituents his best judgment, not necessarily slavish adherence to the will of the people."

"You'd put your judgment first?"

"Not necessarily. I do listen and then decide."

I must have looked skeptical.

"All right, Professor." He smiled again. "I'm listening. Tell me what you think I should do." He held up a hand. "But make it something I can actually do, and tell me why it's a good idea."

He was probably right about insisting that whatever brilliant idea I had should actually be able to be done. I had to think, and I'm never good at thinking when I'm put on a spot, particularly when it's by someone powerful that I don't know.

"Support beauty in the arts," I finally said.

"How would you have me do that? And why?"

I hated being put on the defensive in situations like that. "Because . . . because beauty, it's not the same thing as being popular." I felt like my tongue was tied.

He waited, still looking at me. That embarrassed me, too.

"Art song, what I was singing, that has a beauty. In any time. Even most of the best Golden Age vocals do, but they don't pay much now. I do rezads. I have to, to make a living, I mean." I swallowed, wondering why I was bothering. He'd pretend to listen, and then do what everyone else wanted. But I'd never have another chance. Certainly, no one at the university even pretended to listen. So I plunged on. "When society, government, business . . . when they just give people what they want, it's not art. It's not beauty. It's like the ancient Romans and their bread and circuses. And things get worse, not better. There's more violence . . . isn't that what happened with the first Collapse?" I looked at him.

"Go on . . ."

"I once had a professor who said that you can't improve people or society by pandering to them. You have to challenge them, and give them examples of good singing, and good art, and excellence."

"What if people don't want that?"

"Most people . . . even me . . . we're afraid of the unfamiliar. The good and the truly beautiful in music . . . if people don't get to hear them in school and when they're young, then they'll never change. At the university, they're cutting another course in music appreciation. That's because it's not popular, and the politicians and the bureaucrats listen to the votes. People think music's not relevant. But it ought to be required." With all the effort of singing, my hair had drifted across my forehead. I flipped it back.

"Isn't that dictatorship?" he asked with a quizzical smile.

"We require students to be able to read, to understand economics, to learn about history. Music has been a part of every culture since the Neandertals. Shouldn't they be required to be exposed to something that's been a big part of human history since even before people could write? Shouldn't that be part of higher education? Excellence in the arts is a big part of what makes a society great. Can you name a culture that was great that didn't have great art?"

"Isn't greatness a subjective judgment?"

I could catch the hint of condescension in his voice. I hate people who condescend to me. "That's always what people say when they don't like something. You're in politics. I'm not. Wouldn't you say you know more about politics than I do?"

"I'd hope so," he said with a laugh.

"So why does every politician and every administrator question our judgment as artists and scholars? Why can a businessman or an economist use their knowledge and be respected, but why does every parent and every politician and administrator seem to think they know more about our field than we do?" I was steaming, and I could feel my voice rising and getting harder. I tried to calm down.

"That's a good question. You've obviously thought about it. Why do you think so?"

I ignored the condescension. "Because everyone with any education at all thinks that they can sing or write. When the arts keep getting degraded by politicians who pander to the ignorant, and when the only question is how much money a performer makes, and not how good they are, then the arts suffer. When the arts suffer, we all suffer, because credits are used as the only measure of excellence. Credits don't measure excellence. They only measure popularity, and they're not the same thing." I had to take a deep breath. I was almost panting.

"You offer a good argument as to why I should do something." He gave me that condescending smile again. "What do you suggest?"

"You're the politician. How about something that gives more funds, or grants, to programs in music, with an emphasis on excellence in performing? Maybe a grant program for artists performing the great works of the past. And for seminars that explain that greatness."

"The past? Why not the present?"

"No one's writing great music today. There's no money in it. You have to start with the past. You start with what's written now, and you reinforce mediocrity."

"I can see that you're passionate about your music."

Passionate . . . and stupid. There wasn't any future in being passionate. Dean Donald had made that clear. It was clear once more from the reactions of the tall politician.

"I did listen. And I will promise to think about it." He offered another smile, somehow different. "You do have beautiful eyes, Professor." Then he inclined his head, not quite a bow, and turned away.

"Lots of people would have paid millions of credits to spend that much time with Senator Cannon," Marco said, easing back up beside me.

"That was Senator Cannon? *The* Senator Cannon?" Somehow, I'd never quite connected the man who had just talked to me with the net images of Senator Cannon. Maybe that was because I'd thought of senators as aloof and unapproachable.

"Everyone was watching you, and listening," Marco said. "I wish I had your nerve."

"My stupidity, you mean." There were so many things I could

have said. I could have been far more reasonable, more rational. I could have cited figures, facts, the success that students who knew music had . . . and it had all gone out the window with my stupid passion.

And if he found out that I'd been singing his rezads? Would I lose those, too?

I swallowed. They were probably mostly done, and I'd been paid. But I could have used more creds. I'd contracted with the Brazelton people to have the scanners fixed, and ordered a new formulator, and those two purchases would be putting a big hole in my account.

One of the younger men—with the fixed smile on his face that indicated he was probably on soop—brushed past me on his way out.

I couldn't help but overhear what he said to the woman with him, since he clearly meant me to overhear. "Classical stuff, should have been buried with the composers . . ."

I wished he'd been buried before he'd been born.

Then I looked down at the plate heaped with delicacies. I didn't have any appetite.

I put on a fixed smile as I saw Roberta Clayton approaching.

Chapter 29
Cannon

I was tired Friday morning when I got to my office at the Legislature. That might have been because I got there by seven and because I'd stayed longer at the Claytons' than I'd planned, but Dorn had always been a strong supporter, and you don't keep supporters by ducking out of their functions early, especially not when they insist on talking to you. With Dewey's death, and Heber Smith masterminding Alredd's campaign, and probably

Hansen's, I was going to need every supporter that I could dig up—and every angle I could turn to my advantage.

Rather than look over what Ted had waiting for me, I called up a holo display of the news. NorNews. I liked the tones of the NorNet, even if it had the lowest ratings on the NorAm net. Michael Rasmussen was on the Capital News segment.

"D'Amico has introduced his bill which will restrict the use of rezads to certain periods and certain segments of the broadcast spectrum . . . applauded by the FamilyNow! lobby . . . bill described as a charade by Jared Kirtley, speaking for the NorAm ComFed . . .

"Although the number of fatalities in NorAm from ebol4 is less than originally predicted, the disease remains a threat, particularly for children and those with circulatory problems . . . continues to spread worldwide . . .

"The Agkhanate has repeated its denial that any member of the Talibanate was involved in the nuclear attack on the Russe shuttle Perun . . .

"Halvor Freeman, President of the Martian Republic, suggested that if the guilty were not found and punished, the Republic would have to consider some form of economic sanctions against all Earth, and not just the Agkhanate . . ."

All I needed with the campaign coming up was higher prices and shortages. CerraCraft depended heavily on such imports. How Kemal had managed getting his hands on the company, I still didn't know. I shook my head, but my concern there wasn't Kemal directly, but all the voters who worked there. When all was said and done, credits didn't vote, people did. Too many politicians forgot that. I wasn't about to.

After hearing the news summary, I leaned back in the big black leather chair behind the desk. The singer from Clayton's soirée had intrigued me, puzzled me as well. I laughed to myself. I'd seen the look on her face when her accompanist had told her who I was. Still . . . her words had been unguarded, and worth more than most of what people told me.

What if she were right? I frowned. Surely, we could work out a small program. The FamilyNow! lobby would like something that was traditional and non-rezbased. Educators always liked targeted programs, and I could use some support from the educators. At the very least, it would mute criticism from the leftists, and confuse Hansen totally.

Ted?

Yes, sir?

Have a little assignment for you. See what you can find on funding for classical music studies and performance demonstrations and lectures at the university level. Also, I'd like you to think about how we could set up a small grant program to encourage it. It's the basis of all popular music, even rez stuff, and if we don't preserve some studies of it . . . valuable heritage, you know, that sort of thing . . .

Sir . . . how did you want to approach that? A stand-alone bill . . . ?

No . . . it's not that big an initiative. I was thinking twenty to fifty million a year for the program . . . very limited, no more than twenty programs across all NorAm, and a pilot program here at UDenv, not at Southern. That would be too obvious, but make sure Southern gets into the later list of twenty. We could just add that into the higher ed bill.

Ah . . . I see, sir.

I could tell he didn't. *Ted . . . this is a little winner. Everyone's complaining about the dangerous effect of rezrap and rezpop. We can claim an initiative for pure auditory music and for heritage restoration, and family values. We start it, and have it ready . . . who will oppose it?*

This time I could sense the smile. *I wouldn't have thought of it that way.*

Maybe you could even work something in about how sometimes the small programs are the important ones, that the small things in life are so often lost beside the big issues . . . but the small programs are often what shape people's lives . . .

Yes, sir. You'll want this by Monday, then?

Right.

I was smiling as I leaned back in the chair. The professor would be astounded, especially once I found a way to put her in charge of the pilot program. She'd find that honesty paid, if inadvertently.

She had been beautiful, too, in an intense and yet subdued and passionate way. I could dream, but that was about all.

I snorted, got up, and walked to the window.

Les Kerras for you, Senator.

I'll take it.

I needed to watch Les. So I sat back down at the desk and let him come across on the holo projection.

"Senator. How are you this morning?" Les looked as polished in the holo display as he did on the netcasts, with his slightly wavy brown hair and the boyish smile.

"Just fine." I had a little time, and decided to see what he had in mind, and force him to bring it up.

"Do you know Roberto Tazzi?"

Tazzi had been one of my larger supporters, almost as much as Dorn Clayton. "I'm familiar with him. Why?"

"I thought you'd like to know. His son was killed last night. One of those mysterious drug overdoses. You know, the ones where the DPS hasn't been able to discover any cause, except that the symptoms are OD heart failure?"

"That's terrible." I paused, reflecting a moment. "That's always hard on parents. It's hard on the whole family when something like that happens to a bright young person."

"I understand you might have seen him last night, that you were at a soirée . . ."

"Actually, I did. I'd rather not have my personal life in the nets, Les, but I did talk to him briefly. He mentioned something about wanting to work in politics. He wanted to talk about it there, but it was a social occasion, and I told him to make an appointment here at the office, and that I'd be happy to talk to him." That was almost exactly what I'd said. The young fool had been on soop, and I hadn't been about to discuss something like that in public, especially under those conditions, where anyone could hear, and I didn't want to offend Roberto.

Les nodded. "I can understand that, especially with a rough campaign coming up."

"All campaigns have their challenges, Les. You know that."

"The rumor is that Hansen will be mounting a very aggressive campaign."

"He's a very capable opponent." I smiled, then asked, "Let me ask you a question, Les." I paused, then went on, "Have you heard anything recently about Chris Kemal?" I watched closely.

Kerras frowned, but it had taken him just a moment too long. He knew *something*.

"There are always rumors," he finally admitted.

"I understand. Well . . . we might have some interesting news next week, Les."

"Let me think about that, Senator. If I can come up with something . . ."

"That's fine. Just keep in touch. And . . . thank you for the news about the Tazzi boy. I appreciate that."

"You're welcome."

After I collapsed the holo display, I pulled out the left-hand drawer that held the personal stationery, not the office stationery, but the formal cards with just my name on them, and slowly and carefully wrote out a message of condolence to Roberto and Clarice, using the old-style fountain pen. Almost no one even knew how to write by hand anymore. There were times like this when that anachronistic touch was vital, because it showed more than special care.

I sealed the envelope and wrote their names on the outside, then got up and walked out to the main office.

Ciella, I've got a message that needs a hand courier. Charge it to my personal account, not the office account, I'm bringing it out.

Yes, sir.

When I reached her console, Ciella looked up with that smile. It might have been professional, but I still enjoyed it.

"This is a letter of condolence to Roberto and Clarice Tazzi. Their address is in the file. Their son was killed last night. If you'd make sure this is hand-delivered today?"

"Yes, Senator."

I smiled the paternal smile, then let it slip into an expression of concern. "Thank you."

Little things mean a lot, particularly at times when people are suffering.

Back in my office, I stood by the window, looking westward.

There still hadn't been much feedback on Kemal and Alredd, and that was anything but good. Before long, Alredd would have ads out indirectly attacking me. Two weeks to a month after that Hansen would jump in.

Best that we really pump up the positive rezads over the next week, even though they'd only really begun hitting the nets. The music education bit would help, but that one would have to wait until it was done. That way, it wouldn't be a vain promise, but something I'd already done. That would take Hansen down a bit. Later on, we could hit him with charges that he promised, but I listened, and I delivered.

My smile faded as I thought about Dewey—and Kemal. Dewey'd had his election won, and if Eric were right, Kemal had set someone up to kill him. We really needed to stop Kemal—somehow.

Alicia's research had supplied basic volumes on the space in-dustries. Eric had been right, in that many had been heavily traded. Over the past two years, the equivalent of close to seventy percent of MMSystems had been traded, often in large lots, but not any over one percent. There was no way I had, not without going for a committee warrant or a subpoena, to discover the buyers. Going for either required more evidence than I had.

I wondered if Les Kerras would come up with anything that might help. He knew practically everyone and everything in Denv. Or . . . if I could come up with something, and let Les run with it—that would be even better. That way, we could keep running positive ads and let Les show the connection with Hansen. Then, the nets could keep uncovering things day by day, week by week, that would unveil Hansen's ties to Kemal, perhaps tie him to the unsavory business with McCall and Alredd.

I nodded.

Chapter 30
Chiang

Thursday hadn't been a total waste. Hadn't been as productive as Wednesday. I'd spent some time going over the reports on Dewey's death. My hunches had been right. Someone had tampered with the safety screens on that section of the bridge. Recsat records showed a GSY maintenance vehicle there. Only problem was that GSY could account for all of its repair lorries. None of them had been there. The "repairman" had worn a GSY singlesuit, but the investigation had cleared all of the GSY techs. Recsat records didn't show the face. Repairman had been average size. Nothing special.

All of Brazelton's techs had been checked. All had absolutely airtight alibis. Couldn't have been tighter if they'd been planned. Brazelton himself had been playing the ancient game of golf with—guess who—Chris Kemal. Just the two of them.

Again, highly suggestive. But they were on record on the club's systems, and had been seen by several people. Even the recsat confirmed that they both played all eighteen holes. No way to prove anything, exactly. No way to link the McCall and Dewey deaths, either. Except for nanite system expertise. The Justiciary wasn't exactly fond of circumstantial cases.

No word from CDC on my rezsong suppositions, either.

Talked briefly to Caron Hildeo. She knew nothing, said a great deal of less than nothing, and was extraordinarily pleasant. She had a very plush office at O'Bannon and Reyes, and it wasn't holo-simmie counterfeit, either.

Kugeler didn't call. Nor did Parsfal, and nothing appeared on PrimeNews. Thankful for that. That was how Thursday ended.

Hoped Friday would be better when I hurried in at zero seven-thirty.

"Captain linked. On those ODs," Sarao offered. "It's going to be one of those days."

"Oh?"

"Ernesto Tazzi."

"Son of Roberto Tazzi? The formulator filch?"

"Stet. Was at one of those filch affairs—soirée. You know the kind, with every filch finger food costing more than a hundred creds a gram. Formal dress, very formal. They had an old-style singer with an acoustic piano and an accompanist. Young Tazzi walked out. He got in his electral and went out to the Moulin Noir. Stayed two hours, and left. Made it a good klick before he went down, piled the electral into a tree on the side of the Bryant Guideway."

Sarao had been right. One of those days. Checked my link messages.

When you get in, Chiang, come see me. It's about the ODs. The strange ones.

I took a moment to dig through Resheed's report. The odd-type ODs were up. If Parsfal was right, that figured. More new rezrap shows and larger crowds at the end of the week.

Rezrap? McCall had taken out all the rezrap equipment no more than a year before. Rezrap also increased alkie sales. Who benefited from higher alkie sales?

Sarao?

Yes, Lieutenant?

Have to go see the captain. Like you to see what you can find on something. First, who makes the alkie formulators used in clubs, theaters, places like the Red Moon and Moulin Noir? Second, does the manufacturer get a percentage of sales? Third, who owns the Red Moon and Moulin Noir?

Got it. This have to do with the OD stuff?

Don't know. That was the safest answer.

Had another thought, and linked back. *Also, can you find out if Nanette Iveson or Evan McCall knew the family of a suicide named Erneld Cewrigh? He's in the suicide file that has Al Elcado in it.*

Then I hurried out and up the ramp to the captain's office. She was waiting.

She closed the door and waited for me to sit.

"Sarao told you about Ernesto Tazzi. His father wants an answer. He wants to know why we haven't done anything. I told him that the techs couldn't find any substances but soop in his son's system. He said we'd better, and that it was a disgrace that DPS couldn't get to the bottom of this. You'd mentioned that you had an angle."

Wished I hadn't. But I told her.

She didn't laugh. "It's just crazy enough to be true. How soon do you think you'll hear from CDC?"

"We got an acknowledgment. That's all. Might take weeks for those kinds of tests. Or longer. If they even do them."

The captain snorted. "I'll get the acting coordinator to lean on them. It can't hurt."

We both knew it might not help, either.

"In the meantime, you get to contact some of the possible witnesses at this soirée. Tazzi gave me a list." She extended a copy.

"He ODed two hours later."

Cannizaro nodded. "Politics. That's why you call. I already talked to the Claytons and their daughter."

Politics I didn't need. Neither did Cannizaro. But I'd go through the motions.

"By the way, I got a call from Hans Kugeler. You impressed

him." Cannizaro looked at me. "What did you say? He doesn't impress easily."

"Told him there were three possibilities as to how the McCalls died—accident and suicide, coincidence, or murder. Said that there were problems with each, and that I'd look into all three carefully."

"Did you have to offer murder?"

I looked at the captain, harder than she'd looked at me. "It was murder. Somehow Chris Kemal used Brazelton to kill both McCall and Dewey. Nanette Iveson's death was an attempt to frame McCall. When that didn't work, they killed him." I went on to explain almost everything, including the inside ramp, and the override codes. I didn't mention the linkbugs that hadn't been there, although I was sure that they had been and that Kemal had been monitoring the McCalls.

When I was done, I waited.

"Who have you told this to?"

"No one but you." I held up a hand. "I'm not the only one. At least two newsies know. They came to me. Asked them to hold off."

"And they did?" Cannizaro raised her eyebrows.

"So far. Been three days."

"What did you offer?"

"First look at whatever we make public."

She winced.

"What do you want me to do, Captain? No deal, and we have the nets claiming we're covering up a murder."

"What will you report?"

She didn't ask me to go one way or another.

"Unless things change, we either get enough evidence to indict someone, or we report that there's evidence it was murder, but not enough to link it to any suspect."

"Do you want to announce murder yet?"

"I'd wait. At least till next week. We've already fouled up twice. Then we announce we have done a detailed review, and that we've discovered evidence of a very subtle and sophisticated plot, designed to mislead everyone. We claim delay and distraction because of the death of certain possible key witnesses, such as Marc Oler."

"Can you pin anyone by next week?"

Had to be honest. "Probably not. Maybe never. We've got hard evidence that someone tampered with the systems, and that they were experts. We've got hard evidence that someone wiped all prints all the way down to mini-microscopic levels. Again, experts. Beyond that, it's all circumstantial. Don't even have hard evidence of motive. Might be able to find that."

"We'll meet Monday morning. If this breaks in the nets before that, I'll announce that we're winding up the investigation, and you'll brief the nets Monday afternoon. You can give your newsies an hour."

"It'll keep."

"It might."

That was as close as Cannizaro was going to get to admitting I was right.

So I went back down to my office. Took the hard-copy list of names that the older Tazzi had given Cannizaro. Just wanted to get through the list so that I could say we'd covered those possibilities. Hated the idea of talking to young filch snots.

Made seven calls before something came up. From one of the snots. Male, self-important.

"The singer. That professor. Ernesto hated what she sang. He wanted to talk to Senator Cannon about a job on his staff, but the senator was talking to the professor. They talked a long time, and then the senator left. He looked real thoughtful. She—the singer—she was upset. Had a whole plateful of stuff. She didn't eat any of it, just set it down and hurried out with her piano guy right after that. Ernesto left right before that."

"Did you hear what they were talking about?"

"Not really. She was gesturing and talking fast. He smiled most of the time. The kind of smile you wear when you don't want to upset someone."

The snot didn't have much else to add. After I broke the link, I wondered.

The singer? Didn't sound like she had anything to do with Ernesto. He'd gone to the Moulin Noir for rezrap. But a professor talking to Cannon? Both of them upset? I probably couldn't reach Cannon. I could reach her. She was on the list Cannizaro had given me. Probably ought to talk to her because Tazzi would find out sooner or later, and the filch always cast around for the hired help to blame. Ought to know what her story was, in any case.

Also interested to talk to someone who'd argue with Cannon enough to make him think. Unusual for a soirée where no one remembered anything. Except the older people liked half of what she sang. The younger ones didn't like anything.

I put in a call to her. Wasn't at the university. Tried home. Got a simmie there as well. Left a message. "This is Lieutenant Eugene Chiang of the DPS. I have a few questions about the soirée where you sang last night. Thank you."

Linked to Sarao. *Did you find out about the alkie stuff and the formulators?*

Yes, Lieutenant. In your inlink. Also, FlameTop was performing last night at the Moulin Noir. I haven't found out about the Iveson/McCall-Cewrigh connection—if there was one.

Stet.

I checked through what she'd found. The alkie formulators were manufactured by an outfit in Cedacy, Deseret District— CerraCraft. CerraCraft was a wholly owned subsidiary of CK Constructors. Had been for about three years. More interestingly, CerraCraft had run most of its competition out of business in the last two years, by offering a cheap lease arrangement and percentage of alkie sales. The Red Moon and Moulin Noir were both privately owned. No information available. Had my suspicions, but they'd stay suspicions.

Lieutenant, there's a professor on the incoming. Doesn't look like a professor.

I'll take it. "Eugene Chiang, DPS."

Sarao was right. Holo image showed a slender redhead, silver eyes, slight Mediterranean darkness to the skin. Wore a green suit with matching trousers, and modest silver jewelry. Looked more filch than most filch. "This is Luara Cornett. You left messages for me here at the university."

"Yes, Professor. Last night you were at a function at the Clayton home?"

"I wasn't there as a guest, Lieutenant. I was hired to sing. What would you like to know?" Her voice was melodic, polite, wary.

"You may have heard in the news. About ODs of a mysterious nature. Young man who was at the function died later that night. Looks to be the same."

She frowned. "Outside of my accompanist, and the Claytons, I didn't know anyone there. I usually don't. They don't talk to the hired help, except to give directions or request that I sing a particular song."

"Have you heard the name Ernesto Tazzi?"

"No." She shook her head.

I keyed in an image of young Tazzi. "Here's what he looked like."

She studied the image for a moment, then nodded. "I did see him. He didn't like what I sang, and left early, even before we did."

"How did you know he didn't like what you sang?"

"Most of the younger set don't like either classical vocal or Golden Age vocal, but he made a point of walking by me as he left and making a sneering remark to the woman with him about how the music of classical composers should have been buried with them."

"Didn't that make you angry?"

She laughed. Rueful and sad. "I teach here at UDenv. Sometimes it upsets me, but most of the younger ones are like that. You can't let it get to you. At least some of their parents have taste."

Liked the professor. Couldn't say why. But wanted to know

more. Especially about Cannon. "You said you didn't know anyone at the party. But one of the people there said you had a long
conversation with Senator Cannon."

She flushed. "I'll never live that down. He took me off guard.
I didn't know who he was, and he made some comment about
politicians being more honest than historians. Then, he was condescending to me, and I told him that . . . well . . . let's say I got
very passionate about art and music and suggested it ought to be
taught in greater depth because no culture ever lasted long without great art. He wanted to know what a politician could really
do, and I told him. I didn't even know who he was until after
he left, and my accompanist told me." She shook her head. "I
get passionate about music, but I'm not very good when I'm
caught off guard. That was what the conversation was about.
After that, I was so upset that I couldn't even eat, and I made
Marco take me home."

"That upset you that much?"

"Lieutenant, I was hired help. I probably insulted one of the
most powerful senators in NorAm, and if he spreads it around,
I won't get hired for more soirées. Those gigs are probably a
quarter of my income. Wouldn't you be upset at yourself?"

"I thought you were a professor."

"I'm adjunct faculty here. I carry about three-quarters of a
normal load. I get paid less than half what a full-time contract
junior professor does. I take whatever outside singing jobs that I
can. Except performing live rez stuff."

Interesting, and all probably true. Didn't do much for what I
needed. "One last question. Do you recall anything about young
Tazzi? The man who wanted to bury classical music? Anything
at all?"

Another frown, and a long pause. "He had that fixed smile,
you know, the one so many of them get when they're dosed on
soop. I can't think of anything else."

Tried several more questions, but she couldn't offer more. Almost hated to break the connection.

That was a professor? Sarao inlinked.

Professor and classical singer.

My son gets someone like that when he gets to college and I think I'd worry.

Seemed like a nice lady.

You could use a nice lady, Lieutenant.

Nice, but not my type.

Learned that lesson a long time ago.

Sat at my desk, looking out on a gray noon. More confirmations of suspicions, but no new and hard evidence. Wondered if that was the way both the McCall case and the ODs would end up. Holo dramas—half of them ended when the villain was discovered. Too many didn't follow through on how hard it was to prove what you knew.

Had to find more proof . . . somehow. Some way.

Chapter 31
Parsfal

By late Friday morning, I still hadn't heard anything from Chiang, and I really couldn't go back to Kerras, not until I had something firm. I was working on a "success" story, a piece Brianne was putting together on how a GIL counterfeiting operation had been shut down by the combined efforts of the netops division of DPS and the medical researchers at CMS. It had gotten nasty, with close to thirty people disabled or locked away while the TID larceny took place. Some of the victims would never be the same.

After that, I was supposed to develop some more backstory stuff on a couple of pending appropriations bills that would come up the next week.

Parsfal?

I hated it, but I couldn't help wincing whenever Bimstein blasted a link at me.

I'm here.

Rehm's off today, and besides, you did the stats on the mysterious ODs, right?

I also gave you a background source piece. It didn't hurt to remind the man of what I'd done. No one else would—that was for certain.

Even better. Last night Ernesto Tazzi died in an electral crash. You know who he was? Someone to do with the formulator family?

That's right. Son of Roberto Tazzi. He wasn't killed by the crash, but by one of those ODs. Got a copy of the report. Don't ask me how, but I'm sending it to you. Also, some names who were at the soirée he attended earlier in the evening, and the names of the people he was with when he was at the Moulin Noir. See what you can find in the next hour or so.

You want me to put aside the GIL story?

Of course, good news can always wait.

He was right. The good news gave watchers the warm fuzzies and made them feel good about PrimeNews, but that wasn't why they watched.

I scanned what Bimstein sent. Ernesto Tazzi had probably been killed by a rez-induced OD. There was only one problem with that. We couldn't report it because we couldn't prove it. We couldn't even speculate on it without some scientific evidence. All we had were Chiang's observations, which I couldn't quote, and my conclusions.

I went back to the incoming files and pulled up Bimstein's list. I scanned it. One of the attendees was Senator Elden Cannon. There was a note on that. "Don't contact Cannon on this. Don't mention him."

That was odd, too. If Bimstein hadn't wanted me to contact the senator, all he would have had to do was leave his name off. I laughed to myself. I wasn't thinking. If I contacted the others, someone might well mention Cannon, and then I could have contacted him. He probably wouldn't have returned my call, but that was another question. Was it just that Cannon didn't want to be linked to a ritzy filch soirée? Imagine that—the man of the people, not wanting to be linked to the elite. That also meant that Cannon had contacted Kerras, or the other way around, because Cannon never talked to Bimstein. All of NetPrime knew that story.

I started trying to call names on the list, beginning with the Claytons. I got simmies for the first ten, and left messages. Not a single person broke through the simmie to talk to me. Number eleven was Elfreda Jensen. She actually answered. With the swirled hair that was as stiff as synthstone, she had to have been one of Roberta Clayton's contemporaries.

"I'm Jude Parsfal . . ." I got through the entire introduction and as far as asking about young Tazzi.

"You really don't care about him. You just want a story. There isn't one. He never did any drugs, except a touch of soop. Now, you all want to find something that's not there. It's disgusting."

With that, I was facing a blank holo projection.

I slogged through twenty names, and that was the best that I got.

Finally, I looked at the two names at the bottom, the two names that weren't guests. One was Marco DiMicelli, listed as accompanist, and the other was a Professor Luara Cornett, classical singer. I ran a quick net search on her. She was listed as adjunct faculty, voice and music appreciation, at UDenv. There was a databloc of art song listed as having been released several years earlier, and there was a very short publications list, with several articles. One was on Hugo Wolf, another on Francis Poulenc. I'd never heard of either, but I didn't pretend to know much about music, especially older or classical music, except that I liked what I'd heard, and I did have a modest collection of instrumental works, most of which were pieces composed centuries earlier.

The net search didn't show much else about her, except for older announcements of two art song recitals, and one of another recital scheduled for the coming October.

I wondered if she'd have anything new to offer, but those few filch I'd reached hadn't had much to say. In fact, they hadn't said anything. So I tried her link through the university.

"Professor Cornett? Ah . . . this is Jude Parsfal. I'm a researcher with NetPrime, and I'd like to talk with you for a moment." I waited, looking at the static holo display that showed exactly the same picture as the UDenv catalogue.

Then the image was replaced by that of Professor Cornett. These days, there are few ugly people, only the poor, and those from devastated Afrique and ecologically ravaged Russe. When she appeared in midair, even the holo image was striking, and yet, as I looked at her, I couldn't say that there was a single aspect that was unusual. Dark red hair, mahogany, if you will, with gray eyes, a silver gray. Medium height, neither large nor small breasted, with legs that matched. The picture in the UDenv catalogue didn't do her justice, but I wasn't certain any picture would.

Yet, there was something about her.

"Yes?" Her voice was musical, as it somehow should have been.

"As I told you, Professor, I'm Jude Parsfal with NetPrime. I'm a researcher." At her frown, I hurried on. "I'm not a caster with PrimeNews, or a T-head. I'm just trying to find background information. I understand you sang last night at a soirée at Dorn Clayton's."

"Yes." Her voice was wary, but she didn't look at all surprised.

"Someone else has already talked to you about this?"

"No one in the nets." She paused, as if she were going to say more, but she didn't.

"The DPS?"

"Could I ask you what you'd like to know, Mr. Parsfal?" Her voice was polite, controlled, and yet carried a tone of exasperation. She moved her head in a graceful jerk that flipped a strand of that mahogany hair off her forehead.

"I'm sorry. Let me explain. I don't know if you've heard, but there have been a number of ODs recently. Laboratory studies haven't found traces of any drugs that would cause an OD. Last night, a young man who was at the soirée where you sang left, and several hours later died from that OD. Because he was the son of a well-known man, I've been asked to find out what I can about what happened."

A trace of a smile appeared at the corner of her lips. "Thank you. I could play games with you, but I won't. Was the young man Ernesto Tazzi?"

"Yes. Did you know him?"

She shook her head. "I've never met him, but a DPS officer called just a little while ago and talked to me. He showed me a picture, and I did see this Ernesto at the soirée, just as he left, and just before I left."

"Did he look . . . impaired?"

"Beyond the normal for a young man who could have cared less for a vocal concert?" Her tone wasn't quite sarcastic, almost resigned or weary. "He looked like he'd been on soop. He had that smile that they do. He wasn't, as you put it, any more impaired than he probably was most of the time."

I couldn't help feeling attracted to her, but I had a job to do, with at least two others hanging behind this one. "Did you talk to him? Or did he say anything to you?"

"No. I didn't talk to him." She paused again.

"He must have said or done something for you to remember him out of all those people."

She laughed, and it was like another kind of music, because there was, somehow, intelligence and beauty in the sound. "He wasn't exactly complimentary to classical music—or even the Golden Age vocals. He suggested that the works of all classical composers should have been buried with the composer."

"Did he say anything else?"

"If he did, I didn't see or hear anything."

"I assume that there were no drugs there, except for the alkie and whatever soop the younger people had."

She smiled. "I wouldn't call what they had at the bars alkie. Everything was fully fermented or distilled the long way."

"The kind that would take a month of my salary to buy one bottle?" I managed a rueful twist.

She laughed again.

"Was there anything else unusual?" I asked.

"There wasn't anything at all unusual. Unless you count the fact that there were actually a few people there who appreciated classical vocal music."

"I take it you don't care for rezpop or rezrap."

"For listening or entertainment? No. It makes me very uneasy, and to me there's very little truly musical and artistic about it."

I asked more questions, more than I needed, but I liked looking at her and the sound of her voice, but she really couldn't add more.

When I broke the connection, I thought of Shelley's lines about when soft voices die, music vibrates in the memory. I frowned. Why had she made such an impression on me? She hadn't been flirting. She hadn't been doing much of anything except cautiously answering my questions.

Was it the fact that she had been answering, and not avoiding? That she'd actually been helpful? Or something more?

I didn't know, but I had too much more to find out, and I wasn't accomplishing much. Bimstein wouldn't be at all pleased. I needed to try the accompanist. Maybe he'd seen something and would talk.

And then, there was the McCall thing. I still hadn't heard from Chiang, and I hadn't come up with anything more. Not anything we could cast on the net.

Friday was definitely looking very grim and unproductive.

Urgent! Urgent! Family urgent!

The emergency link jolted me awake. I bolted into a sitting position. For a moment, I just sat there.

Urgent!

Query? Who would be calling at three in the morning on Saturday? And why?

Barbra Saul.

Accept. I had a sinking feeling.

The holo image of Barbra appeared at the foot of the bed. It cast a pearly light across the bedroom. She wore a thin white jacket over a green singlesuit. Her hair was disheveled. Her face was blotchy red, and tears oozed down her cheeks. "Chris . . . Chris . . ."

Marissa turned over, mumbling. "Who? This hour . . ."

"Barbra. Something's wrong." I raised my voice. "Barbra, I'm here. What is it? What's the matter?"

"It's Stefan . . . God! It's Stefan . . ."

"What about Stefan?" I asked. "What's wrong?"

Marissa sat up beside me, and we both looked at Barbra's image.

"I didn't want him to get that Tija. I told him it was dangerous . . ." She stopped and sobbed. "He didn't listen . . ."

"What happened?" I asked again. "Was he badly hurt? What can we do?"

"He's dead, Chris . . . he's dead!"

"Where are you? We'll be right there." I looked at Marissa.

Marissa nodded.

"At home," Barbra stuttered. "I had . . . I couldn't tell . . . everything was burned . . . could barely recognize the electral . . ."

"We'll be right there," I repeated, climbing out of the bed.

Barbra just continued to sob. After a minute, she looked up. "I'm not . . . going . . . anywhere." Then the image blanked.

Marissa triggered the lights. "How terrible." She winced and shook her head. "She cared so much for Stefan."

I took a deep breath. "That was the problem. It's terrible, and she'll never forget. But . . . you know I met with him. He barely listened to me. He didn't listen to his mother. Now . . . everyone's hurt. His mother, his sister . . . any girlfriend he was close to."

"You can't say that to her, dear." Marissa started for her bathroom.

"I know. That's why I said it to you. All we can do is be there." I shook my head. "That won't be enough. It never is."

"You were worried about Stefan, weren't you?" she asked.

"I was. He didn't really seem to understand how the world works. He almost humored me when I was working to restructure that loan he took. As if it happened to be my duty to provide him credits without limit and without work."

"Barbra said you had spent some time with him last week."

"We talked. We even talked about his electral, and I warned him that they could roll if he drove it too fast and tried to corner it too tightly. He said I was just like his mother. I wonder if that's what happened. Barbra didn't say."

"It was some sort of accident with the Tija."

I took another deep breath. "We'd better get dressed and going."

Marissa nodded sadly.

It was going to be a long night—and morning.

The weekend and Monday passed, and nothing happened, except the education bill and our music amendment went through. I even got some unsolicited support from the other side of the aisle. I couldn't say I was surprised. They knew a good thing when they saw it.

Outside of that, and the normal routines, nothing happened, and no one told me anything new. Canthrop didn't have the results from the opening rezads of the campaign. Les Kerras hadn't gotten back to me, and none of my inquiries—official and unofficial—seemed to have had any effect in finding out more about how Kemal was trying to become a major force in NorAm business and politics.

Right after the morning Economics and Commerce Committee meeting on Tuesday, I was leaving the dais when a dark-suited man who'd been watching the proceedings stood and stepped forward.

"Senator?"

"Yes?"

"I'd like to talk with you. I have some information."

"I'm always open to information. You can't get enough of it." I smiled. He looked harmless enough, and he couldn't have gotten through the screens in the committee room if he had been carrying a weapon.

"You were looking for this information. About a certain contractor who's moving into major commerce. Is there somewhere we can talk?"

"My office is as safe as anywhere."

"If someone sees me walking in there?"

"They won't," I assured him. "There are back doors to all senators' offices, for obvious reasons."

He nodded, dubiously. "I'll follow you, if you don't mind."

I understood that.

I walked, and he followed. That gave me an eerie feeling. He joined me when I went down the side corridor, and opened one of the lifts to the back hall above.

Once we were in my office, I linked. *Ciella, I'm back. I'll be in conference for a bit. Don't disturb me unless it's urgent.*

Yes, sir.

The unidentified man looked around the office nervously, his green eyes flitting from point to point. He'd been in a senator's office before. He'd probably been in a committee room before that morning as well.

I triggered the privacy screen, and we were surrounded by the misty gray shield.

"You never did say who you are."

"I'd rather not. If you wanted, you could find out, but there's a certain amount of protection this way."

"I can see that. You said you had some information."

"I do. There's MMSystems stock changing hands, just under the reporting minimums, and it's all going to various trust accounts, with irrevocable trusts."

"Irrevocable?" That was definitely strange. "Who's the trustee?"

"KCF Management."

I'd never heard of it. "Who controls it?"

"KCF Management was set up years ago by a fellow by the name of Arturo Kemal. He was in the fabricating and construction business. For years, it was just a private holding company. The company invested in strictly true blue industrial, infotech, and financial issues. It pays its taxes, reports on time, and operates strictly on the level. About two years ago, KCF began to invest more, in the millions, in the hundreds of millions, and those investments were all in what one might call critical industrial and space-formulation industries. Less than six months ago, large blocs of stock in MMSystems appeared in the portfolios. The closeness to reporting levels triggered the NASR alerts, but since no trust was over the threshold, nothing was done. It was unusual to have so many irrevocable trusts with so much capital in the names of the members of one family, but not illegal. Then yesterday, the paperwork came through to change one of the trusts because the young man who was the beneficiary had died over the weekend. What was strange about that was that he'd collateralized the stock in his trust to take out a large loan. The loan was paid off, not by the trust, but by another entity, and the trust reassigned, with all the necessary penalties, to another family member, a young girl who was only two." He smiled. "You can do that. You just can't ever have it revert to the giver."

"If I understand what you're telling me"—I frowned—"these irrevocable trusts hold the majority interest in MMSystems."

"Not quite. They hold something like forty-six percent. Chris Kemal's personal holding company openly has about six percent." He opened his jacket, very carefully, as if to show me that he wasn't pulling a weapon, and extracted several sheets of paper, which he extended. "The details are there."

I took the sheets without looking at them. They were either what he said or they weren't, and looking at them wouldn't change anything. "Why did you decide to tell me now?" I kept my voice pleasant, reassuring.

"Rumor is out that you decided to look into MMSystems. I saw what happened when you looked into XenoLift. The people who tried to hush things up were forced out of NASR."

So . . . he was in NASR, and that meant that someone there was being pressured not to act. That wasn't surprising, but it was hardly reassuring. Sometimes, the privacy laws had become more of a shield for misdeeds than a protection from government or organizational intrusion.

"I'm more interested in what's happening outside the bureau," I said. "But I won't forget. If you need me to look at something, I'll be here."

He stood. "That's all I have."

"Thank you." I escorted him out to the back hall, and he took the lift and vanished.

Then I went back to the office and studied what he had given me. If all the information happened to be correct, then Kemal was violating the spirit of the holdings laws . . . but not necessarily the letter of the law, unless we could dig up proof that he was coercing the various trusts to vote the stock his way. I'd have bet that there hadn't been any coercion in voting. Not yet.

I had proof of my suspicions, but not proof of wrongdoing. The other aspect of the problem was one of public policy. Relations with the Martian Republic were strained enough, and NorAm—or all Earth—didn't need a cowboy gangster taking over MMSystems at such a time. Still, whatever happened, I'd need to make copies of the evidence and make sure they were in places where others could get to them if necessary.

Ciella, I'm done with the conference. Can you set up a call with Mr. Canthrop?

Within minutes, I had Bill on a holo projection. I liked seeing people. It wasn't as good as being there in person, but a lot better than just a voice or a link.

"The first of the rezads hit the nets last week, but it's taken a while to figure out the results. The initial response is good, but it's too early to tell." He paused. "We'd better hope they're good. Alredd is running against you, Senator."

"I thought he was running for District Coordinator." I knew what Bill meant, but I'd thought I'd try for a laugh or a smile.

"With Dewey's accident, there's no real opposition, and he's picked up on the Southern Diversion. He's claiming that the environment won't hold all the people that the water will support, and that you just want to overpopulate Denv to pad the pockets of your filch friends. The tag line is that they need him to protect Denv against you. It's not worded that way, but that's the message. And because it's national news, the stories are running in Deseret as well."

"We'll have to step up the positive rezads then." I smiled. "Bill, we've added an amendment to the education bill. It's not a big thing, but it's something that people in Deseret District will back. The whole country might back it as well. It's another positive thing, and it's not huge. I'm having Ted send the package to you."

"What do you have in mind?"

"A couple of spin-off ads. Dealing with music, talking about how we have to preserve our heritage, and that sometimes means going against what's currently popular. Also . . . with the Dewey and Hansen campaigns, maybe you could twist it a little. Say that the best music shouldn't be restricted to the filch, but it's a heritage for everyone, and we want to make sure that it remains a heritage for everyone."

"Hmmm . . . might work."

"We've already got it in the bill, and it's on its way to the Executive. She should be signing it within a week."

"What if someone on the other side complains that it's a private project?"

I couldn't help smiling. "No one did, and they won't now. The pilot project's not in my district. That way, I could fight for art, education, and all the servies who've been deprived."

Bill shook his head, but the expression was one of reluctant admiration.

"I'd also like to see if you could use a singer. Luara Cornett, she's a university professor at UDenv, I think. She does classical vocals and art song. Do a clip, and have her talk about it. See if you can do a rez undertone to one of her art songs, whichever fits the Talemen needs . . ."

Canthrop's mouth dropped open, and then he began to laugh.

"It's not that funny, I trust."

He shook his head. "It's not that, Senator. You have excellent taste. Do you know who sings about half your commercials already? It's Professor Cornett. That's how she makes a living. She couldn't do it as a professor."

It was my turn to laugh. For a woman, the professor definitely had spunk—or guts and brains. She had mentioned doing rezads, but I hadn't thought she'd be doing mine. "Maybe you could work that in . . . one of the foremost classical singers in Denv, and she has to make a living as a backrez singer?"

"I'll see what we can do once we get the package." He paused. "Gilligan isn't going to complain about the budget, is he?"

"I'll make sure he doesn't." I could do that. That was easy enough.

After Canthrop, I put in a call to Les Kerras. He was on-screen or something.

So I took the sheets that the NASR junior bureaucrat had provided, made copies, and then began to study them in the half hour before I was supposed to meet with Jo Jaffrey for lunch. She represented the Nengland District and wanted something— probably more support for coastal reclamation.

The Kemal business was looking more involved than I liked, and yet there wasn't even enough information to call a hearing.

Les Kerras for you, Senator.

Thank you. I set up the holo projection.

"You called, Senator?"

"I did, Les. I have some interesting information that I'll be having delivered to you. There are two packages. One is on an amendment we got attached to the education appropriations and passed as part of the bill going to the Executive. It's about effectively preserving an aspect of our cultural heritage. The other you'll also find interesting."

"I'm sure I will, Senator, and I might have some interesting information for you in a day or two. I hope so, anyway." He paused. "Have you heard anything more about these non-drug overdoses?"

"I can't say I have, Les. I might if I were on the health committee, but staying current with all the economic and commerce issues takes most of my time."

"That, and getting reelected." He smiled.

"You do what's best for your constituents, and that should take care of itself." But it only took care of itself if you let them know what you were doing, and if you had the money to get the word to them.

"Best of luck, Senator."

"Same to you, Les."

I collapsed the projection, wondering if Les really had something. Like most T-heads, he was hard to read, especially on a holo image.

I still had to hurry to make lunch with Jaffrey.

Chapter 34
Chiang

Met with the captain on Monday. Nothing new. No news breaks either. Parsfal called once. Told him I had nothing new, but he'd be the first to know. He nodded. I hoped he'd stay patient. Tuesday, I came in earlier. Was there at zero six-forty, before Sarao.

Looked out my window across the Park. Didn't see much except trees and grass. Another week had gone by. Wasn't any further along in finding answers to anything.

Read through Resheed's report. Weekend ODs had gone up—the mystery ODs. No surprise to me. The younger set attended more rezrap over the weekend. But guesses weren't evidence. Ebol4 deaths were going down. Only a hundred more over the week in Denv, mostly northside permies.

Another servie suicide. Young. Jumped off the Elletch Bridge after he'd left the Red Moon. Alkie levels moderate. No other drugs. Checked suicides against the trend. Up—but not to stat significance. Gang riot in northside. Wasn't reported that way, just a disturbance in the park by the community center. Cannizaro didn't like the word "gang." We didn't use it. Smash and grabs had gone down. Made sense. People worried about ebol4. Fewer out and about, less opportunity.

A handful of TIDs, some using the counterfeit GIL technique, some pickup kidnap-style, force the victim to transfer funds to an invisible account. This year, most invisible accounts were in Afrique.

I hadn't heard anything from CDC on the rezrap angle. Still thought rezrap interacted with soop. Wouldn't be something that CDC could prove quickly. If ever.

Lieutenant . . . I'm here. Sarao sounded cheerful on the link.

Good.

I have a message here from Amanda Cewrigh. Get back to you.

Record it and let me know. Try to get her to open up.

Will do.

Sarao was probably better at getting women to talk. I set aside Resheed's report and leaned back in the ergochair. Didn't help much. Had less than two weeks to finish off the McCall review, and I still had nothing that amounted to evidence. Kugeler had been patient. He wouldn't stay that way. Couldn't help feeling that a lot more was going on.

Something that Morss had said weeks ago popped into my head, something about Kemal getting a wad of legit credits. Why would anyone invest in Kemal's enterprises? Kemal as a front? Any super-filch had to know what Kemal was. If they did, it meant they were even more powerful, and that Kemal knew they were. It didn't seem logical. Kemal wouldn't subordinate himself. Few with that kind of wealth would trust him. Shook my head. I was missing something.

Stood and walked to the window, waiting for Sarao to finish with the Cewrigh woman. Clouds were rolling in off the mountains. Late-afternoon rain, probably.

A good twenty minutes passed.

Lieutenant . . . you were right. There was a connection. The recording's on your system.

Thanks, Sarao. Felt myself smiling. Hadn't had much luck, but maybe this would help.

I sat back down in the ergochair and called up the recording, full-size, so that I could see Amanda Cewrigh's face. Then I watched and listened to the whole thing. Had to get a feel.

Then I watched the holo display again. After that, I cut to the critical part.

Amanda Cewrigh wore a blue silksheen jacket and trousers, with a pale off-white loose blouse. Dark-haired, but her eyes matched the jacket. So did the glittered earrings.

"We're still looking into the Iveson-McCall case," Sarao said. "Someone had mentioned that you might have known Nanette Iveson."

"I'm glad someone is looking into it. Evan just wasn't the type to commit suicide. He couldn't have killed her, either. Poor man. He might have been a legal shark, but outside of his office, he couldn't harm a fly. Oh . . . yes, I've known Nanette for years. We went to Holyston together. She was such a comfort when Erneld died."

"She must have been," Sarao said.

The Cewrigh woman shifted on the damask-upholstered chair. "She was a physiological psychologist."

"What did she say?" asked my sergeant.

Amanda Cewrigh frowned. "It's been so long ago. Months now . . . but she said something like Erneld shouldn't have committed suicide. She wondered how anything could have driven him to that. She knew Erneld, you know."

"Do you have any idea who might have had a reason for the McCalls to die?"

Amanda Cewrigh shook her head. "Everyone loved them. And Evan, he was so professional. So was Nanette. That was why everyone trusted them. They never spoke about anything professional. You could count on that. All I ever knew was that he was a privacy solicitor. He wouldn't even tell us his clients. He'd say something like, 'I wouldn't be much of a privacy solicitor if I told you, now, would I?' "

That was it. Nanette Iveson had said that the Cewrigh boy shouldn't have committed suicide. Went back through my notes, and dug up the Cewrigh suicide. A little more than four months ago. Would have bet that Nanette Iveson had pulled out the rez equipment then. No way to prove that, either . . . unless . . .

Sarao?

Yes, Lieutenant?

Sometimes, when filch get rid of stuff, they give it to charities . . . that sort of thing. Can you make some calls? See if anyone remembers a load of high-end personal rez equipment that was donated by either Evan McCall or Nanette Iveson . . . probably about three months ago? A long shot, but I didn't have much else.

McCall had been so tight-lipped that no one knew anything. So was his wife. And both of them were dead.

Decided to put in a call to Kugeler. Didn't like the idea, but he deserved it.

He was in, sitting behind a wide blond desk. He wore a gray jacket over a shimmering gray shirt, with a darker gray cravat. Still had the narrow face that demanded spectacles. His desk was empty. Not one thing on it. He nodded to me. "Do you have anything to report? Or do you have a question?"

"Some of each." I tried a rueful smile. Probably didn't work. "We still have some leads that we're chasing. It's taking longer than I'd hoped. Wanted you to know we're still working."

"Good. Captain Cannizaro said you were tenacious." His smile was worse than mine. "What is your question?"

"Do you know, or could you ask the daughters if there happened to be anyone that their father trusted? Trusted enough to talk to about anything? Besides his wife," I added.

Kugeler frowned. "I don't know anyone, but I didn't really know Evan that well. I can't see that asking that would hurt. Might I ask why?"

"Because I wonder if Evan McCall knew too much." With that sentence I was committing myself at least to a decision of reporting that his death was murder, even if I couldn't identify the murderer.

"You do think it was murder, then?"

"You know I'm leaning that way, Mr. Kugeler. Right now, I have limited hard evidence. Nothing that points to anyone. Only that his death wasn't an accident. At the moment, if you announce it, we'll lose all chance of finding out whether we can discover more."

He nodded slowly. "I will ask Ms. Iveson and her sister, and I will insist that they abide by your caution. Is that all?"

"For now."

I was looking at a blank projection. Collapsed it. I felt better. Still rather go with an unsolved murder than anything else. Also felt I might be safer. Kugeler wasn't the type to let matters rest if something happened to me—or anyone else. Still . . . decided I'd better be careful when I was out.

Sat back behind the desk again, just trying to let my thoughts settle themselves.

Rain began to beat on the outside windows, but it only lasted ten minutes. Fifteen at the most.

Lieutenant, you're getting good.

About what?

Mountain House—they're the charitable outfit that most of the filch give their discards to. Not quite three months ago, they picked up some rez equipment from the McCalls. The dispatcher remembered it because the staff went wild. Everyone wanted it. No one really wanted to put it out for sale in the thrift outlet. So they set a price on it, and let the staff bid on it, and donated the money to the Mountain House fund.

Does anyone recall exactly what it was?

I've got a description. The dispatcher and the manager documented it. They were afraid not to because it was so high end. Worth more than ten thousand creds new, they estimated.

Lock in the description and send someone out to VR it as a visual deposition for evidence.

Will do.

Just hoped no one would ask me how it fit. I knew. Explaining it would be tough, but I didn't want to let that part slip.

Chapter 35
Cannon

Patience was usually rewarded in politics. Few impatient politicians ever lasted, especially in the NorAm Senate. So I sat tight and waited, and smiled, and went to committee meetings, and the Senate floor, and voted, and sent back targeted link messages to constituents, and talked with Canthrop about the next round of rezads. I also waited for Hansen's next round of attack ads. They hadn't appeared, and that bothered me. When someone changes their game plan, you'd better count on their knowing something you don't. Unless they're running out of credits, and Gill had assured me that wasn't the case, that Heber Smith had rounded up more than enough credits to run attack ads for six months.

I'd also heard nothing from Kerras. Canthrop sent me a dataclip to my office link that showed the story Kerras had run on the music education amendment. Nice story, but short. Canthrop had also sent it to Gill, but Gill had sent back a message saying to hold off on using the story and the related rezads until the bill went to the Executive and was signed into law. That wouldn't be for another few days, at least.

Kerras should have had some comment or reaction on the Kemal data, but maybe he'd been tied up with the stories on the Martian Republic's reaction to the latest fabrications coming out of the Agkhanate.

There were times to be patient, and times not to be. This was a time not to be, and on Tuesday morning, I headed over to Ransom Lottler's office. I didn't like doing it, but if you wanted to meet with the chairman of the NorAm Defense Committee, that's where you went.

Almost as soon as I entered his office, a young blonde woman stepped forward. She was almost as beautiful as Ciella, but Lottler chose all of his junior aides on looks. Ciella had been luck for me. She actually just walked in, looking for a job. I'd had Ciella checked out doubly, because I didn't believe in that kind of fortune. Politicians who don't examine gift horses don't last long in office, and I wasn't about to be that kind.

"He's expecting you, Senator Cannon."

"Thank you." I offered the warm and paternal smile. Very paternal.

The door to Ransom's private office opened as I approached, and then closed behind me.

Ransom Lottler looked like an accountant, in his tailored suits and striped shirts, the kind that had been in style on and off for centuries. He had a winning and self-deprecating smile, the kind that announced to everyone that he was just a good fellow who'd been lucky enough to be elected to the NorAm Senate. He stood behind his desk as I entered, but didn't step forward to greet me.

"I hope you've had a good week, Ranse."

"It's just started. I've had better. I've had worse, too. We all have." As he reseated himself behind the desk, he activated the privacy cone. No one else would hear anything, but I had no doubts he'd record whatever happened inside the cone.

I took the seat directly across from him.

"What's on your mind, Elden?" Although he had a soft voice, one that you almost had to lean forward to hear when he talked in private, his expression said that I needed to get to the point. "We've got the PDF commander in front of the committee this morning. Closed session about the problems with the Martians."

"The orbiter nuking or their so-called apology for failing to catch all the debris from that metal asteroid they fragmented two years ago and keep ignoring?"

"Both. We all know that they let some of that debris spiral in toward Earth just to point out what they could do. Now . . . you were about to say . . . ?" His thin eyebrows lifted in inquiry.

"There's a problem with MMSystems, and some of the other vital space-related formulating industries located in NorAm. Some of them are in your district."

"By the way, you handled that amendment to the education appropriations with class. I always have liked the way you've shown expertise in both commerce and education. Too many younger members try to do everything. They all think they know about defense."

I just smiled. He was only five years older than I was. "That's why I'm here. You're the expert."

"I know. Spare me the flattery. What problem?"

"MMSystems is about to change ownership and control. With the delicacy of events with the Martian Republic, I thought you ought to know." Actually, the figures I had indicated Kemal already had control. He just hadn't exercised it.

Lottler didn't bother to conceal a frown. "How do you know this?"

"For now, let's just call it campaign research, Ranse. Under the privacy laws I can't even call an investigatory hearing."

"Whereas I could inquire under continental security?"

"That's your choice," I pointed out. "My hands are tied, practically and legally."

"Not tied enough so that you could let me know."

"You've got a big interest in the next level space tug system." I grinned. "But the designs aren't set in stone. Not yet."

"Are you going to get to the point? What do you want?"

"I don't. Not unless the laws are being evaded."

"That means you think they are."

"It's possible," I admitted.

"Who's behind it? What does it have to do with the committee?"

"If I said what I suspect, it would be considered a violation of privacy," I pointed out.

"Figured you'd make that point. Even under a privacy cone, you never even come close to the edge of the law." Ransom scowled. "If I look into this . . . I'll understand what's going on?"

I certainly hoped so. "I don't know."

"You won't say."

He was right about that.

"That means that whoever's in this has the resources to bring a privacy injunction even against a sitting senator—and probably hammer your campaign as well." He laughed. "Heard about your new positive campaign. It's beginning to make sense."

I'd hoped he'd see it that way. Time for the hook. "The new ownership of MMSystems may not be whom it seems. It looks to be a front, one, shall we say, outside the normal political system." I emphasized the word "outside" just a bit.

For a long moment he was silent . . . considering. "Shit . . ." Ranse shook his head. "If you're right . . ."

"The timing's perfect for them," I pointed out.

"That'd leave all of Earth sucking salt."

Especially his district. I didn't say a word. He'd look into it. He wouldn't like Kemal owning MMSystems any better than the Martian Republic.

He nodded again. "The front people are in your district?"

"At least one of their subsidiaries." That was certainly true. CerraCraft was an open Kemal subsidiary. There were probably others I didn't know about. With the amount of cash that Kemal's black enterprises were bringing in, I had no doubts that there were others. If Ranse brought all that out, it just might put a damper on Hansen's "indirect" fund-raising.

"They're supporting Hansen?"

"That's a guess." They weren't yet, according to Gill, but Ranse didn't need to know that. He needed to think that I was worried about the direct aspects of the campaign. I was, but not the obvious aspects. I was also worried about the continent. It's no great treat to be a senator when times are bad, and I couldn't see any good coming out of Hansen, Alredd, and Kemal.

Ranse laughed. "You'll owe me for this one, Elden."

Unlike some senators, who left the debts there, but unspoken, Ranse was the type to make the point. "On the same terms as your favor to me." I smiled.

"Fair enough." He frowned again. "It might take a few days."

"I understand." I just hoped whatever Kemal was into wouldn't blow open before that. Or that Lottler's inquiries wouldn't be what created the explosion. But I'd rather have a political explosion early rather than right before the election when I couldn't recover as easily. Besides, if it got out in the open, it would make it harder for people to target me personally.

Ransom stood, gracefully, with his accountant's demeanor back in place, and turned off the privacy cone. "I appreciate the news, Elden. Give my best to that lovely wife of yours. I did so enjoy talking to her the other night at the Claytons' affair." He grinned.

"The same to Marge," I answered. "She was most informative about the archaeological excavations in Yucatán. She was talking about the parallels to NorAm. They might be there, you know?"

He laughed, and his office door opened. "She tells me that all the time."

I nodded and turned, heading back to my office. I'd stop there for a moment, before I went to the hearings on Afrique-based credit falsifications and the impact on the NorAm economy.

Sunday and Monday had been hectic. I'd had to work with Paulina and Barbra to set up the memorial service for Stefan and take care of all the loose ends left by his accident. Then I'd had to deal with the delicate situation with MMSystems, and the upcoming annual meeting.

Tuesday morning, Ashtay Massin was in my office, and O'Bannon would be there shortly, with some information I would find of interest. That was his way of saying that I had troubles. I didn't need any more troubles.

I concentrated on Ashtay. "You said you were getting pressure?"

His face was smooth and unworried. "Mr. Kemal, we've had several inquiries and requests for support for members of the existing MMSystems board. I've told them all that KCF Management has been reviewing the performance of MMSystems and will be voting for what it believes to be the best interests of the organization. I've also said that we don't believe that radical change suits anyone."

"And?"

"The price of the stock continues to fall."

"That's the way it is." I made a note for ChrisCo to buy some more. "Too bad we're not speculators. We could suggest that we believe change is necessary. Then, in two days, we could pick up bargain-rate shares."

"NASR would frown on that," Ashtay pointed out. He could have been discussing the weather.

I laughed. "I have no intention of doing that. Or of having you do that. We're not in this for short-term gains or to have NASR look at us any more closely than they already are." I frowned. "We're only removing four members whose terms expire. We're supporting retention of three. And there are seven members whose terms don't expire until next year. That certainly isn't radical."

"That is true, but they do not know that," Ashtay pointed out.

"You can get back to the majors on this. Tell them that KCF will not do anything that will affect the majority composition of the board. That's accurate enough, and it's not something that NASR could claim would fuel speculation."

"It's not factually true, Mr. Kemal."

It wasn't technically true, but it was factually true. KCF's shares and mine could have restructured the board. If I tried a stunt like that, I'd be worrying about whether I'd find myself driven off a bridge. "It is true in spirit, Ashtay, and we both know it. How would you say it?"

"We could say that KCF would not engage in either micro-managing a successful company, or in undertaking anything as radical as the news reports suggest."

"Just the second half. Forget about micro-managing. You raise that, and it suggests that you can."

He nodded. "That makes sense."

"Anything else?"

"No, ser."

When Ashtay left, I leaned back in my chair, thinking, looking out at the faint hazy clouds over the Rockies to the west.

After almost five years, I still couldn't read Ashtay well. He was an excellent funds manager. He was polite, intelligent, respectful, and effective. I couldn't have asked for more. He was also clearly not a Kemal tool, and he'd earned that reputation. I needed that now. But I wondered. Once things were under firmer control, he might be better suited as the number two man in one of the large operating subsidiaries. I didn't want to lose his talent, but I couldn't control him as well as I'd like. And he wasn't family. Now, it had to be the way it was. Later . . . we'd see.

Mr. O'Bannon is here, Mr. Kemal.

Have him come in.

O'Bannon eased in and sat down. He was wearing a maroon coat and a matching tie, with black trousers and a pale pinkish cravat.

I waited.

"I just got a call early this morning. The caller said that Cannon leaned on Lottler to make inquires about large transactions of a certain nature that might have implications for national security." O'Bannon laughed. "More directly, a junior bureaucrat at NASR by the name of Jonathan Ramses visited Cannon. Right after that, Cannon went to see Lottler. Lottler told our boy that Cannon had information that control of MMSystems was going to change hands, and that Cannon hinted that the new ownership wouldn't be Earthbound."

"He said that? How would anyone at NASR know?"

"He doesn't know. He's fishing," O'Bannon said. "No one can know anything except for the securities purchases. He's betting that no one Earthside would advance you credits of that magnitude. Cannon's a pain, but he's sharp."

"Sharp enough to back off from a pointed message?"

O'Bannon thought. "Most people would. I don't know about Cannon."

"A pointed message not directed at him?"

"That might work. If he gets the idea that a lot of bodies will pile up around him, he might figure that no one will want to help him in the future. Power is getting people to do what you want. If people think doing what he wants gets them dead, he loses power. He *might* get that message."

"We'll try that first." I hoped I wouldn't have to try anything else, but if I did, I did. "Anything else?"

"Nothing unexpected."

"How's Hildeo working out?"

"She's very grateful. She also learned more than I'd thought from McCall. She should have everything ready for you by next week."

"Good."

The moment O'Bannon was out of the office, I linked to Paulina. *I'll be going up to the northside plant in a few minutes. Please tell Mr. Grayser to expect me.*

Yes, ser. How long should I plan for you to be out?

No more than two hours. I didn't like to meet with Grayser, but there were times when it was necessary. Wednesday afternoon was one of those times.

Fred and Morrie had the dark green electral ready by the door from the ramps to the garage by the time I got down there.

The drive took thirty minutes, about five minutes longer than usual, because it was raining, and the Northside Parkway system dropped the speeds.

The plant was like any other formulating plant in northside—a grayish oblong with composite walls. There were armaglass windows in the front for the handful of offices there. It used heavy-duty industrial nanite formulators. What we produced there were the complex sections for guideway control units.

The gates recognized me. So did Elron, the armed guard just inside the gates.

"Good afternoon, Mr. Kemal."

"Afternoon, Elron."

"Mr. Grayser's expecting you, ser."

Grayser was the plant's chief of security. His office was at the far left end of the corridor. Although the formulators were supposed to be emission free, I always smelled composite and metals at northside.

Grayser was standing in the doorway to his office. "I got your message." Grayser was an operative. Like the good ones, nothing about him stood out. He was of average height and weight, with average brown hair, not fine or thick or curly.

I nodded, but didn't say anything until he'd closed the door and we were within the privacy cone. I didn't bother to sit down. My trousers just would have picked up the manufacturing dust that wasn't supposed to be there.

"How's Delano settling in?" I asked.

"He'll always be an Ellay wild young guy. But wygs have their uses. He's effective."

"That's good. I need a removal job. Jonathan Ramses. Make it look like a smash and grab or an accident. Ramses works as a junior bureaucrat at NASR. Lives somewhere in eastside."

"That we can handle."

"The other is tougher. We need to send Cannon a message. He still doesn't get it. He's got snoops looking everywhere. Now, he's got Lottler in a position where Lottler's going to have to make some inquiries. If the answers get out, that could make matters more difficult than they need to be. The only way to stop that is to get Cannon to forget it."

"What about hitting Cannon?"

"It won't work. You kill him, and the whole thing will blow. Lottler will squeal like a crashed net. The Dewey bit has everyone looking. Another accident or suicide of someone important, and you won't keep Kerras quiet. If there's any evidence at all DPS will get into it."

"Kerras doesn't know that much. He guesses a lot," Grayser pointed out.

"He guesses well. He also knows more than enough, and he talks to Cannon."

"We can handle him like Ramses." Grayser smiled coldly.

"Less directly. No one cares about an administrative clerk at NASR. They'll look deeper for a senator, or for a well-known T-head. You can push enough people not to root out evidence, but even Kirchner won't look the other way if the evidence hits him in the face."

Grayser tilted his head. He nodded. "Could be. Cannizaro would love to throw her trained dog at this . . . what's his name? Chiang? That's it. The guy doesn't have much in the way of weak spots. No wife, no lover, no family. Lives for the DPS. Guy's a rough-edged, old-fashioned saint."

"So, if Chiang goes down, we have all of DPS and every net in NorAm looking," I replied. "It has to be something more subtle, something only Cannon will get. Something that shows that the next time will be permanent."

"So how do you do that?" Grayser's voice got hard.

"First, you send Cannon a couple of traditional messages. The girl type and a private note. He doesn't get it, you send a second message. One that leaves someone very dead."

"His wife, you mean?"

"No. He'd probably love that. Give him a license to screw everything in sight. He plays at family being important, but he doesn't really know what family is. No . . . more subtle. Some woman he's been making eyes at. Check out those soirées he goes to, either in Denv or in St. George. Find out someone he's done something for, someone he can't even acknowledge. Once you find her . . . that one you can use Brazelton for. Get on it. Needs to be done in the next day or so."

"Too subtle." Grayser shook his head.

"No, it's not. There's no trail. Cannon can't say anything. We can get tougher if we need to, but we won't need to. That way, he calls off Lottler. That sort of thing happens all the time in politics."

"And Kerras?"

"He's been asking for it for a long time. He's due for a heart attack."

"We can take care of that." Grayser smiled. "He's overdue."

"Good." I stood.

Grayser shut down the privacy screen, and I headed back to the electral.

There was still one loose end, but Emile had indicated that was about to be resolved. You couldn't have loose ends in business. That was just the way it was.

The weekend had been quiet, leaving me time to practice—and to think.

The practice had been good, the thinking . . . Well, it hadn't resolved much of anything. I'd thought great thoughts and little thoughts. I still wondered why things happened the way they did. Or why a good student like Mershelle died and one like Synsil, who almost actively fought learning, didn't. Or why the young filch at the Claytons' soirée had all seemed so bored.

As always, I asked myself why creating beauty was so hard. All I'd ever really wanted to do was to sing beautiful music, and I got to do that so seldom. Then, I did get to sing for an audience sometimes, and there were a lot of people who never got any of their dreams.

So few people seemed to understand what beauty was. I kept wondering if it would have been better if I'd been born in an earlier age, before the first Collapse, when music still meant something. None of that solved anything.

The weekend news didn't help much, either. The Agkhanate was blaming the Russeans even more directly for the orbiter bombing. The Talibanate leadership said that there was no way to rein in terrorists when the Russeans had left technology and hidden stealth-protected bases scattered all over Asia. The Martian Republic was considering a metals embargo against all of the nations involved. The ebol4 epidemic was raging through the Amazon basin and southern Afrique. Deaths there were approaching five million. Over the weekend, another fifteen young adults had died in Denv from the mysterious drug overdoses. At that point, I'd switched off the news and turned to my antique visuals of *Carmen*.

On Monday, I'd done what I could. I awakened early and gotten in a good two hours of practice, plus some exercise, and managed to get to the university a good twenty minutes before my lesson with Abdullah. The lesson had been good.

I'd gone to the library to browse through the closed stacks and try to discover some more older sheet music that had never been scanned into the system—in hopes of finding something unique. I didn't. Back in November, I had found a "lost" song cycle of a twentieth-century composer named Britten, called "On This Island"—very haunting and beautiful. I wasn't that lucky on Monday.

Tuesday came and went, with the attendant lessons and class. I hurried home to wait for the Brazelton people to repair and upgrade the conapt's nanite systems, and the malfunctioning scanners. They were punctual, and the bill wasn't totally out of line. I did swallow, but only once.

On Wednesday, I was early in getting to my office, although I didn't have a lesson with Mershelle, because I needed to be there anyway for a series of almost make-work chores for Jorje, like signing hard copies of course descriptions.

There was a message on the system . . . waiting. From Mahmed. Did I really want to hear it? After insulting the senator on Thursday night? Finally, I told it to play and stood next to the Steinway, watching and listening.

Mahmed had a broad smile. Even on the half-size holo projection, that was clear. "You must have made a real impression on Senator Cannon's people, Luara."

I wasn't sure I liked that.

"They asked for you. They want to feature you in a special rezad plugging the need for greater arts and music education. It pays triple because you're faced off in it."

How could I refuse that? A rezad for music at triple pay? But I wondered. Was it the beginning of a pass of sorts? The senator had left me with that comment about my eyes.

I just stood there in the office, beside the ancient Steinway for a moment, then finally pushed through the reply. Mahmed was there.

"Luara! I hoped I'd get you before you started teaching." He was still wearing that idiotically broad smile spread across his dark face. "You did get my message."

"I did."

"You look dubious. Why?"

"I'm surprised, that's all. I met the senator at a soirée where I was the hired help. I didn't think I'd made the best impression."

"You always make a good impression. Then you'll do it?"

"I'll do it." How could I refuse? Besides, I'd been chased around the piano before, and if that happened to be what the senator had in mind, at least he was moving slowly.

"It's a little odd. Do you have the music for a song by Moore that you did at that soirée? Or the Schumann song?"

"I have both." This was getting stranger and stranger. "But neither is short. The Schumann is more than ten minutes."

"They want a short section, thirty seconds to a minute, of whatever you think is the most beautiful as a stand-alone."

"Out of context."

Mahmed shrugged. "It is at least triple pay, and you get residuals if they run it through more than one cycle. Oh . . . and can you wear what you have on? That's what you teach in, isn't it?"

"Sometimes."

"Don't forget the music."

"I'll bring both." I wasn't happy about it, but I didn't feel I could turn the job down. How could I fairly excerpt either work? All I could do was look over the music—after I proofed and signed the course descriptions Jorje had left—and come up with something. And apologize silently to whichever composer I chose.

"Could you make it at noon?"

It was already past eleven, and I needed to look at whatever Jorje had. I was also starving. "Could we make it twelve-thirty? I can stay as long as you need, but noon would be close . . ."

He nodded. "That shouldn't be a problem."

As his image faded, some of what I'd heard finally sank in. The senator was using my ideas in a commercial that he wanted me to sing? Why? He'd been interested, but not *that* interested. And they wanted my image, dressed in the way I was when I taught?

By the time I'd finished with a formulated sandwich in the student center and waited for a shuttle, it was almost eleven-forty. I had a seat on the near-empty shuttle. I marked out three possible passages in the Schumann. I really didn't want to do the Moore. Slightly after twelve, I left the OldTech station and began the fifteen-minute walk along the South Ridge pathway to the older building that housed Crescent Productions.

This time, I remembered the passcode without having to mentally rummage through my linkfile. My steps slowed as I walked down the ramp to the lower level.

Mahmed was pacing just inside the door to Crescent. His smile was one of relief, even as he thrust a sheaf of hard copy at me. "You need to read this first. It's not a script."

I must have frowned, because Mahmed went on immediately. "It's really more of an interview, plus a short take of a song . . . I told you about that."

"That's a long rezad." An interview? Of me?

"We're doing three versions. Long . . . medium . . . short. His campaign guy is going to place the long one as an infoshop with the educational netslots. They'll also be running it as a site-marker."

I shook my head. I had to say something. "That's going to help your receipts."

"Yours, too," he pointed out. "Read through all this, and let me know when you're ready."

I settled down in the worn gray synthleather armchair outside the studio box and read.

The first part was the interview. They'd probably have some gorgeous male with a resonance-enhanced voice in the final version, but Mahmed would just read the questions to me, and there were more than a few.

"Why do you think classical music education is important?"

"Why is beauty in the arts important?"

"What does it really offer students?"

"What would you do if you could . . ."

The scary thing was that while there were suggested responses, the responses were based almost verbatim on what I'd told the senator. He'd either recorded our conversation, or he had a very good memory, and I couldn't have said which.

When I finally finished reading, Mahmed had the studio set up, all in blue, so that they could put the final against any background.

We did the VRing backward. Mahmed had me sing all three selections, several times each, but that didn't take all that long, about forty-five minutes, maybe less.

Shooting the rest of it was agonizing. Mahmed must have asked each question a dozen times, if not more, insisting that I give a better or a slightly different answer each time.

It was nearly five o'clock before he nodded, then smiled. "This is going to be good."

"Good?" "Good" wasn't a word I would have used for a political rezad. I still had to wonder why the senator had decided what I had to say would make a good campaign issue. I walked slowly out of the studio area and gathered up the music, slipping it into the folder I'd brought.

Mahmed followed me. "You really come across on this, Luara. You should have been an actress."

"I wasn't acting. Music's important. I couldn't do that if I didn't believe in it."

Mahmed laughed. "That's why you're a singer. But you're partly an actress. You couldn't sing rezads if you weren't."

That was disturbing, too. Was I acting, selling myself, and my ideals, to survive? Of course I was. I hadn't been given that much of a choice, not if I wanted to sing. I knew that. I'd known it for years. I smiled politely and slipped the folder under my arm.

"The direct pay will be in your account by noon tomorrow." He shrugged. "The residuals won't start showing up for at least a month. It could be longer."

"I understand." I also understood that I'd just made more

credits in one afternoon than I had in the previous four months of working for Mahmed. That meant that now I'd still have extra credits, even after paying Brazelton for the repairs on the conapt's nanite systems.

"There will be another round of rezads for his campaign in about three weeks. It could be sooner. They want you, but those will be like the ones you did before."

"That's fine." At least, I thought it was. Certainly, the thought of being able to pay my bills on time was fine.

Even after I'd left Crescent, Mahmed's observation about my being an actress bothered me. It worried at me all the way back to the OldTech station, and back to my conapt. So did the idea of having my face in a political rezad. There was a difference between singing background vocals and actually being pictured. I couldn't say why, but there was.

Chapter 38
Parsfal

Thursday's big story was that the PDF had found a section of the Super-C underwater base stage of the torpedo-missile that had taken out the Russean shuttle. Bimstein wanted something new there, as well, even after my first crash effort. Before that, I'd just finished another set of weather facts and graphics to help Istancya. Since I hadn't heard anything from Chiang—or anyone else—about the McCall story, and since I'd run out of obvious people to contact, I took a minute to link in on the midday up-date Kerras was doing—before I went back to the orbiter story, while also working my way through the daily news confirmation sheet.

> ". . . quite confident that our technical experts will be able
> to track the source of the components used in the device."

Kerras's voice came in over the clip of an officer in the blacks of the PDF, an officer with a substantial amount of gold braid on the epaulets of his uniform.

"That was PDF Commander Ibrim Fortas. Fortas refused to speculate on a timetable for PDF action. In a related action, Ayatollah Karasi of the Agkhanate denounced the secrecy behind the PDF's actions and said that any attempt to implicate the Agkhanate would result in serious consequences. Karasi refused to explain what those consequences might be.

"The Martian Republic issued a communiqué which applauded the PDF efforts to track down the guilty parties and stated that it would withhold immediate economic sanctions pending the results of the PDF investigation . . .

"NorAm Executive Snowe applauded the restraint shown by the Republic and repeated her pledge of NorAm cooperation with the PDF probe . . ."

I clicked off the news link and sat back in my cubicle. Outside of the reheated orbiter issue, the news week had been slow.

The mysterious ODs were still in the news, but just as baffling as ever. They were now occurring in other large cities, but deaths seemed rare or nonexistent in lower population density areas. There could have been more than a few reasons for that. Cities would get a new undetectable drug—if that were what it was—before other areas. Also, if the deaths were being caused by some sort of strange disease that only hit a small percentage of people, then the deaths would appear more in cities—and they'd be noticed more there. I still thought the rezrap connection was the most likely.

My thoughts kept drifting back to Professor Cornett, and I wondered how old she might be. She wasn't old. That was clear. She didn't have the stiff mannerisms, and she was junior faculty, and when I'd talked to her accompanist, I'd managed to find out that she'd been married once, but that she'd been divorced for at least several years.

I shook my head. A set of words drifted into my mind.

She smoothes her hair with automatic hand,
And puts a record on the gramophone . . .

I laughed. Luara Cornett would never be that absentminded about music. I couldn't help but smile when I recalled her story about insulting Senator Cannon. Passion showed all the way through the professor, even through a holo projection. I could almost see the quick jerk of the head that she used to flip her hair back from her face.

Parsfal?

I managed not to jump out of my chair at the volume of Bimstein's link. *I'm here.*

Know anything about an Edward Smythers, used to be dean of the UDenv Law School?

Smythers? Dean Smythers? I swallowed. I'd meant to follow up on that lead, but with everything else, I'd just plain forgotten. *I know he was once dean there. That's about all. Why?*

He had a small house in southside. Small for southside, anyway. There was a fire and the fuel cell room exploded. He was killed last night.

What do you want me to do?

Not a lot. Just pick up what DPS will release and a short piece summarizing his life. Try to keep it around a minute.

How soon?

Won't run before early evening. Before four, if you can. Feed it to Kirenga. When you're done with that, see if you can put together a follow-piece on how what the PDF has found could lead to whoever nuked the orbiter. Feed it to Metesta. With that, Bimstein was gone.

I should have followed up with Smythers, but that had been around the time of the nuking of the orbiter, and the PDF had been harassing me, and . . . it happened. Except it shouldn't have. But I couldn't operate on regrets.

A quick search of the net revealed that Smythers had lived alone for years. Or at least, there was no mention of a companion or wife or children. He'd retired nearly ten years before. So I began the round of contacts.

The current dean was Wesley Wilson. He was actually in his office.

"Ah . . . Dean, this is Jude Parsfal from NetPrime. I'm trying to find out background material on a former dean—an Edward Smythers?"

"Dean Smythers. He was a fine man. A fine man, and a brilliant mind . . . all of us, the legal community, both scholarly and practical, we will miss him greatly. Dean Smythers was eminently respected throughout the legal and academic communities . . . renowned intellect . . . always accessible . . . a credit to his profession . . ."

"Ah . . . what can you tell me about him personally?"

"Edward was a genuinely good human being, and yet he was able to bring a sharpness of legal focus to the law . . ."

"Did he have any close friends?"

"Anyone who truly knew Dean Smythers knew what a fine human being he was . . ."

I couldn't get him beyond platitudes.

The next three older members of the law faculty that I contacted were all unavailable. Or that was what their simmies proclaimed.

A professor of institutional law named Rajiv Karamchand was somewhat more forthcoming. Karamchand had a long narrow face with smooth tan skin and black eyes that seemed to smile even on the holo display, even as he was talking about Dean Smythers's death. "I'm sorry to hear about it . . . I can't say he was the most popular dean, but he was probably the most effective. Very polite, always courteous, but he didn't put up much with academic rhetoric. He tended to emphasize that litigation should be the last resort, because everyone loses . . ."

"He must have kept in touch with some of his students," I pointed out. "Do you have any idea who I could contact among them?"

"I would think . . ." Karamchand laughed ruefully, sadly. "Of course. He didn't have any family, and with his death in the fire, there wouldn't be any way anyone would know, would there?"

"I'm afraid not."

"He could be quite forbidding, I'm sure you've heard. I know he kept in touch with Sunjay Mohandas and Austin Ohiri and Pamina Sulla. He was probably closest to Evan McCall, but that won't help you . . ." Karamchand laughed regretfully.

"I take it that McCall was something of a scholar, then?"

"Very much so. He was at the top of his class, and his briefs on privacy are legend. Of course, that was one of Dean Smy-thers's special interests, as well."

"Were there other privacy solicitors the dean was close to?"

"None that I know of. Not that many solicitors make it a specialty."

"Is there anyone else who you might suggest who could tell me more about the dean?"

"No. I wouldn't know where to begin."

So I thanked him and started in contacting the three solicitors he had mentioned. Over the next hour I managed to get all of them. That was a surprise, but not a great help, since none of the three could really add too much, but I took clips and wove them together, and sent the fifty-five-second shot to Kirenga. And that left me with a cold feeling in my stomach.

Finally, I called Chiang.

He wasn't in, but I left a message.

Then I went to work on the Super-C follow-up. I still had everything I'd worked on before.

My numbers weren't infallible, but backtracking from the point of impact, it was clear that the missile had been launched into the descending orbiter from somewhere in the neighborhood of the Hawaiian Isles. I'd have also guessed that there was a large private yacht, registered in the name of a dispatriate EurCom filch through an EastInd subsidiary, with a single torpedo tube below the waterline. There were dozens of yachts continually visiting Kauai during the late winter and early spring, and the Super-C technology meant there was no way to determine which had launched the missile. Perfect cover, even from recsats. Again, mostly suppositions, but I'd just package it and present as one possible scenario, and offer that as an example of why the PDF investigation was likely to take a while.

Bimstein would like it. It offered a dig at the filch, and indirectly at both EurCom and the Agkhanate.

Incoming from Lieutenant Eugene Tang Chiang.

Accept. I flipped on the holo screen.

Chiang looked as tired as I felt, with circles under his eyes, and a short lock of black hair falling across a wrinkled forehead. "Mr. Parsfal, I don't have anything new."

"I didn't think you did, Lieutenant, but I do. There was a retired law professor by the name of Edward Smythers, the former dean of the UDenv Law School. He was killed when a fire raged through his conapt this morning. Apparently, he was well regarded, and I was asked to put together a brief news slot. I interviewed several people. One thing that came up twice. His closest friend was Evan McCall, and Dean Smythers was possibly the one man who McCall might have confided in."

Chiang's face stiffened. "When did you find this out?"

"Just before I called you. I didn't want to leave a message." I decided to push just a little, since he'd find out anyway. "His fuel cell room exploded. I can't help wondering if there's a similarity there."

Chiang didn't change his expression. He just nodded. "I want to look into that as soon as I can. Thanks. Be back to you. Our agreement still stands. You get first notice."

Then I was looking at a blank screen. Bimstein would probably kill me if he knew I was sitting on what I had. But he—and I— would be looking at a stiff privacy lawsuit if we broadcast on what I had. And I didn't feel like gambling that NetPrime would bail me out.

I had the feeling that there was definitely a connection between the deaths of Smythers and Nanette Iveson. Everyone who'd died besides McCall had one thing in common. They were people who might have known whatever secret McCall had known as a result of a client.

I frowned. There was something . . . something.

It snapped into place. Caron Hildeo—the junior associate of McCall's. She'd not only gone back to O'Bannon and Reyes. She'd been promoted. So, it had been one of McCall's clients. It had to have been Kemal. Kemal had the connections, and McCall had known something that threatened Kemal.

I laughed to myself. Great . . . just great. All speculations. Not one single shred of evidence, and not even one thing that could be used in a newscast.

It bothered me, and yet . . . what could I do? There wasn't much. So I jotted down two stanzas and dropped them into my personal linkfile.

We have seen it all, what will be,
Yet no one else will turn to see.
We have written out who will fall,
Yet no one else will care at all.

We have no figures on the screen
no way to prove what we have seen
and so the earth will end its days
while ruled and rulers seek self-praise.

With that, and a sigh, I went back to Bimstein's assignment on Super-C. Sometimes, the beauty of truth and research didn't make it to those who needed it.

I hoped Chiang could find more than I had.

By Thursday, I wasn't sure where the week had gone. ODs had gone down again during the week. Nothing from CDC. Nothing more that I could tie to the McCall case. Could feel that things were happening, but no signs showed up in DPS.

Took the white electral. Made another sweep of westside. Came up with nothing.

Came back and found Parsfal's message. Worried about returning the call. Wondered if he was going to blow the story. Called him back anyway. He told me about Smythers's death and the McCall connection. He had good instincts. Wished we'd known about the connection earlier. Sometimes luck doesn't come to you.

Finished with Parsfal, and linked to the system. Searched for Smythers. Only a routine report on the fire. Wondered how much else Parsfal knew. Probably not a lot. Newsies would cast it if they knew anything that a solicitor would back. Neither he nor Kerras were blabbing. Meant they might suspect, but knew less than I did. None of us could prove squat.

Took a deep breath and linked to Kirchner. *Kirchner...* *Chiang here.* Hoped he'd answer. Be easier that way.

What do you need, Chiang?

Quarantine and complete workup on a fire site. Smythers... *this morning.*

There was a moment of silence. *Mind if I ask why?*

Just appreciate if you'd do it. Once we get the results... *let you know. Also, I'll be sending some techs as well, special-* *ized.*

You really think this is linked to McCall?

I didn't answer.

Couldn't be anything else, could it?

Could be... might not be.

Your ass, Chiang.

Better mine than yours.

Kirchner laughed.

I didn't bother with a link on the next. Just rushed out past Sarao.

"On my way to tech. Probably to the captain's office after that." I took the ramps fast. Not a run, but a stiff walk all the way to the tech side.

Duty tech sergeant was Sorgio, not Darcy. Would be a little easier.

"Is Tech Specialist Moorty available for a rush job, Sergeant?"

She frowned, but her face blanked, checking the link. "He's just coming up from the garage, Lieutenant."

"Good. I'll be needing him."

"He's scheduled to—"

"Unless it's the Smythers case, this is priority. You can check with the captain if you want."

"That won't be necessary, ser. We're not that tight now. Will he need a partner?"

"Yes. I'd prefer Alfonso, if you can spare him."

Sorgio smiled. "They're together anyway."

Moorty saw me as he walked in. He grinned. "More of the same, Lieutenant?"

Alfonso frowned.

"Could be," I answered. "There was a fire of suspicious origin this morning. Except it wasn't caught as suspicious until a few minutes ago. Smythers. It's on the system."

Moorty's face blanked as he linked. Then he refocused on me. "Yes, ser. Same drill?"

Alfonso came off the link a few seconds after Moorty, but he didn't say anything.

Waited until they both were looking at me. "I want every aspect of that system checked, even the subnodes. I'd bet that most of the main controls are so much slag or melted rubbish. Lieutenant Kirchner is also sending a team."

Sorgio's eyes flashed between Moorty and me.

"You want *everything*?" Moorty asked.

"Everything that will show whether there was something strange about the systems. Need to know if they were straight or if they were gimmicked. Anything that would show who built the systems, if they were changed, and who changed them. If you can."

Moorty looked at Alfonso. "Seems clear enough. Better get a new kit." He looked at me.

"Trendside will pay," I conceded.

Both techs and Sorgio smiled.

After Alfonso and Moorty left, I went back upstairs. The captain had left while I was sending out Moorty, and she wasn't expected back that afternoon.

Left a link message. *Captain, Lieutenant Chiang here. We may have more developments on the McCall case. Won't know until tomorrow morning, when the lab and tech analyses are done. I'll let you know.*

Then I went down to my office. Sat and looked at the Park for a few minutes. Then linked Sarao. *Can you see if CDC has anything on that rez stuff we sent them?*

I already checked. They've got something.

They do?

Sarao's laugh came across both the net and through the door. *They aren't saying anything. They're looking into it. I asked them when they started, and they said they've been working on it for a while. They'll let us know.*

Thanks.

I could figure out most of the murders. Couldn't prove it. Couldn't figure out why, either. Key was what McCall had known. Kemal was into securities manipulation, but CerraCraft was too small, and he owned it already. He didn't need to manipulate all the stuff KC controlled, like CerraCraft or Brazelton. It looked legit, as legitimate as anything Kemal was into. Why the securities manipulation, whatever it was? Kemal had more than enough credits to ease into most businesses. So it had to be bigger. A lot bigger. The question was still why. And what. Somehow the Cewrigh angle fit, too. Just didn't know how.

Spent the next hours reviewing everything. Didn't learn anything new.

It was sixteen-ten when Sarao linked in. *Lieutenant, Moorty says you hit it. They're on their way back. Estimate they'll be below in ten minutes.*

I'm heading down.

Kirchner came down the ramp right behind me. We both stopped in the garage foyer.

Looked at him.

"You were right. How did you know?"

"It had to be. McCall was always talking to Smythers, but I didn't find that out until this afternoon."

Moorty and Alfonso were the first in. Moorty grinned at me, then shook his head. I understood. I'd been right. Smythers wasn't an unfortunate death. Another murder.

The two homicide types followed them. For a moment, everyone just stood there.

So I spoke. "Let's go to the level-one conference room."

We all walked up. Techs carried their kits.

Room wasn't that big, not with the two techs and the two from homicide and Kirchner and me. Six of us at a round table for four. Kits against the wall. Had to pull in two chairs from against the wall. Techs smelled of fire. All of them had charcoal and smudges on their singlesuits.

"Why don't you start?" I looked at the pair from homicide— Petry and Weems. Petry was a tall and square blonde woman. Weems was new, dark-haired, sallow, shy. Didn't look directly at either Kirchner or me.

Petry glanced at Weems, cleared her throat. "It didn't look like arson to begin with, more like a malfunctioning fuel cell. The fire started around the fuel cell and spread from there. Weems caught it. He found a section of the casing, and it was melted between the inner and outer casings."

"Someone had filled the casings with something?"

Weems nodded, then spoke. Voice was so low I had to jack up my nanite enhancers. "The laboratory should be able to tell us what it was. Something tailor-made to look like insulation, I would guess, ser, and probably corrosive. I'd guess it was designed to eat through inner jacket, and then react."

"The other cells were tailored, too, but more to react to heat," Petry added. "At least, that's what the combustion patterns looked like."

"They'd explode only when the one caught fire?"

Both Kirchner's techs nodded.

Looked to Moorty. "What did you find?"

"The nanite systems were gimmicked, ser. The main box was destroyed, but the last command was frozen in the subsidiary nodes. The defense screens were at full."

"Smythers couldn't get out?"

"The emergency overrides were disabled. You couldn't have gotten through those screens with an orbiter—until the cells powering the screens went. By then, temperature was close to five hundred, even in the coolest places."

"So his house was designed with a separate system for the defense screens?"

Moorty shook his head. "An auxiliary system. A lot of filch places have it. Main system goes down, then a hidden backup system takes over. Usually only lasts for an hour or so. That's to prevent someone from gimmicking the main power system and looting the place."

"Anything else?"

"It was very professional. No hack and splice job."

I nodded slowly. "I'll need a report. First thing in the morning. Trendside will pay the overtime. I want to know everything you found out about the systems. Who built and installed them, if possible, and when they were last serviced, and by whom. That's in addition to the normal arson requirements." Turned to Kirchner. "Can your people do the same sort of thing?"

He grinned. "With you footing the overtime, you'll have it. More data than you ever wanted."

He might have been right about that. Just hoped we could get *something* solid out of all the lab reports. One other thing bothered me. Someone had gone to extremes to avoid the appearance of murder. Almost as if they expected each one would be hushed up so long as it didn't happen to be an obvious killing.

Kirchner didn't say a word until we were walking up the ramp. "This could get tough, Chiang."

"It could."

We both knew it might get worse than that. There were too many bodies and too much technology involved for it to be simple.

Chapter 40
Cornett

On Thursday morning, as I cleaned up after doing my exercises and practicing, I was still wondering about the rezad interview I'd done for Senator Cannon the afternoon before. Why me? Was he just using what I'd said as a campaign issue? Would I feel like I'd been taken off guard once more—and used?

That prompted me to link and check my account. I had to swallow. Mahmed had deposited what he'd promised. The amount was more than significant. That did answer one of the questions. The senator was serious, but now I had to wonder exactly what he was serious about. He'd never contacted me, but did senators do things differently when they chased singers around the piano? Or had I misread him? Was he actually serious about doing something for music? Or serious only to the point of recognizing a good campaign issue?

Whatever it might be, I pushed it aside and finished dressing. I'd decided on a pale green suit with a cream blouse. Except when I was working on sets or something like that, I avoided single-suits.

I had to hurry to make the shuttle. It was sunny and breezy, and my hair flew everywhere. The walks were still almost empty.

The shuttle was still only half as full as it usually was, and everyone stayed away from other people, except those who were already in couples.

Even the campus inside the screens seemed half empty, and the roses were drooping in the area along the walkway as I walked toward the Fine Arts building. It was quarter to eleven as I came down the corridor past the lecture hall and to my office. I only saw two students. I didn't know either.

The office looked as it always did, small and verging on dingy. The single window just didn't provide the light I liked. Even the Steinway seemed ancient, rather than just old, and the nicks on the black finish stood out.

Surprisingly, there weren't any messages on the office system.

I glanced through Amina's file, to check what she should have ready for me. As I recalled it was the Schumann. Just before eleven, there was a knock on the door. It was Jorje. I put the file down.

"Come in."

"I was talking to the dean yesterday," he began, even before the door closed behind him. "He'd asked me to come over to discuss the scheduling for next year."

From his first words, I could sense Jorje was up to something.

"He said he'd been talking to one of the Tazzis. The dean emphasized that the family was one of the strongest supporters of the university, and that Roberto Tazzi was one of the more distinguished alumni. That was just how he put it, and you know how important influential alumni are to the dean."

I just kept listening.

"There was a rumor that you were at a function a week ago where you had a, shall we say, heated discussion with Senator Cannon . . ."

I laughed. "Call it a passionate discussion, Jorje. We were discussing the arts."

"You can be rather . . . strident, Luara, and with funding as tight as it is . . . the dean was most concerned."

I had to shake my head. "Jorje . . . don't worry about it."

"The dean was very concerned, and so am I."

I took a deep breath. "The senator was not unhappy. Whatever I did, it certainly didn't hurt. After that 'discussion,' the senator's campaign hired me to do some singing for his campaign rezads, and then asked me to do a short feature rezad on education." I smiled. "They paid me very nicely. Now . . . do you think that the senator would be doing that if I had upset him?"

For the first time in months, if not longer, Jorje was silent, apparently speechless. Finally, he said, "You're doing rezads for the senator, against education?"

"No. *For* education." With the looming expenses I'd faced a month before, I probably would have done almost any rezad, but I hadn't been faced with that problem.

"You're certain?"

"Jorje. I know what I sang, and I know what I said. I don't know if they will run the ads, but either way, they wouldn't have hired me if the senator had been displeased."

Jorje looked almost disappointed.

I would have liked to strangle him, the little snake, but I just smiled. "You can assure the dean that he doesn't have to worry. Is there anything else?"

There was another knock on the door—a timid one. I looked over Jorje's shoulder and toward the door, then let the system project my voice out into the corridor. "I'll be just a moment, Amina." I looked back at Jorje. "Was there anything else?"

"The dean and I may have to reconsider your position, Luara. We can only be sure of funding through the fall semester."

I nodded seriously, before replying, thankful that I'd thought about the possibility so many times before. "I understand. Funding is always a problem." I paused for a second. "I'll be adding at least one more private student, according to the early registration numbers. Now, if your private student numbers drop off, I can see where that might pose a problem." I shouldn't have said that, but he was the one with the diminishing class sizes. He had all the inspiration of a badly formulated meal.

"The dean will be the one deciding, Luara. It all depends on the funding."

I nodded once more. "I understand perfectly, Jorje." I certainly did. Neither Jorje nor the dean wanted any surprises. They also didn't want adjunct faculty thinking for themselves, or suggesting that either Jorje or the dean was wrong.

"I'm glad you do, and I'll be telling the dean that there won't be any problems from the senator." With a smile, he bowed slightly, and left.

If there were any problems, I'd definitely hear about them, and I'd probably be on the street for unprofessional behavior. Unprofessional would be defined as conduct that harmed the university. That was a judgment call. There wasn't any effective way to appeal that, not unless I'd brought in a huge grant or had a student winning some international award. Neither was very likely at that moment.

Probably I should have been more conciliatory, but I was getting tired of being conciliatory.

I pulsed the door to keep it open after Jorje left. After a moment, Amina entered.

"Is anything wrong, Professor Cornett? Professor Ibanez . . . he looked upset."

"Nothing beyond the normal. He's worried about the music section's budget for next year." I smiled. "Are you warmed up?"

She nodded.

"Then start with the Schumann." I settled at the keyboard.

Amina stood facing the Steinway as I played.

After the first phrase, I could see that her jaw was tensing up. "Stop!"

She looked puzzled. Amina had a wonderful voice—most of the time. With her height, her fair skin, her jet-black hair, and a presence that lit up the stage when she appeared, she could go far—even in our artistically challenged times. Sometimes, though, she tried too hard.

"Feel your jaw. You're locking up. That keeps your mouth too closed."

She nodded. She understood.

"Let's try it again." I began playing the Schumann.

The same thing happened again, and I stopped playing. Every so often she backslid. I couldn't figure out exactly why, but it usually happened if she'd missed a lesson or if she'd gotten too tired. Or upset.

"What's the matter, Amina?"

She just looked down. "My brother. He's with the ERC in the Amazon. We can't reach him on his link, and no one can reach his team. He was supposed to report back to the base on Tuesday for updated nanomeds . . ." She burst into tears.

That was the end of the singing part of the lesson. After that, I let her talk. With the amount of tension in her body, a lesson wouldn't do any good for either of us. She'd keep tensing up, and reinforcing a bad tendency. I'd end up tense as well. The problem was simple. Almost every emotional and physical problem can affect the voice, one way or another. I could certainly understand her tenseness. Her brother was missing right in the middle of that part of the world where the ebol4 epidemic was the most virulent.

She kept talking. When she left, she seemed less wound up, but she had every right to be worried, and there wasn't anything I could do about that.

We hadn't taken a full hour. So I didn't have to rush to music appreciation.

While I went into the class less hurried than on many days, after an hour and a half of trying to explain the importance of the Romantic Period and to get the class to show some understanding of the differences between the outlook and structure of the Classic and Romantic Periods, I was exhausted.

I even managed to ignore the whispered comment: "What difference does it make? They're all dead."

I just reflected that the young snot who made it would also be dead, in time. There wouldn't even be music by which he'd be remembered. Even if the beauty of the classical works were remembered only by a handful of artists and musicians, that was enough.

I held to that thought. I'd been fortunate enough to understand the beauty of pure classic acoustic music, and I'd even had the privilege and pleasure of performing it. Perhaps it was a small candle in the darkness, but it was my candle, and my light.

That thought was harder to hold through my two o'clock lesson with Rachelle. She was a blonde beauty with a great natural voice and a doting filch family ready to pay anything to make their daughter happy. Unhappily, for reasons unable to be remedied by either education or nanites, in learning voice, Rachelle had the attention span of a flea. Yet she excelled in pure scholastic efforts.

"Open your mouth . . ." I don't know how many times I said that in the fifty minutes of that hour, but it felt as though I had every two minutes.

After Rachelle left, I just sat in my office chair for a good fifteen minutes. I was too tired to do anything else. I didn't feel like braving the old stacks of the library, either, seeking out forgotten music. I just gathered myself together and walked to the shuttle.

It was about two-thirds full, instead of being cramped. I actually got a seat.

When I got home, the system announced immediately, *You have two messages.*

From whom?

The first is from Brazelton Services. The subject is: About Your System. The second is from Mahmed Solymon at Crescent Productions. There is no subject.

I frowned. Brazelton Services. They had repaired the scanners and done the maintenance on the conapt's nanite systems just on Tuesday. What else? *Accept Brazelton.*

The image was a generated one—a handsome man in a repair uniform.

"Please give us a call. We recently upgraded your system, and we have been informed that several of the components have been reported to us as substandard. These could result in potentially dangerous problems. There will be no charge to you. Please call us—"

Just what I needed. I called.

"This is Luara Cornett—"

The image cut to a short-haired man in a maintenance single-suit. "Thank you for calling back. Would it be all right if we sent out someone right now to replace the defective components?"

"That would be fine." Of course, it was all right. I just wished they'd done it right to begin with. They probably wished the same thing.

"Someone will be there within the hour, and thank you very much."

I cut off the image. Like everything else, even repairing my systems was more complicated than it had to be. I went to the next message. *Accept Crescent.*

Mahmed's image filled the foyer. "Luara . . . I thought you'd like to know. I've had two calls about you, one from the Crayno Agency and one from an outfit I've never heard of—they're not even in the book. They both are interested in your doing rez work for them. Crayno wants to test you for something with high-end professional services. They're very reputable. I did give them your name and link code. The other outfit called itself Jaguar Promotions. I took their number, but said you'd get back to them. If you want it, let me know. I've also attached several of the earlier rezads. Since they're being run in Deseret, you probably wouldn't see them. I thought you'd like to see. I assume we're still on for Tuesday. See you then."

If I wanted the number? Mahmed knew I wasn't anywhere close to filch. That meant he didn't trust the Jaguar people. If he didn't, I should find out why before following up. Since the

Crayno people had to contact me, I really couldn't do anything about them but wait.

I debated about watching the rezads, but finally gave in.

The first image was that of the name Cannon, against the red, white, and blue stripes of the old Republic. I guessed he was wrapping himself in the ancient flag. Then came a series of images showing the senator in various places and actions.

The voice-over resonated through me.

"Cannon for Deseret, Cannon for the people. For all the people, all the time . . ."

The rezad went on to suggest that Cannon was a people's senator. Absently, I wondered how much of a people's senator, but I got caught in the closing song and music.

The scary thing was that I'd sung the words that had run behind his image. After hearing just one rezad, I almost wanted to vote for him. And I didn't care all that much for him.

The second one was clearly for a more Hispanol audience, but that touched me some, as well. The third was close to rezrock, and left me cold.

Still, the impact of the first two bothered me. I still wasn't sure I liked the man, or what he stood for, but I might have voted for him right after hearing the ads. With a shiver, I link-pulsed off the message link.

After Mahmed's rezads, I needed something to get my mind moving in another direction. I settled on NorNews as the least objectionable, while I set my new formulator on Jamaican Jerk Chicken.

". . . headlines for the next hour. Fatalities in SudAm from the mutated ebol4 virus have now exceeded six million. The Martian Republic apologizes for asteroid debris, but suggests it needs Earth technology to ensure it doesn't happen again. More mysterious ODs last weekend, and no cause in sight . . ."

I pulsed the selector to the weather, to anything less depressing, and hoped the chicken wouldn't be too long. I also hoped that the Brazelton techs wouldn't be too late.

Chapter 41
Chiang

I didn't sleep well Thursday night. Was in the office by zero six-thirty on Friday. Went back over what I knew, what the files and evidence showed. Tried to figure out the missing connections. The Cewrigh thing nagged at me. Nanette Iveson had said that Erneld Cewrigh shouldn't have committed suicide. I sat there for a moment. That set of pieces snapped together. Not in a way that I could prove, but it made sense. *If* my suppositions about what resonance did were correct.

The captain didn't call me. Saw no reason to call her until I got the tech and homicide reports.

Instead, went back to the day-to-day business of trendside. ODs were rising, including the mystery ones. They would through the weekend. TID- and GIL-related frauds were declining. Assaults and disturbances were still down. Made sense. Fewer people out because of the ebol4 scare, and people stayed more in their own space.

Sarao showed at seven hundred. *I'm here, Lieutenant. Any news? Still waiting for the reports.*

Found a message from Cannizaro asking for a formal report of some sort on Ernesto Tazzi. Took me a minute to recall. What the captain meant was that she needed something for political cover. More than the facts. Started in on that. Took more than an hour before I had down all that I could prove. Added a section that said CDC was looking into aspects of the OD problem. Decided against sending it. Hoped we'd get an answer from CDC before the captain leaned on me.

Moorty's here, Lieutenant.

Have him come in. Checked the time. It was zero eight-forty.

Moorty looked like he'd spent all night up. "Lieutenant." He extended a databloc and a bound hard copy. "I figured you'd need both."

We both smiled.

"You're right," I told him. "Have to meet with the captain about it. Is there anything else in it?"

"That we didn't cover last night?" He frowned. "There were some of the same basic routine twists in all the jobs."

"Routine twists?"

"Just the way the circuits are put together, programmed. Looks like the same tech did them all."

"Anything else?"

"Lieutenant, you got Brazelton—the company, anyway. There were defective modules and deadly program routines. The fuel cells had been tampered with, and there was circuitry there to make them fuse. Circuitry evaporated, but"—Moorty smiled— "the heat etched some of the components on the stone clear as a photo. The house was a death trap if anything happened." He gestured to the databloc I held. "It's all there."

"Thanks. Appreciate it. Lots."

"Just get them."

Hoped I could.

Fifteen minutes later, my office door opened. Kirchner didn't announce himself. Just walked in. Looked at me. He had a hard-copy report and a databloc as well. "Good thing for me you don't dice."

"Murder by arson?"

"Cut and dried, once you look beneath the appearances. Smythers tried to ram a chair through the window and broke the legs of the chair. That's a pretty good indication he was trapped, and that the overrides were disabled. The autopsy of what was left of lung tissue shows certain particles. He tried to put out the fire. There were buckets there. We found the melted remains. The fire didn't burn the whole place."

Frowned at that.

"The kind of heat that would melt stuff should have burned more than it did. That means it was set with a high temperature substance in the walls of those fuel cells. But all of the incendiary burned before the backup power cell for the defense screens failed. High temperature, and then the temperature dropped. Smythers asphyxiated, fell, and was burned. There should have been more carbonization of his body. There were lots of little traces, but they weren't obvious unless someone looked closely."

His grin was off-center. "You can have this one, Chiang. I wouldn't go into any dark halls for a while, maybe a long while."

I just looked at him.

"You've known this all along, haven't you?" he asked.

"Some of it. Had to prove it, though."

He nodded and was gone.

Put in a call to the captain. She was still out, meeting with the acting District Coordinator. Asked to meet with her as soon as she returned.

Then I read through both reports one more time. Evidence was clear in parts, not so clear in others. Moorty and Alfonso had solid evidence that Brazelton had installed "defective" components that had caused the death of Smythers. The earlier reports would support the same for McCall and Iveson, not quite so strongly.

The reports on Dewey were weaker yet. Evidence for tampering with the guideway system that had killed Dewey was suggestive, but not ironclad. I thought we could get Brazelton there on fraud or negligence—substandard original equipment.

Homicide had more evidence from the Smythers fire. Technical explanation was involved, but solid. Lots of details—particles in Smythers's lungs, compounds deposited and melted into the composite frame of the house, restriction of oxygen flow. List was long. Hoped it would be long enough.

Took the datablocs out to Sarao.

"Could you have two more hard copies made?"

She lifted her eyebrows.

"I want one. The captain needs one, and we'll probably have to provide one to a solicitor."

"You're that close?"

"I'm hoping."

Back in my office, I tried to figure out why Kemal wanted all the victims dead. It couldn't just be the OD and Cewrigh links. That would have been annoying, but not a reason for murder. McCall had known something else. Wondered if I'd ever know.

Chiang, this is Captain Cannizaro.

Yes, Captain. Think we have a breakthrough on the murders of McCall, Iveson, Dewey, and Smythers.

Smythers?

Need to come up and explain.

Give me five minutes.

Yes, ser.

Went out front to talk to Sarao.

"Still nothing from CDC?"

"Not a thing, Lieutenant. Do you still think there's something wrong with resonance music?"

"Something very wrong." Wasn't about to say what. No point in it.

"You think CDC can find it?"

"Hope someone can." I shrugged. "Time to go see the captain."

"Good luck, Lieutenant."

Need that and more. Walked up the ramp. Didn't hurry.

Cannizaro was waiting. Door was open. She looked tired, more tired than Moorty. She'd look worse before it was over. Dark circles under the black eyes. Blonde hair was limp. Worry lines looked etched with black wire.

Door closed behind me. Privacy barrier blanketed us.

"Before you brief me, Chiang, did you get my message on the Tazzi case?"

"Yes, ser. Drafted a report. Like to wait to see if we get an answer from CDC."

"CDC?"

"We asked for some special analysis. Don't know whether it will help."

She nodded slowly. "I'd forgotten. We can use that. I'll tell Roberto that my people have even enlisted the expertise of CDC. Either way, it can't hurt. It shows we're trying everything. What about the newsies? Parsfal—was it?"

"He's the reason we have a case. He called yesterday. Said Smythers had died in a fire. Smythers was the former dean of UDenv Law School. Smythers was McCall's only confidant. Parsfal didn't think the fire was an accident. It wasn't." I handed her the two hard-copy reports. "Tech and prelim homicide forensic reports."

"This is going to provide some answers on the McCall case?"

"You won't like them, Captain."

She sighed. "I *never* like anything you do on cases like this. No one else does, either. That means you do a good job. Now tell me what I need to know."

"Brazelton did the McCall protective system. Put in unauthorized codes, overrides. We have a report on that. The same kind of work was done at Smythers's place. The techs found prints on the back of the system box at Smythers's house. Fresh prints. Prints might be Brazelton's. Also a new control submodule. New *faulty* module."

"So?"

"Have to have special equipment to insert submodules like that. Rest of the box was five years old. One of the components wasn't manufactured until six months ago. Same company that supplies Brazelton. The guideway components are used by both GSY and Brazelton, but GSY doesn't use the same control system as Brazelton does for domestic systems."

"That's not enough to prove it's murder," Cannizaro pointed out.

"Could get Brazelton on one or two counts of negligent homicide . . . cost him his licenses . . . and a few other things."

Cannizaro looked directly at me. "You could."

"Could also see if he'd drag in Kemal on a plea."

"What good would that do?"

"Brazelton's guide systems were the ones that failed in Dewey's death . . . and in Nanette Iveson's death. They weren't the originals in either case. Then the Smythers's case. At least three counts of being an accessory to homicide . . . that's three separate and discrete violations. That's cause for permie treatment. At a minimum, it allows for use of truth nanites even under privacy law."

"For a street lieutenant, you have a nasty mind, Chiang." For the first time, she smiled. "Go try it."

"Yes, ser." Couldn't help smiling. Only one problem. Doing it was harder than telling the captain.

"You can hold off on the Tazzi report until next week. And the McCall report." Captain looked up at me again. "Get on with it. Keep me informed."

"Yes, ser."

Walked down to trendside to start the legalities to call in Brazelton for questioning.

Chapter 42
Parsfal

By Friday morning, I was stewing. Almost a week had passed, and I'd gotten nothing from Chiang. Bimstein had been on me all week about one thing and another, and I was about ready to break the McCall-related stuff, regardless of my promise to Chiang.

I hadn't more than walked in the office when Istancya was standing there. Her face was frozen, as if she'd had bad news of some sort.

"What is it?"

"Les Kerras died last night."

"What?"

"They think he had a heart attack."

"People don't have heart attacks anymore. Not many do," I added. "Where?"

"In his office." She looked down. "Bimstein just linked. He said Paula Lopes would be taking over for him for now."

Parsfal!

I winced. *I'm here.*

We need an analysis of the impact of the economic sanctions the Martian Republic just proposed. I'm sending over the draft they sent to the NorAm Executive. Need something within the hour. Feed it to Metesta.

"Bimstein?" Istancya whispered.

I nodded.

I'll do what I can.

Do better than that. With that, he was off-link.

"Bimstein," I said slowly. "He wants an economic and tech analysis of the economic sanctions being threatened by the Martian Republic. He wants it now. He didn't say anything about Kerras."

"Les doesn't matter, now." Istancya gave a small sad smile. "He was a disposable T-head. The news must go on."

I nodded. Then, I walked slowly into my cubicle and sat down in front of the console. Les Kerras . . . dead? A heart attack in his office? I had my doubts. Bimstein hadn't said a word about Kerras, as if he were already forgotten and cremated.

There was a set of lines in my mind . . . not mine . . . but those of the Irish bard.

The years to come seemed waste of breath,
A waste of breath the years behind
To balance with this life, this death . . .

No one even had a moment to spare to consider Les Kerras. Or what his life meant.

I sat there in front of my console, taking a moment before calling up whatever it was that Bimstein had sent. I looked at the console. It had been moved. Not a lot, but just a little. I frowned and started to sit down. Then I looked again.

There was an envelope wedged under my console. I eased it out.

My name was written on it—Jude.

Finally, I opened it.

Jude—

If I'm still here, just keep this for reference. If I'm not, you know what to do. KCF Management = Asset and control dump for trusts held by the children and grand-children of Arturo Kemal. Irrevocable life trusts to each child. Each trust holds 4.5% of the stock in MMSystems. It's not that simple. Each trust owns 55% of the stock in another holding company, and in some cases, two. There are ten trusts in KCF. Sketched out the pattern on the next sheet.

Chris Kemal holds 5.5% percent of the MMSystems stock outright . . . also is the executive officer of KCF (aka Kemal Children's Fund) and of his own personal holding company (ChrisCo).

All the secondary holding companies are operated by Kemal family members or by trusted subordinates.

Irrevocable trusts not considered "controlled" by the giver or trustee under NorAm law. Privacy law prevails.

McCall was the one to set this up, before he left O'Bannon and Reyes.

Also . . . found sizable transfers from the Nauruan National Bank to one of Kemal's holding companies—ChrisCo. Sizable means nearly a billion credits over a year. NNB is the bank that handles the Earthside funding for the Martian Republic. Couldn't confirm. That's because NNB is the only large financial institution that has refused transparency in the case of suspected criminal activities.

NASR is hiding things. Don't know what. No one there will talk. Not officially. Cannon knows some of this, but I don't know what he'll do. If anything happens, let Chiang know. In person. I couldn't reach him.

Clearly, Les had set out what he'd known in a hurry. But why me?

I looked at the two thin sheets behind the scrawled letter. Then, I looked again.

"Istancya!"

She darted into the room.

"I need a favor. A big favor. Les left me something, and I have to go to DPS. Bimstein wants an economic analysis of the economic sanctions threatened by the Martian Republic. I told you that—"

"I'm not an economist," she protested.

"I know. I can rough out the numbers, and the salient points in a few minutes. Could I *beg* you to polish them and send them to Metesta?"

"You beg so well, Jude." She laughed ruefully. "I'll do what I can." She paused. "Is what Les left you important?"

"He thought it was. But I can't take it to Bimstein without DPS clearance."

"You'd better get busy on the numbers. I'll watch and ask questions."

She stood behind me as I worked and tried to explain what I'd done and why. The numbers weren't my best, but they were in the right district, so to speak. The threatened sanctions would hit Afrique the hardest, then EastAsia, and the SudAm. That made sense, because those continents has less advanced formulator technology.

I threw together two charts and a colored map, and then gave Istancya a hug. "Thank you!"

"You owe me." She said it warmly.

After that, I went down the hall. Kerras's office was open.

Rehm was standing there. He looked at me. "All his files are gone. Bimstein wanted me to check. There's nothing there. Someone wiped them. Or maybe Bimstein transferred them."

"That's strange." It wasn't, but it was better to say that it was. "You'd better tell Bimstein."

Rehm frowned. "Would you want to tell him?"

"No. But he asked you to look." I offered a sympathetic laugh. "Better you than me." As I went back to my cubicle, I had to laugh again, if quietly and ruefully. Kerras's console and files had been carefully erased, of everything. No one even thought that there might be something else left.

"I thought you were going," Istancya said.

"Loose ends. I'll be on my way in a minute." Then I scanned the sheets Les had left into the system and set it to fire off copies under certain circumstances. The addressees included a number of people, including a couple of senators.

I did take an electrocab to get to DPS.

I got stopped in the DPS foyer by the automatic gates and a simmie that declared I wasn't cleared. So I put through a call from there to Chiang.

Of course, all I got was his simmie.

"It's urgent." That must have been a code word because a brown-haired sergeant appeared.

"Yes? May I help you?"

"This is Jude Parsfal, and I'm stopped down in the lobby. I need to see Lieutenant Chiang, and it's very urgent."

"I'm sorry, Mr. Parsfal, but he's tied up right now."

"The last time I had to wait to get to him he was not happy, Sergeant. Tell him I have some information that he needs urgently. I do mean urgently. About the McCall case."

"I'll see what I can do."

I stood there and watched the empty space where the holo projection had been.

The sergeant's image reappeared.

"He'll link with you. He says to keep it short."

"Is he here in the building? This shouldn't go too many places."

Another pause and blankness before the sergeant reappeared. "Come up to the third level."

I had barely reached the third level, where the sergeant whose image had instructed me sat behind an arc of consoles.

Chiang appeared. He looked disgruntled.

"What do you have, Parsfal?"

"Some more information on why—"

"This way." He turned.

I followed him back into his small office. Before he could say anything, I handed him the hard copy. "Kerras died last night. He left this hidden for me. I don't think his death was as natural as Bimstein does. All of Kerras's files were wiped. McCall set up the holding companies that are buying MMSystems. That's hard. Kerras also got far enough to think that Kemal was fronting for the Martian Republic in buying MMSystems."

Chiang scanned the hard copy. A cold smile crossed his face. "This is good. Do you know where Kerras got this?"

"Someone at NASR I'd guess, but I can't confirm that."

"We're getting close." He looked hard at me. "Not a word. You say one word, have you cited for every minor offense you make for the rest of your life."

I glared back at him. "Senator Cannon already knows some of this. If he goes public, we have to. You can't make my life much worse than Bimstein can if someone else gets this. I've played square with you longer than any other researcher or T-head would. I can't sit on all this much longer. Hours at the most."

The lieutenant actually sighed. "Figured as much. Hold off three hours, and I'll give you what we have. It's more than you have."

I thought. Three hours. It would take me an hour to put what I had in usable form. "I'll try for three. I can give you two for sure."

"Try hard, Parsfal."

"I'll try, but that depends on Senator Cannon and the other nets, Lieutenant."

"The longer you can hold, the more I'll be able to give you." He folded the two sheets. "If you want that story, I need to be moving." He just stood there looking at me.

"Thanks, Lieutenant. I'll give you as much time as I can." I had the feeling he'd give me a lot—if I could hold out. Whether I could was another question.

I walked out of DPS wondering where it would all lead.

Chapter 43
Cannon

When I got into the office at nine-thirty on Friday, with only a half hour before committee, there was a message on my private line. The image was that of Les Kerras. He was flushed, breathing hard, and he looked awful.

"Senator . . . you might want to check the fund transfers from the Nauruan National Bank to the various Kemal holding companies, especially ChrisCo. I'd guess that the Martian Republic is fronting Kemal to take over MMSystems so that they can have greater control over the next generation fusion tug systems.

"If I'm not here, talk to Jude Parsfal, not Bimstein or another T-head. Parsfal knows plenty . . . maybe more than I do."

That was it. Kemal fronting for the Republic? The man had neither ethics nor common sense. I didn't expect ethics from him, but how could he trust a world who could throw asteroid fragments across the entire Earth? Or who threatened economic reprisals whenever the slightest thing went wrong?

I tried to reach Kerras. All I got was his simmie.

A half hour passed, but he didn't get back to me. I didn't know Parsfal, and hesitated to call him yet.

How could I do anything? If I made a charge like that against Kemal, I'd be liable for privacy suits, damages . . . you name it. That didn't take into account the boost it would give Hansen. He could charge that I was seeing imaginary enemies everywhere, that I had gone paranoid, and was attacking the man who had saved and expanded CerraCraft.

The hardest lesson in politics is to do nothing until you know what to do. The second hardest is to figure out what to do when you're standing alone. I'd figure it out, and I wasn't about to go off half formulated.

With no answer from Kerras, I headed for committee. I was turning toward the members' entrance when a young newsie accosted me. She was attractive—and aggressive. She charged past to Jaffrey, almost into my face.

"Senator Cannon! Senator! It's been said that you believe women should remain in the home, or even if they work that they should remain secondary to their spouses. How would you address that?"

Where had that come from?

I laughed. "Each person should run his own life. I don't tell people how to run their lives. That's the great thing about NorAm. We allow people to be free. Each family should work out who is responsible for what. Not the government."

"But your wife's career has been secondary to yours. Is that something you decided for her?"

I shook my head and offered a smile. A warm one. "No one decides for Elise. She is a most capable woman. She chose to be a talent assessor. She could be a senator." I paused, drawing out the silence for a moment. "If she happened to be the fortunate one. If she happened to be the senator, then you'd be asking her why my career was secondary."

Several of the other newsies laughed.

"Now . . . if you'll excuse me. There is a committee meeting."

I slipped through the members' entrance and into the back room.

Jo Jaffrey came in after me. "Have you been making speeches on the sanctity of the nuclear family again, Elden?"

"I haven't said a word. Not one." I laughed. "Not in years." I'd learned that lesson early. I didn't have to be taught twice.

"Then your opponent must have." She smiled. It was an understanding expression.

"You, too?"

"Not this year. Two years ago, they caught me when I suggested that not all coastal protections were well thought out. I was charged with returning to the bad old days of coastal tourism and exploitation."

We headed into the committee room. I still wondered. The newsie hadn't smelled like Hansen, and Hansen wouldn't have raised that issue. He lived in Deseret District as well. Of course, Kemal could have raised it for him.

The committee meeting was mercifully short. We had a markup of the technical amendments that would conform product definitions for a series of minor nanite formulator components to world standards. We finished in less than an hour, and twenty minutes of that was because Silvio Berta had to question each provision.

Just before I left the back room, a Senate messenger handed me an envelope. The outside bore the imprint of Margot Halensek, the senator from Saskan. I took it, but didn't open it. That wasn't a good idea in a public venue.

The time was eleven-fourteen when I stepped back into my office. I came in through the front. It was easier that way, because everyone knew I was back in my office. I looked at Ciella first.

"Ciella? Did I get a call from Les Kerras?"

"No, Senator. It's been quiet this morning."

"Thank you." I linked Ted, because the door to his small office was closed. It usually was. He liked quiet. *Ted, I'm back. Anything I should know?*

The Education Department staff agreed to accept the wording on the Music Grant pilot program, and to the pilot program at UDenv. They also accepted the conditions—that the administrator of the program be a solo performer, currently employed there in either contract or adjunct status. They even bought the regional centers—including the one at Cedacity. The bill and report are scheduled to be signed on Monday.

Good. Thank you. I'll be in for a while.

Once I got to the office I pulsed the door shut and opened the envelope. I couldn't imagine what Halensek wanted. It had to be some sort of invitation or formality.

It was neither, and it clearly wasn't from Margot. Inside the envelope was a hard-copy story, with a picture, and a small square of paper folded shut. I read the story first.

Eastside Denv resident killed in smash and run on East Ridge shuttle platform. Jonathan Ramses was the assistant to the Deputy Minister for Information Services of the NorAm Securities Registry . . .

The picture was that of the man who'd given me the information about Kemal. I unfolded the paper. I almost had to pry it apart. There wasn't much there, just a few words.

You've been warned. It will get worse if you don't stop.

As I watched, the paper crumbled into dust. So did the picture, leaving only the hard copy of the news story.

I could feel my temperature rising. Kemal! The audacity of the man.

Elden? The link was on my very private line, the one only Elise had.

Accept. I wondered what the problem was.

"So I could be a senator?" Elise laughed, not quite kindly, her image seemingly scanning my office. She was calling from her home study. That was normal on Fridays, because she didn't go into the net offices except on Tuesdays, Wednesdays, and Thursdays.

"You certainly have the brains for it," I said.

"I don't see her."

"See who?"

"The sultry research clerk who linked here looking for you."

I froze inside.

"So . . . she is there." Elise's voice turned hard.

I shook my head. "I got a warning just a while ago. A note in an envelope. It scanned as clear, but it was the kind that turns to dust a few minutes after you open and read it. Someone wants me to stop asking questions about something. The last line was something like, 'If you don't stop, things will get worse.'"

For a long moment, Elise studied my face. I could feel it even through the holo link.

"I believe you. I actually believe you. You have that stunned look. I've only seen that expression a half-dozen times since we were married—like when you found out Emma was a girl. Or when—"

"Elise . . ."

"Elden . . . just be careful." Her voice actually softened. "I'll see you tonight."

She was worried, and Elise never worried.

Someone with a message from Jonathan Ramses.

I froze for a moment, then clicked on the recorder. *I'll take it.*

I'd never seen the woman on the screen. I'd have bet no one else ever had, or ever would, that she was a special simmie, although her physical assets were certainly astounding, and clearly available.

"Eldie, dear . . . you're spending way too much time worrying about things that don't matter to your district. Why, if you didn't worry so much about those, you might have more time for me."

"Who are you?" I might as well ask.

"Eldie baby, you *know* . . ." The "know" was delivered with a practiced pout. "You *know* what you need to do."

And she was gone.

I sat down behind the desk. Kemal was worried. He wouldn't have gone to such lengths otherwise. What else might the man do?

I put in a holo link to Gilligan on the direct private line, not the office lines that were all monitored.

"Gill, Elden here." I didn't know why I said that. He could see me.

"What now?" Gilligan was a square man, with a square and honest face under short blond hair. He was also the best political operative I knew. That was why he worked for me. I always went for the best.

"What have you heard?"

"About what?"

I just looked at him.

"Heber Smith is getting lots of credits. Probably from Kemal. Some will go to Alredd. More will go to Hansen."

"What else?"

"There's a rumor that you're looking where you shouldn't, Elden."

"Would you mind telling me where you heard that?"

"I didn't. Someone whispered it to Allie just as she got on the shuttle here in St. George. She didn't see who."

"I'm getting messages here, the blackmailing kind."

"Blackmail? Isn't that old-fashioned, Elden?"

"When sultry-looking women I don't know have my private home number and holo there, and holo my office, asking for Elden . . ."

Gill winced.

"When I get questions in the Senate corridor from a newsie set up to pounce, suggesting that I'm an ancient chauvinist who wants to keep women shoeless and at home . . . when I get disintegrating notes suggesting I back off . . ."

"I'll see what I can find out."

"Good."

Next came a link to Lottler. He wasn't in. Or he wasn't answering me. I suspected the latter.

I tried Canthrop. He was in.

"Senator. I've just seen that rezad on education—the one with the professor. We ran a few focus tests on a couple of selected markets. You've got a real smash there. I don't know why, but it is. I'd like to drop it into the rotation . . ."

"Ah . . . fine. Go ahead." I forced a smile. "Have you picked up anything? Anything odd?"

Canthrop frowned. "Not that I can recall. Crescent Productions did tell me that several agencies were interested in Professor Cornett—both for her singing and as an upscaler."

I frowned, because I was getting an override signal from Ciella. *Yes?*

Senator . . . we thought you ought to know. There was an announcement that Les Kerras died last night, apparently from natural causes . . .

Thank you.

"All right, Bill. If you hear anything strange, let me know."

He was still looking at me curiously when I broke the connection.

I laughed. Sometimes the choices are made for you. *Ted . . . would you and Sam come in?*

Then I linked to Pagel.

Pagel . . .

Yes, Mr. Chairman?

I want an immediate subpoena and information search warrant under committee seal, citing economic security, requesting the details of all fund transfers of greater than one million credits from the Nauruan National Bank to all NorAm banks and securities firms.

Senator—

Pagel . . . it's a matter of NorAm security.

The courts . . .

We'll see what the Justiciary says . . . I didn't care what they said. This one was a winner, and if it weren't, then I'd be as dead as Kerras. *I want that subpoena, and I want it out this afternoon. It's that important.*

Yes sir. I'll . . . we'll get it out. As I talked, I dug out one of the packets that held the information Ramses had given me.

By then Ted and Sam Wicker, my media aide, were standing on the other side of the desk.

"Sit down."

They did, looking even more puzzled than Canthrop had.

"Ted . . . Sam . . . I need an immediate release, and I want it to go everywhere. Here are the guts. The Martian Republic has been attempting to buy control of MMSystems through the front mechanism of using a NorAm citizen and the holding companies and trusts of his family." I handed a copy of the packet to Ted. "Those are the details."

I let them look over the information.

"Ah, sir . . . can we confirm this?" Ted's voice was apologetic.

"You don't have to worry about that, Ted." He didn't. It was my office, and my career, if it didn't work out. I'd trade both for my life, if it came to that, which it wouldn't if I were willing to make the trade. "We also need the following information in the release." I cleared my throat. "Within days of receiving this information, from two different sources, both sources died under suspicious circumstances. Because of the serious implications of the information, under the emergency powers of the chairman of the Economic and Commerce Committee, I have requested an economic security subpoena of the relevant financial records. Uncovering the sordid details is vital at this time . . ." I let the words trail off.

Both looked stunned.

"Oh . . . the two sources are Les Kerras of PrimeNews and a Jonathan Ramses of NASR. They're both dead, within hours of each other."

Ted looked at Sam, and Sam looked back at him. Neither looked directly at me.

"Go on. You've got enough to finish it and polish it. I want to see something in no more than an hour. Sooner, if you can. Go!"

They still had that stunned expression when they left.

Then I put through a call to Elise. She was there.

"What is it, Elden? You have that grim look."

"Elise, dear . . . this has turned very nasty. For the next few hours, until I call you, you'd better stay home, and make sure the defense screens are on full."

"You have done it now, have you?" Her smile was rueful.

"I don't know. I'll let you know."

"I hadn't planned to go anywhere, but I'll check the screens. Do take care, dear."

"I will."

After we broke off, I got up and walked to the window. I wasn't about to leave the office until the release was everywhere. That was safest for me and for Elise. It might actually be better for the continent. Whether it was the end of my career was another question.

But that was the beauty of politics—the big gamble. Sometimes, it paid off.

Chapter 44
Chiang

I'd just sent the warrant for Brazelton's arrest and questioning down to Kirchner. Also requested a forensic autopsy on Les Kerras.

Kirchner didn't complain about Kerras. *Brazelton, Chiang? He's a house cat among cougars.*

Got evidence to prove he's more than that.

You really think he'll take a plea? They'll kill him.

He doesn't, and I've got enough to turn him permie.

I told you before—I'm glad it's you. You want a pickup to custody, right?

You got it. Make it quiet and quick.

We're on the way.

Sarao came in on the link as I broke with Kirchner.

Lieutenant, there's a newsie here. He's the same one as before—Jude Parsfal. He says he has something urgent for you.

Parsfal? *I'll link and see what he has to say.*

Sarao was back in less than a minute. *He's here in the building, down in the foyer. He says it shouldn't go on system.*

In the building? Could have been a gambit, like Kama's chess tricks. Parsfal didn't seem the type. Never know, but I couldn't just throw him out. *Send him up.*

When he got to trendside, Parsfal was breathing hard. Looked worried.

"What do you have, Parsfal?"

"Some more information on why—"

"This way." I walked back into the office, tripped the privacy screens. Turned and waited.

Parsfal handed me two sheets of copy. He went on to explain why he thought Kerras had been killed, what the sheets meant, and how Kemal was involved.

We were close, but I needed time. Told him so. He wasn't happy. Promised me two hours maybe three.

Parsfal left. I looked at the sheets. The credits made the guideway contracts look like crumbs. Hard to believe what Parsfal had said about Kemal fronting for the Martian Republic. But Kemal would do it—if it meant credits. He'd gut his own sister.

All I could figure was Nanette Iveson had discovered something. That had made McCall skittish. Maybe enough that Kemal couldn't chance McCall undermining his deal for MMSystems. Kemal got titular control. Morss had been right. With that many credits, Kemal could have gone straight. What I didn't *know* was what Nanette Iveson had discovered. My bet was that it was some rez effect. Laughed to myself. No proof there was such a thing. Might never be. Didn't look like it mattered. *If* we got Brazelton before Kemal found out.

Kirchner's dets did. Within the hour. I'd gotten the rest of the legalities as lined up as I could. I was waiting outside the IR when they brought him in. He wasn't impressive-looking. Medium brown hair, medium size.

Brazelton looked at me. "You're Chiang, aren't you?"

"Lieutenant Eugene Tang Chiang to you, Mr. Brazelton."

"I'll invoke my right to a solicitor. I have no intention of answering any questions without him."

"That's your right. You will be held in maximum solitary restraint until he arrives." I smiled. "For your own protection, you understand."

He didn't say a word. He did stiffen.

"Take him down to maxsec. He gets a comm to his solicitor. No one else."

Kirchner smiled. "Our pleasure."

After they left, I linked to Cannizaro.

Captain, we've got Brazelton. He's mute until his solicitor arrives.

Is that a problem?

Might be. Have a tip that info on Kemal is about to break. Securities scheme to take over the space-formulating outfit—MMSystems. As a front for the Martian Republic.

Don't tell me you dug that up, too, Lieutenant?

No, Captain. Rumor is that NetPrime did. Might have cost Les Kerras his life. Requested a forensic autopsy.

Chiang . . .

Yes. Captain?

I'll either be DPS commissioner, and you'll be a captain—or we'll both be reprimanded, demoted, and retired. That's if we survive that long.

I'd already figured the second half of that.

Let me know. Cannizaro broke the connection.

Brazelton's solicitor arrived in less than a half hour. Jakob

Flemmerfeld. Head man in the top firm of criminal solicitors. He was waiting by the IR when I got there. Blond, hard blue eyes, and a no-nonsense manner.

Brazelton hadn't been brought up from maxsec yet.

"Lieutenant, I must protest—"

"Counselor . . . we are acting to preserve Mr. Brazelton's life and safety. He is being charged with several class-one felonies. He is also an accessory to even greater criminal actions. We'd like to keep him safe. Wouldn't you?"

"Are you suggesting—"

"Suggesting nothing." I nodded toward the four dets escorting Brazelton. Didn't smile. Kirchner had them all in full nanite screens, overlapped to protect Brazelton.

"Rather dramatic, Lieutenant," Flemmerfeld observed.

"Effective. Shall we go?" Gestured to the open IR door.

Just the three of us in the interrogation room. Me, Flemmerfeld, and Brazelton. I activated the privacy cone.

"Might I ask the offenses with which my client has been charged?" Flemmerfeld was most polite. That kind was dangerous.

I handed him the hard copy.

Flemmerfeld looked over the list. "I trust you have admissible evidence."

"We wouldn't be having this little meeting, Counselor. Not without hard evidence." I turned to Brazelton.

"Simple enough, Brazelton. We've got you. We can link you to Edward Smythers's death. We've got forensics on everything from your equipment to proprietary override codes. We've got replacement of fuel cells with defective units . . ."

Brazelton didn't say a word. Neither did his solicitor.

"We don't have to prove intent. We've got three solid cases of homicide. Nanette Iveson, Evan McCall, and Edward Smythers."

Neither one still spoke.

"Just a few of the counts. We can also add unauthorized maintenance on the guideway that contributed to Coordinator Dewey's death. Both Alredd and Senator Cannon will be happy to use that. Don't forget perjury . . . you offered a signed deposition on the nanite system dealing with the death of Nanette Iveson. Either one, and that would make four."

I handed the folder to the solicitor.

"All theory, Lieutenant."

"Nope. We did it thorough, Counselor. Proprietary equipment. Faulty proprietary equipment. No one else has it." I grinned. "If it's not, then I can bring five counts of fraud."

Brazelton didn't say anything. Didn't turn pale. Just stiffened.

I waited. "I'll get it one way or another, Brazelton. Once you become a permie, I'll ask you, and then, after I've got the information, we'll just release you onto the street."

Brazelton looked at the solicitor. "Out."

"You're entitled to representation . . ."

"Out."

I release the privacy cone. "I believe your client has asked you to leave for a moment, Counselor." That told me who was paying for the solicitor. Also told me not to trust the legal ethics of Flemmerfeld, Hayes, and D'Aboul. Already didn't trust O'Bannon and Reyes.

"What do you want?" Brazelton finally asked once I'd reactivated the privacy cone.

"You know who I want."

"You're asking the stars."

I just smiled. "Then you take the fall. You lose everything. We still get Kemal. It just takes longer. You think Kemal will let you walk around?"

"If I do . . . then what?"

"I'll push for two counts of negligent homicide, house restraint for one to two years, provided you agree to resign and sell all interests in the business."

Let him think for a while. Just stood there.

"I have one condition of my own," Brazelton finally said. "You lock me up until Kemal's taken care of. I'll take maxsec."

First time had someone who was filch or near filch wanting to be locked away. Understood why. We could do that.

"I have a condition in return."

Brazelton looked up.

"I want the name of every system repair job you've made since November, name and address, and I want it now. Your boys can link it through to the console outside."

Brazelton shrugged. "You can have them all. Better have your friend Kama fix one in the next day or so, though. Cornett, Luara, professor type."

"Why her?"

Brazelton shrugged again. "Don't know. Orders." He sighed. He didn't look like he did know.

Wondered how much else we'd never know. That could wait. I released the privacy code and linked to Sarao.

Have an urgent job. You take a tech team to the house, conapt, whatever of Professor Luara Cornett. Try and get her. Tell her not to enter the house. Get Kama. See if he'll make sure the system is done right. I'll pay—if I have to.

The professor? What does Brazelton have against her?

He doesn't. Kemal does. We don't know what. Like to have the professor alive so we can figure that out.

I'm on it, Lieutenant.

Then I stepped out into the corridor, leaving Brazelton inside.

"This is unusual," Flemmerfeld said quietly.

"Counselor, your client has agreed to provide certain information. In return for that information, once it is received and documented, DPS and the District Advocate's office will accept a plea of guilty to two counts of negligence leading to death, and request divestiture of the business, and a house arrest of two years."

Flemmerfeld didn't turn a hair. "I see. Then perhaps we should call in the District Advocate and make sure that this is established legally. I would also be remiss if I did not request what information you are required to divulge."

"Most of it's in the folder," I pointed out.

"Two of those are weak cases."

"They're strong enough that your client has no desire to see them to a full trial," I pointed out.

"Before we proceed, might I speak with him alone?"

Kirchner stepped forward. "You have every right to that, Counselor. We will insist on a full body scan." He nodded, and one of the homicide dets appeared with a scanner.

There was a muted squawk.

"He has a penknife and two old-style pens in his pocket," the tech announced.

Kirchner held out his hand.

Flemmerfeld surrendered both before he entered the IR.

He wasn't there long. He came out with a false smile. Looked at me. "You must have been most persuasive, Lieutenant."

"Just let the facts speak, Counselor."

"You'll send the agreement to me before you present it to my client, I trust?"

"Of course." Could see that he hoped we'd blow the procedures. "We intend to follow the DA's requirements to the letter."

"Very good, Lieutenant. I'll be looking for the agreement." He turned and walked toward the ramp down to the garage.

Sarao . . . Then I realized she was gone. Turned to Kirchner. "Could I impose on you to have someone call in someone from the District Advocate's office for an immediate sealed and authenticated deposition? And for the plea agreement."

"I'd be happy to have Janis request that." He looked in the direction of the departed solicitor. "You trust him as much as I do." He grinned. "You couldn't trust him any less."

"You think he's off to tell Kemal?"

"No. He'll tell O'Bannon. That's another form of insulation." Kirchner tilted his head. "You aren't authorized to offer a plea, you know?"

"I know. You really think the District Advocate is going to do better?"

Kirchner laughed. "Your ass."

I walked back into the IR.

Brazelton looked up.

"We'll have someone from the District Advocate's office here in a few minutes. Draw up the plea agreement. Means you have to make an authenticated deposition of what you did."

"A confession?"

"Call it life insurance. If Flemmerfeld knows the information is authenticated, there's less incentive to try to remove you. Becomes one more offense against Kemal. Possibly against Flemmerfeld."

Brazelton looked doubtful.

"Not pressing. You've got a few minutes to think about it." Left him there, guarded by the four dets.

Headed up to my own cubicle. Needed to get to Parsfal before that blew. See if I could keep it under control. Didn't get that far.

Kama came in—on link relay.

Eugene, I'm on my way to some professor's conapt. What exactly am I doing?

Saving her life from another nanite malfunction death. Why her? I don't know. Send the bill to Brazelton's outfit. If they won't pay, I will.

I can do this if they won't. But my price to you is that chess game.

I laughed. *I can afford that.*

Don't forget it.

After Kama broke link, I tried Parsfal. He was in. Even on holoscreen, he looked tired. Like me.

"Ah . . . this is Jude Parsfal."

"Lieutenant Chiang, Parsfal. Here's what we have. We have someone charged with the murders of Edward Smythers, Evan McCall, and Nanette Iveson. Can't tell you who for about an hour, maybe two, until the DA's office completes the legalities. I don't know how it will work out."

"Work out?" He looked puzzled.

"There will be a conviction. I'm not sure whether it will be murder, manslaughter, or homicide through culpable negligence. We have evidence that establishes who did it in all three cases."

"What about Kemal?"

"The suspected perp is linked to Kemal. You can have that on background. Don't have any problem with your using what you showed me, but we can't comment on that. You need to make that clear."

"I can see that, Lieutenant." He stopped. "Ah . . . about the other nets?"

"What other nets?" Shrugged. "If someone calls me, then I'll have to answer. Have no interest in doing a release until we know more."

Parsfal smiled. "Thank you, Lieutenant."

"I'll give you one other thing. Background only. Luara Cornett—professor at UDenv. She was also targeted. We don't know why, and the most we'll get there is intent to harm. Do you know why she's in this?"

He looked blank-faced. The way I felt.

"That's off the record. But . . . you follow it up your way, and we won't pay any attention. You might talk to her." Could see some interest in his face.

"Thank you."

"Have to get back to work." Broke the connection.

Cannizaro wouldn't be happy about NetPrime, but I could claim Parsfal already had most of the story and had done us a favor by sitting on it a week. He deserved a few hours before the others got to it. Deserved more, but a few hours was all I could give. Had to give that much or none of the nets would cooperate the next time. If I made it to a next time.

Wondered how he'd handle the story—and the professor.

When I got back to NetPrime, I hurried up the ramp and back to Istancya.

"How did it go?" I asked. "Did Bimstein bitch?"

She looked up from her console, and from what appeared to be something on education. "I fed it through. I haven't heard anything."

Parsfal? Where have you been?

I winced and mouthed to Istancya, "Bimstein."

She nodded as I walked back toward my cubicle. *Following a story. Didn't you get the the sanction stuff?*

It was all right. Need a follow-up.

What sort?

Which multilaterals are going to be hit hardest? Regional impacts within NorAm. Political fallout here in Denv. That sort of thing. Set it for Paula and feed it through Metesta.

Time?

Whatever you can do in the next hour.

Again, I was holding a dead link. I still didn't have a full story, or anything close, and I had Bimstein wanting stats that weren't easy. I compromised and sketched out a story about Kemal based on what I already had. Took almost a half hour.

Then I really started scrambling. It was more like an hour and a half before I fed the economic stats to Metesta.

I got maybe ten minutes back on the Kemal business before the link chimed, *Incoming from DPS, Lieutenant Eugene Tang Chiang.*

Accept. I hoped Chiang had something I could use and not another request to hold off. I flipped on the holo projection. "Ah . . . this is Jude Parsfal."

"Lieutenant Chiang, Parsfal. Here's what we have . . ." He went on to tell me they had a suspect in three murders, including those of McCall and his wife, and that there was a link to Kemal, and that I could release most of what he'd told me.

I couldn't quite believe I was getting a DPS go-ahead, even if informally. I couldn't help smiling. It might only be for a few hours, but we did have an exclusive. "Thank you, Lieutenant."

"I'll give you one other thing. Background only. Luara Cornett—professor at UDenv. She was also targeted. We don't know why, and the most we'll get there is intent to harm. Do you know why she's in this?"

"No." I hadn't the faintest idea. I'd talked to her, been intrigued by her, but having an argument about art with Senator Cannon didn't give a reason for Kemal to want her dead—unless Kemal thought she was the senator's lover—and he should have known better.

"That's off the record. But . . . you follow it up your way, and we won't pay any attention. You might talk to her."

"Thank you." I still wondered why Chiang had fed that to me. Guilt? Was he trying to give me something extra?

"Have to get back to work."

With Chiang's last words, I was looking at a blank projection. I collapsed it.

I started to work in the DPS angle.

Incoming document from the office of Senator Cannon.

Display, store, and print. I sat up with a jolt.

The Cannon release was similar to what Les Kerras had left for me, except there was more detail, and more rhetoric. Cannon also sent through a sound bite clip. I ran that up on the holo display.

"The Martian Republic has acted in bad faith. It has used a NorAm citizen to gain control of MMSystems. MMSystems is a key to the future of all Earth. It is a vital deep-space industry. This act is deceptive and despicable.

"So are the actions of Mr. Chris Kemal. By acting as a front for the Martian Republic, he has either allowed himself to be used knowingly. Or he has been totally incompetent. Either way, his actions have endangered all of Earth in the years to come."

I couldn't believe what I was hearing—a sitting senator denouncing the chairman of a major NorAm multilateral, and releasing numbers to prove it.

Bimstein! We've got a major story.

What? Better be good.

Two parts. First, story I was chasing. DPS is charging someone linked to Kemal with a string of murders—Iveson, McCall, and Dean Smythers. Second, Senator Cannon is denouncing Kemal for fronting for the Martian Republic in buying control of MMSystems—the deep-space tug formulating and manufacturing outfit.

Who else has got it?

Everyone will have the Cannon statement. We've got the exclusive on the murder counts.

Who did they charge?

DPS won't say. It's still in process. A high officer there confirmed that there was an arrest, and they have a suspect in custody, and that suspect is linked to Chris Kemal.

Do what you can. Do it quick.

I put in a call to Chiang.

"Yes, Mr. Parsfal?" I could see the strain on his face.

"Can you tell me who's been charged?"

He looked at me, thought for a moment. "Emile Brazelton. It's public now, but no one else knows. No calls from other newsies. That's all I can say now." He paused. "There won't be anything new over the weekend. Check with me midmorning on Monday."

"Thank you."

He broke the connection before I could. *Bimstein . . . they haven't released it, but DPS confirmed they've charged Emile Brazelton with three counts of murder.*

Go with it. Get something to Paula in the next ten minutes.

I couldn't have thrown what I had together if I hadn't already done most of it.

The feed had barely run through Metesta when Bimstein was on the link.

Parsfal! You got confirmations on this?

Cannon sent us the sound clip. Lieutenant Chiang gave the confirm on Brazelton, and on the murder charges. Don't think we should name him. That's why I said a high official at DPS.

All right.

Good by you?

Fairly good.

Chiang said there wouldn't be anything new from DPS till Monday. I've got one more lead on the story. Might be a follow-up. I'll be out for an hour or so.

Take a remote and stay on link.

Will do.

I'd spoken before I'd managed to see if I could even locate Luara Cornett. She wasn't at the university, but I was lucky. Unlike most filch, and in some ways she seemed filch, or maybe that was because she had an air of unattainability, she had a listed address in eastside. Actually, it wasn't listed directly, but the link codes from the university gave her home codes, and NetPrime's database revealed the conapt block for those codes, with an address. There were only ten conapts in it, and I could knock on ten doors.

Should I go out there?

How could I not?

Friday hadn't been a good day, from the beginning. I'd overslept. I'd had trouble getting time to practice because Raymon had called. He wanted me to come to dinner on Saturday night. Then he'd told me about all the problems he and Felycia were having with Terese. She'd just turned thirteen and wanted to know why she couldn't do what she wanted.

The westbound shuttle was more crowded than in previous days. About a third of the people wore masks, the kinds that had microbe blocks. There hadn't been any masks when the ebol4 epidemic first hit. Now, it was over, and people were wearing masks. The masks should have been sent to SudAm or Afrique. They might still have done some good there.

I barely made it to the administration building at the university in time for my eleven-thirty appointment with Dean Donald. I wasn't looking forward to it. It was the second meeting with the dean in something like two weeks. Some years I hadn't met with him once. Deans usually don't deal with adjunct faculty.

Malenda glanced up as I entered the office. "Professor Cornett, he said for you to go in. The door's open."

I walked in, very carefully.

"Would you please close the door, Luara?" Dean Donald looked up from his console and smiled. "The administrivia never ends."

I wasn't surprised. He kept creating much of it, and most of it was unnecessary.

"Please sit down." He kept smiling. He waited until I sat in the center, black-trimmed, red synthleather chair. "I've been talking over next year's budget with almost every member of the Arts and Humanities faculty. As I am most certain Professor Ibanez has discussed with you, the arts face truly parlous times. The trustees have required that we implement a ten percent reduction in overall costs for the College of Arts and Humanities."

"Professor Ibanez stated that was the reason for reducing the number of sections of music appreciation." I had to wonder what the meeting was all about. I'd already protested the cuts, without any effect. The dean didn't even seem to remember our talk.

"This raises the question of whether we should continue private studio voice lessons at the university. Private voice lessons are just not cost-effective, Luara. The rez-prep class is, and the large sections of music appreciation are."

"Do you intend to cut out voice training?"

"Oh . . . no. Not at this point, certainly. But . . . unless enrollments for the courses of the College of Arts and Humanities improve, or we receive other funding sources, I cannot say how long we can provide a dying discipline."

I forced myself not to snap back. I took a slow and deep breath and flipped back my hair. "I see." I did see, all too well. "It seems to me that this is a self-fulfilling prophecy, Dean Donald. The arts must be experienced in person to be fully appreciated. The university requires less in personal class experience, and the appreciation of the arts declines. The university then cuts personally attended classes in the arts more because enrollment declines."

"It is a sad situation, Luara, and you have described it accurately, but that is the way it is, and the way it will remain, I fear, unless matters change in a way I must honestly say I do not foresee."

"So why don't you simply require more in-person courses, both in the arts and in other fields?"

"We cannot remain competitive if we do."

"It's been my limited experience that quality is always competitive."

"Only the quality that people want, Luara. Only what they are willing to pay for." The dean smiled, condescendingly, and stood. "I fear we will not resolve this debate at any time in the foreseeable future, but I did want you to know the situation, and to understand that if changes must be made in the future, they will be in no way personal." He kept smiling.

I stood. I was so angry that all I could do was nod politely. "Thank you, Dean Donald." It might not have been personal to him, but it was to me.

He was still smiling when I left.

I was steaming. I decided not to go back home, but to check my office. It was old-fashioned, but I'd never linked the office and my conapt. I still felt that unless the university wanted to make me full contract, they didn't deserve instant, around-the-clock access. I really felt that way at that moment.

The first message was from Mahmed. He was smiling, but it wasn't a condescending expression. "Luara, I just wanted to confirm that we're on for three-thirty on Tuesday. If that's a problem, let me know. It will be a long session. Cannon has some new ads he wants to record. We may have to schedule another session on Wednesday. I hope you can do that."

I called him back, but only got his simmie.

"Mahmed, three-thirty is fine. I can do Wednesday at three or later."

The second message was from a tall blonde woman.

"This is SuEllen Crayno of the Crayno Agency. Mahmed Solyman of Crescent Productions provided your codes. We'd be very much interested in talking to you. If you're interested, please let me know."

Was I interested? How could I not be interested, with Dean Donald suggesting that he was just dying to throw me out once he could figure out a way?

I called back, and got a simmie of SuEllen Crayno.

"This is Luara Cornett. I'd be interested in talking with you. Mahmed spoke very highly of your agency . . ." I left my home codes as well.

After that, I checked the system for memos and documents. The only thing of interest was a note from the library to inform me that the section I'd been searching manually was scheduled for purging in June. Purging? Just because no one wanted to take the time to scan the information or read through it? There was no way I could search it all by June. How many other songs or song cycles were there, like the Britten cycle, that would be lost forever? There might not be any, but I had no way to know.

Still, I had to try. So I went back to the stacks and spent three hours. I found nothing. Then, I got a sandwich from the student center and ate it before I walked to the shuttle station to head home.

The shuttle was almost full. Except for the handful who still wore masks, it was as if people had forgotten that two weeks before ebol4 had been raging across the continent. I didn't look at anyone. I still couldn't believe what the dean had said. But I could. Beauty didn't matter. Education didn't matter. All that mattered were little numbers on a screen that said the only way to be perceived as a good university was to do what every other university did, but more cheaply. Or cost-effectively. Or whatever.

When I got off the shuttle, I should have been calmer. I wasn't. I walked . . . so fast it was almost a run . . . to my conapt. When I reached the lane, and the pseudo antique sign on the brick wall that announced "Eastside Courts," I slowed, then stopped short of the group just outside my door.

Two DPS techs were waiting for me, and a DPS officer of some sort, a small and wiry woman. She stepped forward. "I'm Sergeant Sarao, DPS." She pronounced her name as if it were spelled "sorrow." "We'd called you at the university, Professor. We're here because there may be some problems with the nanite system in your conapt."

"I just had it repaired. They've been here twice this week."

"It wasn't repaired correctly, according to the man who did it," the sergeant said. "It's very dangerous. We'd like to request that you wait here with us. A master technician from Westside Physical Systems is on the way."

"What's wrong with the system? What did they do?"

"We don't know. We've been told it's dangerous."

That was all I could get from the sergeant. So I stood in the afternoon spring sunlight, getting hotter inside and out. I waited and watched, glad that I didn't have any appointments with Mahmed or the Crayno people that afternoon and that I wasn't going to Raymon's until the following night.

An electrolorry appeared and eased into the lane toward us. Just like the sergeant had said, it bore the emblem and name of Westside Physical Systems. I'd never heard of it. But if someone were out to get me, they could have done it with a lot less than three DPS officers and a contracting tech.

The man who got out wore a spotless white singlesuit, with glistening black boots. He was tall, way over two meters, with a Polynesian cast to his broad face. He stepped forward to the sergeant. He carried a small case.

"Kamehameha O'Doull, at your service—and Eugene's—Sergeant Sarao." He turned to me, and smiled broadly. It was a friendly smile, the first one I'd seen all day. "You must be Professor Cornett. You wouldn't know, but I heard the recital you gave two years ago. I came with my niece, Anna Lilekalana."

I didn't recall him, but Anna had been a good student. She'd transferred to Southern University in Cedacity, and she'd even sent me a message or two. "How is she doing?"

"She just did her senior recital. It was very good, and she thanked you in the program." The big man's smile faded. "If you will show me your conapt, and the systems box, we'll see what we can do."

"Ser . . ." interjected Sarao gently, but firmly, "we'll need to record and authenticate what you find."

"I thought as much."

I must have opened my mouth.

"Evidence," Sarao said. "We'd like to make sure we have a record of an attempt."

She didn't say what kind of attempt, but my stomach clenched. I'd just assumed it had been sloppy or careless maintenance. Sarao's words suggested someone had been out to hurt or kill me. But who? I doubted that it was Senator Cannon. Jorje had been mad at me, and the dean wasn't exactly pleased, I was certain, but neither had the expertise to work on nanite systems. They also wouldn't have spent the credits to have someone else do it.

I found myself opening the door, and then standing back. "The system boxes are in the closet to the right of the foyer."

Sarao stayed with me on the front porch of the conapt. The two techs took in recording equipment.

"Professor Cornett?"

I turned.

A man hurried toward me. He wasn't that much taller than me, but he was muscular and broad-shouldered, and his eyes were gray-green. "Ah . . . Professor Cornett . . . I'm Jude Parsfal." He looked at the sergeant. "I'm glad you're here. Did Lieutenant Chiang send you?"

Sarao nodded.

I looked from one to the other. They both knew something I didn't. Jude Parsfal had interviewed me about the soirée, but what was he doing at my conapt? "What do you want?"

"To make sure you were safe. I thought DPS would be here, but when I called your office, and you weren't there, and when you didn't answer your home link, I thought I'd better come out."

I just looked at him.

"Let me ask you a question, if you wouldn't mind?" he asked, almost gently.

"I can't stop you from asking."

"Did the Brazelton people fix your home nanite system?"

I couldn't believe what he was suggesting. "Did you know, and you didn't . . . ?"

He shook his head, violently. "No. It's not that. I just heard from Lieutenant Chiang, and I hoped he told you, but I wanted to make sure. That's why I called everywhere and came out here."

"I'm all right." I wasn't sure that I was, but I wasn't about to admit that to a near total stranger.

"I'm sorry. I didn't mean to upset you."

I could see the relief on his face. In a way, it was touching. He'd really been worried about me. Someone I'd only talked to once, but he had taken the time to make sure I was all right.

I looked at the sergeant and then back at Jude Parsfal. "Could one of you two explain?"

Sarao spoke first. "I think it would be better if Mr. Parsfal explained. He can say more."

"Ah . . ." Jude Parsfal cleared his throat. He looked down for a moment. "It's like this. I think it is. Mr. Brazelton has been taken into DPS custody, and he has been charged with various crimes. I believe that murder is one of the charges. The evidence which I know about suggests that he modified the nanite defense systems of several people so that their fuel cells caught fire and that the screens held them inside, and they died of smoke inhalation or something like that."

"How . . . horrible . . . " I shivered. "But . . . why . . . I don't even know the man. Or was he just . . . killing people at random?"

"We don't know for certain," the news researcher said. "It might be as simple as the fact that you spent some time at a party with Sentator Cannon, and someone thought you might be closer to the senator than you are. There's some tie-in with the senator. He's just issued a press release suggesting that Mr. Brazelton's multilateral superior has been involved in significant wrongdoing involving the Martian Republic."

From the sharp look on the sergeant's face, I could tell that was new to her.

"Because I argued with a senator?"

Parsfal laughed. "Anyone who argues with a sitting senator is considered close enough to matter because everyone else is too busy currying favor." He paused. "The senator listened, didn't he?"

"He seemed to," I admitted. I didn't want to mention the re-zads, but it might help. "I'd done a few rezads for his campaign, but he didn't know that. Then, after that, I mean, after the argument, his campaign asked me to do some more, and even a special one about education."

Jude Parsfal frowned. "That could be the Hansen tie-in."

Both Sarao and I waited.

"Kemal has been backing Senator Cannon's opponent. If you were making a difference in the way his ads were working, I wouldn't put it past Kemal to have you removed. Kemal doesn't hesitate to remove obstacles, especially if he thinks he can get away with it."

I had to admit I hadn't the faintest idea who or what Kemal was.

The big technician from Westside Physical Systems walked out onto the front step.

Sarao turned to him.

"Eugene was right. There was a problem there," he said. "Your techs are finishing up documenting and authenticating the changes to the system. I need to get some replacement covers for the fuel cell." He looked at me. "Everything will be all right. Once they're finished, I'll make sure it's done the way it should be."

"Thank you." I still didn't have any idea why someone would want to hurt me. The only person who'd truly gotten furious with me had been Michael. That had been years earlier. Besides, he'd been dead before the Brazelton people had worked on the system. Jude Parsfal's explanation made as much sense as anyone's, but that was scary in itself. Being targeted to be killed because you helped someone win an election?

The Westside technician nodded, then turned and walked toward his lorry.

"I don't want to drag you into this"—Parsfal looked almost sheepish—"but I'd like to mention this as a possibility—without using your name. Would you mind if I slipped something into the story about how it appears that others involved in Senator Cannon's campaign were apparently also targeted?"

"I don't know. I don't want people to know, or to think that I might be involved with the senator. I only talked to him once, and that was because I was the hired help at a soirée."

"I'm only asking," he said quietly. "I wouldn't even put your name or your gender in the background story—just a mention of a key technical and advertising support person who was also targeted, but escaped."

I felt uneasy about that, but I'd have felt uneasy about saying no, too. "Just so you keep my name and direct background out of it." I flipped back my hair, and then felt nervous about that as well.

"I promise." He smiled, warmly, and it wasn't all professional. "If I don't get back to NetPrime, my boss will have my skin." He inclined his head. "It was good to meet you in person, Professor, and I'm very glad that you're safe. Please take care."

"I will." What else could I say?

As Jude Parsfal walked away, Sarao grinned at me. "He likes you. I've never seen a newsie bend over that way to protect someone. He's sticking his neck out to keep you out of it."

"I wouldn't know." I didn't, but it did seem strange that a newsie I'd talked to once would double-check on me while the people I worked with were trying to get rid of me and my job merely because I'd spoken my mind.

Chapter 47
Kemal

Friday night, after dinner, I was standing on the balcony of the family retreat in Aspen. I was looking toward the twilight-shrouded and early-leafing trees. On those slopes, centuries before, there had been skiers carving their way downhill through a much colder spring.

"What are you thinking, Chris?" Marissa slipped up beside me.

"Oh . . . not much. It's good to get away from Denv at times." There were so many details, and so few people who seemed to understand that multilaterals and families had few differences. Discipline and love—those were what held both together.

"You don't mind being here?"

"I'm happy to be here with you." And I was. Marissa was more than any man deserved, and she'd always stood by me, and never tried to manage the business side of things.

There is an urgent call from James O'Bannon.

Marissa looked at me. She could sense the link. "Do you have to take it?"

"I'll be quick."

She kissed me on the cheek. "I'll wait here."

I walked into the small study and flipped on the holo display. I wanted to say that it had better be important. I didn't have to. O'Bannon knew better.

O'Bannon's image filled the small study. He wasn't laughing. "I just got a call from Jakob Flemmerfeld. Brazelton was arrested and put in custody by Lieutenant Chiang just a few hours ago."

"Not nanite restraint? No house arrest?" That was bad. Very bad.

"Actually, Brazelton is under maximum security. He's also accepted a plea bargain, against Flemmerfeld's advice."

"What are the terms of the plea bargain?"

"For him to reveal what he knows about you. It's more elegant than that, but they're coming after you, Chris."

"Start doing what you can."

"We already have." He looked hard at me. "You might think of taking a trip. Off Earth."

"That would show guilt. What am I guilty of? Building a heritage for my family? Trying to revitalize businesses that were crashing? Creating jobs and better transport systems?"

O'Bannon nodded. "I'll keep close to the matter. Nothing will happen soon."

I had my doubts about that. But I smiled. "That's the way it is." I shrugged.

After O'Bannon broke the connection, I glanced toward the door. Then I smiled. Marissa was waiting, and there wasn't much else I could do. Not at the moment.

Everyone would be waiting, watching, hoping to push me into

doing something reactive and stupid. That was the last thing I should be doing.

I opened the study door and walked toward the balcony, Marissa, and the waiting evening.

Chapter 48

Logic and rationality are like three-edged blades, and two of the blades wound the user more than the third wounds the enemy or benefits the user.

The so-called rational analytical approach embodies a fundamental flaw, a flaw that has consistently and historically either been ignored by both rationalists and scholars or minimized. This flaw is the assumption that matters, feelings, or occurrences that cannot be described rationally or quantified objectively are of such little significance that they will not affect the outcome of the analysis. Further, such "nonrational" feelings or occurrences are all too often termed "irrational" and thus dismissed as beneath consideration.

In attempting to evaluate all too many human situations, in practical terms, there is indeed a difficulty. How does one quantify love or hatred, exaltation or depression, patriotism, or beauty? How can one present any of these "objectively"? How can one weigh the impact upon human conduct? Upon economic or political behavior?

The problem is merely made worse by the rationalists who dismiss those who cannot present their case or argument objectively and rationally. Failure to present a case in rational terms does not mean that the case does not exist; it only means that either the presenter cannot provide a logical format or that the case is not susceptible to logical presentation. By insisting on an objectively rational case, the rationalists impose what can best be called "the tyranny of logic."

Solicitors and attorneys at law have historically been the leading tyrants of logic. We have seen through the ages how totally unjust, unmerciful, and irrational laws and judicial decisions have been reached through pure logic and rationality.

Moreover, the tyrants of logic question the value of the so-called irrational. Of what use is great art? Beautiful music? Inspiring architecture?

In point of fact, any decision—indeed, any organization or culture—which does not incorporate emotion, passion, and other so-called irrational factors will in the long run fail, because the absolute reliance upon quantified facts and pure logic reduces the intelligence of the decisions of that culture. The evidence of history demonstrates that few strong societies have existed transgenerationally without an internal culture embodying irrational elements such as love, beauty, art, and music.

Yet, from the centuries preceding the first Collapse through the present, supposedly intelligent men and women have striven to ensure that the decisions that they make are grounded in absolutely quantified facts and pure rational logic . . .

> Exton Land
> From "The Importance of Irrationality"
> *Etymology Quarterly*
> June, A.D. 2364

Marissa and I woke around nine. We decided to eat breakfast on the enclosed sun porch. The morning sun there warmed the room. The miniature lemon trees along the east wall gave the room a moist and fragrant feel.

Marissa set down her coffee. "You didn't sleep that well. Are you sure you're all right?"

"There are some loose ends . . ."

"I heard about Emile Brazelton's arrest. It's on all the news nets. Some of them are saying that it's tied to your takeover of MMSystems."

"I'm sure it is. They don't want me to have the company." I laughed. "That's clear enough. They'd charge me with anything from child abuse to murder if they thought it would keep me from taking over. That's why O'Bannon called last night. I told him to get ready for the worst."

"I thought it might be something like that." Her hand reached across the table and squeezed mine. "It's going to be bad, isn't it?"

"Yes. I didn't want to bother you with it. I just wanted to enjoy the weekend." I had wanted that, and I'd enjoyed the evening with Marissa. We hadn't had too many evenings like that in the past months. There would be few ahead either, I feared.

Marissa turned. Fred had knocked on the door frame.

"Mr. Kemal? There's a Mr. Massin for you. He said it was important."

Marissa raised her eyebrows.

"I'll try to make this quick." I'd said that the night before, but nothing was likely to be quick in the days and weeks ahead.

I nodded to Fred. "Show him to the study." Ashtay probably had bad news as well, especially if he'd traveled from Denv to find me. I took a last sip of coffee, then rose from the small table.

I smiled at Marissa. "Don't leave. I'll be back."

"I'll be here, dear."

I'd been so lucky with her. She was beauty itself, and I'd never forgotten that, not over all the years. With a smile, I walked to the study.

Ashtay was standing beside the bookcase that held the leather-bound pre-Collapse books that few knew my father had collected over his lifetime.

"Good morning, Mr. Kemal."

I closed the door, and then eased behind the desk, where the screens there would protect me from anything short of ultra-ex. "Good morning, Ashtay. I imagine it must be important for you to come all this way on a weekend. What is it?"

Ashtay turned. "You should know. I'm not Ashtay. I talk like him. I look like him. I'll register as him."

I studied the man who said he wasn't Ashtay. He registered as human, but he could have been a clone. The scanners didn't show any weapons. "What do you want?"

"To tell you that the game is over. The risk has become too high for the Republic. The agreement is terminated. Your family will be safe."

"What—"

Blinding white flared from Ashtay. I tried to drop behind the desk, but the whiteness flared through the screens. Then . . . blackness . . .

Chapter 50
Chiang

I had duty on Saturday. Used the monitors to check on Brazelton every hour. Sometimes more often. He was safe, healthy, bored. Scanned the news nets. Nothing more than what Parsfal had gathered on Friday. Speculation, but no new facts. Agkhanate claimed that the Martian Republic had staged the attack on the orbiter itself. The Republic denied it, claimed that the Agkhanate was trying to escape its own guilt.

With a flash and an urgent warning, the advance summary report arrived on my console at eleven hundred. I read it twice. The important words were simple.

> ... explosion at private retreat of Christopher Kemal ... ultra-ex suspected ... Only casualties ... Kemal and unidentified male ... no GIL identification on record for unidentified male ... preliminary gene screen indicates probable clone ...

I read through the report and checked a few more things. Then I got ready to link to the captain. She wasn't going to be pleased.

On Friday night, we had a clear path to Kemal. By Saturday, all we had was Brazelton. Brazelton didn't know anything more than what he'd done. He'd worked directly for Kemal. No other links. No proof, and with the privacy laws we had nothing.

I used the priority code to link with Cannizaro.

Captain, this is Lieutenant Chiang. Urgent override.

What is it?

Kemal's dead. Part of his Aspen place was blown up. He was in that part. DPS checked out all access to Aspen. Limited. Filch-expensive limited. DPS there found two bodies in the debris. Kemal's and an unidentified male with no GIL ID. Kemal's wife swears he was in his study. Upset and then some, according to the report. Only craft that couldn't be tracked was a private orbital shuttle—registered to EraseCo. Out of Nauru. Registration was false. No such craft, no such registration.

We've got Brazelton, and nothing else, then?

That's the way I see it. Clear that Kemal was fronting for the Martian Republic. They saw what was coming and removed him. No ID on the killer. Bet it was a clone loaded with non-reflective ultra-ex, but can't prove that, either. Privacy laws mean we can't trace back. So we can report that Brazelton claims he was hired by someone else, but that someone is dead. Means that no one will know the details. No hard proof.

That will satisfy Kugeler . . . mostly. His clients don't care so much about a Justiciary verdict as a clearing of their parents. Even over the link, Cannizaro didn't sound displeased.

Doesn't bother you, Captain?

Not much. With the Russean orbiter mess, both the PDF and the NorAm Senate will be happy that the Martian Republic isn't dragged into the headlines again. Everyone knows Kemal was a bad actor, and he's gone.

Oh . . . and one thing more. Les Kerras was murdered. Simple poison that mimics a heart attack. Kirchner is investigating how he ingested it, but we probably won't find out. I paused. *Lot of bodies for no real solutions, Captain.*

But these actors won't try it again. The Senate will be watching for another Martian takeover, and Kemal's empire will fragment. We'll talk about it Monday. In a week, almost everyone will have forgotten.

I wondered about that.

Those were my orders. I sat there and began to go through all the dispatches and records I'd neglected. Just went through the motions—until I came to the CDC document. Not even a response to our request. Just a report that had come in with all their other drek. Read over it. Bottom line was that the combination of exposure to heavy amounts of resonance music and "soop" selectively overstimulated the heart muscle in certain individuals with specific genetic profiles. Such overstimulation led to fibrillation and then heart failure. Rezrap also could cause depression in certain genetically susceptible individuals and was heightened by alcohol.

Just a report. Slipped back to us.

Couldn't help mumbling. "Didn't even give us credit." I wouldn't even get reimbursed for the rez stuff I'd bought and sent to CDC.

Wondered who'd actually won in the whole mess. DPS escaped without a disaster, but wouldn't have called it a victory. McCall's wife had probably been tipped off to the alkie-rezrap connection for suicides by the Cewrigh woman. She'd told McCall. McCall had let that slip in some way, or even brought it up. Kemal had removed McCall's wife and tried to frame McCall, and then set up the suicide as a double insulation. Kemal hadn't wanted anyone to look into his dealings. Not with the MMSystems deal in the works. So the McCalls had been expendable, and no one really cared except their children.

NorAm Senate avoided embarrassment. So did Kemal's family. The rezrap would go on. There would be warnings, but kids would still die. CDC would point out it was a small percentage. Filch parents would screen their kids. The others would take their chances. Kemal's "heirs" would keep making credits on alkie and ignore the suicides and ODs. So would the soop makers, and trendside would keep score.

Sat there, thinking.

For a moment, had an image of the professor—true beauty. Laughed. I'd seen Parsfal's face. Never seen a newsie that worried.

Latest crisis was over. I'd have to get back to everyday trends.

. . . and I still owed Kama that game of chess.

Chapter 51
Cannon

At nine-forty on Monday morning, Ransom Lottler stalked into my office, barely behind Ciella's quick link.

Senator Lottler—he looks stern.

I smiled as long as the door was open. I didn't sit in front of the desk, but settled behind it. There were times to be a sheep, and times to be a bullheaded ram. I did activate the privacy screen.

He still wore the ancient-style pin-striped suit, but the mild accountant had vanished. The soft voice hadn't.

"I had thought you had more sense, Elden. A subpoena for economic security? Where did you come up with that idea? The leadership . . ."

I just grinned. There wasn't much else I could do. Besides, I knew it would irritate him.

"Go ahead and grin . . . Never have I seen anything more high-handed. You know that continental defense security takes precedence over everything. Economic security . . . what's that?"

"Ranse . . . let's look at this rationally. You can either support me, or you can oppose me. If you oppose me, I'll have to point out that you knew this more than a week ago and that you did nothing. I'll even go under truth nanites."

"You would . . . you actually would, you goody-goody. What are you going to do when the Martian Republic threatens that embargo?"

"They won't. You can issue that subpoena for all the records of NNB and for the ownership of MMSystems. It wouldn't be a good idea, I admit. Not now, but you could, and you could suggest that to the Executive and to the appropriate individuals in the Republic's government. I don't think they'd want that information public."

"You have an answer for everything . . ."

"And," I went on, "you can also point out that the new fusion drive for the space tug still happens to belong to MMSystems, which is a NorAm business. You might suggest that we're happy to cooperate, and that in return we'll overlook their heavy-handed attempts to steal Earth technology."

Lottler laughed. "You're not going to do anything?"

"Not a thing more." I'd done what I'd had to, and I'd been fortunate. Others hadn't been, and someday I wouldn't be. But, for now, I had been.

Lottler's laugh faded. "You won't always be lucky."

"None of us are."

"See you on the floor. By the way, Marge liked your amendment on music. I even voted for the bill when it came up."

He probably had. I hadn't checked.

"This afternoon." I did stand and see him out.

Then I went back to the office and checked over the committee business for the morning.

For all the infighting, for all the threats, veiled and not so veiled, there was still a beauty in politics—because it worked. It worked better than violence, and better than anarchy, even if it did verge at times on chaos. And I was good at it.

Even the professor would see that.

Chapter 52
Cornett

At dinner on Saturday night, Raymon had listened to my story about the conapt systems. I wasn't sure he really believed me, even after the news reports about Christopher Kemal's death in an explosion. I wouldn't have believed me. After all, why would someone that powerful want to kill an unknown music professor?

By Monday, the whole business still seemed unreal. Whether it was unreal or not, I still had to make a living, especially while I could. So I took the shuttle in and taught Abdullah. He had a good lesson, as usual.

After he left, I spent some time in the office, reorganizing my sheet music. Then I went to the library and continued my almost-vain search for lost art songs. I didn't find anything new, but I did find an ancient copy of "Silent Noon"—a Rossetti sonnet put to music by R. Vaughan Williams. I already had a much newer copy, but finding that confirmed my desire to keep plowing through the material the library was going to discard.

I went home and ate. Tuesday, I was up early, practiced an hour, and made it to the university by ten to get ready for Synsil's lesson and my music appreciation class. I'd barely draped my shawl over the coat rack—it was still too cold not to wear something and too warm for a coat—when the system announced, *Incoming from Ted Haraldsen, office of Senator Elden Cannon.*

What he did want? Would he have an explanation of what happened on Friday? *Accept.* I flicked on the half-sized holo projection. Ted Haraldsen was tall and thin and blond, another version of the senator.

"Professor Cornett? This is Ted Haraldsen from Senator Cannon's office. The senator asked me to give you a call."

"Yes?" What did Senator Cannon want from me? I didn't feel like being chased around the piano, even indirectly by one of his aides.

"The Senate passed the education legislation last week and sent it to the Executive. Yesterday, the Executive signed the bill. The new law will establish a grant program for music demonstration programs. It also establishes a pilot program at UDenv." The aide actually grinned at me. "I'll be sending the details to you, but you should know that the language effectively establishes you as the administrator of a two-million-credit pilot program."

I couldn't help swallowing. Me?

"We'll also be sending a copy of this to the university. Is there anyone who should get a copy besides President Hinckle?"

"Dean Wharton Donald is the dean of the College of Arts and Humanities."

"Wharton Donald? I'll make sure he gets a copy, too. Do you have any questions?"

Questions? I had more than a few, but not the kind I could ask. "Uh . . . I probably will, but this was a surprise to me."

"I understand. I'll leave my codes if you have questions."

After he finished, I just looked at the blank holo projection for a good three minutes before I remembered to collapse it. Me? The head of a grant program with a bigger budget than the entire music section of the college? Because I'd had the nerve to stand up to a senator?

I shivered. Standing up to him had almost gotten me killed.

I printed out what the senator's office had sent and read through it. The language about the administrator of the initial pilot program at UDenv was very specific, yet in a general way. The way it was written, there wasn't anyone else at the university who could be the administrator, but it didn't actually name me.

I read through it all a second time. The words didn't change.

Incoming from Dean Wharton Donald.

I debated for a moment. *Accept.*

"Professor Cornett, I just heard about your success in landing a major grant program for the university. Both President Hinckle and I are so pleased, and I wanted to let you know that you will be receiving full contract status, beginning immediately."

Once more, I wasn't quite sure what to say. Why full contract? Then I understood. Program administrators had to be full-time contract professors or administrators, and the pilot program was a five-year grant. I'd bet my contract would be for five years as well. "Thank you, Dean Donald. I had talked about the problem of needing more music demonstrations to Senator Cannon. I have to say I'm pleased that he listened." Then I lied. "He said he wanted someone with my background to handle the first pilot program, and I'm certainly looking forward to it."

"Oh . . . so are we. It's quite a well-funded program. Quite well funded."

"I'm looking forward to working out the details with you, Dean Donald. The senator wanted this to be a very hands-on demonstration program." I hoped my smile wasn't too forced. "His staff asked me who besides the president should know, and I insisted that you should also be notified." I managed not to gag at that. It was true.

"I am most appreciative of your concern, Professor Cornett. Perhaps we could meet later in the week."

"I'd be more than happy to meet. What about Friday morning?"

We agreed on eleven on Friday, and he offered three more congratulations before saying good-bye. I just sat there. I was certain that Dean Donald was intimating to the president, without actually claiming it, that the program had been the result of his wisdom in retaining me at a time of financial shortfalls.

He could have that.

With a full-time contract position, I might actually be able to reclaim the Altimus from Raymon's garage and use it at times. Then I wouldn't always have to take the shuttle. I might be able to enjoy a few more small luxuries in life—like speaking out once in a while. I might even have time for some sort of a social life—if I could find anyone who still looked for beauty in the arts.

Chapter 53
Parsfal

Monday came, and I'd done nothing about the professor. But I kept thinking about her. Finally, on Tuesday afternoon, after writing out the lines I'd agonized over all morning on a plain white card, I took personal time, and headed for her office. According to the university class schedule, she was there. I hoped she was.

I made a stop. The flowers were roses, and real, and very expensive. I didn't care.

The university's gates accepted my NetPrime ID. I had to ask directions to the Fine Arts building, but I managed to find it.

When I got near her office, I could hear someone singing. Then the singing stopped, and resumed, and stopped again. I didn't know too much, but she was clearly giving a lesson. So I found a bench a ways down the hall and sat down. My palms were damp.

Was I insane? No . . . life was too short, and the beauty of words alone, even the words of the Irishman, was not enough. Words needed song for full expression.

After about fifteen minutes, a student emerged. She walked slowly.

I waited a moment, and then hurried to the door, keeping the flowers behind my back as I knocked.

"Yes?"

"Ah . . . this is Jude Parsfal. I . . . have something for you."

After what seemed an endless moment, the office door opened. She stood there, her silver-gray eyes somber, yet dancing. Then she twitched her head slightly, and flipped back a few errant strands of that mahogany hair deftly.

"These are for you." I handed her the bouquet of yellow roses. "They're real hothouse roses. Not formulated."

The professor's mouth opened. "Why . . . ?" She looked at me quizzically, perhaps even appalled.

"Ah . . . I'm not . . . well . . ." I handed her the card that went with the roses. I watched as she read the words I'd written for her.

No wind whispers, disturbs your fingers,
perfect hands where perfection lingers.
Your unsung song spins in my mind
seeking words I still cannot find.

I watched after others did you wrong,
and never heard your favored song,
yet scarce can find the strength to bring
strong warm words for you to sing.

So these flowers do I proffer
as but gesture, beginning offer.

She looked up, a faint smile on her face, a smile that could have meant anything.

"I know," I said hurriedly. "It's not good poetry, and you don't even know me, except through a few interviews. It's not like Yeats and his gong-tormented sea. But . . . I wanted it to be about now and you, and not the misty past. And . . . I didn't want to just let you sing for people who didn't care, except that you were a decoration." I paused. "We might have a chance to be more than hired help. Newsie researchers are hired help, too." I stopped. I was talking far too much.

She smiled. It looked like more than a professional expression. "I'm still hired help. I have to do a rezad in less than an hour. Would you like to come with me? We could go somewhere afterward for something to eat, if you wouldn't mind."

Mind? "I'd be delighted. Thank you."

"Thank you. Let me get my shawl."

Somehow that was fitting—a singer with a shawl.

I couldn't speak poet's words. All I could do was smile back. It was enough.

About the Author

L.E. Modesitt, Jr., is the author of The Saga of Recluce, The Spellsong Cycle, and other popular fantasy and science fiction novels. He lives in Cedar City, Utah.